MASKS WORN *by* MAGICAL WIVES

HIYODORI

Contents

1

Here and Now

"You slipped away from me," said Nemesia's guard. "I've been terribly negligent."

He shoved her through the secret entrance. Nemesia stumbled out across the warm snakeflint floor.

She whirled, trying to catch his eye. She wasn't quick enough: her guard darted out of sight like a mouse disappearing through a hole. The painted panels of the wall closed up seamlessly behind him.

She stood alone in the Abbess's chamber of contemplation—ostensibly a room for private meditation. In reality, the Abbess often used it to receive important guests.

Nemesia had never been one to flush in mortification. But the floor under her bare feet felt momentarily hotter. She couldn't remember how to pry the wall panels apart. She'd never snuck in here by herself before.

What was she supposed to do now?

Hide yourself. See how it plays out.

She ducked behind a decorative folding screen, almost tripping over her robes in the process.

To most visitors from Above, this room would seem gigantic. According to the norms of Below, it was barely more than an antechamber. Cozy and intimate.

The main doors were needlessly wide and went all the way up to the soaring ceiling. A smaller human-sized door had been cut into one of them like a flap for a restless dog.

The pet door swung inward.

It was exactly the right height for the Abbess. Her guest ducked to follow her through.

Nemesia stopped peeking out from behind the screen. The potted plants on either side might help block their view of her. Hopefully. Both were fake, formed of green branching cave crystals.

As for herself, all she could see was pebbled snakeflint and the silvery-white silk of her unfamiliar robes. Tension threatened to clog her ears.

A faint tremor came through the floor each time the Abbess thumped her staff. Nemesia balled herself up and felt extremely foolish. Here she was, a woman of thirty-four, a veteran of life Below. She'd chosen an atrocious hiding spot.

The Abbess's staff stopped thumping closer. She must have reached the low table at the center of the room. The floor below it was deeply recessed, allowing visitors to dangle their legs. The Abbess would always kneel, her feet flattening neatly beneath her.

The Abbess had a voice like a frog with a cold; her guest sounded younger and clearer. "The King wants you to get married." The Abbess was skeptical. "Why should he care if you're married or single?"

"Ask His Highness," the guest said, unbothered.

"Have you been neglecting your duties? Does he expect a wife or husband to whip you into shape?"

"If it's all the same to you, I'd prefer a wife. Also, I'd be impressed if anyone can whip me into shape. That isn't the reason he ordered me to marry."

"Enlighten me," the Abbess said coldly.

"There's been too much fighting."

"...Fighting?"

"Duels at sunrise, brawls at banquets, scuffles out in front of the corner store. Over me."

"I don't follow," the Abbess said, even more coldly.

"Ladies who love me—and men, but mostly ladies—keep getting into fisticuffs. It's a perennial problem."

"So the King, in his Snake-given wisdom, thinks you can stop this by getting hitched."

"It might work. I've never been married before."

"Fascinating," said the Abbess. "Your quest for a wife brings you Below because...?"

"I'm thirty-eight, Venerable Abbess. Sometimes the symptoms start early. Everyone will breathe easier if I'm partnered with a quality extinguisher."

Nemesia had ended up in just the right place, at just the right time. This was her chance. Her guard had pushed her so she wouldn't lose her nerve.

"I can see how that would benefit you," the Abbess said cynically. "This quality extinguisher you seek—what's in it for her?"

The guest laughed.

"I can offer the lucky woman a life of relative leisure. A rent-free home Above. She doesn't need to love me. It's better if she doesn't. She just needs to like me well enough to live with me—and help tamp down my magic."

Nemesia's legs had gone stiff. When should she announce herself? All she could imagine was getting up too quickly and falling on her face.

The Abbess reluctantly mentioned a couple Maidens of the Snake who might be interested in life Above. She described their capability as extinguishers.

Every member of their sect could neutralize magic to some extent. But exact scores rarely came up in conversation.

"Venerable Abbess," said the guest, "I hate to toot my own horn—"

"No, you don't."

"These ladies all sound perfectly pleasant ... but I'm the most powerful maenad in centuries. You might use your fingertips to snuff a candle. You wouldn't use them to snuff a bonfire. Tell me about your strongest extinguishers. I want someone who won't ever need to fear me."

The Abbess said: "Your criteria keep growing more complicated. You want a top extinguisher? There's one right in front of you"—Nemesia jerked, almost knocking the screen—"but I'm over eighty. I would rather sacrifice myself to the Snake than babysit a feckless young maenad."

"Perhaps I can have it all," the guest—the mage, the maenad—said cordially. "What about her?"

"Who?"

"The person skulking behind you."

Nemesia's head hadn't poked out above the top of the screen. It wasn't thin enough to show her shadow moving, either. She could've sworn she'd been silent.

Now she had no choice but to show herself.

She straightened her legs. She emerged from behind the tall folding screen and the crystal plants that flanked it. Her naked feet tracked no anxious moisture or dust; the snakeflint floor erased all traces as she walked. It was still warm, like the flat back of a living creature, and had a slight give to it.

A birdcage veil covered her eyes. She kept her gaze lowered to the subtle scale pattern of her robes, a barely-there shimmer. Only after reaching the table did she glance at the kneeling Abbess and her seated guest.

The guest's mouth curled. "You were holding out on me," she said to the Abbess.

Nemesia, flinching, braced herself for fury.

2

2

Eden the Maenad

IN THE PAST, there had supposedly been other types of magic users. Now there was only one. Maenads. Raging mages. Some called them berserkers. Which was confusing, because successful maenads could control otherwise uncontrollable magic. They'd learned to master the berserker within.

"K. Eden—Kuchinashi Eden," the Abbess said without pleasure, indicating her guest. The surname came first.

Next she introduced Nemesia: "M. Nemesia."

"M for Meifu?" said the maenad called Eden. "Just like you, Venerable Abbess."

"All Brood members take the same surname." Two small piercings glinted beneath the Abbess's grim lower lip: pointed studs like protruding fangs.

"So what's your score?" Eden asked Nemesia.

Nemesia looked at the Abbess. She had no idea, really. The last time she'd taken an extinguisher test was before she formally joined the Brood at thirteen. Before she came to live Below.

The Abbess dragged her staff closer with bony fingers. It was carved from whitish wood and resembled a pair of twining serpents. Most people from Above never realized that those shapes were actually snake-sized worms.

Her staff at the ready, the Abbess said: "M. Nemesia is a nasty little sneak who has great difficulty following simple instructions."

"Then perhaps I ought to take her off your hands."

"I can't recommend her as anyone's wife. Nemesia, go—"

Eden the maenad sprang to her feet. She managed this with startling speed, given that her legs had been trapped in the recess below the table.

The Abbess stared resentfully, still kneeling with her bare toes tucked primly beneath her, still grasping her staff of worms.

"You meant to hide her from me," Eden said. "Who's the sneak, Venerable Abbess? I want your best, if she'll have me."

Nemesia took an involuntary step back.

Eden came forward in slippers—generic guest slippers with the ammonite-shaped mark of the Brood. Her robes were masculine: mostly black, belted low around her hips. Tasseled epaulets capped her shoulders. A new trend from the lands Above?

She was somewhat taller than Nemesia, with tawny skin and a perplexing mix of gold and black hair. In her left hand she held an object like a short military baton.

She lifted Nemesia's half-veil, flipping it to cover her hair.

Her courteous smile dropped away. Her face was vivid, capable of shifting in an instant from amusement to distaste. "You look..."

No one said anything further. Eventually Nemesia filled in the blank. "Yes?"

"You have eyes like a snake."

"That's nothing special in the Brood," the Abbess interjected.

Eden indicated Nemesia's wrists. "May I?"

Nemesia pushed back her sleeves. On both her wrists were twin marks like a snakebite. She stooped to lift the hem of her robes, too. She had matching birthmarks on each ankle.

"Those are the starkest stigmata I've ever seen," Eden said without moving.

"You can't have seen many," the Abbess said peevishly.

All clerics had at least one such birthmark. Their order went by any number of names: the Eternal Brood, Irreversible Sisters (regardless of gender), Maidens of the Snake (likewise) ... but they were most commonly known as the Bitten Brood.

"You heard my age," Eden said to Nemesia. "How old are you?"

"Thirty-four."

"Really! Must be the lack of sunlight down here. All of you have incredible skin. You, too," she said gallantly to the Abbess.

"Bite me," the Abbess spat.

Eden ignored this. She addressed Nemesia again. She had one slightly crooked tooth; it peeped out when she spoke. "The King of Now insists that I acquire a spouse. Are you available? Would you like to live Above?"

Nemesia's throat had gone all dry and pinched. "I would," she replied at the same time that the Abbess said: "She's not available, and that's that."

"Are you already married?" Eden inquired.

"...No."

The Abbess glowered up at both of them.

Nemesia tugged her veil down over her eyes.

Eden took her hand. "You have every right to refuse, of course. Will you marry me?"

"Yes." It came out in a croak.

The Abbess stumped to her feet, seething. She lifted her worm staff and jabbed Eden's calves with it, rapid as a fencer.

"Ouch!"

"You stupid, stupid woman. M. Nemesia will be useless. She hasn't gone Above in years! Leave her Below where she belongs."

"Take me away," Nemesia said in a rush.

Eden pulled her closer and gave the Abbess a chivalrous nod of apology.

The staff thumped Eden's shin several more times. But for all her spite, the Abbess didn't call for guards.

Her eyes—keen as ever behind drooping lids—met Nemesia's for just a moment. No winking. No acknowledgment. Just pure scorn, so convincing that Nemesia felt a little sick to see it. But her heart hammered a victory beat in her hollowed-out chest.

Everything had gone according to plan.

3

Two Days Ago

Two DAYS PRIOR, a slightly different group had gathered in the same chamber of contemplation.

Nemesia and the Abbess knelt at one side of the low table. Nemesia's guard stood back by the elegant screen and crystalline plants: arms folded, silent and anonymous.

Three ceramic cups of delicate green tea rested on the table. All were small—no handles—and glazed with a pattern of reptilian scales.

The Abbess smoked a bark pipe. It looked like a paper party horn, going straight and stiff when she exhaled, curling in on itself when she inhaled. The guard made a few attempts to wave smoke away from Nemesia's face before retreating to his post.

Across from the Abbess sat a man with both feet planted firmly in the dark recess beneath the table. His name was D. Sholto.

Daiya Sholto.

He was hefty, thick-necked. And yet his generously proportioned body didn't seem to go together with his miserly head or his gaunt, bony face. He might have stolen his skull from a starving stranger.

The Abbess removed her pipe. Her breath smelled of incense.

"The choice is yours," she said to Nemesia.

On this day Nemesia had worn red robes—as was her custom—and no veil. Her hands tensed in her lap.

"I can do it," she said.

"Good," said D. Sholto. "Then—"

"I don't want her to know that I'm a Bride."

Sholto stared at her with narrow black eyes that looked too small for his face, which in turn looked too small for his wide shoulders and wider torso.

"That's your biggest selling point," he said.

Ten years had passed since Nemesia's previous sabbatical: the last time she'd gone Above. She could think back on it without much pain. All that remained was a twinge of humiliation.

She'd spent a year Above. Each Bride of the Snake did, once every decade.

She'd been twenty-three. She'd fallen in love.

At the end she'd revealed that she wasn't just an ordinary cleric of the Bitten Brood. It didn't mean they couldn't be together. It didn't necessarily mean she'd have to go back Below forever. But Tanyu had looked at her with such dread when she explained about being a Bride.

Now she said: "I'll marry whoever you like. Just don't tell her I'm a Bride of the Snake."

Sholto grabbed his tea—his hand all but swallowed the cup—and knocked it back like a shot of liquor. "K. Eden loves stealing other people's women. She loves hoarding treasure. She would leap to take the bride of a god."

"Why do you hate her?" Nemesia asked.

"None of your concern."

"Among other things," the Abbess said dryly, "K. Eden jilted his sisters."

"Multiple sisters?"

"Apparently."

"That's irrelevant," Sholto snapped.

Nemesia wondered when this jilting had occurred, and how old his sisters were now. Sholto had introduced himself as a retired maenad, which ought to put him somewhere north of forty.

At twenty-three, Nemesia had been easily consumed by love. At thirty-four, she couldn't imagine where anyone would get the energy for multiple torrid affairs, whether simultaneously or in rapid succession.

Sholto looked at her more closely. "Plenty of Brides get married on sabbatical. Some even stay married, and stay Above for the rest of their lives. The Abbess claims you're her most potent extinguisher. Will the Snake be reluctant to let you go? Are you really that special?"

Nemesia and the Abbess exchanged a look. The Abbess blew her curly pipe straight, making it point at Sholto like an insulting finger.

"M. Nemesia is a four-bite Bride," she said. "Someone like her only comes around once every few generations. But if she truly wants to participate in your schemes, the Snake won't interfere."

Sholto relaxed, mollified. After going over all the practicalities, he spent the rest of the meeting demeaning K. Eden's character. He called her spoiled, shallow, and too powerful for her own good. She had the favor of the King. Deceiving her would be a victimless crime.

He complained bitterly about the resilience of her reputation. "She goes to brothels ... and she spends all night teaching board games to high-class courtesans. They have a wonderful time—and for some reason, everyone in the city knows it!"

Nemesia kept her thoughts to herself.

The Abbess, for her part, focused on hammering out the details of what D. Sholto could offer the Brood in exchange.

Technically speaking, the Snake provided for all those Below. The problem with this was that the Snake sometimes had a skewed notion of practical human requirements. When you desperately needed toilet paper, a chest of ancient coins would be cold comfort.

The Snake took care of them, but industry and noble families helped make up the difference. Most especially the Daiya family, who had already invested considerable sums to help redevelop facilities for tourists from Above.

After Sholto departed, the Abbess set down her curled-up pipe.

"If you agree, I'll milk his offer for all it's worth," she said. "But you can still back out."

Nemesia shook her head. She'd been dubious until she heard Daiya Sholto say he would triple his donations. That changed things. That made it more than a matter of her own selfish whims.

In a moment of weakness, she'd once asked the Abbess if she could skip her next sabbatical altogether. She could endure and even enjoy life Below as her memories of Above grew ever more distant. Going back Above would make the contrast so much worse.

"The Snake needs memories of society and sunlight," said the Abbess. "Everything each Bride brings back after a sabbatical—every scrap of lived experience— helps the Snake understand us. You know this better than anyone."

She leveled an unsympathetic look at Nemesia, who had knelt at her feet. "You *could* refuse to go on future sabbaticals. It's your life. Take risks, if you must. But I won't be held responsible. You'll have to explain to the others why you get an exception. I won't pretend that the Snake slithered up and told me in a vision."

The Bitten Brood secured placements for Brides spending a year Above: housing, work, everything. Facing the prospect of her second sabbatical, Nemesia had already become inconveniently picky.

She didn't want to return to her old workplace. She couldn't risk running into Tanyu. She didn't want to take some other job where she would be a burden to those around her.

She didn't want to become mired in impossible hope.

Daiya Sholto knew that the King had ordered Eden to find a spouse. He'd arranged for associates to drop hints about how it might be smart to wed an extinguisher.

"The trick is to make it seem like it's all Eden's idea," he'd said. "Let her pluck your poor downtrodden extinguisher out of obscurity."

At first Nemesia had worried that he was trying to hire her as an assassin. No matter how many women Eden might have jilted, Nemesia wouldn't murder her. She wasn't trained for it.

But her role wouldn't involve any physical violence. And she could hide the fact that she was a Bride of the Snake.

She'd have to remember to stop wearing red.

4

From Below to Above

NEMESIA HAD a single packed bag, which Eden now carried: her baton in one hand, and Nemesia's luggage in the other.

Nemesia's guard lurked in a corner. Eden waved in greeting, but he turned his head. Usually he had more of a sense of humor.

"I'm the most gifted living maenad within the Shell," Eden said. "Not the greatest of all time, to be sure, but the best you can get nowadays. I'll keep her safe."

The guard continued to act like a statue. His features were hidden by the fringes of his hood.

The Snake's magic anonymized every guard Below. Shadows obscured their faces. Their voices and their stature all blurred together. Beneath their uniforms, they could be any age or gender. Only their unique badges distinguished one guard from another.

After returning from her first sabbatical, Nemesia had been seized

15

by paranoia each time she met a new guard-in-training. She'd wondered: could this be someone she'd met Above? She'd wondered, against all reason: could this be Tanyu?

Bag secured, she and Eden left to wind through the warm sprawling corridors that led to the exit. The guard stayed behind.

Nemesia led the way, still barefoot, holding embroidered cloth shoes and loose white socks with a thin ribbon to tie at the ankle. She would put them on before climbing the stairs.

Eden watched her with the intensity of an art dealer trying to identify a forgery.

Nemesia cleared her throat. "Is there something…"

"On your face? Yes. You have enviable eyebrows."

"I try," said Nemesia, who had never thought much about her own eyebrows. There weren't many mirrors Below.

"You don't have fangs."

"No."

"Can you inject venom with your teeth?"

"Not as far as I know."

"Your guard didn't like me very much," Eden remarked later, as they ascended the great spiral stairs that ran from Below to Above. "Should I have given you a chance to say goodbye in private?"

"It's fine. Our guards mostly keep to themselves."

They were alone on the staircase. In reality, there might be swarms of commuters and tourists traveling up and down alongside them. Each individual group would always appear in isolation.

That was just how the stairs worked. Stray too far from your companions, and you wouldn't see them again until you emerged Above or Below.

The steps were as wide from end to end as a row of seats in a stadium. Wide enough to accommodate a massive stampede of humanity. They had no guardrail to keep you from toppling off the edge into nothingness. Wise travelers stayed in the middle.

Eden kept drifting over to study the walls of the shaft.

The art there was too immense in scale for human eyes. It mostly looked like swirling abstract lines. It had a way of changing over time, old drawings retreating and new drawings surfacing like patterns traced in sand by fierce wind.

Frequent commuters became familiar with common motifs. They could glance at a mysterious curve and identify it as delineating a naked human heel. If they kept climbing, they would know to look out for the lines of a long shapely leg. Passengers on the stairs were ant-sized, at best, compared to the figures on the wall.

First, learn everything you can, Daiya Sholto had said to Nemesia. *Her habits, her spending, her vices, her blind spots.*

For the past decade, ever since she returned from her first sabbatical, Nemesia's interaction with outsiders had been extremely limited.

Wide-eyed teenage novices trickled Below to join the Brood each year. She helped mentor them. Guards cycled in and out, too. She could deal with anyone within the context of the Brood.

Which didn't help much now. She didn't know how to talk to Kuchinashi Eden. And as soon as soon as they started climbing the stairs to Above, Eden shut her mouth and gazed at the lines on the curved walls as if she'd forgotten Nemesia was there.

Nemesia wasn't sure what to make of her. But then, maenads were known for their unpredictability.

"Those lines weren't drawn by humans," Nemesia said, since brooding wasn't getting her anywhere.

"They weren't?"

"Human artists might have created smaller drafts, once upon a time," she amended. "The Snake amplified their work."

"The lines look carved," Eden said, "but they're actually painted. Or is it the other way around?"

"Depends on the day."

"I was trying to see if there were any depictions of the Snake itself."

"No one ever depicts the Snake," Nemesia said, startled.

Eden traced a squiggle on the air with her forefinger. "Not even by just ... drawing a snake?"

Only someone who'd lived her entire life Above could crack a joke like that.

A week had passed since their first meeting. The Abbess adroitly negotiated to ensure that Nemesia's departure would sync with the start date of her second sabbatical, although she made up some other excuse to get Eden to agree. Only Brides went Above on such a regimented schedule, and Nemesia was determined not to be known as a Bride.

Eden seemed blissfully ignorant of all things Below. Otherwise, she would never have asked about art of the Snake.

Below was an unmappable warren of caverns sized for an indescribable god. Only Brood members could navigate its passages without guidance: their snakebite stigmata led them true.

It was never cold, and there was plenty of ethereal light, much of which had no obvious source. Tourists sometimes became nauseous from the dizzying ceiling heights, the impossibly tall doors, the unnatural acoustics.

The journey up and down the spiraling stairs would vary in length for different travelers. You could descend for what felt like hours and arrive Below only to find that less than a minute had passed.

Yet even elderly folk could make the trip without hurting their knees. The gravity of each step propelled you subtly to the next. So subtly that most people failed to notice they were being helped along.

"It's difficult to use magic Below," Eden said.

"You tried?" This came out in a yelp.

On second thought, there was no stricture against it. Most maenads simply wouldn't think to use magic unasked.

"Just a bit. Felt like exercising with a weighted vest—and weighted ankles, and wrists, and everything else."

That made sense. Snake-bitten clerics were blessed with the ability to suppress magic, and Below was the realm of the Snake, which had powers of its own. (Above was also the realm of the Snake. Just less overtly so.)

"But these stairs aren't strictly Below," Eden said. "Let's take a shortcut."

She handed over Nemesia's bag. Then she shook out the other thing in her fist.

It wasn't a baton at all.

It was a compact folding umbrella.

Eight ribs sprang apart like the legs of a spider. The dome of the umbrella turned out to be semitransparent—a colorful imitation of stained glass.

"All maenads have our chosen props," Eden said with easy confidence. "I've always liked collecting parasols and umbrellas. So many different designs. How can you pick only one?"

They were still very far down. The diffuse illumination around them was similar to the snakelight that dwelled in certain chambers of the Brood. A slippery light that swam sideways, like swirling currents of water. It borrowed from the stained glass hues of Eden's umbrella. It flung shadowed echoes of color across the vast pale steps in illogical splatters.

None of this could account for why Eden's dark eyes now looked auburn, touched with red. Or why the steps hummed underfoot, as if the two of them were insects crawling inside a musical instrument.

"Try not to extinguish me." Eden said.

Nemesia nodded. She clenched her hands together inside the long sleeves of her robe. Surrounded by the inaudible drone of rising magic, she surrendered her wariness, her clumsy consciousness of her covert mission, her anxieties about going Above.

Eden twirled the umbrella on her shoulder, and the stairs changed shape.

It happened in a series of frozen images, pages from a flip book. Chunks of the staircase rose like fossils hacked from stone, reassembling into wild helixes in the colossal dark well at the center of the shaft. A vertical tunnel large enough to accommodate the Neverending Snake.

"How are you doing that?" Nemesia blurted.

Eden shot her a quizzical look. "I'm a berserker. I haven't the faintest idea."

"What do you do when it rains?"

A shrug; her umbrella bounced on her shoulder. So did its cascade of vivid shadows. "It's just an assistive device. I can open a parasol without opening my magic."

During her previous sabbatical, Nemesia had spent a lot of time around young maenads. Mere children.

In her cumulative two decades Below, she'd sometimes taken shifts at one of the Brood's sanatoriums for retired maenads. On average, the residents looked a good deal older than the likes of K. Eden. They would never use magic again, if they could help it.

So in many ways, she was more familiar with maenads than your average citizen of the kingdom Above. But she'd never seen a practicing maenad at the height of their power.

The tassels on Eden's shoulders stirred in an unaccountable breeze. Freed slabs of rock floated in open space, a jumble of coruscating ladders.

The original spiral steps were such a rich source of material that they remained surprisingly intact, albeit with missing trenches here and there.

Eden used her shining umbrella to gesture toward the nearest of the hovering blocks. "Take my arm," she said. "Just don't dampen my magic."

This structure she'd built was comparable, in some ways, to an open-riser staircase. But the airy gaps between stepping stones seemed much too wide.

Nemesia clutched Eden's arm. She had a vague sense that each step forward covered enormous distances. Ambient light sparked against Eden's umbrella, casting prismatic shards down through the black space between steps.

There was a distant whooshing of water. Nemesia could've sworn she saw a narrow boat pass far below. She peeked at the divine art on the walls, but she still couldn't make out anything except incomplete lines.

In a rush, the sunlight from Above became screamingly bright. Her eyes teared. Eden held her umbrella low over both of them. Its stained glass pattern cast only the faintest of shade, but it was better than nothing.

They'd reached the top step of the coiled staircase. The main staircase, not Eden's invention.

Nemesia peered down the shaft. For most of the journey, it appeared like a straight shot from bottom to top, but up here it flared to form a funnel. Like the spiraling mouth of a sunken mine.

It looked exactly as it always had. No flying hunks of bone-colored rock.

"That was just for us," Eden said. She closed her umbrella and tucked it back in its small black pouch. She seemed like the sort of person who would never struggle to refold a map.

Nemesia brushed breathlessly at her silver-white robes, just to have something to do. They were completely unsullied.

The air Above tasted harsher and tangier than the air Below. There was more wind, more smoke, more dust, more voices, and a million more scents.

Below, Nemesia felt the constant weight of the invisible Snake like an endless cramp in her soul. It wasn't unbearable. It was just *there* in a way she only noticed after experiencing the lightness of stepping Above.

Under other circumstances, she would have been dwelling on memories of failure from her first sabbatical, or her reflexive shyness at the sight of the sky. But she was still dizzied by Eden's torrent of magic, and so that was the first thing she asked about.

By reputation, at least, maenads were stingy with their power. It took a lot out of them.

"It does hurt," Eden said, although she hardly looked winded. "It's exhausting and unpleasant."

"Then why—"

"Because I love it."

"Even if it pains you?"

"There are people who love running ridiculous distances, sometimes all around the perimeter of the Shell. There are people who run until their nipples bleed from chafing. Doesn't that sound awful?"

"Um, yes," said Nemesia.

"Even so, long-distance running is a perfectly acceptable pastime. So what's wrong with loving magic? It's not for everyone, but it's for me. And I'm good at it."

She took back Nemesia's bag of clothes. "My turn to carry this. Ah ... your eyes changed. That's why you left your veil behind, isn't it?"

Nemesia's snake-slit pupils only manifested Below—as was usually the case for Brood members with that particular symptom. Up Above, her eyes were nothing remarkable.

"Your eyes changed, too," Nemesia said. They no longer held that maddened hint of red.

"I put my magic back to bed," Eden said lightly.

They made their way along the rim of the circular chasm that led Below. Once they left, they began to see other people wandering down the off-white stairs.

There were alternative ways to get Below, but this entrance was the largest and best known. The chasm was ringed by flapping banners with the ammonite mark of the Brood. Further out came dense rows of shops and stalls selling trinkets and food—fermented camelid milk, fried tofu, roast pigeon.

A steam organ caterwauled in the distance. Eden pulled Nemesia smoothly through the ruckus.

She stopped upon reaching a small forgotten square that had made a half-hearted attempt at turning into a city park.

A tree with scant dirt around it grew next to a formation of threadbare bushes. There was a bench with a broken back, and a rusted pump, and a water fountain in the shape of a raccoon. Its paint had flaked off in a way that made it look exceedingly rabid.

Nemesia stood in the shade of a house with small triangular windows. She drank in the scenery. At last her breath caught up with her.

"You live here?" she asked.

"Oh, I'm way out in the countryside. Maenads usually get housing far from the city, and far from each other. We're supposed to ensconce ourselves in peaceful, relaxing environments."

"I know. But you seem unconventional."

Eden grinned a little. Her gaze fell to Nemesia's wrist. "You were called to life Below," she said. "You prefer life Above?"

Maybe she wouldn't prefer it—not anymore. She hadn't been Above in ten years. It would be a relief if she turned out to hate it.

"I was born Above," she answered.

"So was I," Eden said waggishly.

She spread her arms. Her black sleeves swung dramatically. Behind her, the crazy-eyed raccoon fountain glared like a silenced prophet.

"Welcome back," she proclaimed, and that was when it finally sank in.

Nemesia's heart raced ahead as if tripping downhill. She'd fought to knead away her elation, to grind all these spiky feelings into flatness. She was Above once more—it filled her lungs—and she would be devastated to leave again at the end.

5

The Hypothetical Assassin

NEMESIA WAS COLD. Her feet were coldest of all, even stuffed in the socks and embroidered shoes she'd brought from Below. No native warmth rose from the pavement of this forgotten square. She moved sideways into a block of sunlight.

It wasn't all bad. The cold made her tingle with life. The city rooftops looked stunningly lucid after she dabbed at watering eyes. It even felt novel to sniffle. Her nose kept running and running, shocked by the fullness of the air.

Eden's face moved as if fighting a smile. She slipped Nemesia a pack of tissues.

It was February: the first month of the new year. (People followed the same calendar Below, but there were no seasons, and no one ever shivered.)

At twenty-three, Nemesia had embarked on her first sabbatical in much the same way, stepping up into the lingering chill at the start of the year. Then, too, she had chosen not to be openly known as a bride.

She remembered fluttering banners at the top of the stairs. She remembered a bottomless sense of possibility. She'd originally gone Below at the age of thirteen. Ten years later, returning Above had felt like visiting fairyland.

Nothing so terrible had happened at the end of her first sabbatical. Just a little heartbreak. But she'd begun to see that her heart was a faulty door. It couldn't open many more times, and it couldn't open far.

Who can compete with the Snake? Tanyu had said to her.

Kuchinashi Eden didn't know it yet, but their marriage bargain would end a year from now, together with Nemesia's second sabbatical. As to whether Nemesia stayed Above afterward—that would depend on her own actions, and Daiya Sholto, and the Snake.

Unaware of all this intrigue, Eden patted the flaky raccoon fountain. She waited for Nemesia to finish blowing her nose.

Then Eden beckoned her onward. They passed between long, narrow apartments stacked two to three stories high.

Political posters were stuck all over retaining walls and garden fences. The candidates wore smiles or scowls of grim determination. One had put on a highly realistic crocodile mask. One was clearly just someone's spotted pet dog, with a grin that showed several rows of extra teeth.

The faces and typefaces changed from year to year, as did the candidates' unpronounceable names. There were always posters, but never elections. The parties being advertised seemed entirely fictional.

When Nemesia grew old enough to question this, a Brood sister had explained to her that the ubiquitous political posters were fragments from dreams of the Snake. Or a reflection of the world beyond the Shell.

In its observations of the world outside, the Snake must have gained the impression that such posters were a proper component of a thriving civic society. It didn't matter that the kingdom within the Shell was in no way a republic. Imaginary candidates smiled on garden walls because the Snake thought they belonged there. And because the Snake thought that, hardly anyone looked twice.

Consider the migratory geese that could sometimes be seen crossing the sky, even though they had no way to leave the Shell. Consider the miraculous shipments of grains and fruit that grew nowhere on local soil. The Snake's logic could be hard to follow, but it gave them lives of abundance.

Look humble, Nemesia told herself as she and Eden crossed through unfamiliar neighborhoods. *Look bashful. Look harmless.*

This didn't require much in the way of acting skills.

Was there a similar litany at the back of Eden's head? What would it be—look proud and carefree? That confidence seemed to come to her as naturally as Nemesia's reticence.

Eden walked briskly, her back tall and unprotected.

It would have been easy for Nemesia to conceal knives in her generous sleeves. If she were a real assassin, she could whip a blade out right now, quick as a cobra. The wildest of magic would fail to stop it. Eden would bleed out in the street, her power extinguished, unable to heal her own wounds, Nemesia's hand covering her mouth to staunch her screams.

Maybe such thoughts just didn't occur to people who'd lived their whole lives Above.

Nemesia had come of age in the care of the Brood. Maybe living with a sect that worshipped a fanged and poisonous deity would inevitably make you more inclined to think of morbid possibilities.

Citizens from Above had little concept of true poverty or physical misery. They harbored a vague awe of the past Empire that had helped birth their wondrous Snake. Beyond that, they knew nothing about world history. They could hardly even remember a time before the current King of Now. They would forget all particulars of the previous king whenever a new one got installed.

Eden stopped by a roadside shelter with walls on three sides and a peaked tile roof. Across the street was an abandoned house swaddled in brown vines.

Nemesia sat on a bench inside the shelter, perplexed, and quietly stretched her ankles.

Most of the signs on the walls bore stern warnings about the necessity of picking up fallen fruit. HARVEST PROMPTLY: IT'S THE LAW! and so on, with a lot of forced rhymes.

She leaned closer to scan a wanted poster for someone called Oddscale. The art was weirdly flattering. The figure wore a roguish scarf rendered in faded black brushstrokes like a curl of smoke.

Oddscale...

She'd heard that name numerous times during her first sabbatical, too. She had her own stories about Oddscale—who was a vigilante hero to some, and a criminal to others, and who always gave city residents something to talk about.

She turned, meaning to ask for news of Oddscale's latest exploits.

The words died on her lips.

"This is an omnibus stop," she said.

"That it is," Eden agreed.

"I've never—"

"Never?"

Nemesia stood up.

"Omnibuses are extremely safe," Eden said.

Except that people sometimes vanished while riding them. What sort of people? Those closest to death—so you could never use an omnibus as an ambulance—and those without strong connections Above.

The Abbess warned Brides about this before she sent them off on sabbaticals. "You only have a year," she'd say. "Even if you've made friends, your bonds might not save you from the depths of an omnibus. There are plenty of other ways to travel."

Wind jostled the nest-like vines around the house across the street. Nemesia's feet—suffocating inside those unaccustomed shoes—felt colder than ever.

Eden observed her patiently. "You're afraid to ride the omnibus."

A dried-up leaf scurried between them, then blew itself into a blind corner of the shelter.

Nemesia said nothing. She would only betray herself if she gave some weak explanation.

She locked eyes with a wrinkled caricature of angry fist-swinging fruit. It was half-covered by the Oddscale poster.

Eden took her by the elbow. "Let's go there." She pointed at the nest house. "The bus wouldn't have been very romantic, anyway."

As they finished crossing the street, an omnibus appeared in the distance. It was a great clacking, whooshing thing with too many legs to count, and a dark iridescent beetle body, and windows as transparent as a glasswing butterfly. The passengers inside looked like gray ghosts staring out.

6

A Provisional Marriage

BEHIND THE abandoned house sprawled a tangle of barbed wire and thorny roses. The blooms had turned brown and papery.

"It's a touch overwrought," Eden said wryly. "Wait here."

She walked along the wire fence, occasionally bopping a droopy rose with her fist.

Nemesia glanced up at the vine-wrapped house. An exterior staircase jutted out from the highest floor. It stopped midair, leading nowhere.

There was a rustling down by her feet. A wide, short snake scooted out from beneath the overgrown veranda. But it moved more like an inchworm, and it was as thick around the middle as a legless cat.

And it had eyelids. It blinked up at Nemesia. She blinked back.

"You found a mudling?" Eden, coming back over, sounded incredulous. "Aren't they famously shy?"

The mudling wiggled in warning, then—somehow—spontaneously

leapt as high as Nemesia's shoulder. It plunged back down and rolled vigorously out of sight. Startled birds flew out of the house above.

They watched the darkness under the veranda for another minute, but the mudling refused to reemerge.

Eden showed her over to a section of the fence where roses and barbed wire swirled into a shape like a wreath: an unnaturally perfect hole, almost as tall as Eden herself.

Forbidding magic stained its circumference, making it something you would instinctively glance away from, like a half-eaten carcass. Once Nemesia made an effort to pay attention, the magic let her be.

"Do you have wormholes Below?" Eden asked.

"Of course."

"I suppose Below isn't necessarily any smaller than Above. Perhaps it's larger." She took Nemesia's hand. "Be careful. This one stings."

The wreath-like wire and roses framed only a view of an abandoned lot. The houses in the rest of the neighborhood were as clean and pretty as freshly frosted cakes.

Eden ducked through the hole. Nemesia, pulled along by her hand, twisted sideways to keep from snagging her bag.

She felt nothing when she crossed the threshold.

They emerged on the front step of a cottage with a green sod roof. There was nothing else in sight except rich rolling land. No omnibus stops, no vivitaxis, no city buildings, no ammonite flags, no signs of humanity. And no hole to show where they'd come from.

Eden coughed and winced and thumped her chest. Once she'd recovered, she cast a measuring look at Nemesia.

"Didn't bother you?"

"Not at all."

"Lucky." She sighed. "That used to be a perfectly pleasant hole. I had to make it obscure and uncomfortable. Used to get too many nosy intruders." She motioned at the cottage. "It's larger than it looks. Here, I'll take your bag. Give me just a minute."

She disappeared inside.

The front door was as round as the wreath of roses. It had been draped with festive streamers of delicate molted snakeskin, crispy and colorless and already turning ragged. Perhaps they'd been hung for Nemesia's sake. A welcoming gesture, like fresh flowers in vases.

A staircase marched up the side of the house, terminating at a stretch of empty wall. Elsewhere, a single turret poked up above the roof, looking about as tacked-on as the symbolic stairs.

Most houses up here had at least one staircase to nowhere. They were rooted in very old beliefs, possibly older than the Snake itself. A ploy to misdirect demons and devils.

There were no such vestigial staircases Below, where the Brood felt that the Snake's protection ought to be more than sufficient.

Eden popped back out and ushered her inside, saying they were ready to process the basic paperwork.

Nemesia had an impression of an uncomfortably stretched-out hall. The ceiling was not low, but she found herself hyperaware of its presence. Her feet were in house slippers now, still all covered up. For a time, human-sized rooms and corridors would seem just as smothering as wearing shoes.

She'd lived Above until she was thirteen, and she'd gotten by just fine during her first sabbatical. She'd learn to ignore it.

An apple-sized lump squatted on Eden's right shoulder. Before she had a chance to ask about it, they entered some sort of study, or maybe a library. Slender trees grew outside all the windows.

"My dear Warden," said Eden, indicating an old man behind a desk. "The seneschal of this fine establishment. Just call him Warden, as I do. It's a sign of respect."

Nemesia uttered a tentative hello. The Warden grunted.

Eden gestured at her shoulder. "And this lovely lady is Pimiko. My crabantula."

On closer inspection, the whorled lump was a big spiral snail shell made of semitransclucent material, like dark smoky glass. A cluster of fuzzy legs peeped out of the opening.

Nemesia said hello again. The crabantula didn't respond.

"Our Warden will see to all your day-to-day needs," Eden said. "But first, let's get that contract delivered. I'm sorry for the lack for ceremony. We need to hurry up and appease the King."

The Warden had a long narrow face that looked as if it might fit effortlessly between the bars of a cage. He wore robes in deep, serious hues—black and humorless blue.

"Where's your witness?" he growled.

"Where indeed? I hope she's ready." Eden raised her voice as though speaking for the benefit of someone unseen.

"I'm a guest," said someone behind Nemesia. "I never signed up for this."

The woman in the doorway had two short horns growing from her head like rogue bones.

"What do you think of my wife?" Eden asked pleasantly.

The stranger gave Nemesia a long, hard look.

Nemesia stood very still. Her stigmata burned like mosquito bites on both wrists and both ankles.

"You either chose extremely well for yourself, or extremely poorly," the stranger said. "Time will tell." She had singularly pointed teeth. More like a shark than a snake.

Eden wore an odd smile. "You can at least bless our marriage."

"I refuse. Ask someone else."

"Come on, now. It's our wedding day."

"Your wife will bless your union, if you turn out to be deserving."

Eden chuckled. The horned woman flicked her nails, urging them to get on with it.

The Warden donned a set of heavy eyewear with protuberant lenses. A jungle of bendy long-necked lights descended from the ceiling, making the desk look like an operating table. He misted a tray with a glass spray bottle. Something writhed, then went still.

He opened a case of utensils that resembled a mix of tattoo needles and tiny makeup pencils.

Eden shifted closer to Nemesia, speaking softly. "He's a trained scribe of letters. It's more difficult than it looks. Ever tried it?"

"No," Nemesia lied. "I can write with a pen on paper."

"I can, too. What a coincidence."

"But I was never allowed to inscribe a scrollworm."

"I've heard that scribes from Below have high standards."

Indeed—the Brood often poked fun at missives sent from Above. As far as Nemesia could tell, though, the Warden would've held his own among the snootiest scribes of her acquaintance.

He hunched low over the anesthetized scrollworm on his tray, tattooing its unfurled skin with torturously cramped writing.

"This is a provisional marriage," he said through his teeth. He didn't look up. "The initial term is one year, as stipulated by your Abbess. The contract can then be made permanent, or dissolved without penalties. Eden, show her the details."

There were several paper copies on the desk before him. Eden plucked one free and began pointing out each clause in order.

At the other end of the room, the horned woman ran her fingertips over the door frame like a bored cat looking for something to scratch.

Nemesia had no concerns about the marriage contract. The details matched everything she'd already gone over with the Abbess.

The Warden paused his work and inquired—this time in more formal language—whether she agreed to be legally wed to the maenad known as Kuchinashi Eden.

Nemesia consented. The horned woman reluctantly bore witness.

No one signed anything. A transcript produced by a sworn scribe would mean no less than the royal seal of the King himself.

Without touching, without kissing, without looking each other in the eye, they were officially married. At least for a year.

"Congratulations," the horned woman said in tones of doom. She whisked herself out of the room. There was something strangely weightless about how she walked, as if her feet never fully touched ground.

"Will the King be satisfied if it's only provisional?" Nemesia asked.

"We hardly know each other well enough to make it permanent from the start. After all"—Eden smiled charmingly—"you might come to loathe me. Plenty of other ladies have before."

"Were you married to them?"

"No. But what seems tolerable at first might become quite intolerable with time. Look—it's about to go."

The Warden unpinned the paper-thin skin of the scrollworm. It immediately rolled itself up again, like a living cigarette.

His face creased in pain as he straightened his back. The surgical lights retreated toward the ceiling.

A narrow tube was clamped to one leg of the desk. In it rested a misshapen lotus pod affixed to a sturdy artificial stem. The pod was dry and brown, with hazelnut-sized wads of colorful fabric stuffed in every socket that had once held seeds.

The Warden used a pair of tweezers to pluck one such ball—bright red with white stitches—out of the lotus pod. He inserted his docile rolled-up scrollworm in the exposed hole. It disappeared like Nemesia and Eden stepping through a frame of barbed wire at the edge of the faraway city.

"The King will know you've followed orders," he said as he plugged the hole again. He didn't sound much more cheerful than the woman with horns.

7

Separate Bedrooms

EDEN TOLD THE Warden to rest. She claimed she would give Nemesia
a tour of the cottage.

Her idea of a tour turned out to consist of pointing vaguely at various
flights of stairs and telling Nemesia: "If you can navigate Below, you
won't have any problems up here."

In the meantime, Nemesia reclaimed her bag. She tried asking about
the horned woman.

"Oh, she's not a very sociable sort," Eden said airily.

The crabantula on her shoulder began to creep ever so slightly out
of its shell. Its eyes were a cluster of obsidian dots, all but hidden by the
thickness of its fur.

Nemesia, mesmerized, forgot to ask if the horned woman had a name,
or at least a title. Like the grave-looking Warden. Or the crabantula ...
Pimiko, was it?

Eden halted before an arched door. "There's your bedroom."

"My bedroom?"

"I like having some space to myself. Figured you might, too."

Nemesia started to open the door. "Are there any rules I should know about?"

The crabantula shrank back inside its shell until only its hairy claw-tipped toes remained visible. "Rules?" Eden echoed. "Like what?"

"Things I shouldn't do. Places I shouldn't go."

At this Eden drew herself up a little, one hand on her low-belted hip. "No, no. Go anywhere you want. Open any drawers you please. No forbidden rooms in this house. You can even run away, if you like."

"I wasn't planning on it."

"I'll have to come after you at least once, to save face. But if you run away again after that, no one would expect me to drag you back against your will."

It took a lot of work for Nemesia to keep her thoughts off her face. "Why would I run away? I wished for a life Above."

"Did you?"

"Why else would I—"

"Huh. Could've sworn that you were being coerced."

"You thought that," Nemesia said slowly, "and you still didn't hesitate to marry me?"

Eden moved nearer. The wood floor creaked underfoot. The ceiling was too high to reach up and touch, but to Nemesia it felt oppressively close. There were faded shapes all around them—antique wallpaper or painted panels—but she'd been too lost in her head to perceive the decor.

"Your Abbess hid you in plain sight," Eden said without a trace of a smile. "She wanted me to find you on my own. So I'd be more likely to pick you."

Nemesia's wrists prickled.

"If you think that's true…"

"I do."

"Then why did you choose me?"

"I like knowing who the spy in my house is."

Nemesia had envisioned buried bodies, closets full of skeletons, secrets locked in a basement or attic, questions she was never supposed to ask, doors she was never supposed to open. She'd worried about getting caught. But not on the very day of her arrival.

"And that," Eden concluded, "is why we're going in separate bedrooms. Tell our Warden if you need anything, or if you'd like to send out any scrollworms. Keep in mind that he's a rather accomplished cryptographer."

She stepped back, her gold-bleached hair swinging. It was tied loosely, with a bit of cord that looked ready to slide right off. Pimiko, face hidden, gripped her epaulet with minuscule black claws.

Nemesia's fingers felt numb around the handle of her bag. She couldn't comprehend why Eden wasn't throwing her out.

"Aren't you glad we got that out of the way?" Eden said. "Now you can relax and get down to spying, or performing acts of subtle sabotage, or whatever else you've been tasked with. Now you can enjoy your stay. I hope you do—I have to admit, I love it here."

She said all this without the faintest tinge of irony.

Afterward—alone and dazed—Nemesia closed the door of her new bedroom. She stared out across the furniture without seeing a thing.

Her mind kept jumping back to earlier moments. To the fat mudling that had popped out of nowhere, as if to warn her. To the sloughed snakeskins draped about the front door like a laundry line of white fishnet stockings.

She'd interpreted the skins as a misguided gesture of kindness or superstition. But other Brood members might have viewed them as a taunt. Maybe she was supposed to have been gravely offended.

The Bitten Brood frowned on using real-life snakes to symbolize their Snake, which of course was something entirely different. The Neverending Snake. The Snake That Ate the Roots of Time. It was in no way comparable to a backyard adder.

Actual snake leather was naturally out of the question, both Above and Below. But she'd heard of shed snakeskin being repurposed for charms and jewelry. There was no malice in that—nothing but entrepreneurial reverence. The Brood would turn a blind eye.

In any case, the tourist district Below sold all kinds of goods with suspiciously squiggly motifs, from kitchen towels to earrings. The Brood might claim such designs were wholly abstract, but everyone knew what they were meant to look like.

Nemesia began unpacking. Several dark wooden chests with elaborate iron fittings were lined up against one wall. Every compartment was empty. The bed was sunken into the floor.

Her feet ached from walking on hard ground in the city, and they still felt as though they would always be cold.

She looked out a window and saw large angle trees dotting lazy hills, their thick branches bent like a sharp succession of elbows. Round sculpted clouds squatted along the horizon like craggy scoops of ice cream.

Somewhere beyond all this lay the Shell that separated their self-contained kingdom (both Above and Below) from the rest of the world. Nemesia had never gone close enough to see it in person.

She opened the hidden compartment tucked deep in her bag. The contents—a vial of dessicated scrollworms and her own miniature tattoo kit—remained undamaged.

In some regards, it was easy to lie to those from Above. They couldn't know that almost every Maiden of the Snake was trained in inscription. No one Below would rely on her to prepare a formal letter, but she was competent enough to teach the basics to younger novices.

She sat back on her heels and considered what to do next.

Was there any point in proceeding as planned? Eden already knew she was up to no good. And yet—so far—Eden seemed to have no intention of kicking her out.

Unlike Daiya Sholto, Nemesia had no personal reason to resent her new wife. But when she thought back on how coolly Eden had looked at her in the hallway, it was with an unaccustomed flare of irritation.

You think I'll be so ineffectual that you won't even try to stop me. You think it's safe to let me snoop.

Part of her wanted to prove Eden wrong.

She didn't see Eden again later that day, or that night. She tried to have dinner with the Warden, but he vanished after serving her.

She found a bathtub down the hall from her room. It took some wrangling to produce warm water. Bathing springs Below were always hot and clean and fresh, without any funny levers or handles or calcified metal dials.

She kept hearing isolated drips, a strange plinking that echoed from within the walls around her. But she couldn't find any soft spots, and she didn't smell any rot.

She laid herself down on her sunken bed quite early. It was close to the same size as her bedding Below. Just right for one person.

The windows had interior shutters, which she'd closed to block out starlight, but she still couldn't sleep. That watery dripping in the walls hadn't stopped yet.

It was the sound of magic percolating, she concluded. The building's windy rasping came from its innate magic, too. So did the nearly undetectable sensation of the floor tilting gradually from one side to the other, struggling to make itself perfectly level, never quite satisfied.

She had no clue where Eden was right now, or where she customarily slept.

You can run away, she'd said. Was that a suggestion? An invitation? A trap?

Down Below, Nemesia had never been lonely. Even through cavern walls, she could always sense other Brides. It felt like they were all hatchlings cradled in the same nest.

She missed her guard, too, although he'd only been with her for the past couple years. Everyone called him Roc, because the badge he wore depicted an open-winged bird.

This had initially spurred a lot of good-humored debate. Some thought his bird looked more like a phoenix, or an eagle. Some argued that a roc wasn't a proper bird at all; it was a different sort of aerial titan. Older sages—who remembered legends of rocs eating giant serpents—found his nickname ominous. But it was easy to say, and Roc himself liked it, and so it stuck.

A restless layer of Nemesia's mind remained in constant motion, like running water. She recalled more meaningless bits of the day so far. Floating stone steps. The icy ground beneath thin-soled shoes. Eden stepping gracefully among spiky weeds in her dark mannish robe. Posters of nonexistent politicians, and of the hero Oddscale.

But Oddscale was real. For almost as long as the Snake had been around, there had been a shadowy figure known as Oddscale—played by different people from one generation to another. The Snake had convinced itself that society needed silly political posters, and that true justice required the presence of a masked vigilante.

As a child, Nemesia had secretly dreamed of growing up to be the next Oddscale. She bore four snakebites, after all. More than anyone else alive. But instead of becoming a hero, she'd turned out to be a Bride.

8

Teeth

THE NEXT DAY, there was still no sign of Eden. The Warden set out a breakfast of sweet pumpkin porridge loaded with red beans and rice cakes. It was so filling that Nemesia almost rolled right back into bed.

But the Warden soon made himself scarce. So she donned a robe with fewer layers and a simpler sash than the day before, and she started exploring.

The architecture of the cottage seemed distinctly illogical. The corridors stretched out to comical lengths, as if forgetting how much space the layout really required. This didn't bother her; she was accustomed to the vagaries of winding tunnels Below.

The majority of rooms appeared to be in actual use. All of them—even combined together—could have easily fit inside the Abbess's chamber of contemplation.

Nemesia found only two that had been set aside for storage. Both were crammed from floor to ceiling with excess furniture. Vintage dining chairs, speckled mirrors, a billiard table, wood cabinets subdivided into tiny drawers. You could fit a single preserved stag beetle in each pull-out compartment, and not much more.

The storerooms looked too haphazard to hold evidence of dark secrets. Which might actually make them an excellent hiding spot, but there was a real risk of getting buried alive. She resolved to search them last.

The house had a small elevator, too. She rode it just once. It was obnoxiously slow.

She kept getting confused about the total number of floors—two or three, or four? Whatever the case, the highest level was only accessible via the elevator or the basement.

She figured this out after locating another set of stairs behind the laundry room. They marched off into darkness, as if connecting to a sub-basement.

These stairs were well-lit, but their shadows were in constant motion. Wire cages had been installed around each light, and within those cages, flecks of brightness veered about like giddy moths. They were spaced out along the walls with dizzying irregularity.

Clover grew from the seams between each step. Perhaps it fed on the same old thrumming magic as the sod of the roof, which also supported throngs of wildflowers and the occasional slender sapling.

She didn't hesitate to walk down the stairs, and she wasn't surprised when they deposited her on the uppermost floor of the house.

The Warden's room was at ground level, and Nemesia's room was on the second floor. Eden's room seemed to be all the way up top. Pimiko the crabantula clung motionlessly to the wall outside her door.

Nothing happened when Nemesia slid the door open. It wasn't locked. The dripping sound in the walls strengthened, like rain hitting a skylight. But it was sunny outside, and sunny in Eden's bedroom.

She had an extravagant loft bed, neatly made up, with a hammock strung in the space beneath.

An astonishing variety of umbrellas and parasols hung from high wall hooks arranged around the perimeter of the room. Overhead, exposed ceiling beams were carved with segmented ridges like an earthworm.

A framed picture rested on an old-fashioned vanity. The girl in the picture looked young. Well under twenty. Over her robes she wore a cross-back apron—a style of garment usually reserved for students. She had chin-length black hair tucked behind her ears, and she wasn't smiling.

She stood by a twisted pine tree that loomed taller than the nearest building. It was staked to the ground with cables stretching out in four different directions, like a tent without fabric.

That tied-down tree tickled Nemesia's memory. Had she seen it during her last sabbatical? Or much earlier?

Who was this girl to Eden? Nemesia scrutinized that serious face, bare of cosmetics, and finally the answer came. In a spot where others might place images of dear friends, Eden had chosen to display a lovingly framed portrait of her younger self.

She'd expected Nemesia to come sniffing. She might very well have left the picture out for Nemesia's benefit. There were few other personal effects in evidence.

There was no sign of the horned woman, either.

Anything truly important would be hidden in multiple ways. Locked in a fireproof safe, for instance, inside a magically sealed-off room.

With its structural oddities, the house would have been difficult to capture on paper. Nemesia contented herself with cobbling together a rough mental map. Then she turned her attention to hidden spaces.

The first-floor drawing room contained a striking display of vintage robes, each strung up on a plain black rod to show its pattern to best effect. Nemesia maneuvered carefully between them. She followed the sound of dribbling water to a blank stretch of wall.

She extinguished the magic on the wall. Temporarily, not permanently. All it took was a pointed thought.

Behind the illusion awaited a magical supply closet. Or perhaps a dumping ground.

Dried lotus pods lay strewn like animal droppings in a corner. She turned one about in her fingers. It didn't seem usable for sending letters.

Most of the remaining space was taken up by a dusty chest of drawers. The wood was black with age. Parts of it looked downright charred.

On top of the chest was a second chest, half as small as the first. On top of that was a third chest, half as small again. And on top of that—

It just kept going. Vertigo seized her. She crouched and opened the lowest drawer.

Empty.

She reluctantly pulled open the next drawer, and then the next drawer, and the next.

The drawers got smaller. Soon she had to rise on her toes. She couldn't see inside: she stuck her fingers in and scrabbled around. Every single compartment felt empty.

At last she came to the highest one she could reach without fetching a stool. She groped uselessly at the lip of the drawer. She was already starting to draw back when her fingers snagged on something cold.

It felt like a necklace. Perhaps a lumpy strand of pearls.

She brought her hand down and found herself clutching a fistful of brassy human teeth.

9

The Scriptorium

DEEP BELOW, there was an area known as the undersky. The main entrance was blocked by an imposing stone door that no one knew how to open.

Brides entered the undersky through a much smaller hole, a round aperture like something bored by a carpenter bee. Its exact location changed from day to day, although it never drifted far from the impenetrable door.

If you could see that entrance, and step through it, you were deemed a Bride of the Snake.

On the other side of the hole, there was still a stone ceiling. It was rough and unfinished, and overall less impressive than other vaulted ceilings Below—some of which teemed with masses of giant human figures.

Such sculptures protruded too far to be called reliefs. They appeared to be falling all at once, grabbing each other by the ankles, faces contorted with terror (although you'd have to use a spyglass to perceive such details from the ground).

The undersky had none of that. No stone mobs cast down from the heavens. No monumental line art, like in the stairwell to Above.

The undersky had no floor, either. As its name might suggest, the floor seemed to be made of sky. When you walked about, it felt like walking on air. Night never came, but the light would sometimes shift as if paying tribute to sunrise or sunset. There was no land to be seen, just endless layers of clouds.

At thirteen, Nemesia entered the undersky and was thus deemed a Bride. But she forgot to come back. The Abbess had to send in six other Brides after her, ranging in age from eighteen to eighty-five. A full month had passed by the time they extracted her.

She thought she'd only been inside for a few minutes. She remembered the wind and the golden light from below, the blue expanse, the weightless sky around her bare feet, the clouds folded in on themselves with pink cavernous shadows. She remembered the mind-scorching presence of the Snake. She remembered understanding each and every one of its names. She knew what made it the Snake That Ate the Roots of Time.

She barely remembered her own name, or anything that had happened Above during the first thirteen years of her life. The Abbess scolded her, saying she was far more vulnerable to the undersky than other Brides.

She wasn't allowed back down there until she'd spent several years practicing all the Brood rituals meant to cultivate self-possession. She learned meditation techniques. She learned to extricate herself from the immeasurable weight of the Snake.

Whether you were lost in the undersky or lost in magical Snake-given dreams, the first step was to remember yourself. The second step was to stop panicking. It was like trying to save yourself from drowning.

Maybe it was because of her familiarity with the immensity of the undersky, and the unseen immensity of the Snake. Maybe that was why Nemesia gazed down at the string of human molars she'd found in a secret drawer, and she didn't make a peep.

She jiggled the teeth in her palm, thinking furiously. They were either metallic replicas or real teeth with a metal coating, roots and all. Like chocolate-dipped strawberries.

She wasn't an expert on teeth—or other bones, either. But she had seen strands of preserved teeth before. They were designed to be just long enough to use as a necklace. Of course, no one within the Shell would actually wear human teeth like jewels.

Below, near the door to the undersky, there was a vault where the Bitten Brood stored artifacts from outside. Not just from Above. From outside the protective magical Shell that surrounded the entire dominion of the Snake.

It wasn't the only such collection. The palace had one, too, as did a few museums of curiosity in the city (although many of their artifacts were fraudulent). Some private citizens kept antiquities from outside as family heirlooms.

Nemesia was only personally familiar with the Brood's vault. Had she glimpsed this exact necklace there, or something very like it?

She backed away from the wall. The latent illusion snapped back into place, hiding the tower of chests. She retraced her steps among the silent standing robes. Each had a small placard with notes about its design and date of creation. She didn't stop to read any.

Even if she'd never seen a string of teeth before in her life, even if she'd had no prior knowledge to suggest that this object came from outside, she would have known. It didn't belong here. It didn't belong anywhere inside the Shell. All her deepest instincts warned her.

Eden, too, should have known that her extinguisher wife could unlock any area hidden with magic. Either she was extremely forgetful, or she simply didn't care if Nemesia found this necklace.

Maybe she'd bought it at a black market auction. Maybe it was a gift from a lover. Maybe everyone knew that Eden the maenad liked jewelry made of pulled teeth.

Nemesia had only brought a limited number of scrollworms. She'd better learn more before sending Sholto her first report.

She hid the necklace in her room.

Over the next few days, she sometimes found the Warden cleaning. He was slow and thorough. The house itself took care of crumbs that fell on large flat surfaces, like tables or carpets. It ignored dust caught in small crevices, such as the worm-like grooves carved all over the ceiling beams in Eden's room.

She attempted to fish for Eden's whereabouts. The Warden proved so unresponsive that she had to give up on subtlety.

"Where is she?" Nemesia asked.

"What do you care?"

"I'm her wife."

"Hah!"

That was, evidently, a complete sentence. The Warden went back to fussing with miniature trees in shallow pots. He kept some indoors, but the majority were outside, crowded all over multi-level benches made of weathered gray wood.

As he went about his duties, Nemesia kept following him around and asking after Eden. To no avail.

He must have spent decades climbing stepladders to wipe at the molding. He didn't appreciate Nemesia's urgent offers to help. But the sight of him teetering atop a ladder, skinny arms outstretched, was rather more than her conscience could bear. Besides, if they worked together, he might warm up to her. He might tell her more about the house, and about Eden.

This hadn't yet come to pass. The Warden remained gruff, and said little. Pimiko kept appearing in random corners: sometimes with her legs fully extended, and sometimes hiding deep in her shell. She wasn't very vocal, either.

Nemesia, for her part, kept forgetting that she was supposed to get the Warden talking. She was too accustomed to spending time in companionable silence with fellow clerics.

In the process of assisting him, however, she managed to take a closer look at the library.

Of all the rooms in the house, the library and the kitchen were generally most likely to be occupied by the Warden. She could make up excuses for poking around the kitchen—she could pretend to be desirous of water, or tea, or a midnight snack. She'd exercised more caution about invading the library.

Perhaps *library* was the wrong word for it, anyway. The Warden mainly used it as a scriptorium. Sometimes he scribbled away at scrollworm skin while Nemesia wiped invisible fingerprints off the glass-fronted shelves holding books and boxed scrolls.

Who would he send so many messages to in Eden's absence? Maybe he was paying bills for her. Or writing boilerplate replies to angry letters from ex-girlfriends.

By pretending to make herself useful in the scriptorium, Nemesia began to learn the Warden's routines. She deduced when she could come back unobserved.

She put this to the test on a cloudy afternoon. The Warden would be busy receiving deliveries of fresh vegetables, tofu, rice, and other standard kitchen supplies.

Alone, she walked casually into the scriptorium. She did a circuit of the room to make sure Pimiko wasn't lurking anywhere. Eden might be using the crabantula to keep tabs on her. Perhaps Eden could peer out through those tiny alien eyes, or sense the air stirring furry bristles.

Fortunately, Pimiko's size and gleaming shell made her much easier to spot than a regular house spider. The scriptorium seemed clear. Nothing watched Nemesia except the lotus pod by the desk, all its hollows plugged with silken spheres like soft marbles.

A few of the Warden's thick-leaved houseplants were arrayed near the window. One had started to flower.

She went over to the shelves. The protective glass doors were sealed with magic. It seemed like a tricky sort of spell, intended to admit only Eden or the Warden.

Nemesia, being an extinguisher, could bend the magic apart to let herself in—like turning the steel bars of a cage into flexible rubber. (She could also have simply snuffed the spell out altogether, but she didn't want to leave an obvious trail of destruction.)

She inhaled the scent of old paper. She examined books and scrolls of folklore about demons and elves. Scripts for famous old plays. Compilations of hundreds of ghost stories and urban legends. Tall tales of Oddscale. Scholarly tomes about magical theory.

There were a surprising number of texts with a historical bent. A lot of them focused on the Antemaenad: the first maenad, the greatest maenad. She'd shown that it was possible to control wild magic, to tame the berserker within. She'd led the Blessed Empire to victory in distant lands.

Surviving stories of the Antemaenad were mostly pure myth. In that sense, these fit right alongside nearby collections of classic supernatural tales for children.

Mixed in with this were occasional memoirs from people who claimed to have ventured outside the Shell. They had slipped away in their dreams, they said, led by a sacred serpentine guide. Or they were abducted by monsters. Or they stumbled through a mysterious door and found themselves stranded on foreign shores.

That sort of travelogue was rarely reliable. Nemesia skimmed titles until she reached one that she couldn't read at all.

A chill went down her back.

This book looked newer than most others, but it was completely indecipherable. The lettering on the page had nothing in common with any written characters she'd ever learned.

The Brood vault also stored a selection of books with unreadable text. Books from outside the Shell. They were printed in languages that no one from Above or Below had any idea how to parse.

She didn't take the foreign book. She closed up the shelves and retreated. Her slippered feet remained steady, but her pulse felt violently uneven. Soon she would have to compose her first message to Daiya Sholto.

10

The Warden

SHE PREPARED her report in her room, then stole back to the scriptorium after dark. The kitchen looked steamy; the Warden was busy.

She poked her scrollworm through the lotus pod. Afterward, she recorked the seed hole with its silken cloth stopper.

When she heard footsteps at the door, she had just enough time to take several big strides away from the desk.

Soft evening lights had come on when she entered: a host of little lost flames caught near the ceiling like bugs in cobwebs. Those lights were pure magic. She could cut them off if she wished.

But what then? She'd stumble around, blinded. She'd walk straight into a bookshelf, or straight into the Warden himself.

So she left the lights on. She positioned herself by a hanging scroll painted with a wash of monochrome ink.

"We don't have art like this Below," she said without turning her head.

Artwork Below was usually grander in scale. Like the great fields of rock formations and sparkling gravel that Brood sisters raked into ever-changing patterns day after day, year after year.

The Warden shuffled toward her. "What were you doing?"

"Admiring this—"

"Before that."

"Looking for something to read."

"The shelves are locked."

"The doors are glass. I can see titles, at least. I'll let you know if there's anything I'd like to borrow."

The Warden regarded her frostily. He was smaller than her, shriveled with age. She was lucky to have heard him in the hallway—he always doddered around in split-toe booties, quiet as a creeping cat. He wore dark, practical clothing, sometimes with odd motifs like a moon-colored spider on his back, or a single forlorn tree growing from the hem of his jacket.

Luckily for Nemesia, life with the Abbess had thoroughly inoculated her against any fear of grouchy elders.

"I married into this household," she said evenly. "My wife told me I can go in any room, for any reason. Was she mistaken?"

"I'm not paid to have opinions."

"Do you wish I'd never come?"

"Hmph."

They seemed to be at an impasse. At least he hadn't openly accused her of treachery.

"Did Eden tell you my name?" she asked on impulse.

"I drew up your marriage contract," he said slowly, as if she were stupid.

"Ah. Yes. May I have your name, then? She never told me."

He blinked at her owlishly.

A tremor went through the corrugated flesh of his face.

Was he having a stroke?

"M. Withers," he said in a voice she'd never heard before.

"M for—"

"Meifu," he replied. Immediately, and lightly. "Same as you. Meifu Withers. Like Meifu Nemesia. Like Meifu Balsa. Can't believe old Balsa's still the Abbess."

Nemesia gaped.

Beneath the glow of the hovering evening lights, the Warden transformed.

He straightened his back. He dipped his hand in a little jar on the desk—which wasn't ink, as she'd assumed. It must have been some kind of hair serum. After applying it, he removed his old-fashioned glasses. He pulled a svelte new pair out of his sleeve.

He cleared his throat.

"I'm only sixty-one," he said. "Decades younger than Balsa."

Nemesia was flabbergasted. "You're ... you're from the Brood?"

His face scrunched back into sour lines of the Warden she knew. It wasn't magic. It was just an extraordinary feat of physical acting.

Then he merrily collapsed into the chair behind the desk. He plunked one foot atop his knee and slipped his house boot halfway off. He tapped meaningfully at his bare ankle.

He had a snakebite birthmark, reddish-purple against pale skin. Nemesia knew at a glance that it was real. Brood members could always tell.

He bore the same surname as all other ordained clerics. He was a Maiden of the Snake, a true Irreversible Sister.

"What should I call you?" she asked, clinging to protocol.

"Keep calling me Warden. It's one of my favorite roles." He fixed his footwear. Then, more contritely: "Did I have too much fun with it?"

"With what?"

"Playing an archetypal old hardass. You're one of the Abbess's favorites, aren't you? Figured you could take it."

Human pettiness lost much of its edge after years spent like a flea, huddling against the invisible bulk of a divine beast.

"You fooled me," Nemesia said sheepishly, "but the Abbess is harsher."

He smiled like a boy. "Whew. I was afraid I'd overdone it."

She'd looked at him and seen an ancient loyal servant, bowed by time, gruff and craggy and resentful of outsiders.

Now he took bottled oil from a drawer and began tending assiduously to his salt-and-pepper beard. This worked wonders to smooth and sharpen it, but the smell made Nemesia sneeze.

"What are you, exactly?" she said.

"The Warden of this storied house."

"I get that, but—"

He spoke like a narrator introducing a play. "Back in the days of a different Abbess, I requested to be stationed Above. Took on work looking after maenad residences. Eventually I ended up here.

"In a house drenched with generations of magic, it helps to have someone around who can turn bits of it off. Like an emergency plumber. If the magic goes wrong, I can't fix it, but I can keep it from bringing the whole building down."

"So you faked being a bitter old grump ... just for sport?"

"Did my act remind you of home?"

"Where's home?"

"I took most of my inspiration from Balsa."

Nemesia was frankly too baffled—and too impressed—to be upset. She'd rushed to rescue him when he tottered up ladders, terrified he might shatter his hip (or his head). In the days since her arrival, he hadn't once broken character.

"Eden knows you're from the Brood?"

"I'm an extinguisher. All wardens are."

"Oh."

The Abbess could have warned her, Nemesia thought sourly. Was this supposed to be common knowledge? Most people—whether from Above or Below—would never have occasion to peek inside a maenad residence.

"Eden knows what you're really like?"

"Of course."

"Did you plan this out with her?"

"Nope. Not a word."

"She didn't seem surprised when she brought me to meet you."

He flexed his wrists. "She's seen me play that kind of Warden before."

Eden hadn't mentioned that her live-in seneschal wasn't always so crabby. She'd made a point of not saying his real name, either.

"Did you discuss me with the Abbess?" Nemesia asked.

"She sent a letter exhorting me not to trouble you." The Warden chortled. "I owe my allegiance to the Bitten Brood and the Snake. Not old Balsa.

"The bones of this cottage date all the way back to the Antemaenad," he added, abruptly serious. "Some even claim she lived here. True or not, there's a lot to look after. Housework keeps me busy. I won't be your friend, but I won't be your enemy, either."

He would know perfectly well that Nemesia had been taught the same rudimentary skills as other clerics. So much for pretending she had no training as a scribe.

Had he already guessed that she was a Bride? Had the Abbess told him outright?

"I can keep helping you, if it's actually helpful," she said. A peace offering. "If I'm not just getting in the way."

"Sure. I'm always happy to finish up early." He rose, moving much more flexibly than before, and tucked his chair back into the writing desk.

"My real passion is community theater. Practical effects only. No magic. The whole acting thing, playing a role—it didn't come out of nowhere." His posture briefly reverted to that of the older Warden.

"Ah."

"I used to play Oddscale on stage. One of the old apocryphal variants. A dashing gentleman thief."

He mimed tossing a scarf about his neck. Nemesia suppressed a laugh. Even without props, he looked the part.

"That's how I first met Eden."

"Really?"

He twirled on the carpet to face her, as dramatic as a starring actor. His newly neatened beard would have been officious-looking on most men, but on him it came off as puckish.

"She was still in school," he explained. "My troupe went to her reformatory. Did a charity performance in the garden."

Despite being located Above, maenad schools were all run by the Brood. And they were always called reformatories. Young maenads needed to be thoroughly reshaped before they could safely rejoin society.

Raging mages were berserkers by nature. It took years to learn to hold in their magic. In Brood reformatories, staffed by extinguishers, they could master their power without hurting themselves or others.

"She saw you perform," said Nemesia, "and she went to say hello after the show?"

The Warden shook his head. "None of the kids were allowed to talk with us. She told me about it much later. Once she was old enough to leave the reformatory for weekends and holidays, she found us again. She watched a bunch of plays at outdoor festivals."

He drew a circle around his wrist. "Maenads in training wear a wristband. It turns bright red if their magic leaks. Hers never turned red, but my costars noticed her anyway. Weren't any other teenage maenads in the audience.

"Once she got permission from her teachers, she began to volunteer with our troupe. She had real potential as an actress.

"But she became a lot busier after graduating. Eventually she stopped performing. She still helped with costuming and makeup and set design for as long as she could. She was always very interested in behind-the-scenes work."

This was all new information. Eden's total absence from her own home had made it impossible for Nemesia to get to know her.

Of course, Eden had every reason to keep their interactions to a minimum.

"Why is she avoiding me?" Nemesia inquired. Mostly out of curiosity about how the Warden might answer.

He tipped his head from side to side, stretching his neck.

"Most maenads reach the peak of their magical mastery in their twenties," he said. "Some start losing control as soon as their early thirties. It's exhausting, holding your magic in when all it wants to do is go berserk. It's a battlefield best suited for youth."

"Like athletics."

"More like the game of Go," he corrected. "Some elite players peak later. There's plenty of individual variance. K. Eden is still going strong, for the most part."

"But she's shown symptoms of deterioration?"

"You're an extinguisher, and a much more capable one than I am," said the Warden. "Old Balsa made that crystal clear. If something ever happens—if I can't stop Eden—then you'll have to."

"What should I watch out for?"

He pondered for a moment, then lowered his voice. "Her dreams slip out at night. That's often one of the first symptoms."

"Is that why she's avoided sleeping here?"

"Maybe she doesn't want you to see it yet."

"Would you give her a message?" Nemesia asked. "Tell her to come have dinner with her wife. At least once."

The Warden snorted. "No, thank you. You can tell her yourself." He briskly explained how.

11

The Emergency Egg

LATER THAT NIGHT, Nemesia went to Eden's room. She took the chair in front of the vanity and turned it to give her a view of the bed.

The loft and the hammock below it were both empty. The only illumination came from thick pillar candles trapped under glass bell jars. The wicks appeared unlit, but something flickered and shone inside the creamy wax.

The Warden had tossed her a keychain. It had no keys attached, just a dangling metal socket that affixed itself, claw-like, to the tip of a speckled pink bird egg.

After telling her how to use it, he shooed her off, saying: "It's past my bedtime."

Nemesia had brought the necklace of metal-plated teeth from her room. She laid it on Eden's vanity. She closed her fist around the pink egg, squeezing as hard as she could. At last it broke.

Nothing oozed out. When she opened her fingers, the shell had been reduced to dry empty shards—as thin as flakes of paint, although it had taken considerable force to shatter.

A second later, invisible magic ricocheted out of the wreckage. The eggshell put itself back together, fragments leaping to form a seamless pink whole. She set it aside.

The keychain was supposed to be an alarm mechanism. A way for the Warden to call Eden if, say, the house suddenly collapsed and trapped him.

The light of the fireless candles billowed as if in a gust of angry wind. Something stirred in the loft.

Nemesia climbed up on the chair just in time to witness the metal tip of a parasol piercing through made-up bedding.

The parasol rose smoothly out of a tucked-in blanket. It pointed at the ceiling like a lance.

Next came a raised arm gripping the parasol's handle, followed by the rest of Eden. She pulled herself up as though grabbing at the edge of a swimming hole.

Once most of her had swum up through the mattress—as if it were no more solid than mist—she tossed her parasol aside. Nemesia ducked. It sailed past her and caught itself nimbly on an empty wall hook.

Eden made a sound of annoyance. The blanket had re-solidified around her ankle. She wrestled with it as if trying to shimmy off slim-cut pants.

Her foot popped free. She looked across the room at Nemesia, still standing atop the chair by the vanity.

"I take it that no one's been hurt," she said.

"No accidents, and no emergencies," Nemesia affirmed.

"Where's the Warden?"

"He went to bed. What were you doing?"

Eden stopped midway down the stairs to the loft. She sat comfortably, legs outstretched.

She wore a wrap jacket (without her usual epaulets) over trousers, but no shoes. She must have come from someplace indoors.

"What was I doing?" she said. "Reciting poetry by moonlight. What else? I might ask you the same thing. Did you browbeat our poor Warden into surrendering his emergency egg?"

Nemesia stepped down off the chair. "I know his name now," she said, "and he gave it freely."

"The egg or his name?"

"Both."

Eden ran both hands through her hair, golden except for where the roots at the top of her head spilled down like spreading ink. She eyed Nemesia speculatively.

"Took you a while to make him break character," she said. "It's been about a week since he inscribed our marriage."

"We could have skipped that whole charade if you'd told me that he belongs to the Brood."

"I didn't want to take away his fun."

Pimiko scuttled out from the underside of the loft and hopped onto Eden's arm.

"You used your pet to spy on me," Nemesia said.

"Only sometimes." There was a certain tired bluntness to her manner, as if she couldn't be bothered with artifice.

"Why would you marry me and then immediately vanish?"

"I'm here now, aren't I?"

"You weren't here yesterday, or any day before that. You left me to my own devices." Nemesia tapped the re-formed egg. "I could've burned the house down."

Eden rubbed her forehead.

"Are you really going to complain about having too much freedom? Have you been lonely—is that it?"

"I never asked you to flee your own home."

"I was just being polite," Eden said wearily. "Didn't you find it easier to search the premises without a maenad breathing down your neck? I had things to do."

"Were you planning to stay away until I dragged you back by force?"

Eden put a hand over her mouth, concealing a smile. "Well, it's nice to feel wanted."

"Even by a stranger?"

"Everyone starts off as strangers."

It was easy to imagine her using that line on someone else. Daiya Sholto's unfortunate sisters, for instance.

Nemesia swept the string of teeth off the vanity and held it out, molars jangling. Eden's only response was a slow blink.

"This is an artifact from outside," Nemesia said.

"Not everything in this house is mine. Generations of maenads have—"

"There's a book from beyond the Shell in the scriptorium, too. Not even hidden. Shelved right in the middle of your collection."

Nemesia hadn't realized how outraged she was until she heard it in her own rising voice. "You stole these artifacts out of our most sacred vault. That's why you came Below. That's why you pretended to want a spouse from the Brood. You needed a pretext to enter our sanctum. The Abbess welcomed you as a guest!"

The artifacts had historical resonance, but no special power of their own. The Brood would not be deeply wounded by the loss of a couple fragments from its collection—although scholarly types would lament it.

Nemesia was not a scholarly type. She couldn't begin to guess at how an appraiser would determine the value of an unreadable book or a necklace of human teeth (real or molded). The violation of trust was what stuck in her craw. This was the sort of wicked deed that Oddscale the hero ought to punish.

Eden got up and picked her way down the rest of the stairs from the loft. She came across the floor. She stopped in front of Nemesia with the brassy teeth dangling between them.

"There are artifacts from outside the Shell in private collections, and in the palace," she said, unhurried. "You know that? Then you must be accusing me because you think you saw these exact pieces—or something like them—in the custody of the Brood."

Her finger brushed the lowest-hanging tooth as if plucking a single taut string on a musical instrument. "Even if I stole Brood treasure the very day we first met, why would I proceed to plant it right where you could find it?"

"Maybe you took a lot more," Nemesia said stubbornly. "You could have already sold the rest."

"Ask your Abbess if anything's gone missing. Get the Warden to shoot her a note."

"I will."

"Good."

"In the meantime"—Nemesia shook the teeth like a rattle—"explain this."

"Want that necklace for yourself? Keep it, if you like. Consider it a wedding gift."

"That's not—"

Eden put her hands on Nemesia's shoulders and gently steered her out of the way, then stepped up to the mirror.

"Let me get comfortable. Then I'll tell you."

She transferred Pimiko from her arm to the vanity, near the framed portrait of her younger self.

She began removing jewelry—thin gold earrings and bracelets and rings and necklaces, so dainty that Nemesia hadn't noticed her wearing them. Meanwhile, Pimiko's furry legs explored the desktop in a series of cautious, mincing steps.

Eden's wrap jacket was slipping off. She wore a sleeveless top beneath it. *This person is your wife,* Nemesia thought, briefly overwhelmed by absurdity. *You've never even touched her shoulder.*

"I went missing," Eden said.

"You ... what?"

"For three years. Between the ages of thirty-three and thirty-six. I remember none of it," she added casually. "Just blankness. Like a night of too much drinking, except it came on without warning, and it lasted for years. At first—after returning—I thought it was payback."

"Payback for what?"

"All the mischief I've made. At any rate, I reappeared three years later. I had no memories of my absence. Instead of memories, I had artifacts from outside. So I kept them."

She pulled open a drawer and began dropping bits of jewelry into a cloth-lined tray. "In three full years, not a single person saw me anywhere in the city or the country, Above or Below. I must have been spirited outside the Shell.

"I seem to have sacrificed three years of my life for a couple of useless curios. And not any old three years. I'd have been delighted to trade in chunks of my childhood. But those particular years might otherwise have marked the height of my magic-using career. That's an irreplaceable loss."

She soundlessly rolled the drawer shut. Pimiko, on the desk above, went still and tense.

"I'm thirty-eight now. I've had time to get over it." She shrugged off her jacket. "Mind if I change?"

"It's your room," Nemesia said automatically.

She tucked the toothy necklace in her sleeve. Eden had said she could keep it, and it felt like evidence of ... well, of something.

It took her several extra seconds to understand that Eden had every intention of fully disrobing.

"Don't you all bathe together Below?" Eden said. "Sorry—didn't mean to startle you. Avert your eyes if you must."

That felt like a challenge. Nemesia stared fixedly at the umbrellas and parasols hung on the wall like works of art. Some umbrellas could block the sun, and some parasols could stave off rain. Either type would work just as well, presumably, when it came to unleashing Eden's magic.

"Now that I think about it," Eden said, as soft as rustling cloth, "the Brood does have a reputation for spiritual purity. There's a lot of erotic writing about showing Maidens of the Snake how people in the world Above express their virility."

"That's obviously fictional."

"Oh?"

"We're clerics, not children."

"I'm glad there's no need to worry about modesty, then."

"Focus on changing," Nemesia said with asperity.

Eden bent over (rather unnecessarily). Nemesia welded her eyes to the wall display. Clear umbrellas and richly painted oil-paper umbrellas; parasols with curved bamboo handles and parasols collapsed into a case small enough for a pair of glasses.

Her throat felt stuck in place, as if it had forgotten how to swallow.

Eden glided past her and rummaged through a chest. She came back wearing a thin robe decorated with a couple large multi-tailed goldfish. They were scattered about, lost in dark water.

"You lied," Nemesia said.

"When?"

"You claimed to need an extinguisher, but you already have one."

Eden fetched a hairbrush out of the vanity, startling Pimiko. "I never lied about being in search of a spouse. I'll take any number of wives, if that's what's required to make the King stop losing sleep. So far, it seems like one will suffice."

"How nice for you," Nemesia said woodenly.

"I was telling the truth about needing another extinguisher, too. Forget about the King. In less than two years, I'll be forty. Unless I work extremely hard to prove myself, I'll be obliged to retire."

"Is that a bad thing?"

"I'm not ready to let go of my magic. I might not be ready for years. I need an extinguisher who can age alongside me."

Nemesia crossed her arms. "Our marriage is provisional."

"Are you already planning to leave?"

Eden finished running the brush through her hair, then started plaiting it. Her question hung in the air unanswered. She didn't push for a response.

"You might not be cut out for this gig." The mirror caught her smile. "The part of it that involves subterfuge, I mean. I wonder—what's your promised reward?"

"Nothing to do with you."

This came out sounding harsher than Nemesia intended. She meant only that she had no personal vendetta.

Maybe Eden understood that. Or maybe she was impervious to barbs. She tied off the end of her braid and looked over her shoulder.

"If I were you, I'd pretend to be falling in love," she advised. "I'd throw myself into the role of a blushing bride. One might argue that we're decades too old for that. But people from Above are primed to think rather strangely of those from Below. Remind me, how old are you? Thirty-three?"

"Thirty-four."

"Doesn't matter. Bat your eyes, make some reference to how peculiar it feels to see the sky every day, and they'll think you're a simpering innocent. The Warden could give you acting tips."

Nemesia failed to see the point. "It won't work on you, will it?"

Eden sat sideways in the chair by the vanity, one hand laid idly on a corner of the desk as if inviting Pimiko to nibble her fingertips. She looked up through her lashes. "You let yourself into my bedroom. That seems like wifely behavior."

"I'm not trying to lay a honey trap."

"See, you shouldn't tell me that. Don't disarm your bombs before you set them."

"You already know I've got ulterior motives," Nemesia said, exasperated. "I won't press my luck."

"Snake Almighty. I can't believe they sent a rank amateur to seduce me. These amorphous enemies of mine ought to know better."

"No one said anything about seduction."

"What did you think you were supposed to do? You're my wife!"

Eden threw up her hands. She was clearly joking, but Nemesia didn't feel much inclined to laugh.

"It won't work," she repeated.

"Who's to say it won't? I already walked into one trap. I saw you crouching behind the Abbess's screen, waiting to be caught. The extinguisher of my dreams—such a convenient discovery! And I asked for you anyway."

"I can see why you give the King a headache."

"Do you want to stay?" Eden asked suddenly.

Nemesia wondered if she were about to get evicted. "I'm supposed to stay for a year."

"Not that. Here. Tonight."

Eden regarded her with innocent dark eyes. The sleepy glow of flame-free candles was kind to her skin. She reached sideways—without looking away—and retrieved the Warden's egg as deftly as a pickpocket. The keychain hung precariously from the tip of her finger.

"We're married," Nemesia said, "but we've never spent a full day together. We've never even had dinner."

"Ah." Eden looked contrite. "You're a believer in dinner before bed?"

"One doesn't have to lead to the other."

Eden laughed, low and quiet, and yet it struck Nemesia like the victory bell at the end of a fight.

"Tomorrow, then," Eden said. "I'm sorry I kept you waiting."

<h1 style="text-align:center">12</h1>

<h2 style="text-align:center">The Other Lotus</h2>

NEMESIA STASHED the teeth from beyond the Shell in her bag again. She left her bedroom shutters open, expecting sleep to elude her.

The night sky was clear, freckled with stars. The Shell arced invisibly in the distance: closing everyone in, keeping them safe, as it had for many hundreds of years.

The realm of the Snake was not devoid of suffering, or hierarchy, or injustice, or grief. Yet there was no truly abject deprivation, no violent tribal clashes, no senseless wars of succession.

Some in the Brood thought the entire marauding history of the Blessed Empire had been meant to lay the groundwork for this final enclave. Whatever the reason, the Empire had shrunk and shrunk and boiled itself down until all that remained were the lands that came to be surrounded by the Shell.

Everyone agreed that one day the Shell would crack. One day this paradise would come to an end. One day the Snake would sally forth into the mysterious outer world. After all, eggs were made for hatching.

But everyone also agreed that such a day was still a long way off.

Nemesia left the windowsill and put herself to bed. She could sense the ceiling even when she closed her eyes. It hung there like a threat.

There was still almost a full year left before the end of her second sabbatical.

If nothing changed, she would live out the rest of her life according to the same cadence as other Brides of the Snake. Ten years Below, one year Above, again and again.

There was only one way to break that cycle: get a loved one from Above to petition the Snake for your release.

It wasn't necessarily encouraged, but some Brides chose the opposite. They gave themselves over to the Snake completely. They would walk down into the undersky and never come back.

There were never more than ten living Brides around at any given time. The timing of their sabbaticals had almost no overlap. The whole point of a sabbatical was to immerse yourself in life Above, to soak it up like a sponge for the avid Snake. Not to cling to the company of those you already knew from Below.

Most importantly, they weren't called Brides because the Snake wanted them for amorous reasons. The Snake was beyond such things.

To some extent, so were they. While in residence Below, they found it extraordinarily difficult to form profound attachments. Romantic or otherwise. Even years-long friendships were tinged with a certain quality of pleasant detachment.

The hormonal squalls of adolescence passed without incident. Nemesia remembered being wracked by vivid, shocking dreams, but nothing bled over into waking reality. The nearness of the Snake filled every open space in her psyche.

When she went Above for her first sabbatical in her twenties, she'd felt freshly molted, all tender skin. She'd been jarred to find herself wondering what people thought when they saw her. She ruminated painfully over things she had or hadn't said. She wished she could leap back in time and redo clumsy encounters.

The Brood's god was called the Snake That Ate the Roots of Time, and yet she usually attempted not to dwell on its nature. Only when living Above did she yearn to take that time-twisting power in her own hands. Only when living Above did she make mistakes that cut to the quick.

She fumbled, she stammered, she went tongue-tied with embarrassment or longing, she struggled to calm her racing mind. And she couldn't get enough of it.

She didn't want to disappear in the undersky. If only there were some other way she could stay Below for the rest of her life. It would hurt much more to keep going on sabbaticals, to feel herself made raw all over again, as if part of her had never aged past twenty-three. The more she tasted Above, the more she would miss it.

She'd spoken of this with other Brides. Most seemed content with the interminable back and forth. Some had numerous friends Above, but they'd never asked anyone to petition the Snake. The cycle added a pleasing rhythm to their lives—and the older they got, the faster it passed. Besides, with long gaps between visits, they rarely ran out of things to talk about.

Ten years ago, Tanyu had asked if Nemesia loved her, or if she loved the idea of being freed from the Snake.

Those words spread like ink in water, tainting a year's worth of memories. Had she been so giddily drawn to Tanyu because she perceived a chance to escape?

For her first sabbatical, Nemesia had asked to work with children, remembering the teachers who'd raised her in a Brood-sponsored crèche. (She'd been born with bite marks, but no one went Below to formally join the Brood before the age of thirteen.)

The Abbess had found her a placement as an assistant counselor at a maenad reformatory. She didn't actually do much counseling—or extinguishing, for that matter. She'd taken care of children too young for their magic to pose much of a threat.

She'd fantasized about making such an impact on a child's life that they would beg her to stay. Still, you couldn't ask a three-year-old to stand up to the Snake. Even Tanyu—a grown woman who'd loved her—had faltered in the end.

She hadn't told Tanyu about being a Bride until her year was almost up. She couldn't imagine getting that close to someone with thoughts of the Snake hanging over their heads from the start.

For her second sabbatical, she'd declined all jobs involving children. She'd have to say goodbye to them after a year. She'd have to explain why she couldn't come back.

She hadn't wanted to meet more new people, new friends. Even if she hid the fact that she was a Bride, she might start hoping for one of them to free her. Every relationship would be poisoned by that secret expectation.

"Your conscience balks," the Abbess said. "You feel like a courtesan trying to convince a wealthy customer to buy you out. Tell me, do your four stigmata force you to make everything four times as complicated? Other Brides view their sabbaticals as a fun vacation to a foreign land."

"But I can't," Nemesia said. "I can't."

"Satisfy Daiya Sholto, and his patronage might persuade the Snake to let you go. Even if he petitions for you as part of a tit-for-tat deal."

"I doubt it."

"There are historical precedents," said the Abbess. "The Snake is more generous than you think. And more arbitrary—arbitrarily lenient, as well as arbitrarily harsh. You know this. There's plenty of reason to hope. The biggest hurdles have always been the ones you set up inside your own head."

"That doesn't sound hopeful at all."

"Regardless, you've got to spend a year Above." The Abbess blew into her bark pipe, making it wheeze like a broken noisemaker. "The high nobility have certain rights, and more influence than they deserve. Rich and titled people have always been able to bend the rules. This too is an immutable aspect of human society, as conceived by our Snake.

"Perhaps you'll sense that once you ascend the stairs to Above. Daiya Sholto's sponsorship might really procure your freedom."

"If I make enough mischief to make him happy," Nemesia said.

"If Kuchinashi Eden is as terrible a woman as he claims, then you might want to go above and beyond. Judge for yourself. A year is a year, no matter how you spend it. Whatever happens, I'll get that promised funding out of him. Trust me."

It felt like a very long time had passed since their last conversation.

The next day, Nemesia and the Warden wrote to the Abbess, asking if any artifacts had recently gone missing from the Brood's treasure vault. They included a detailed description of the tooth necklace and the unreadable book.

Nemesia went for a walk afterward, venturing far enough that she lost sight of Eden's house. She laughed when thick mudlings sprang out of the brush to roll beside her.

A herd of huge fluffy camelids grazed along the crest of distant hills. She held her head a smidge higher after spotting them. They had such dignified silhouettes.

Gnarled threads of smoke curled off isolated incense trees, the same type used to produce the Abbess's pipe. Better yet: butter-yellow wintersweet bloomed in the shade of grassy knolls. She could've spent hours basking in its scent. Nothing so flowery grew Below.

Tanyu had once taught her the names of countless trees and plants. She was surprised to still remember so many on sight.

When she returned to the cottage, hands and toes made clumsy by seeping cold, the Warden passed her a letter. It wasn't the original, tattooed on worm skin. He had already flash-transferred it to a more legible sheet of paper.

The Abbess stated firmly that nothing was missing. There were multiple artifacts that might match the ones they'd described, but all remained secure in Brood custody.

Later, during tea, Nemesia recalled that lotus pods were usually set up in pairs. One for sending, one for receiving.

There was only a single lotus in the scriptorium.

She asked the Warden where he and Eden kept their receiving pod.

He chuckled. "Your wife won't tell you?"

Nemesia had already searched the house as thoroughly as she could, storage rooms and all. She'd checked inside every compartment covered up with magic. She'd walked through walls disguised by illusions, most of which led nowhere special. She'd slashed past layer after layer of rusty power until she located a (perfectly functional) sauna without any physical doors.

There had to be other hidden spaces, ones concealed without any magic whatsoever. The receiving pod for inbound letters would be stored there. Perhaps along with other secrets and compromising information.

She hadn't the faintest idea how to look for trap doors rendered invisible by virtuoso feats of carpentry. She might spend years tapping on floors without finding a thing.

"You're thinking of stalking me till I lead you there." The Warden sounded gleeful. "Too late. Eden left you alone for a week. Now that you've sought her out, she'll keep you busy. I'll have plenty of time to check the mail without anyone watching."

"Well," Nemesia said, "thanks for telling me."

As always, she offered to help him cook. As always, he refused. She brought the Abbess's letter back to her room and began laying garments on the sunken bed. She didn't have many choices, but she found herself oddly stumped about what to wear to dinner.

13

A Dinner Date

THE WARDEN placed colorful drinks in front of Eden and Nemesia. Each came garnished with a cocktail umbrella.

To Pimiko—who had her own place setting—he gave a shallow dish of water and an umbrella of exquisite black lace.

Eden raised her eyebrows. The Warden bowed and shimmied backwards out of the dining room, smooth as a dancer.

Nemesia removed the paper parasol from her glass. "Is it edible?"

"You can certainly try." Eden idly opened and closed her own umbrella, one-handed.

"Perhaps for dessert."

"These have essentially no alcohol, by the way," Eden said after a sip.

"Really?"

"Maenads and heavy drinking don't mix."

"Ah."

"If you'd like yours stronger—"

"It's good," Nemesia said truthfully.

"I suppose the Brood isn't very big on imbibing, either."

"Not many wild parties Below."

For a few moments, they drank in silence. Pimiko scooted forward, half-sitting in her water dish to sup. Her part of the table was set with artful layers of absorbent placemats.

The Warden had styled the dining room like a restaurant. A large table had come apart to form several intimate two-seaters. Nemesia, Eden, and Pimiko shared one. The others held flower arrangements, water pitchers, and a profusion of candles lit with real flickering flames.

There were no candles on the table they ate at. Instead, the Warden had planted something like a snow globe. Rather than faux snow or quaint scenery, it was filled with a swirl of magical fire.

Nemesia held her hands over the globe. Only a pleasant warmth made it out through the glass—nothing searing or dangerous. She amused herself by dimming it, making the magical flame shrink down to the size of a fingernail.

She felt Eden watching her, and pulled back. Light washed over them as fire filled the globe again.

Eden flicked at her toy-sized umbrella as if playing with a lighter. Each time she snapped it open, a prick of red entered her eyes, like reflected coals.

"That triggers your magic?" said Nemesia.

"An umbrella is an umbrella, regardless of size. It functions like a stage cue. I could release my magic with a jacket tossed over my head, if I needed to."

The hint of burning coals vanished as she shut the little umbrella. She laid it down. Then she reached in her sleeve and extracted another one. She spun it between her fingers.

"I always keep a couple handy," she explained. "Can't take the big ones everywhere. Besides, people recognize me just from the silhouette of my parasol. I'm less intimidating when I appear empty-handed."

She stashed the umbrella back in her sleeve. "Also, not to brag," she said, "but I made these."

"By hand?"

"The Warden can craft them, too. We make sure to keep plenty of stock at home."

The Warden returned, as if summoned by the sound of his name.

He came carrying a small bamboo cage. Inside were several pale brown crickets. He caught them with chopsticks, and held them out to Pimiko one by one. She snatched up his offerings with queenly grace.

"Crabantulas aren't strict carnivores," he said as they watched her eat. "Plump pre-fed prey is a special treat."

"She doesn't eat pests around the house?" Nemesia asked.

He shook his head. "Insects hardly ever get in. Too much old magic. Previous maenads must have really hated uninvited guests."

"Well," Eden said after he left again, "I'm sure that whetted your appetite."

They finished their drinks. Then she leaned around the table to get a look at the full length of Nemesia's robe.

It was dyed to resemble the undersky: white clouds and rich blue near the lower hem, gradually giving way to darker fabric above. Those who had never seen the undersky might take it as representing the transition from day to night, or a cross-section of the real sky and upper atmosphere.

"Lovely pattern." Eden raised her empty glass in tribute. "Those are good colors on you."

"You'll see a lot of it if you spend more time at home," said Nemesia. "I didn't bring many robes."

"We'll go get you something new, then. Before you meet the King."

The Warden brought out a salad of crinkly cruciferous leaves and ultra-curly stems. "No crickets," he proclaimed as he served them.

Next came a delicate dish of poached fish—snakehead, he said.

Nemesia was not a quick eater. Eden seemed to be pacing herself to avoid finishing far in advance. She kept setting down her utensils to inquire about life Below. She was particularly intrigued by the Brood's anonymized guards.

"They feature in several classic romances of mistaken identity. Did the Warden tell you how we first met? Yes? Some years later, I played a Brood maiden who falls in love with a guard who turns out to be her long-lost childhood friend."

"That wouldn't happen in real life."

"Which part of it?"

"Where do I start?"

Eden laughed. "No, I get it. People don't come to the theater for an accurate depiction of the Brood. That playwright might never have set foot Below."

She leaned back in her chair. "Your guard didn't seem terribly fond of me."

"When did you see him?"

"When I went down to fetch you, remember? Are they all that standoffish?"

"They may look and sound the same," said Nemesia, "but that's just magic. They aren't a collective."

Many Brood guards liked to make music. Even those with zero past experience. They all seemed the same when they sang—but some subliminal part of your ears could still tell who really knew how to carry a tune.

True individuality came to the forefront when they took up a guitar or a flute or a zither. No magic could disguise the clumsiness of a novice player. They were thrilled to sound like themselves, even if it meant that some of them sounded terrible.

Between bites of snakehead, Nemesia told Eden about the guards she'd known best.

The first Brood guard she ever met was the one who took her Below at thirteen. The identity-blurring magic wasn't effective Above. He'd kept his hood up, but she caught glimpses of his face as they made their way toward the stairwell. He had appeared quite old. Fatherly, even.

His unique badge was emblazoned with a reptilian silhouette. She called him Iguana until the Abbess corrected her: his badge was supposed to represent a chameleon.

Because she'd seen slivers of Chameleon's true face, she found herself thinking of the other guards as male, too. Their uniforms muffled most differences in gait. But sometimes, from the corner of her eye, she noticed Chameleon limping. Was he one of the oldest guards in the Brood? Was he hurt? She never quite worked up the courage to ask.

When she came back after her first sabbatical, Chameleon was gone, his tour of duty complete. He took his fiddle with him.

Why had he ended up serving as a guard in the first place? She'd always wondered, and then she'd wondered if maybe she'd be better off not knowing.

Roc—her latest personal guard—was a more recent arrival. He'd come Below about two years ago.

He had been something of an oddball from the start. It was remarkable, actually, how different one guard could seem from another.

The first time they spoke alone, Roc had asked if she wanted to run away from the Brood. He offered to help. Nemesia gaped.

"Right, I know it isn't allowed," he'd said, "but I figured it would only be polite to ask. No one's ever asked you before, have they?"

Eden was a masterful listener. They had almost finished the heartiest course (stewed goat and dates) by the time Nemesia realized how much she'd been talking. And yet she'd failed to bring up the one thing she'd wanted to say.

Pimiko had retreated partway inside her shell. Subtle vibrations and clinking from the table, sounds traveling through air—what did any of this tell her?

As Nemesia glanced over, Pimiko rose up on splayed legs. Her clustered eyes rose, too, attached to protuberant stalks like those of a crab. They waved and twisted in an exaggerated show of flexibility, then retracted.

"First time seeing that?" Eden asked. "Pimiko knows all kinds of tricks."

She plucked her closed cocktail umbrella off the table. She held it out towards Pimiko as if issuing a challenge with a very small sword.

Pimiko's legs remained still. Something else shot out of the shadow of her shell—a dark blur—and retreated just as quickly.

Eden's umbrella had been snapped cleanly in half.

"You don't want to know what her claws can do to a finger," Eden said. "Or a throat, for that matter." She saw the look on Nemesia's face. "Oh, she knows you belong here—she won't hurt you. Unless you come at her with a hammer."

Nemesia refocused on the fiery snow globe. No more distractions.

"You wanted me as an extinguisher," she said. "That's why you came Below."

"So you're satisfied that I didn't come to pilfer artifacts?"

"Nothing's been reported missing. The Abbess confirmed it."

"Nice lady."

"Don't say that to her face," Nemesia muttered.

Just beyond the nearest door, the Warden snickered, then covered it up with a theatrical cough.

"You haven't asked me to do any extinguishing," Nemesia continued. "It's common, isn't it, for wedded folk to get cold feet?"

"Preferably before the wedding. Not after."

Eden fiddled with the halves of her broken cocktail umbrella. "Truth be told, I've never enjoyed having my magic muffled."

Nemesia cast a glance at the door. "You already live with an extinguisher."

"He's here to guard the home front. I don't take him to work with me. Which is what I'll inevitably need in the future."

"Take me along with you, then," said Nemesia. "Start getting used to it."

"Didn't realize you were so eager to help."

"I'm running out of things to do here."

Eden looked puzzled. "Don't clerics live very quiet lives Below? You shouldn't be so easily bored."

"I can only riffle through your underwear drawer so many times."

"Why, I thought you'd come equipped with an endless to-do list. Shouldn't you get around to—oh, I don't know, planting evidence of treason or something?"

"Shouldn't you try to keep me so busy that I don't get a chance?"

Eden sighed. "Having a wife is a lot more work than I thought."

"You're stuck with me. Might as well make use of me."

"True," Eden said easily. "I said you could sabotage me, but I never said I would let you succeed."

The Warden swept in to clear their plates. He left a dish of small candies wrapped in wax paper. The whitish ones were sweet milk candy; the pinkish ones were flavored like salty-sour pickled plums.

"He doesn't usually prepare a dessert course." Eden sounded apologetic. "That's my fault. Don't have much of a sweet tooth."

"I can live without cake."

"They were generous with dessert back in the reformatory. Always gave us treats after hard bouts of conditioning. I wasn't the only one who came to hate ice cream."

Eden popped a plum candy in her mouth. Then she sat up and began interrogating Nemesia about her work history.

Nemesia had been raised Above in a crèche, one owned by the Brood. As she got older, she'd started helping out around the nurseries and classrooms—doing odd jobs, watching little ones—but that all ended once she turned thirteen.

Ever since she departed for Below, she had primarily served as a Bride of the Snake. The Brood took care of her, and she received a stipend, but there were no deliverables associated with being a Bride. No performance reviews. No overtime. Certainly no risk of layoffs.

She'd planned on claiming that she'd worked in the tourist district. She rarely went there herself, but she'd spoken with Brood sisters who ran hotels and trained tour guides.

At last she cracked, having run out of generic things to say about landmarks and hospitality and private saunas. She resorted to mentioning that she'd also worked Above for a bit in her twenties.

Eden's face suddenly went neutral. No more spark of playful interest. "Where? Back at the crèche that raised you?"

That would have been a better answer.

"At a reformatory," Nemesia said. There was no reason to feel cold. The lights in the room were rich and warm. The banks of candles and flowers on the other tables made it seem as if they were dining at the center of a secret altar, offerings piled up all around them.

Eden didn't react at all to the word *reformatory*.

"Which one?" she said simply.

"The one on Downcastle Street. A few blocks away from my crèche." Once again, it didn't occur to Nemesia until after she'd spoken that maybe it would have been smarter to lie.

She pictured a much younger Eden posing by an impressive pine tree.

That tree. It stood on a remote corner of Downcastle Street. Way past the crèche where she'd spent her childhood, and past the reformatory where she'd worked during her first sabbatical. She would never have gone that far along the street as a child. She remembered the tree only because she'd seen it while walking with Tanyu.

"Is that the reformatory where you...?"

"That's the one." Eden was all smiling nostalgia. "I would've graduated long before you showed up as a teacher, of course. When did you say you worked there?"

"Ten years ago."

"Exactly ten years ago?"

"Just about."

"Then you were there for the kidnappings."

She pushed the candy dish toward Nemesia, who took one without thinking.

14

Ten Years Ago

DURING NEMESIA's first sabbatical, Oddscale began abducting children from the Downcastle Street reformatory.

None of the toddlers in Nemesia's care got taken. An eight-year-old girl disappeared first. If Oddscale hadn't claimed responsibility, the staff would have assumed she'd run away on her own. Which wasn't unheard of, although no children ever escaped for long.

The other abductees were several years older: ten, eleven, thirteen, and so on. For each stolen child, Oddscale left behind a shred of gray-black fabric and a note inscribed on scrollworm skin, dry and crackly and rolled up like a candy cigar.

These letters hadn't come through a lotus pod. Why use scrollworms, and why let the parchment dessicate without proper treatment? (At least the worms hadn't suffered for it; their skin could be shaved off painlessly, and it always grew back.)

The notes were, as a result, very difficult to read. Oddscale must have wanted the administration to struggle.

The text denounced specific teachers and monitors—denounced them by name, and demanded that the Brood remove them. No missing students would be returned until all remaining staff abandoned traditional punitive policies.

If even a single kid had gotten snatched away from an ordinary school, their kin would riot.

However, young mages and Snake-bitten children had one key commonality. As soon as their magic (or stigmata) emerged, their parents would turn distant. Indifferent. They would be most pleased to promptly surrender their child to a crèche or a reformatory. They never harbored any regrets.

It was better that way, wasn't it? The Snake made it feel natural.

If you had a bitten child, or a magical child, of course you would give them up. It was like finding a lost wallet stuffed with cash. Any moral person would turn it over to the authorities. You'd feel a brief glow of righteousness. You'd discovered that wallet by happenstance, but it had never been yours.

In a few years, you might start to forget that the whole thing had ever happened.

Nemesia had manifested snakebites from the moment of her birth. Her parents had probably held her for a few seconds, if even that, before passing her off to Brood-affiliated nurses.

She'd been lucky. Sometimes snakebites popped up later in life. And a maenad's wild magic might not appear until they were considerably older. There were children who got tossed into a reformatory for the first time at the age of nine.

Better to always have some inkling of your fate than to grow up surrounded by a family that would inevitably turn on you.

The Snake made the separation easier for affected children, too. At the Downcastle reformatory, Nemesia's charges soon stopped calling for mamas and papas, aunties and uncles, siblings and grandparents and everyone else.

That didn't mean they hadn't lost anything. But this was how the world worked inside the protection of the Shell.

So when Oddscale kidnapped young maenads-in-training, no mob of terror-stricken relatives came to beat down the school doors.

The staff faced a different set of pressures. People feared for public safety. A maenad with incomplete conditioning was a berserker with no restraints. If they got loose, they might go on a magical murder spree. They might explode in the middle of a crowd.

Public opinion shifted once word got out that Oddscale was involved. Oddscale was, after all, a hero with a storied history. An ally to common folk. A champion appointed by the Snake.

Perhaps some students—or many students—had been mistreated. Perhaps the institution itself was what needed reforming.

At first, Nemesia hadn't known what to think. She hadn't been there very long, and her class of toddlers took up all her attention.

If the other staff seemed aloof, she could understand why: they knew she would be gone in a year. They were kind enough, and they respected the fact that she didn't like to make a big deal about being a Bride.

But she had never wandered into one of the upstairs classrooms and watched them attempt to teach absolute self-discipline to growing mages. She had never witnessed the techniques they used to extinguish children mired in the magical and physical throes of berserking.

No one invited her to read Oddscale's notes. She heard the details much later, once rumors spread to the rest of the city. Only then did she learn about how grim-faced teachers would sit on raging eleven-year-olds, simultaneously flattening their magic and crushing their breath out. Oddscale claimed that children had died of this in the past. Hardly anyone would ever know, because there were no kin left who remembered them well enough to mourn.

A terrible heaviness filled Nemesia's gut, and for the rest of the year, it never quite left. Her coworkers had always been on their best behavior when they knew she was watching.

The Abbess came Above to visit the reformatory. She personally interviewed students and teachers alike.

Nemesia couldn't prove it, but she'd begun to think Oddscale was right. Certain colleagues seemed to regard their charges more as violent criminal inmates than as growing children who had absolutely no one else in the world they could turn to for help.

There were other things she only noticed after the kidnappings started. The unspoken shadows that cast a chill over innocuous conversations. The abrupt silence that ensued when she walked in on a room of laughing teachers.

When she saw children looking tired and wretched, when she saw children who seemed cowed or sullen, she'd assumed it was because being a maenad inherently involved a certain degree of loneliness and misery. They had to spend years painfully grinding their frenzied magic into a state of utter submission. There were no shortcuts. No one could rescue them.

Likewise, she'd assumed her fellow teachers and counselors were all infinitely good and patient, and never had a bad day, and never came to loathe their berserking wards, and never egged each other on, and never grew numb to cruelty.

She'd been oblivious, and naive, and far too trusting.

Maybe there was no truly humane way to transform little wild mages into maenads with adequate self-discipline to safely graduate. But it could still be better. Even if the process would inevitably involve struggle and suffering, it could be so much better. Nemesia swore to that from the bottom of her heart. She invoked the name of the Snake, and the Abbess believed her.

Her sabbatical came to an end before Oddscale returned any stolen children. They did all come back eventually: the Abbess succeeded in reforming the reformatory. Enough so, at least, to satisfy the people's hero.

Sometimes Nemesia felt guilty about refusing to go back to the Downcastle reformatory. She could have spent her second sabbatical there, instead of leaving with Eden.

She would've been a much better caretaker the second time around. She would've known what she was doing from the start. She would've kept a watchful eye out for the older children, too.

She could've ascertained for herself that the reformatory really had changed for the better—and had stayed that way, even a decade later.

Oddscale would step in again if any maenad children were needlessly suffering. She told herself this, but an old shame still collected in dusty corners of her soul.

The reformatory was all tangled up with her memories of Tanyu, too. She had first met Tanyu—a contracted landscaper, no personal affiliation with the Brood—right there on the reformatory grounds.

They'd gotten to know each other during long walks all over Downcastle Street. After the first few abductions, Tanyu had reluctantly told her everything people were saying about the reformatory and those who worked there. She turned to Tanyu when there was no one else she could trust.

For all she knew, Tanyu still came by all the time: trimming trees and unruly hedges, sweeping leaves, laying down mulch, planting row upon row of perky new annuals. The reformatory had always been beautiful on the outside.

15

Extinguishing

NEMESIA SMOOTHED OUT her crinkled candy wrapper as if it were a piece of scrollworm skin. Her shoulders felt rigid.

Who had been in charge of Eden's conditioning? Perhaps someone Nemesia had worked with—years after Eden's graduation—one of those late-career teachers she'd initially looked up to.

Any moment now, Eden would say something further about the reformatory.

But she didn't.

She deposited her broken cocktail umbrella in the candy dish. "Vesper says—"

"Who?"

Eden raised her hands to her head and stuck her forefingers out like horns. "Been avoiding you, has she?"

"About as much as you have."

"I came for dinner with you, so I win," Eden said obscurely.

There seemed to be no tactful way to phrase her next question, so Nemesia settled for simplicity. "Is she from outside?"

"Outside where?"

"You know."

"Would you believe me if I said no?"

Their eyes met.

Sometimes, very rarely, people slipped out through the Shell without meaning to. Sometimes, just as rarely, visitors came in from beyond.

Such visitations were largely the stuff of dreams and stories. No one would run around shouting excitedly about mysterious outsiders. No one would capture them for study or attempt to establish diplomatic relations. Future visitors might not show up again for generations, anyway.

They were treated with generosity, like lost travelers. Sometimes they turned out to be clever fraudsters from inside the Shell. Sometimes they could only speak in senseless tongues.

In many cases, they lingered for only a night or two before vanishing. Brood sages theorized that the Snake used these foreign visitors as a test of hospitality. So it was just common sense to be courteous to eccentric strangers. If you were lucky, the Snake might reward your kindness.

Of course, most such visitors were human. Eden's guest seemed like something else altogether.

Eden said: "Vesper and her—mate? Is that the right word?"

"There's two of them?"

"They know a great deal about what lies beyond the Shell."

"Could they have brought in those artifacts?"

"The teeth and such? Like a cat carrying in a dead bird? No—I had them on me when I came back from my three-year disappearance. My guests just arrived recently."

"You must have shown them your book," said Nemesia.

"Oh, yes."

"Then—"

"Vesper has no interest in translating," Eden said dolefully. "She called it stupid. An obsolete propaganda piece from a faraway continent. I was hoping it might be a cookbook."

"Has she looked at the rest of your library?" Eden owned a lot of travelogues and memoirs and confessions. Sagas of accidental journeys beyond the Shell.

"Of course. I made her go through and tell me what seems right and what seems totally made up. It got depressing, though."

"What did? Having answers?"

"I've been beyond the Shell, too," Eden said. "So what was it all for? I remember none of it. Yet I've experienced that greater world. I must have—where else could I have been when I vanished?"

"Kidnapped by Oddscale?" Nemesia blurted.

Eden stared blankly at her. Nemesia shrank. She'd had decade-old abductions on the brain.

Eventually Eden said—as if this were a serious theory—"Some people might claim I had it coming."

She grinned. "But I'm pretty sure Oddscale usually makes your sins very clear. If you've got to be punished, at least you'll know what it's for. No hero has ever shown up to denounce me."

"The horned woman," Nemesia said, desperate for a change of topic.

"Vesper? What about her?"

"Could you have first met her outside the Shell?"

"She denies it," said Eden. "Never saw me before. It's a big world out there."

"She could be lying."

"To what end? At heart, she's a rather straightforward type."

"In your estimation."

"I'm a good judge of people, and magical creatures that look like people. Even the King says so."

Eden rose from her seat. She reached over to trace the spiral whorl of Pimiko's shell. "Good night, my pretty." Then, to Nemesia: "We've spent long enough digesting. Let's go water the house."

She didn't explain what this might entail. Nemesia didn't inquire, either; she figured the answer would soon become apparent. They thanked the Warden for dinner and headed down to the basement.

Eden cut past the laundry room and began descending the final set of stairs. The clover that sprouted from cracks in the steps turned toward her as she passed, as if she were a living blaze of sunlight.

On the top floor, they stopped by her room to fetch an umbrella.

"What about the one in your sleeve?" Nemesia asked.

"We'll want a full-size model for what's about to happen next."

Eden stood beneath her array of umbrellas on hooks, looking up. They were way out of reach. At one end of the room awaited a rolling ladder on tracks, the type that might be used in a professional library.

She didn't go for the ladder. Instead, she pushed at the wall right in front of her. High above, a single long umbrella leapt from its hook and fell into her waiting hand.

Her chosen umbrella was plain and clear, no pattern whatsoever, with a curved black handle. She hooked it over her wrist.

They proceeded down one of the house's signature hallways (unrealistically long, with few doors).

At a dead end, Eden raised her right foot. She brought it down on the carpet with all her might. There was a crack, as if she'd stomped straight through the floor. Nemesia's heart jumped like a grasshopper.

A rope ladder dropped from the ceiling. "No magic," Eden said slyly. "No need for it. I can play this house like an instrument."

After ascending the ladder and a short, convoluted staircase, they emerged inside the turret at the back of the cottage. Nemesia admitted that she'd thought it was just decorative.

"You can come back on your own if you find the right place to stomp," Eden said.

She pulled Nemesia out onto a narrow uncovered balcony. They went through a glass door disguised as one of many tall windows.

They were now higher up than the green sod roof that covered the rest of the house. It spread out before them like a peculiar peaked meadow.

The balcony had no furniture. It didn't offer room to do much more than stand side by side. Eden gestured at the pinnacle of the turret behind and above them. "Parts of the structure date back to—"

"The Antemaenad." The greatest mage of all time, and the first to conquer her own berserking magic.

"The Warden told you? No surprise there. He's proud of being stationed here—more than he'll ever admit."

Eden opened her clear umbrella. She draped her free arm around Nemesia, nonchalantly drawing her closer, as if there were no other reasonable way to share it.

"It's mostly magic," she said, "but it would still make us wet. Enjoy the music."

In the post-dinner darkness, rain fell on the house, soaking the woolly turf of the roof. Mossy sprouts shot up wherever rain landed, more silver than green. Entire tussocks and bushes puffed into being.

Everything growing from the roof gave off a faint luminescence.

A melody formed as raindrops struck the transparent umbrella, sliding away the moment Nemesia's mind began to grasp it. The music passed through her, eluding capture, leaving only the impression that she had heard something beautiful.

Eden's voice was barely audible beneath the rain-song. "The reformatory made me hate ice cream, among other things. But funnily enough, it never made me hate magic. Guess I could live without one of those, but not the other."

They listened to the rain for several more minutes. An entire miniature forest had germinated from the grassy field of the roof.

Fearful creatures—mice, or deer not much larger than mice—darted through the underbrush. Shrubbery bowed and swished like weeds in a tumbling river. Yet the rain dropped in straight lines, without any hint of wind.

"The hardest part of using magic is the part where you have to stop."

Eden faced straight ahead, eyes on the lush roof. "My parasols and umbrellas function as a psychological go sign. But it doesn't work in reverse. Takes a lot more focus to reel the magic in than to let it out."

Her arm around Nemesia exerted the same gentle pressure no matter how much magical rain came down.

Nemesia wondered aloud why maenads weren't paired with extinguishers by default.

"In the field, not just at home?" Eden shrugged as she spoke; Nemesia felt it. "The Brood can't spare that many Maidens of the Snake. We're short on wardens as it is. The whole point of putting us through all that grueling training is so we learn to grapple with our magic alone, for as long as we can."

She looked sideways at Nemesia. "Go on," she said. "Make me stop. Should be easy, right? We're already touching."

Nemesia reacted like a dog told to heel.

The rain ceased.

Stark silence followed, a silence that seemed almost violent in its suddenness. The plant life on the roof shrank and drooped, newly obedient to gravity. Blades of grass as thick as broadswords flopped under the weight of the water gilding them. Motionless drops clung to the clear dome of Eden's umbrella.

Eden didn't say a word. Her arm remained steady around Nemesia's shoulders, but the umbrella began to tip forward.

Nemesia hastily seized the handle, trapping Eden's loosening hand beneath hers. Eden's fingers felt—not cold, exactly, but as if they had no temperature at all.

Extinguishing wasn't supposed to be especially traumatic for an adult maenad with full mastery. But Nemesia didn't actually have much experience with dousing magic from a living body.

At the reformatory, she'd been one extinguisher of many. Three-year-olds couldn't exude enough magic to cause serious trouble, and no one called her for help with older students.

Had she come down too hard? Had she crushed Eden's magic in the same way as the worst reformatory monitors?

Eden blinked, then, and lowered the arm that had been holding Nemesia close to her side. She patted absentmindedly at the hands clenched around the umbrella handle—both Nemesia's and her own, as if she'd forgotten it was hers.

Nemesia let go.

Eden lowered the point of the umbrella to the balcony floor, still dripping, and wrapped it shut with the attached snap-button tie. The luminescence of the green roof kept fading, moment after moment, but there was still enough light to make out suggestions of movement.

"You're good," she said, as if praising the umbrella. "You're very good."

"You aren't hurt?" Nemesia scrabbled for words. "How did it feel?"

"What matters is that it worked," Eden said mildly.

She glanced up, holding the wrapped-up umbrella like a walking stick. "It wasn't painful," she added. "The next time you stop me, you can do it in just the same way."

"When will the next time be?"

"A couple hours after sunrise." She waved at the black sky. "Come back inside. You'll want to get some sleep first."

16
Worranges

EDEN DIDN'T STAY the night. She never did. But when Nemesia followed the scent of hot soup to the kitchen, there she was again, perky and bright-eyed.

"No one ever expects me to be a morning person," Eden said smugly. She paused, chopsticks pinching a slice of rolled omelette. "Is that why you look so betrayed?"

"You always make me have breakfast in the dining room," Nemesia said to the Warden.

He jabbed an unrepentant thumb at Eden. "If she insists on eating with the help, I can't stop her. She's the boss."

"Then what am I?"

He pretended to be hard of hearing. Nemesia gave up and took a seat at the counter.

Odd corners of the kitchen were occupied by a menagerie of wood and ceramic figurines. Camelids, yaks, mammoths. Even mudlings. Nemesia eyed them while drinking down a bowl of salty soup.

After breakfast, as they stepped out the front door, she noted that someone had removed all those festive snake-shed streamers. Either the Warden, or the wind.

Eden linked arms with her, guiding her toward a structure hidden among the trees out back.

It looked like an oversized picture frame, a gilded antique rectangle. Its shape echoed the pristine ninety-degree bends of angle tree branches.

The gold paint was weathered, but the frame held fast. Preservative magic kept it from rotting.

Eden pointed with her parasol—another one long enough to use as a walking stick. "If you had your fill of prowling around the house, why didn't you go spend time in the city?"

"Do you keep your darkest secrets in the city?"

Eden snorted.

The frame surrounded an open-ended wormhole. Nemesia could have walked through at any time, but it would be a one-way trip. Without magic of her own, she could only visit its last recorded destination. Which might be helpful for tracking Eden, but not so helpful for getting home again afterward.

Today Eden wore an outer robe with a pattern of austere blossoms and bones. The bony parts were detailed animal skulls, each depicted as finely as a fancy peony.

She unfurled her parasol. It was dark, with a generous hanging fringe of ecru lace.

Half-finger gloves clothed her hands. She ran one down the side of the frame, as if daubing on a fresh glaze of magic. Then she crossed through, disappearing as she went. There was enough space to hold her parasol at full mast.

Nemesia stepped over the bottom of the frame, too.

On the other side, Eden awaited her on a path between farm fields—some abandoned and some half-harvested, with birds preying on the remainder. The sky had only a few careless clouds. They looked like brushstrokes of watered-down white paint.

A lazy wind rippled at the lacy trim of Eden's parasol. Nemesia adjusted the shawl she'd brought for warmth.

"We're closer to the city now," Eden said. "Might see buildings if we went up on those bluffs."

"Is that where we're going?"

"We're heading out to an orchard. Ever had a worrange?"

"A what?" Nemesia thought she might have misheard.

"A worrange. A worry-inducing tangerine orange."

"...Doesn't sound very appetizing."

Eden twirled her parasol. "There's a market for it. Not enough to sustain this orchard, though. The owner died without heirs."

Nemesia still didn't understand why anyone would plant multiple trees of worry-inducing fruit.

As they walked along, Eden said: "For most people, a worrange is a one-off novelty. A fun, stupid thing to try with fun, stupid friends. Might give you a horrible stomachache."

"Hm," said Nemesia.

"Is it so hard to believe?"

Eden tipped her parasol sideways as if to block out curious eyes, although there was no one in sight except a cluster of camelids.

"If you already feel like crap, eating a worrange will make you worse. It'll turn discontent into outright despair. But you'll know that if you wait a few hours, the worst of it will vanish.

"And it does. The weight comes right off your shoulders. Of course, once the worrange wears off, you just go back to your original baseline.

No actual change. It makes endless gray days seem to momentarily ease their chokehold. It creates the temporary illusion of feeling lighter."

"The artificial lifting of artificially induced distress," Nemesia said.

"Not that I would recommend it in lieu of therapy."

"Have you—"

"We maenads aren't supposed to consume worrange products, anyway. We're technically barred from anything that might affect our state of mind."

Eden did an abrupt double-take. Her voice lightened. "Nemesia, you've got fans."

Multiple mudlings had shimmied their way out of a forsaken field. When Nemesia and Eden resumed walking, the prancing mudlings kept pace.

"I haven't done anything to provoke this," Nemesia said, resigned.

"Isn't there a parable about how mudlings are the Snake's most loyal disciples? Like recognizes like."

"Are you calling me a mudling?"

"You're a true apostle of the Neverending Snake." Eden edged a few paces away, trying not to frighten Nemesia's followers. "If you trained them to do tricks, you could put on a show. In fact—no need to train them. Just look at them go."

The mudlings turned limbless cartwheels. They bounced themselves off the dirt-packed path like rubber balls.

Mudlings had been largely responsible for Nemesia's first conversations with Tanyu. Not long after she came to the Downcastle reformatory, they'd begun plaguing the grounds.

Since—at least mythologically speaking—they were precious servants of the Snake, not even a mortally exasperated groundskeeper would try to poison them. Only the most humane of traps would do, and humane traps weren't all that effective. Mudlings were capable of acrobatic feats that defied both their stumpy anatomy and common sense.

Seeing Tanyu at her wit's end, Nemesia went to apologize. Tanyu had been baffled when she claimed responsibility. She didn't mention being a Bride—it wouldn't have helped. Neither Brides nor general Brood clerics had a reputation for luring in elusive mudlings like a trash can attracting crows.

That was why they got to talking. And that was why they started taking walks together, testing how far away Nemesia could lead her latest crop of groupies.

Once Tanyu acknowledged the mudlings' inexplicable attraction to Nemesia, she stopped viewing them with enmity. Suddenly she seemed to find them endearing.

Ten years later, and here Nemesia was again, this time in the countryside instead of the city, with a different woman and a different batch of mudlings.

Her entourage stopped cavorting only when the worrange grove came in sight. They began to back off. Some rolled sideways like squishy logs, and some humped away like big mournful caterpillars. Soon weeds concealed them all.

"Smart critters," Eden said approvingly.

She put one arm out, warning Nemesia not to proceed any further. She tossed her open parasol up in the air. It hung there obediently, casting an ovoid shadow off to their right.

The orchard whined like a dog.

The worrange trees varied in height. Some were shorter than Eden, and some were twice as tall. The shortest had slender boughs so laden with fruit that their tips touched the ground.

There was, overall, more fruit on the ground than in the trees. Browning fruit, molding fruit, soft and misshapen fruit. Empty curls of peel lay scattered about like a murder scene.

There was a reason the city put out public service announcements telling people to harvest promptly. But Nemesia had never seen it for herself.

The abandoned worranges had sprouted lips and teeth and scraggly hair. They crawled blindly, splitting open and biting at the ground. Others scooted along on fleshy protrusions that looked all too much like human toes. A stench hovered over the orchard: an irreconcilable mix of sweet citrus, sharp rot, and sweaty feet.

"We came just in time," Eden remarked, unperturbed. "They haven't gotten smart enough to leave their grove yet."

"What will you—"

"Watch," she said.

The ground beneath the fallen harvest was covered in crabgrass and old leaves. Eden's magic rippled through the topsoil, shaking it out like a bedsheet. The worranges cried like human infants.

A moment of stillness, and then a churning demon of decay surged up between two rows of trees.

At first it looked like a single beetle the size of a yak. Later, it looked more like millions of smaller beetles had conglomerated into a facsimile of a larger body, all moving and consuming as one.

It harmed nothing except worranges, which it devoured with alacrity. If it ran straight through a tree, its solid-seeming body would part like liquid, individual beetles tumbling down through the branches in thick waterfall streams before regrouping.

When its mouthparts opened, Nemesia glimpsed a hellish red light.

"Er … did you just summon a devil?"

"Don't worry about it," Eden said blithely.

As the creature ate up masses of old worranges, steam poured out through the seams of its ever-shifting bulk. The air already smelled drastically better—purged, like after a rainstorm.

Soon Eden's beast had picked every last worrange off every last bough. Its mouthparts pulsated, looking for other rotten things to eat. Perhaps it had developed a taste for humanoid hair and teeth.

"Thought you might shriek or run," said Eden, who was doing neither, as her composite beetle loomed closer.

"Did you want me to?"

"Not particularly. It's good to know that you don't scare easily."

"I'm a Maiden of the Snake," Nemesia said with cold dignity—the way she imagined the Abbess might say it.

The beetle had swollen from the size of a yak to the size of a mammoth. Its mouthparts clacked greedily. Its body gave off a hissing sound like a kettle. But Nemesia had lived in the embrace of a much larger and more terrifying presence.

"If I end this enchantment myself, I won't be able to do anything else today, magically speaking," Eden said. "Too risky. Too tiring."

"And if I end it?"

"We'll get to tackle the next chore in my backlog. This very afternoon."

So the reward for completing a task would be more work. Such was the way of the world.

The floating parasol rotated sedately above them. Eden held her arm out. Nemesia took it.

Eden seemed to be under the impression that extinguishers used physical touch to deactivate magic. (Perhaps as a result of her experiences at the reformatory, where teachers did tend to rely on corporeal measures.)

Nemesia had never needed to make direct contact with her target. At the moment, though, she saw no benefit in issuing a correction. She tucked their arms together more firmly.

The hulking beast shuffled closer. It was a pointillist aggregation of swarming components the size of a ladybug. They buzzed so softly and in such great numbers that their noise seem to rub itself into being against the underside of Nemesia's skull.

She wished it all away.

The great beetle collapsed inward, returning to soil and crabgrass and scattered leaves. Eden's parasol descended, lace fluttering like a windblown skirt.

They both instinctively reached to catch it. Eden got there first.

"I wonder if I made myself love magic because of how much more miserable I would have been if I hated it."

She whirled the parasol shut. "I wonder if I'm reluctant to let go of magic because of how much I went through to master it. But so did everyone else, and most maenads are happy to retire by forty."

"Not everyone has to feel the same," said Nemesia.

"Exactly. When I actually use magic, I stop worrying. Who cares about the reason? Who cares if it drains me? How could I not love it? The best part is that it's still wild. I don't really know what I'm doing, or the mechanics of how it all comes together. I just know that I've caused it—with my power and intention—and the results are magnificent."

She swept her closed parasol toward the orchard as if conducting a symphony. The beetle-like construct had vanished, taking every last tumorous worrange with it. The reek of rotten citrus and unbrushed teeth had been driven out, too.

"Very tidy," Nemesia said.

Eden looked askance at her, then broke into a grin. "You're not impressed."

"I meant that as praise," Nemesia protested.

"I took it as such." Eden offered her arm again. "You've been helpful. You know what that means—"

"More work?"

"If you're willing. It won't always involve fruit with teeth and toes."

17

The Over-Under

THEY WENT TO lunch in Yolk City. Eden had booked a eighth-floor restaurant with an impressive view of the central stairwell to Below and the densely packed market around it.

Nemesia—being unfamiliar with much of the terminology on the menu—told Eden to order for both of them.

As she said it, she wondered how payment would work. She'd never gotten in the habit of carrying much cash. She had a billfold and a coin purse tucked in her robes, but how much did it actually add up to?

Prices might be different from ten years ago. Or not. The Snake's presence warped the economy in inexplicable ways.

Eden caught her furtively counting off 1,000 scale bills. "No, I've got it," she said. "And by me, I mean the government. Maenads get to live like nobles without ever having to enter the lottery."

They were seated at a counter-style table, side by side, facing full-length

109

windows. Eden reached in Nemesia's sleeve and fished out her coin purse, which was stamped with the ammonite emblem of the Brood.

"Were you trained as a cutpurse?" Nemesia asked.

"I would make a good purse snatcher, wouldn't I?" She shook Nemesia's scales out onto a spare napkin. "Let's play a game."

The coins were shaped vaguely like their namesake. Nemesia had always thought they resembled guitar picks. (Down Below, many Brood members had more day-to-day contact with musical instruments than monetary instruments.)

Each scale was stamped with a king's face—men and women, young and old. Some were long forgotten, and some were the King of Now.

Every citizen of the Shell could recognize the King of Now at a glance. Even if (like Nemesia) they had never seen him in person. Conversely, even if a previous king sat beside you at a bar, you would never realize who they were. The Snake granted past kings an absolute mask of anonymity.

Eden taught her a game of memory that involved flipping coins face-down, mixing them, and taking turns trying to pick out the King of Now.

The reverse side of every coin bore the same symbol, a figure eight inside a circle. A stylized hourglass. Nemesia assumed the oldest coins would feature defunct kings, but this led her astray. Some of the most discolored were the most recent, as if they all aged at different rates.

They played a precarious stacking game, too, until their tower tumbled down. Then Eden showed off sleight of hand tricks, making coins disappear and reappear without magic.

"I'm a real sharpshooter when it comes to coin-flicking," she said wistfully. "Best not demonstrate here, though."

The restaurant was called The Over-Under. When they first came up, Nemesia had asked if the staff took wagers.

"They aren't bookmakers," said Eden. "But it does attract a playful sort of crowd."

They'd walked past diners intent on card games and compact board games. A solitary artist scribbled away at a sketchpad, ignoring his lunch.

Once they settled by the window, Eden nodded at the crevasse below. Market stalls coalesced around it like the rings of a tree trunk.

"That's where The Over-Under gets its name from."

"Ah."

The pedestrians caught in those rings seemed to move inexorably in the same direction, water circling a drain. In truth, only a small percentage would venture down the stairs. Most were just there to shop.

Now Eden flipped Nemesia's scales face-down again, one by one. "Would you like to meet anyone from Below?"

"Why?" Nemesia said, wary.

"Thought you might be lonely."

"I haven't even been Above for two full weeks."

"Feels like longer." She balanced a coin on the end of her thumb. "Want to visit the market? We rushed past it before."

Nemesia imagined the monotone shuffle from booth to booth, head swiveling, trapped amid all those people like the little beetles that had joined to form a worrange-eating magical beast.

"I like seeing the market from a distance," she admitted.

"So do I," Eden said, with evident relief. She swept the scales back into Nemesia's coin purse.

Nemesia had little memory of eating. She'd been focused on the hypnotic mass of humanity churning around the stairs to Below, and the equally hypnotic interplay of Eden's fingertips and glinting coins.

The Over-Under specialized in food in disguise. The first dish she'd been brought was a bowl of clear broth and colorful river rocks. They'd turned out to be some sort of meat and root vegetable construct.

After all their plates had been cleared, Eden ordered cake.

"You don't care for dessert," said Nemesia.

"I don't. But I like seeing what they come up with."

While they were waiting, she led Nemesia over to a wall of portraits and autographs.

"Recognize anyone?"

Nemesia scanned the display until she spotted an actor wearing the widest hat she'd ever seen. He had a beard down to his waist, as thin and sharp as a javelin. The print was signed by *M. Withers*.

"The Warden," she said. "Are you here, too?"

Eden waved this off. "He's a titan of community theater. Compared to that, I barely count as a dabbler."

One frame stood out from the others. Instead of faces or human figures, it held a flat-pressed scrap of dark cloth.

Nemesia recoiled. The scrap was snake skin—flayed, not shed. Skin made into leather.

The scales lay flush alongside one another, without any overlap. The whole gray-black pattern glistened with hints of rainbow iridescence.

As her first spasm of revulsion faded, she saw that the torn fringes where the scales ended looked like regular fabric. A cunning imitation. But it felt inexplicably alive, or akin to evidence of life. Like the taxidermized tail of an escaped lizard.

"Odd-scaled snakes have skin like this," Nemesia said.

Eden tapped the glass. "Read the caption."

There was a note sealed inside the frame. The text was small and faded, and light glanced off the glass at just the right angle to obscure it.

"Did Oddscale write that?"

Eden shaded the note with her hand, leaning around Nemesia to peer at it. "This is from the restaurant owners. A testimonial. See the stamp where they signed it? Well, you were half right. The black scrap is Oddscale's calling card—a sliver of the notorious scarf. A character like that, they usually leave their card in advance." She motioned as if dropping a handkerchief. "As a warning. Repent, or be punished.

"In this case, it couldn't have been planned. There was a hostage situation right here in the restaurant. A disgruntled former noble acting out."

"Oddscale swept in to save the day?"

"Seems so. All hail our shadowy savior. Must've left that rag as a parting gift."

"I wonder if Oddscale is a person at all," Nemesia said.

"Oh?"

"Maybe Oddscale is ... a vessel for the will of the Snake."

"Is that the Brood's opinion?"

"Or—an offshoot of the Snake itself, in human form. A lesser incarnation. A projection of its magic. If no one sees much of Oddscale's face, maybe there's no face to see at all."

She would normally have kept this sort of speculation to herself.

Eden was looking at her strangely. No, not at her: past her. She might have stopped listening midway though.

"Ah—our cake is here," Eden said happily. She turned her back on the wall of souvenirs.

Their dessert took the appearance of a gnarled hunk of wood, slightly smaller than Nemesia's fist, frilled with shocking orange mushrooms.

"Better not serve this to children," Eden muttered. "Might train them to eat random woodland fungi."

The filling had a rich bitter depth to it, with only mild hints of sweetness. It was curiously gratifying to watch Eden go back for a second bite—although she stopped there and told Nemesia the rest was hers, if she wanted it.

"Did you never think of marrying for love?" Nemesia asked as she whittled away at the trompe l'oeil cake.

"Anyone I married for love would poke around about as thoroughly as you have, I think. Out of simple nosiness, if not malice."

"Or out of wanting to know and understand you."

Eden flipped her dessert fork sinuously from one finger to the next. "Perhaps. Makes me squirm to think of it. The older I get, the harder I squirm."

"But you sought me out yourself."

"This is different. This is more of a business arrangement, with mutual benefits and risks. When you search my drawers, you're just taking your due."

"What if I wanted us to behave like real wives?"

"We are real wives," Eden said.

"Provisionally."

"What do wives do, anyway? Aside from the obvious."

Nemesia didn't have much of an answer for that one. "What do professional maenads do day after day?" she countered. "You said it wouldn't all be worranges."

Eden told her about fighting monsters, finding lost pets, assisting fire brigades, repairing wormholes, and so on.

If no other urgent tasks arose, she'd patrol the edge of the Shell. "That's how we'll spend the rest of our afternoon," she said munificently. "A nice leisurely stroll along—"

A server approached, making a beeline for their empty dessert plate. Eden grabbed Nemesia and lunged away from the window seats. Nemesia stumbled, bewildered. Eden kept scurrying for the door, but a second server cut her off. He presented her with a folded missive.

Eden's face fell. She slunk back over to Nemesia and said in longing tones: "We could just pretend I never got this."

"The entire restaurant saw you. What is it?"

"Nothing important."

Nemesia stared daggers at her, mentally channeling the Abbess, until she recanted.

"It's an emergency summons," Eden said reluctantly. "These go out to every available maenad. There's a good chance that I won't be the first on the scene."

"I extinguished your devil this morning," Nemesia said. "You didn't have to do any work to banish it. You're in peak condition. You love magic. Go use it."

"Yes, but—"

"You called yourself the most gifted living maenad within the Shell."

"Did I really? That sounds like hyperbole."

"We'll go help," Nemesia said firmly, "and we'll go together."

18

A Sinkhole

SHE'D SPOKEN TO Eden the way she might speak to a newly arrived novice, some gangly child fresh off the stairs from Above.

Initiates were rarely homesick for long. Still, the enormity of the Brood's caverns made them timid. They became terrified of getting lost—even if Nemesia assured them that their stigmata would lead them true. Sometimes you had to be painfully stern, or else they would never learn to make their way around on their own.

Eden was not a fearful Brood novice. Eden just enjoyed using magic on her own time, on her own terms. She took advantage of her seniority to snap up assignments with lengthy deadlines, and she completed them in any order she pleased.

The Warden later confirmed that she had a habit of dodging urgent summons.

"I plan things out!" she protested. "I don't do well under pressure."

"Nonsense," he said. "You never had any trouble being an understudy."

Eden slumped across the kitchen table. "If I take all the hard work, younger maenads will never get a chance to grow."

"If you never take any hard work, you'll never set a proper example." He looked Nemesia in the eye. "You did the right thing," he said, nodding crisply. "Don't listen to her moaning. Sometimes she needs a good kick in the—"

"Why must you be so cruel?" Eden said plaintively.

"Without further proof of great deeds, you'll be forced to retire at forty."

Eden flinched. "No talk of that until after the gala. You promised."

All this came later that evening, after they dragged themselves home. After Eden mournfully answered the summons she'd received at The Over-Under.

Upon leaving the restaurant, she opened her parasol and drew a temporary wormhole: a large lopsided circle in empty air. It shimmered, warping with heat.

They stepped across swiftly. It felt like walking through a ring of fire. Eden kept a firm grip on Nemesia's wrist, pressing at her bite marks as if to staunch bleeding.

The wormhole spat them out downtown. The air reeked of hot pepper. Nemesia immediately started sneezing.

A sinkhole the size of a public swimming pool had opened in the street in front of a restaurant.

A maenad in his late teens rushed tearfully over. It was all his fault, he sobbed. "I was just—I was just trying to scale up the recipe!"

Eden froze.

The sniffle-filled pause stretched out so long that Nemesia felt compelled to intervene, despite her sneezing and her dearth of credentials. Eden gawked as if she'd never seen someone weep in her life.

As Nemesia attempted to formulate soothing words, Eden thawed. She patted the boy gingerly on the back.

After some questioning, they determined that no one was actually hurt. A few onlookers had leaned too far over the edge—but he'd already scooped them out, none the worse for wear.

All in all, he hadn't been very successful at cordoning off the scene of the incident. People still sat about in steamy rubble, cheerfully chatting, sipping from bowls passed out by intrepid restaurateurs.

The sinkhole was, in short, a giant hotpot. Icebergs of tofu protruded from savory broth. The liquid roiled with red currents of pepper paste. There were heaps of cabbage leaves larger than bedsheets. And onion slices, too, cooked to glistening translucence.

Eden got the younger maenad to calm down and move away.

"He shouldn't have let anyone eat that," she said under her breath. "What if it turned them into cows? Then he'd really have a reason to cry."

"Could it do that?"

"You never know."

"It does smell good."

Eden shot a baleful look at the long lines of would-be customers. "Did you see how much they're charging over there? They didn't even cook it!"

"Is there anything I can extinguish?" Nemesia asked doubtfully.

"No—this is all magically inert. The act is complete: he already generated a lake's worth of hotpot."

"Could your devil eat it?"

"My devil has no tolerance for spice."

Nemesia, upon request, went to borrow an empty bowl from the restaurant chef. After leaving it with Eden, she worked to herd away all the gawkers.

Meanwhile, Eden shrank the lake of molten hotpot down to the size of a single serving, leaving a wet jagged crater coated with peppery sediment. She handed her filled bowl over to the junior maenad.

"Dispose of this," she ordered.

"How...?"

"Any number of ways—you have magic! Just don't let anyone taste it. They might very well explode."

She jabbed the air with the end of her parasol, as if goading a gargantuan invisible beast. The road put itself back together: slowly at first, then faster and faster.

Some minutes later, the sinkhole had vanished. Eden snapped her parasol shut and threw herself down on a bench in front of a barbershop.

There were several stacked cages of colorful birds arrayed outside the shop window, off to the right of the bench. Perhaps to attract customers. They were piercingly vocal.

The hotpot place across the road currently had a queue trailing halfway down the block, although it was late for lunch and early for dinner. Eden said cynically that rumors of the sinkhole would keep business booming for at least the next couple weeks.

The parakeets chirped knowingly.

"Was that tiring?" Nemesia asked.

Eden massaged fretfully at the back of her neck. "Shrinking it wasn't difficult. Just takes concentration not to shrink everything else in the process. But look—I pulled it off. Good as new."

The cobblestones had been relaid with stunning regularity. But they hadn't previously been shaped like smooth interlocking scales.

There also hadn't previously been a film of reddish dust clinging to the mortar. As for the ambient smell of hotpot ... it may have predated the sinkhole, considering the restaurant across the way, but it probably hadn't always been so pervasive.

When all was said and done, Eden spent more time reassuring the culprit than she'd spent on fixing his mistakes. He kept wringing his hands.

"He won't get in serious trouble," she told Nemesia on the way back to the cottage. "We're good at punishing ourselves all on our own." She sighed and added: "A lot of maenad work is just cleaning up each other's messes."

It was a good thing, they agreed, that one couldn't simply dig a hole through the ground to Below.

"Imagine how your Abbess would react if the Brood got showered in soup," Eden said.

They both smelled distinctly spicy even after returning home, bathing, and reconvening in the kitchen. The Warden sniffed the air and named the exact restaurant that Eden had rescued.

She groaned. She instructed Nemesia to be ready for another outing tomorrow. Then she tottered towards the basement. Only Pimiko dared to follow.

She didn't show up for dinner. She didn't sleep at home that night, either.

From the next day onward, she periodically whisked Nemesia away for maenad assignments. Around the house, though, Nemesia was still more likely to run into the Warden.

Now that he was no longer playing a self-assigned role, he became chattier than before. And louder. He did vocalization exercises while chopping vegetables, and sang show tunes out in the garden.

Once Nemesia asked him about a song he'd been bellowing up and down the stairs. (Which he was perfectly capable of climbing, as it turned out, although he used the elevator for his cleaning cart.)

"Oh, that one?" he said once she'd hummed a few bars. "It's from *The Archetype*. An older musical. Extremely popular."

"What's it about?"

"The rise of the Antemaenad." He grinned impishly. "Eden joined in for a couple performances of an abridged version. Twenty years ago, maybe."

He taught Nemesia the lyrics. His nostrils flared when she said she'd never seen a musical. "Well, we'd better fix that," he said darkly.

He'd loosened up enough to let her wander freely in the kitchen. In quiet moments, she pretended to be an art restorer, scrupulously dusting the animal figurines that paraded about the countertops.

Past a cascading veil of hanging potted vines was a half-hidden cabinet—which, of course, Nemesia opened.

It was tall and dark and cool inside, without any interior shelving. It contained just three things: a vial of worrange extract, a wine-size bottle of worrange bitters, and a jar of worrange marmalade.

She heard the Warden approaching. It was too late to hide, so she showed him the marmalade. "Who eats this?"

"Not I," he said, "and not the boss."

"Who, then?"

"Our plants." He pointed at the pots that trailed vines low enough to brush their shoulders. "Gives them a dose of healthy anxiety."

He looked at her straight-faced. He was too much of a professional to crack under pressure.

Cold air leaked continuously out of the cabinet until Nemesia closed it. The bottle of bitters looked less than half full. She wasn't sure about the extract, although it had felt very light. The marmalade, on the other hand, seemed barely used.

Maybe it had proven too sweet for Eden's taste.

"The plants won't mind if I try some."

His brow furrowed. "Your wife might mind."

"She said she wouldn't have any work for me today."

Nemesia began preparing a slice of toast. The Warden made no attempt to physically stop her, but he was quite clear about the fact that he didn't endorse it.

She finished eating, put back the marmalade, cleaned crumbs off the table, and went upstairs to lie down.

Her heart raced, and her stomach clenched. It was like the opposite of the undersky, where nothing hurt because nothing mattered, most especially not the tiny invisible speck of a thing called *you*.

With worrange jam in her belly, it felt as though the whole world had shrunken down to the aimless crawling ants of her thoughts. As if there were nothing more urgent than the dizziness in the depths of her ears.

Her mind quaked.

She had always belonged to the Snake. She had always been a thing of the Snake. The bracing vitality of everyday life Above was just as much a hallucination as the cramping anxiety brought on by worranges. If she longed for fresh air and fresh experiences, it was because the Snake sought fodder for its dreams.

What right did she have to be here? Why did she want so badly not to be seen as a being already claimed and possessed?

She didn't really believe that Daiya Sholto could pry her away from her destiny. No matter how well she pleased him. The Snake would allow for a certain degree of corruptibility in human society up Above, sure, but why would it ever relinquish one of its Brides to a backroom deal?

If Nemesia herself didn't think it was possible, then the entire effort was doomed from the start.

The Abbess would let her go through the motions anyway. The Brood would benefit from Sholto's donations. Besides, Nemesia had nothing better to do, did she? She still needed to while away the greater part of a year Above.

If she didn't at least pretend to cater to Sholto's requests, she would be left shambling incoherently from one day to the next, dreading the inexorable countdown to the end of her year. When her sabbatical was over, she would go back Below. All this churning apprehension and yearning would be extinguished like a candle dipped in a bucket of water.

After her first sabbatical, she hadn't missed Tanyu. Not truly; not viscerally. Down Below, thinking of Tanyu had sometimes felt like remembering a half-forgotten classmate. Perhaps that was a sign that their connection would never have been strong enough to survive the Snake.

19

The Shell

THE MENTAL TUMULT receded, leaving her drained. A bitter marmalade aftertaste lingered in unreachable crevices of her mouth.

Her jaw ached. Her body had gripped all her bones like a fist, terrified of losing control. She looked with interest at her trembling fingertips.

Downstairs, she sprinkled salted sesame seeds over a palm-sized bowl of rice. She ate it by the sink, gazing mindlessly out a light-filled window.

The Warden sang—more mutedly than usual—in the long reverberating corridors between rooms. He seemed disinclined to mention her worrange experimentation to Eden, which was just as well.

Nemesia didn't bring it up again, either. Instead she asked him to transcribe a letter to Roc, the guard she'd left Below.

Her fingers stopped palpitating as she dictated her message in the scriptorium. The relief was immense, although she wouldn't personally consider it worth the price of purchase.

She waited several days for a reply from Roc, but none came. He'd claimed he would be there when she returned from her sabbatical; maybe he'd counted wrong. Maybe his term had already ended.

He'd encouraged Nemesia to take Sholto's deal. He'd told her she had nothing to lose. But Nemesia knew neither his face nor his name. She would have liked to call him a friend, except that she wouldn't recognize him even if he showed up as a waiter at The Over-Under.

Her note, inscribed by the Warden, said that Roc had been right. This was a good place to spend her year. This was a kind house, if somewhat peculiar. She didn't know what would come of it in the end, but she was glad she'd followed his advice. She was glad to be here.

She didn't understand how much she meant that until she heard herself telling the Warden what to say. The post-worrange high might have made her more effusive than usual, but the feeling behind it was true.

She mentioned to Eden that she might be expecting a response, although her expectations were low. She used this as a pretext to inquire about the missing receiving pod.

"If any letters come in, our Warden will make sure you get them," Eden said.

"Can't I check for myself?"

"Trust me, it isn't worth the hunt. You'll never find the mailroom on your own."

"Then show me."

Eden cackled in amusement. "You're the undercover agent here! I won't do your job for you."

After this, Nemesia focused more on looking around outside. She'd reached the limit of what she could accomplish indoors, short of using a sledgehammer on innocent walls.

She'd come to live with Eden and the Warden at the start of the new year, which fell in February. Now it was early March, a couple weeks away from the equinox. On sunlit days, it grew warm enough to start opening windows.

Nemesia, accustomed to the heated floors and seasonless comforts of Below, would have preferred it warmer still. But she appreciated the novelty of shivering under open skies. During brisk walks, she might eventually loosen her overcoat or shrug off her shawl.

Eden often took her on patrol along the rim of the Shell. The terrain there was prone to frequent fluctuation. Eden would point out teethy new cliffs, or trees unceremoniously dumped upside-down, roots in the air, as if deposited by a storm.

Nemesia dutifully wrote each observation in a logbook borrowed from the nearest border town.

There were many, many border towns. They dotted the vast circle formed by the Shell's intersection with solid earth. Roads ran from the border to Yolk City like spokes on a wheel.

Not all such roads were heavily trafficked. Reliable wormholes seemed difficult to establish close to the Shell, but maenads would come by once a week or so and set up temporary portals, like a low-frequency ferry.

Tanyu used to suggest taking a trip together, spending a few romantic nights along the border. The reformatory kidnappings started before those plans could come to pass.

Eden's eyebrows shot up when she first learned that Nemesia had never seen the Shell. "Our Warden thinks I should take you downtown and get you caught up on pop culture—but that can come later. I've always liked Shell duties, anyway."

She carried an oyster-white parasol. It curved up to a peak like a dollop of meringue. The point on the end was as long as a carving knife.

She had opened it not to use magic, but simply to shade her head.

She would have held it out over Nemesia, too, but Nemesia was happy to bask in sunlight.

They climbed a grassy ridge, and the Shell came into view. It was not a distinct object one could see from afar, like a mountain or a river. It was more of a mirrored effect in the air, throwing back the illusion of a pastoral landscape.

The mirror reflected no living animals. You could walk up to it without ever seeing yourself on the other side. No one came that close, though. It exerted a repulsive force. Even if you tried to go straight, it would turn your feet.

Nemesia extinguished the repulsion—only a little of it, like waving steam away from her face. She stepped up to the invisible wall where the scenery doubled. She stopped just short of touching it.

Higher up, the mirroring faded. The sky didn't reflect the ground. But the Shell was still there, transparent, curving over the land like a contact lens.

The repulsive field would close up again as soon as she left, rolling together like a mass of fog.

She couldn't guess what would happen if she extinguished part of the Shell itself.

"Want to try?" Eden said from behind her. "I can probably fix it."

"Probably?"

"I've never seen a breach before. It does happen, though. Fissures form, like in melting ice. The Shell usually plugs its holes on its own."

"Let's not go looking for trouble," Nemesia said—to herself, as much as to Eden.

A breeze tugged at Eden's parasol. The kind of wind that might sweep along a lonely shore.

"I picked Pimiko up near the border," Eden said.

"You just saw her crawling around?"

"Many years ago. Someone tipped me off. Told me where to find her."

"Who?"

"A random passerby. At first I was more suspicious than grateful. She'd clearly been raised as a pet. Figured my informant had to be the person who dumped her."

She shut her parasol to stop the wind from trying to steal it. "I see you doing math on your fingers. Yes—she's over twenty. Crabantulas live a long time. Especially out of the wild."

Pet abandonment wasn't the only possibility, she explained. A lot of treasures washed up along the rim of the Shell. Some came from outside, borne in by an intangible magical tide, and some were conjured wholesale by the Snake. Only the Brood could tell the difference with any authority.

Pimiko might have appeared together with other mysterious treasures—crates of nameless fruit that no one knew how to eat, iron pots with layers of seasoning that shone like glass, shoes that would never give anyone blisters.

Most border towns had grown organically in places where treasure washed up on a regular basis. Open warehouses caught hauls of mysterious trinkets like submerged cages for trapping crayfish.

Between towns, treasure-hunting hobbyists prowled along the uninhabited border, though they didn't necessarily find much. Sometimes Eden had to break up squabbles between rival groups.

The hardest day of the month came on quite suddenly. They arrived at a border town and found it in a screaming state of chaos. Another maenad, in the process of troubleshooting a wormhole, had accidentally transformed twenty-one local residents into angry bluebirds.

Nemesia counted off each missing townsperson as Eden converted bluebirds back to people. *One, two, three ... nineteen, twenty, twenty-one—*

Eden kept going.

Nemesia leapt forward and grabbed her, one hand clamping down on each stiff epaulet. Her umbrella went flying like a hat snatched by a gale. The rumble of her magic died out.

Nemesia had lunged before thinking. It shouldn't have been necessary to touch her at all. Now, somehow, it felt safer not to let go.

They both looked at the twenty-second blackbird, whose claws had warped into short fleshy hands ... or long-toed feet? Hard to tell.

It was a chimera, a bird grafted onto the chubby severed fists of a baby. It lay on its side, overbalanced, cheeping weakly, turning pitiful circles as its fingers (or toes) pushed clumsily at the dust beneath it.

"Let go," Eden said levelly. "I'll undo it."

"Can you?"

"I can't leave it!" she snapped, rounding on Nemesia, who held her ground out of sheer astonishment.

Eden let out a controlled breath. She removed Nemesia's hands from her shoulders, one at a time. She fetched her umbrella. She dusted it off.

"No one would begrudge me for summoning emergency backup," she said. "But no other maenad could put this poor bird to rights any faster."

Nemesia stepped back. Eden restored the bluebird. It flew off, beclawed once more, and rapidly vanished from sight.

As soon as the bluebird took flight, Eden caught at Nemesia's hand. Nemesia halted all the possibilities of magic that brimmed around her, quick as shutting a door. Eden startled a little, stumbling, saying nothing.

Around midday, they staggered out of town with feathers in their hair. The wormhole was back in working order, and the townspeople were all accounted for. They wrote an incident report in the local logbook before fleeing.

Eden flung a borrowed picnic blanket beneath a stand of blackthorn trees. The white buds were round and full. She hung her umbrella from a low bough—upside-down, still open—and declared that no one would bother them.

Indeed, no one did. Treasure hunters meandered past without a glance.

"I found your guard the other day," she said abruptly.

Nemesia sat up. "Roc?"

"The older one. He served Below, and then left you. He plays the fiddle."

"Chameleon. How did you—"

"I can't arrange a meeting," Eden said, apologetic. "I was discreet. Didn't approach him directly. But I did learn a couple facts of interest."

Criss-crossing branches cast a lattice of shadow over her half-golden head. Since their first meeting, her roots had grown longer and blacker.

The chill of the ground seeped up through the blanket, making it feel almost damp.

"Tell me," Nemesia said.

"He's a serial debtor. After bankruptcy proceedings, he worked over a decade Below to pay his dues. Except..."

She unhooked her umbrella from the tree, half-closed it, and used the pointy part to draw a line in the mossy dirt beyond the blanket.

"It hasn't happened yet," she said. "He's taken on an avalanche of debt. But he hasn't served his sentence. Not Above, that is."

She sketched more hash marks and arrows, kneeling to wield her umbrella like a giant pencil. "Do you get it?"

"Do you?"

"Somewhat. Tenuously."

The Snake could shake time up like dice in a cup. The Snake could shift decades about as if restringing a necklace.

"Chameleon already served his time Below," said Nemesia. "I was there for part of it."

She borrowed Eden's umbrella and moved to the opposite side of the blanket to start a fresh set of drawings. Two parallel lines: one for Above, and one for Below. She carved a vertical mark down the middle.

"This is the present moment."

"Here and now," said Eden.

"In the present, the timelines of Above and Below are aligned."

"As far as we know."

"Right. As long as both lines balance out in the long term, they don't always have to match up."

"Not for everyone, I suppose."

"Chameleon played a guard Below." Nemesia shaded a block on the left half of the lower line. In the past. "Above, here and now, he hasn't yet departed to serve his sentence. In the future"—she shaded a block on the right half of the upper line—"he'll go backwards in time to work for the Brood."

"One day, even further in the future, he'll pop up Above again. He'll finally remember you."

"I still won't know his face," said Nemesia. She'd seen hints of it, but she didn't trust her memory.

Eden crawled across the blanket for a better look at her diagram. "So there were two of him in the past. His younger self, merrily incurring debts Above—and his older self, working them off Below."

"But why would he want that?"

"He's delaying his tour of duty until his children grow up. Once the wait is over, he'll be absent from their lives for years. Serving in the past can't change that." Eden wiped soil off her umbrella. "Bet it wasn't his choice at all."

"Why would the Snake shift his time around unasked?"

"To maintain consistent staffing levels?"

"I don't think the Neverending Snake cares about workforce issues."

"For your sake, then," Eden said easily. "The Snake pushed Chameleon's service backwards because it wanted him to meet you. Not just at any age—when you first went Below. The Snake wanted to give you a father figure."

"A father figure without a face?"

"He obviously made some kind of impression." She began folding up the picnic blanket. "I've seen diaries from people who stumbled outside the Shell and came back to find that a century had passed. We're all subjects of the Snake That Ate the Roots of Time. Maybe some of us lurch back and forth across decades by accident. Like slipping on ice."

She shot Nemesia a quick smile. "Sorry. Time travel is always a tedious topic."

"The Brood has a different definition of tedious. This is nothing."

Eden chortled. "It isn't professional to mix business with pleasure, but we *are* married. I'm glad if my yammering doesn't bore you to tears. I haven't done much else for you."

"You've given me a place to stay," said Nemesia, "and interesting work, and interesting stories."

Then she heard herself ask, quite spontaneously: "Do you want to know who hired me?"

"Would you tell me?" Eden sounded scandalized. "Just like that?"

"It depends."

"Well, don't. You need more experience before you establish yourself as a double agent. Or—perish the thought—a triple agent."

"Or a quadruple—"

"Let's stop there." Eden tossed over the folded-up blanket, forcing her to catch it. "I have guesses. Even if you outright told me, I could hardly take your word for it. So save the double-crossing for later. Keep things simple."

"You blew my cover the day you brought me Above," said Nemesia.

"I don't know if it's possible to get any simpler."

They started to descend the mossy slope. Eden caught at her shoulder, telling her to stand still, and plucked one last blue feather out of her hair. She blew it away. It rode the wind for a surprisingly long time, twirling about. They watched all the while, as if they had a duty to see it land.

20

Horns and Chains

BETWEEN EXCURSIONS with Eden, Nemesia searched the grounds around the cottage.

She felt no personal loyalty toward Daiya Sholto. His vendetta seemed out of proportion with Eden's alleged crime (toying with the hearts of his sisters, was it?).

But now she'd been here for a month, and simple curiosity won out. Whatever Sholto had sent her to uncover—she wanted to discover it for her own sake.

As for whether or not to tell him ... that could be a separate decision.

There were no fences to demarcate the official borders of maenad property. The Warden's garden transitioned seamlessly into boundless wilderness. If you could even call it that. Everything in sight had been influenced by generations of resident magic. True wilderness would surely have been more combative.

So: Nemesia could stride across meadows for hours without glimpsing another human soul. Yet no brambles tore at her ankles.

Where there was grass, it grew low and tame—and, for this time of year, oddly green. Where there were trees, dry matted leaves spread out at ground level, forming a light-splashed delta of endless paths. As if a crew of foresters had cleared the way.

Every babbling stream came equipped with stepping stones, and none were slick with dangerous mud.

The water was wide and clear and gentle. In some places, it became so shallow that the backs of well-fed carp protruded from the current, brown and glistening.

Dapper ducks glided about as she crossed, some all white and some all black. Arm-length mudlings bounded madly from bank to bank. Even shy caecilians—which looked like a cross between snakes and worms—poked their heads out of the soil to watch her. She had to be careful about where she stepped.

Eventually she made her way to a natural well surrounded by forested slopes. It was another kind of sinkhole, stunningly blue and deep, with no obvious tributaries. The shape of the land had cunningly concealed it from view.

There were people down there.

She descended a tumble of boulders that formed a sort of incidental staircase. Below came a wide, flat shelf of rock covered with a sheen of moisture. The sinkhole opened abruptly in the middle of this shelf, as stark as a gouged eye.

The woman with horns sat with her legs in the water. She wore a single-layer loose robe, carelessly tied, and didn't seem to care if it got wet.

She wasn't sitting on a rock. She rested on the air above the water's surface. As Nemesia approached, she leaned back on splayed hands, fingers comfortably braced against nothingness. A second figure floated face-down beside her.

"She's not drowning," said the woman with horns. "Just relaxing. What do you want?"

Nemesia found herself suddenly tongue-tied.

The figure in the water began to glide around like a crocodile. Ridged shapes broke the surface. Then a human forehead and unblinking dark eyes rose into sight. The trailing ridges turned out to be long chains, although Nemesia had never seen a metal chain that could float.

The horned woman was still waiting for her answer. "Well?"

"I won't come any closer," Nemesia said. Partly to avoid getting her shoes wet. Partly to reduce the risk of falling in headfirst. Partly because—

"You're not afraid of us," the horned woman said. All hints of mirth had left her face. "You're not afraid of being eaten. You're a lot more territorial than I thought."

Nemesia stood on a dry slab of rock above the azure sinkhole. She stood with her hands in front of her, as if solemnly awaiting a pronouncement from the Abbess.

Her clasped hands shook.

Not, as the woman had correctly inferred, with fear.

Her hands shook with the urge to extinguish.

These people were outsiders. These people didn't belong in the Shell. She didn't know if they were really people at all, but they had magic. If they had magic, then there was something in them she could crush like a bug, pinch like a candle wick, dowse like a flame.

"I won't say no to a fight," said the woman with horns and pointed teeth.

Nemesia shook her head mutely.

This baseless aggression—it was just a reflex. The Abbess had taught her to be more than a creature of instinct. These were outsiders, yes, and probably inhuman, but they were also peaceful visitors. They were Eden's guests.

"All I want to do is talk," she said, and she tried to mean it.

The horned woman shrugged. Her companion swam in idle circles, watching silently. The chains kept swirling, too, forming complex tracks as they dragged their way through the water.

Nemesia spread her shawl on the rock beside her and took a seat. "Did you come inside the Shell by accident?"

The woman looked bored. "We have some familiarity with sealed cities. And barriers."

"There are other places like the Shell?"

"There have been, at times. Nothing to do with here."

One of her dangling ankles moved, kicking underwater. The swimmer stilled, then parted the surface as if diving in reverse, slipping casually up to sit cross-legged on a cushion of invisible air.

The swimmer was girthy with muscle. She wore what might have been either a two-piece swimsuit or sporty undergarments. Inorganic chains grew directly from her flesh, dangling off her back and shoulders and stomach like extra limbs.

The woman with horns and the woman with chains faced Nemesia, one mostly dry and the other dripping. They didn't look much alike except for the fact that, very briefly, they both wore expressions of identical pity.

"How long will you stay?" Nemesia asked, ill at ease.

"Not for years," said the horned woman. "We won't be here long enough to watch your Shell hatch."

Nemesia had a sense of time running out. As if, from the beginning, she had been granted a limited number of questions.

"Do you know Eden's secret?" A stab in the dark.

The horned woman laughed. "It's nothing shameful."

"Has she really been outside the Shell?"

"Not yet. Maybe she'll leave in the future. Time can get scrambled here. Time outside the Shell and time inside the Shell might not match up, either.

"Makes me wonder," she added offhand, "what will happen when it hatches. Will anything be left alive in its shards? Will every last maenad get devoured by their own magic? You, at least, have nothing to worry about."

Nemesia's snakebites twinged.

The woman with horns waved a dismissive hand, nails glinting. (The woman with chains had given her a reproachful look.) "Never mind that. Your Shell won't crack for a while to come."

She turned away, looping an arm around her companion's neck. Those long chains swished in the water like trailing fingers. A shy, pleased sort of gesture. Or so it seemed to Nemesia.

"I found a necklace of teeth," she said hastily. "An artifact from beyond. What does it mean?"

The horned woman glanced back. "Could be a symbol of brutal subjugation. Or it could be a symbol of loving commitment from a mage."

Both women dove into the sinkhole like seals, flawlessly synchronized, splashless. No bubbles rose in their wake. They went to depths far beyond the outer boundary of Nemesia's vision.

A few scattered fish still circled the rim, hoping for a way out. Nothing else remained. Nemesia got up and dusted off her shawl.

There were already a few things that she had decided against reporting to Daiya Sholto.

For example: Eden had a history of eating worrange products, defying the edicts meant to keep maenads away from mind-altering substances.

She didn't have definite proof, though. She couldn't see how it was any of Sholto's business if Eden ingested worranges to make herself miserable, or if she sought the burst of relief that came after the effects wore off.

What else? Eden claimed to have spent years outside the Shell. She'd brought back physical evidence, if not memories. She was currently hosting two guests who themselves hailed from outside the Shell—and who said she'd never actually left at all.

Nemesia wasn't quite sure how to characterize Eden's guests. They weren't demons. Stairs to nowhere on the side of a building wouldn't be sufficient to fool them.

Were they gods from the outer world, peers of the Snake? No. They were too small, and too tangible. The essence of the Snake could not be fully contained in a physical body.

Perhaps they were avatars for a fragment of something greater. Perhaps the outer gods had sent them inside the Shell as observers. Like how the Snake kept sending its beloved Brides on sabbaticals.

If they were just here to observe the realm like guests of honor at a concert, that might explain why the Snake seemed largely unperturbed by their presence. Although Nemesia had no idea where they went when they were nowhere to be found, or what they did when no humans were watching.

21

The Archetype

Nemesia saw the visitors more frequently after that conversation by the hidden well.

At sunset, she might spy them atop the turret. They hovered like hummingbirds come to feed on a flower.

Sinuous chains would stir soundlessly against the dying light of day. Blink, and for a flickering moment, the smaller woman would be crowned with the stabbing antlers of an elk.

In mid-March, Nemesia woke to the sensation of something poking her cheek. She cracked her eyes open. Grayish light leaked in—just enough to see a black blur of spidery fur and legs on her pillow.

She told Eden over breakfast. "If I reacted badly, I could've lost my nose."

"No one got hurt." Eden appeared entirely unconcerned. "Pimiko approves of you, and so do I. Even our gargoyles—"

"Our what?"

Eden pointed at the ceiling. When Nemesia looked at her blankly, she raised her arms in a turret-like triangle. "They've been skulking about the rooftop like gargoyles. I think they're rooting for you."

She made Nemesia come over to the windowsill. Pimiko crouched between figurines of land krakens, trying to blend in.

"Did you see her paw pads?"

"I'd just woken up," said Nemesia. "I was woozy."

"Look now." They both crouched down, putting themselves at eye level with the sill. "The tips of her legs are pink, see? They make a shape like tiny puppy paws. Ugh, my heart."

"I thought you were going to show me something important."

"There's nothing more important than crabantula toes."

Eden vanished later that morning, claiming she had an appointment. When she returned, it was a bright and windy afternoon, and Nemesia was attempting to stomp her way up to the turret. She still couldn't locate the right spot on the hallway carpet.

With all that noisy tromping, minutes passed before she noticed Eden leaning on the wall behind her.

"At this rate, you'll break your foot. Or the floor." Eden spread her hands. "At least wait until after the Snake Moth Gala. The King expects me to bring you."

"That's…" Nemesia searched her memory. "Around the equinox, isn't it?"

"About a week from now. Which means it's time to go shopping."

When they came outside, the Warden was sweeping the front stoop. He fixed Eden with a gimlet eye. "Got your tickets?"

She swung her sleeve at him. "Right here."

"If you'll be passing City Hall—"

"Not now," she said. "We'll deal with that later."

"Deal with what?" Nemesia asked as they left.

Eden didn't feign ignorance, at least. "I'll be thirty-nine this fall. I have to apply for an extension of my magic practitioner permit. The standard period of permission expires..." She waited expectantly.

"At forty."

"Right on. You can get two-year extensions till you're sixty, and one-year extensions after that."

"Has there ever been an active maenad over sixty?"

"No. By then, maybe I'll actually want to retire."

Nemesia recalled snatches of past conversations. "The Warden thinks you should hurry up and apply."

"There's still time," said Eden. "I'd rather focus on debuting my beautiful wife at the Snake Moth Gala, so as to reassure our ailing King."

She clearly didn't want to talk about it anymore, but Nemesia persisted. "Who decides whether to renew your permit? The King?"

"If only. It'll be a cadre of bureaucrats. They aren't nearly as fond of me. More to the point—" Eden stopped, looking vaguely aggrieved, and gestured at her head. "Don't you notice anything different?"

They were on a wide, gracious boulevard. The paving stones locked together like a jigsaw puzzle. Outdoor diners kept dragging tables and chairs—which seemed to be only loosely affiliated with any given eatery—to chase the warmth of the sun.

Eden tilted her neck one way, then the other.

"You got your hair done?" Nemesia guessed.

It looked exactly the same as before. Perhaps just a fraction blonder and shinier. Her roots still showed in bold black streaks.

"If I never got it touched up, it'd be dark past my ears. Roots usually grow out in a straight line, you know—not these artful streaks. This look takes a lot of maintenance."

"So why bother?"

Eden didn't answer. She nudged Nemesia toward a store without a sign out front. It could have been anything. A members-only bar. A private office. A criminal safehouse.

It turned out to be a one-woman clothier. Eden gave the owner a series of rapid instructions.

"Something simple," Nemesia added while the clothier looked her over.

The type of robe they sought didn't require much in the way of measurements. That part of it was done quickly, and with a light touch. The clothier then vanished into a back room, leaving them to pore over books of fashion plates.

The shop was extremely quiet, even with restaurant-goers hauling furniture on the street outside.

"I brought enough clothing from Below," Nemesia said in a whisper.

"It's all very nice," Eden replied genially, "but it won't look good if you show up in an old Brood robe. People will think I'm mistreating you. Now, you might not care much about my reputation—"

"Er," said Nemesia, who was reasonably good at maintaining long-established lies, but still fumbled when it came to fibbing on the spot.

"—which is the correct attitude," Eden continued. "I don't care much about my reputation, either. That, however, is more or less why I found myself in need of a spouse."

She flipped pages. "If we make a decent showing at the gala, society will be forced to swallow the fact that I have a wife and that—by all appearances—I cherish her.

"If I don't bring you wearing something fancy, they won't just mutter about me. They'll question the Abbess's judgment, too. You don't want that."

All this time, Nemesia had been mystified about why Eden (and the King who backed her) was going to such lengths to rehabilitate her image. Perhaps it all had some basis in truth—her philandering, the squabbles and duels she'd sparked along the way—but such matters seemed rather too petty for royalty.

If Nemesia were crowned ruler of all the Shell, she wouldn't interfere. She'd let Eden face the natural consequences of her own fornication. That seemed fairer than trying to stifle her notoriety with a paper-thin marriage that might evaporate after a year, anyway.

But Eden seemed to claim the King as a genuine (if exasperated) ally. The King must have known, then, that she hoped to keep practicing magic after turning forty.

Maybe—like the Warden nagging her about her application—this semi-forced marriage had been the King's attempt to smooth the way. The palace bureaucrats who would decide her fate might consider more than just the words written on her plea for an extension. Officially or unofficially, they might take everything else they knew about her into consideration, too.

In theory, maenads could do just about anything so long as they maintained a tight grip on their magic. But officials wouldn't think well of you for trailing an army of lovelorn paramours, or being slow to respond to emergency summons.

The King wanted to boost Eden's chances without overtly intervening—which might make the bureaucrats hate her, and would only complicate future extensions. Especially since no one King of Now could last forever.

Daiya Sholto, in contrast, wanted to sink Eden. He'd be delighted if Nemesia walked into the gala clad in rags.

There were other ways she could play into his hands, no matter what she wore. She could visibly cower; she could feign injuries; she could try to run away in front of everyone. Was this what Sholto expected? Well, he hadn't said so. She wouldn't act based on imagined instructions.

As Eden turned more pages, Nemesia unthinkingly reached out to stop her.

"You like this style?" Eden said. "So do I. But it's a little outdated."

The current page showed a woman with two-toned hair just like Eden.

"Is that you?"

"Does it look like me?"

The woman in the fashion plate was fair-skinned.

"No. But that hair..."

"I'm a trendsetter." She said it with a hint of self-mockery. "Some years ago, all kinds of people tried replicating my hair. Nowadays it's quite passé—for everyone except me. Can't beat the original."

"Why did you—"

"—start dying it?" She pulled over another lookbook. "When I was way younger—just a kid, really—I kept getting compared to the Antemaenad. I'm a generational talent, sure, but those are enormous shoes to fill."

"I thought the Antemaenad had light hair, too."

"That's the funny thing. No one knows precisely what she looked like. The record is extremely confused. On the bright side, no one thinks she had an obvious dye job."

"No one talks about her having a crabantula or carrying parasols, either."

Eden snapped her fingers. "See? You get it. All I have in common with her is magic. Same as any maenad."

The tailor reemerged, arms laden with bolts of cloth, and the three of them began debating the finer points of formal design.

22

At the Facade

THEY APPROACHED the theater an hour before sunset. At the Warden's urging, Eden had gotten tickets to a professional revival of *The Archetype*.

Nemesia said: "If you'd prefer not to see it—"

"Do you want to skip the show?"

"No, but..."

"But?"

"It's a story about the Antemaenad, isn't it?"

"It's not that I can't stand hearing about her. I just don't like being measured against a legend." Eden finished folding her parasol. "Come this way."

Arm in arm, they walked together down the center of the promenade.

The theater was fronted with fearsomely thick columns dripping in vines. Slender waterfalls spilled through greenery, as in a jungle. Carved ogres guarded eagle-size nests. Elaborate stairs to nowhere graced every floor. Some vestigial staircases curled like snakes around the central pillars.

Nemesia didn't understand until they were close enough that they should have heard rushing fountains and the bleats of parrots peeping out of tree-like holes.

"It's flat," she said, astonished.

"They call it the Facade Theater for a reason."

What she had taken for ground-level gardens turned out to be a series of standalone painted pieces, cleverly spaced out to disguise the entrance from afar.

According to Eden, the building facade was made up of numerous panels, too, carefully fitted together for a seamless appearance. They got fully switched out several times a year, to mark the change of seasons. There were other minor updates from day to day, or even from morning to evening.

"See that monkey?" Eden pointed. "Before noon, he's up in the opposite corner, fighting a lion with boxing gloves."

"What's the building like underneath?"

"Smooth and blank."

They navigated around the garden props, which had a top coat of magic, like a thin layer of sealant. Just enough to stave off fading and weathering.

"With more magic, they could make it more convincing," said Nemesia. "Or the entire effect could be achieved with magic alone."

"It wouldn't be the Facade without this enormous fake front. Anyway, illusions are more sustainable when they have something real at their core."

Inside, the lobby was an expanse of sweeping purple carpets. Sunset light fell magically through the covered facade.

The entire front functioned like a two-way mirror. Look back, and the avenue was laid bare—only slightly dimmer than outside, as if viewed through a layer of grayish glass. Nothing interrupted the vista except slim scaffolding.

They'd taken less than three steps when several someones chorused, "K. Eden!" and "Kuchinashi!" and "Kuchinashi Eden!"

"Where have you *been*?"

"You cheeky little—"

"—thought maybe you decided to vanish for another three years again."

"You won't believe what they're saying about—"

"—almost *stabbed* him. For you, she said. All for you."

Soon enough, every last set of eyes landed on Nemesia.

"And who's this?" asked a gentleman with a scarlet-mottled neck. It might have been a rash, or simply the heat of excitement.

"A friend? A girlfriend?" asked a lady.

"Your flavor of the month?"

"Your soup of the day?"

Eden snaked an arm around Nemesia's waist. "M. Nemesia," she said brightly. "My wife."

Nemesia watched with interest as jaws dropped and eyes bugged out.

"Everyone thought that was just a ridiculous rumor. Everyone!"

"A lot of ridiculous rumors about me prove to be true," Eden said.

Someone was guffawing. "Snake Almighty, can't imagine this lasting. We ought to take bets."

Eden's fingers rested very lightly on Nemesia's hip. "I'm sure I won't hear about anything of the sort," she said in a cool, clear voice. "Not a whisper. That would be far beneath you—all of you."

She made a few additional remarks: looking each of them in the eye, naming names. She sounded both profoundly courteous and profoundly threatening. The actual words coming out of her mouth could have been anything. She bid them a cheerful farewell—"Enjoy the show!"—and swept Nemesia away across the purple-carpeted lobby.

They met with several similar interruptions before reaching their seats in the mezzanine. Eden kept smiling, but a certain murderous edge had started to creep into her tone.

"It's no less than I deserve," she muttered to Nemesia, "but I wish they'd leave you out of it. I'm sorry."

"Doesn't bother me," Nemesia said honestly.

In her early twenties, she'd cared very much about how strangers Above looked at her, what they said, what they thought of her. Apparently that had been a passing phase.

Eden twisted vindictively at their ticket stubs. "This theater attracts a high-end crowd. I should have warned you. Posh types are incurably nosy."

Even the balcony seats looked close to full. People packed into gated standing areas off to each side of the floor, too. They looked younger and less formally dressed than the rest of the audience.

Eden, catching the direction of her gaze, patted the armrest between them. "All seats are paid, and all are equal. But anyone can come watch from the standing zones for free."

"There must be an upper limit." Nemesia tried not to imagine the crowd crushing itself on the barricade.

"They take a set number of walk-ups per day. Other slots get raffled off in advance. It's a very different type of viewing experience."

The lights dimmed. Magic flooded the floor, swirling around their ankles like lukewarm water.

"Whatever you do," Eden had said earlier, "don't extinguish anything inside the Facade."

So she let it snare her senses. It dragged her forward, like a fish in a net, and all of a sudden she seemed to be utterly alone in the theater.

Alone, and positioned right in front of the stage. Somewhat higher than the actual orchestra-level seats. She could look straight out and see everything, as if the set had been crafted solely for her perspective.

She still felt the plush purple cushioning under her thighs. Her solitary seat floated in a black sea without voices or rustling, without any trace of perfume from other rows.

Without Eden, either, until she reached for the armrest and found a hand already waiting there.

It was as though Eden came back into being the moment Nemesia touched her. Eden, and no one else.

"You didn't say this would happen." Nemesia felt little need to whisper. All evidence suggested that no one in the imperceptible audience would be able to hear them.

"It came up about five times in the safety announcements," Eden said, amused. "You weren't listening. Did you scream? First-timers often scream, even if they know what's coming."

"It reminds me of Below."

It really did: that unseeable vastness yawning behind them, an expanse that made the bright jeweled island of the stage seem small and intimate.

If she wanted perfect isolation, all she had to do was release Eden's hand.

Music swelled. Nemesia kept holding on.

"You can sing along," Eden said. "The Warden taught you the entire songbook, didn't he?"

"I came to hear professionals. I can hear myself anytime I want."

On their way here, Eden had commented that major theater companies put on a totally different type of show than the amateur troupe she used to perform with.

This wasn't an expression of humility. She meant only that they pursued a separate art. Magical extravaganzas at the Facade had little in common with stripped-down performances of practical stagecraft. With planning and practice, the Warden's troupe could perform anywhere—outdoors in city parks, at tiny venues in border towns, at a maenad reformatory.

But this particular magic-drenched production of *The Archetype* could only take place at the Facade. It was calibrated for a massive seated audience who would all feel themselves to be the only one watching. The actors sang directly to Nemesia. They looked her in the eye.

Multiple different people played the Antemaenad. They switched out nearly every scene. Artful lighting, costuming, and magic made it feel natural. Her face and stature and hair were in flux, but Nemesia knew her at a glance every time.

Mythologized stories like these were the closest most civilians would come to ingesting any meaningful nuggets of history. It was about as far from the facts as a fairy tale.

When the lights and the remainder of the audience returned, she realized she'd been touching Eden's hand (or wrist, or sleeve, at varying times) for hours. Remnants of music still rang in her ears.

They waited until most others had filtered out of their seats. Eden smiled and waved to passing acquaintances—who clearly wanted to talk with her, but couldn't quite bring themselves to swim backwards through the current of the crowd.

The standing-room-only areas emptied, too, before Eden got up. "Let's sneak out through the gift shop."

They were just about there when another knot of extremely well-dressed men and women descended on them. Current or former nobles, Nemesia guessed.

"No need for you to put up with this," Eden said in her ear. "I'll just be a moment. Hang out by the pamphlets."

Nemesia gratefully slipped away into the shelter of the shop. Some items were marked with eye-popping prices. A custom silk robe hung on the wall, hand-painted to match the current face of the building.

She studied a rack of cheaper prints and cards that each replicated a single panel of the outer facade. Some hailed from other seasons, with traces of melting snow, or a profusion of flowers as purple as the lobby carpet.

Orchestral music from *The Archetype* piped itself off a score book that lay open on a pedestal marked *Not For Sale*. The pages turned on their own, flicking like a bird adjusting its wings.

Nemesia hummed to herself like the Warden.

Someone came over to examine the prints beside her. She moved to make room.

It was a woman with neat dark hair down to her shoulders. Quite a bit longer than before. She wore a modest sweater and slim pants.

Tanyu had never cared for robes.

23

Evening the Scales

THE SONG CURRENTLY playing was a rousing tune about destined conquest, one meant for the whole company to sing together.

The music book turned another thin page of its own volition, as placid as a duck in water.

Tanyu looked older. Anyone would, after a decade. But Nemesia had no trouble reading her face. Shock, guilt, grim obligation, wishing she could pretend not to notice.

Nemesia wasn't making an appropriate expression, either. Her own face had turned to stone.

"Meifu," Tanyu said, which was worse than any other name or combination of names she might have chosen to use. She winced when she said it—she had never been good at covering up how she felt.

"Tanyu!" cried Eden, coming up out of nowhere. "My wife told me all about you."

Nemesia hadn't told her a thing.

Eden introduced herself. "Kuchinashi Eden. A humble maenad."

"You're married?"

Tanyu sounded strangled. Nemesia felt much the same way.

"We're still newlyweds," Eden said warmly. "I ventured Below on royal business—top secret stuff. It was love at first sight."

Her eyes sparkled. Her smile shone. Nemesia, in contrast, stood there with all the vivacity of a block of wood.

Anyone else would have succumbed to the radiance of Eden's golden hair and singular focus. But Tanyu was on a mission. She steeled herself. She looked straight at Nemesia.

"Does she know?" Tanyu asked.

Nemesia had to say something. But there was nothing natural she could possibly say here. She had to move, then. She had to knock over the rack of prints. Or fall headlong into the self-playing musical book. She had to stop Tanyu from talking.

No. She had to take Eden and leave, now, with or without an excuse.

She reached for Eden's sleeve and found herself clutching air.

"Careful, there," Eden said, farther away than expected. She tapped a big man in a small aisle, asking him to turn sideways. A child darted through the opening.

"Mama!"

The child latched onto Tanyu's leg. Nemesia glimpsed checker-print clothing—a simplified robe set—and dark brown hair in a flat, shiny bowl cut. She couldn't tell if she were feeling a million things at once, or absolutely nothing.

"Great show, wasn't it?" Eden said to Tanyu. "Have a lovely evening, both of you." She fluttered her fingers in a goofy farewell until the serious-faced child broke out in a smile.

It was night outside. Nemesia forgot she had a shawl: she carried it in her arms like a kitten until Eden plucked it away and arranged it around her shoulders.

Eden seemed wholly at ease. She pointed out a constellation (one that even Nemesia already knew). She told Nemesia to watch her step as they traversed one wormhole after another.

At last the city lay far behind them. The living roof of the cottage rippled in the dark. Rope-like vines swayed invitingly from the eaves.

Nemesia moved automatically toward the circular door.

"Let's even the scales first," Eden said. "It's not quite time for bed."

She opened her parasol. Nemesia had thought it was a plain black model, but now the underside glowed with stars. Not so brightly as to drown out the real stars above. It was just enough borrowed light to see where they stepped.

As they skirted around the garden of angle trees, warmth wafted down from the starry bowl of the parasol.

"You did a background check on me," Nemesia said bitterly—all the more so because she had no reason for bitterness.

"There wasn't much to check," Eden said. "You've spent a lot of your life Below."

Does she know?

Tanyu must have imagined Nemesia falling in love again, getting entangled, getting married—and still concealing her identity. Waiting till the last possible moment to reveal herself. To say, in other words: *Face down the Neverending Snake. Win me from your god.* This was what *I love you* meant from the lips of a Bride.

The worst part was that Tanyu wasn't entirely wrong. No, the worst part was that Eden already knew, didn't she? She was just too considerate— to the spy in her own household!—to put it into words.

"Whatever it is you're worried about," Eden said, "Tanyu never told anyone."

Because she'd had no reason to. Nemesia had vanished Below. She might feel differently now that she'd met Nemesia up Above again—this time with a spouse.

It didn't matter what Tanyu said, though. If Eden had pinpointed the timeline of Nemesia's past habitation, she'd have seen that it fell neatly into a tell-tale pattern. Nemesia should have known she would investigate.

"Your Tanyu isn't married." Eden appeared to be addressing the stars under the rim of her parasol. "She left her old landscaping firm. She struck out on her own. Then she adopted a kid from the Downcastle crèche."

Nemesia touched the marks on her wrist. Not every crèche-raised child had a snakebite. The Brood took in other children without guardians, too. This tended to slip her mind; when she was young, she'd assumed everyone in the world was marked.

"Tanyu always wanted that," she said.

"To raise kids?"

"To go independent." She laughed. It didn't feel forced. "She never said a word about children."

A sweet, fresh scent hung over the hills at night. Maybe it was just that she noticed it more without wide skies and daylight to take her attention away from the taste of the air.

So much had changed for Tanyu in the space of ten years. She was strangely glad to see it, to overwrite the stricken face in her memory. Tanyu probably hadn't thought of her for ages before today.

She ran her fingers through chilly air outside the heat beneath the parasol. She felt exposed, like a diaphanous creature crawling out of the safety of an old cocoon.

"Want a chance to catch up with her?" Eden asked.

Nemesia shook her head.

"Let Tanyu live her life. Your new wife shouldn't be seen with an ex."

"Some would say it serves me right."

"Why have your romances made you so many enemies?"

"I blame the Antemaenad."

"...................."

"That was a joke," Eden said. "Kind of."

"I don't get it."

"I may have started double-booking love affairs because the Antemaenad was famously chaste."

"You've let lovers fight over you," Nemesia said—although to her, this was all hearsay. "You've hurt people."

"I calmed down a lot over the past decade." Eden flashed a sliver of a smile. "But I don't deny it. You can pursue your case with a clear conscience."

They had come up to a slick black pond. Eden caught at Nemesia's elbow to keep her from stumbling in. Every so often, a quiet splash resounded just within earshot, but the water remained still enough to reflect the colors of the stars. Black and white ducks were curled up to sleep, heads hidden: some floating, some nestled on rocks.

"You spoke of even scales," Nemesia said.

"That I did."

"You know far more about me than I know about you."

Eden raised one hand, finger crooked, to make the shape of a stunted horn. "Vesper once mentioned that folks outside the Shell don't think of our Antemaenad as any kind of berserker. To them she was simply a mage—the greatest mage. Unmatchable."

"This isn't about you."

"Perhaps," said Eden. "I don't usually share my thoughts on our esteemed forerunner. Not with friends. Not with bedmates. Not even with fellow maenads.

"I'd read the same thing before, in some dusty old book. I didn't remember till I heard it from Vesper. I might have read it many times, and never retained it. But I remember this: our ancestors had other names for the Antemaenad. Some called her the Deceiver."

"A compliment," Nemesia said.

"She showed herself to the rest of the world, but none of them could really see her." She glanced at Nemesia. "This isn't new to you."

"The Brood favors history over any other field of study."

"Why?"

"No one else can effectively study it. And we serve the Snake That Ate the Roots of Time."

"So learning about the past aids the Snake's digestion?"

In starlight, Eden's face and hair retained hardly any color. She looked like an ink wash painting, all gentle shades of gray.

"History gathers Below," Nemesia said. "Most people Above can't hold it in their minds. It filters down to pool around us like water draining through soil. We're a repository of things forgotten."

"An underground reservoir," Eden murmured.

She gave Nemesia her arm. An implicit request for extinguishment.

The starlight in her parasol winked out. She closed it one-handed. Something dripped among the bent rushes that lined the pond.

"We maenads sculpt ourselves into vessels of wild magic," she said. "When you're a child locked in a reformatory—in the process of being sculpted—none of it feels good, and none of it feels right.

"People say the Antemaenad blazed a path for us. But when you talk to Char and Vesper, it's obvious that the Antemaenad in their stories used other types of power, too. She mastered wild magic, and she mastered the tame, predictable, consistently replicable magic of other countries. She isn't an archetype that anyone can embody in full."

Vesper: the woman with horns. Char: the woman with chains.

Perhaps now Nemesia would stop forgetting their names.

"There's something I've been meaning to ask," Eden said, facing the dark water and the motionless ducks.

Nemesia tensed. "What?"

"Who's allowed to speak with the Neverending Snake?"

"Anyone can pray."

"No, not that. Certain members of the Brood can speak with the Snake, correct? The Abbess, I'd assume. The ones called sages. Brides for sure.

"How about outside the Brood? The King of Now. Maybe Oddscale. Those who seek the release of a Bride. Is that it? Regular citizens can't ever apply for an audience?"

"Is there something you want to say to the Snake?" Nemesia asked.

A calculating silence. Then: "If I get forced into magical retirement at forty, I'll definitely want to file a few complaints."

"I can help you leave a message with the Abbess."

"Why, thank you," Eden said, flippant. She turned towards the house. "Let's go back. Our Warden won't sleep till you tell him what you thought of the show. Are your eyes used to the dark now? Tread carefully."

The encounter with Tanyu felt like something that had happened weeks ago.

Eden knew, tacitly, that she was a Bride. Eden knew, and didn't care. Why would she? Their marriage was a play put on to satisfy the King and society.

It might reflect badly on her if Nemesia took off after just a year of wedded life. But by then, Eden would surely have gotten the answer to her application. She'd have bought herself another two years to work out the details of her next extension.

She didn't care if Nemesia was a Bride—because she didn't care, in the end, whether Nemesia stayed or went. She wouldn't feel used or manipulated. There was nothing pure in their relationship that could be ruined by the looming presence of the Snake. There was nothing there at all.

Nemesia, grasping this, experienced a relief more potent than the absolution that might come after digesting a worrange. Eden was unfailingly kind, good-natured, and accommodating. And she had always seen that Nemesia had ulterior motives. She had always seen Nemesia as a threat.

Eden might be vulnerable to the machinations of Daiya Sholto. But she would be utterly immune to the pressures that came with loving a Bride. Whether this was deliberate or an accidental stroke of genius, the Abbess couldn't have placed Nemesia with anyone better.

24

The Snake Moth Gala

The day before the gala, a courier delivered a large package from Eden's clothier.

They unwrapped their new robes in the drawing room. Eden ran her fingers along extra-long trailing hems. Her magic would keep them from collecting dirt or dew in the royal gardens.

"It's got to be subtle," she said. "That's the real mark of skill. Your train can't float too high off the ground."

She gave Nemesia a quick overview of what to expect. "The morning will be taken up with tedious private ceremonies. We'll show up in the afternoon—that part's more lively. You'll have a moment or two to speak with the King. Might have to wait around for a while first."

It seemed that the morning rites were mostly for the induction of new nobles. Departing nobles had already been honored in a ceremony of their own.

The Snake was of the firm belief that human civilization demanded stratification. It made that built-in stratification more equitable by rotating families in and out of the uppermost crust of society. Everyone knew what to do if they won the noble lottery: milk it to the last drop, until their seven-year term expired.

On the day of the Snake Moth Gala, Eden asked how Nemesia would feel about taking the omnibus. "No wormholes exit right at the palace."

"We"—she still choked a little on the word *Brides*—"we aren't supposed to."

"You've lived over a month with me and the Warden. Don't you think we would miss you?"

"I don't know if a marriage of convenience counts as a deep connection."

Eden removed Pimiko from her shoulder. "The omnibus doesn't eat up every last loner, or there'd be a lot more disappearances."

"Maybe you just don't hear about them."

"Possibly. What serves as protection—actual attachments, actual relationships, or just simple faith? Is it enough to believe that you'd be missed if you vanished?"

"Seems unfair to reward false confidence," Nemesia muttered.

"Who says anything has to be fair? Maybe that's what happened to me at thirty-three. Maybe I got erased from the back of an omnibus." Eden made some final adjustments to Nemesia's robes. "No matter. We can hoof it."

They stepped out of a wormhole at the far end of Jigsaw Boulevard. After a spate of unseasonably warm days, it was colder now, the sun occluded by clouds.

For a time, they walked parallel to a vivitaxi lane. It was filled with fine gravel, like the dry gardens of the Brood. Insectile vivitaxis left intricate rippling patterns as they shuffled past.

They were less capacious than an omnibus, but they could expand accordion-style to fit multiple families at once. From a distance they looked deceptively unhurried, trundling along without a care in the world.

The Abbess had not advised against riding vivitaxis. Still, Nemesia was relieved that Eden didn't suggest it.

"Ever been to the palace?" Eden asked. It was currently a mountainous outline on the horizon, past the noble district.

"I've seen it from afar."

"You're not nervous?"

"Should I be?"

"People will be politer than at the Facade," Eden said. "We made our appearance there in order to plant a few crucial seeds. By now, word will have spread. They'll have gotten the idea that I'm quite touchy about you."

Nemesia kept getting distracted by her clothing. She had never worn this style of robe before. It dragged regally behind her—although, as promised, the silk remained grime-free.

The outermost layer was all black and gray and silver, with circles and crescents meant to evoke the phases of the moon. The only color came from her inner robes, red and lavender and blue and other rainbow hues peeking out from her collar and sleeves.

Eden, for her part, wore rich mustard yellow. Her robe had dark reddish accents, shapes like long-beaked birds and alien flowers. Her hair hung loose, a different shade of gold than her clothing. You could spot her from a block away.

Before they left the house, Nemesia had helped straighten the fringe of Eden's epaulets. They were a dark rusty hue—in some lights, almost black.

"Did you need these?" she'd asked. "You're not bringing Pimiko."

"At this point, it's just part of my signature look."

"No umbrella, though?"

"Might get too crowded." She reached inside her sleeve and showed Nemesia the toothpick handle of a drink-sized paper parasol. "I'm still equipped for emergencies."

As always, the palace lay half in ruins. In the days of empire, it had merely been a minor countryside castle. So went the thinking among Brood scholars, at least.

But it was without a doubt the most regal structure in Yolk City. Urban explorers stayed away from the ruined half not because it was royal property or because it was primly roped off, but because it had been taken over by an enormous colony of so-called palace cats. They were exceedingly ill-tempered and bushy, and they dwelt nowhere else within the Shell.

Few attempts were made to reclaim any feline-occupied territory. The royal family only ever consisted of the King of Now, who didn't need the extra space, anyway.

Most of the building was constructed from some pale bluish substance that blended with the sky. It looked grandest around sunrise and sunset—and on dull cloudy days, like today.

The Snake Moth Gala would primarily take place outdoors. The gardens had many wide decks and courtyards, and paths that could fit four omnibuses side by side. Visitors took tea in lakeside pavilions, or rode self-propelled boats, or ate canapés around tall mushroom-shaped tables.

Just inside the north garden entrance, a bronze rendition of Oddscale caught Nemesia's eye. She wouldn't have recognized it if not for the unmistakable scarf.

"The sculptor took some liberties," Eden said drolly.

Oddscale's face had been rendered as a craggy blob. The limbs were eerily long and skeletal, and the torso twisted down to a wasp-like waist. The feet were a combination of blocky hooves and coiled springs.

Nemesia leaned down to read the pedestal, careful not to trip on her robes. In summary: "Oddscale saved several kings from assassination."

"Rote attempts," Eden said dismissively. "It's just one of those things."

"One of what things?"

"Society needs a noble class, and if you've got kings, then you've got to have assassins, too. Never mind that there are no obvious benefits to killing the King of Now. The Snake will just install someone else in their place. One King is very much like the next. So you really can't be too hard on obligatory assassins."

"As long as no one dies."

"Yes. All right, M. Nemesia—I can finally show you my skills."

She walked Nemesia over to a courtyard filled with games.

Competitors flicked coins at bulls-eye targets on the far bank of a rectangular pool. Coins that hit the target left bruises—neon-toned blots that faded like the slow light of a firefly. Both the scales that flew true and those that fell short bounced down to form glittering piles at the bottom of the water.

Eden hit the exact midpoint of every available target, just to show off. Elaborately robed nobles began to cheer for her by name.

Music warbled from some other corner of the garden, drifting over like shreds of fragrant smoke. Nemesia situated herself behind a wall of spectators. She was surprised at how quickly Eden came and found her, despite being ambushed by well-wishers every couple of steps.

Someone put an arm around Eden's neck. She removed it gracefully, saluted at a friend across the way, spun and shook a man's hand, then snagged Nemesia and sailed off with her.

They passed rings of keen-eyed courtiers engaged in lofty games of shuttlecock. The players called for Eden to join.

She laughed them off, fluttering the ends of her sleeves in dismissal.

Nemesia found herself inclined to believe that Eden had, as claimed, been less of a libertine in recent years. A significant proportion of her admirers were young—in their early twenties—and overwhelmingly peppy. Perhaps some of the thrill had faded as she grew older and her followers stayed the same age.

More mature types watched her, too, but they weren't as obvious about it. They seemed content to appreciate the light of her presence in the same way they appreciated the artful standing stones placed throughout the garden, and the peach-colored swans that had lived at the palace so long that they'd forgotten how to fly.

"If you're wondering about the secret to my popularity," Eden said—already with a note of exhaustion—"it isn't just my looks."

"It isn't?"

"Hah. No, it's just that most maenads avoid socializing as much as possible."

"And you don't?"

"I do like my quiet time. Even then, I'm more sociable than all the rest of them combined. Haven't seen a single other active maenad here, have you? Keep your eyes peeled. They'll be few and far between. They've got the perfect excuse for it, too. We're all in a delicate truce with our magic—can't do anything to upset it. If that means no carousing, so be it."

She sucked in an abrupt breath.

"What?"

"Stubbed my toe." She locked arms with Nemesia and set out for a narrower path between low-spreading trees.

Nemesia glanced back, scanning the topiary. Daiya Sholto stood with his arms in his sleeves, grimly observing a shuttlecock match. A handful of elegant women flanked him.

"Who was that?" she asked as Eden drew her behind a craggy shelf of rock.

"Who was who?"

"The man with the small head."

"A noble," Eden said shortly.

"You didn't run from any other nobles."

The decorative rock was pocked with more holes than a honeycomb. An area in the middle had been polished flat and engraved with famous poetry. Eden looked at it pointedly, as if she would rather take questions about ancient literature.

"His name is Daiya Sholto," she said after Nemesia refused to relent.

"I've heard of the Daiya family."

"Have you, now."

"They've invested a lot of capital Below."

"Won't last much longer. They're on the final year of their term as nobles."

Nemesia affected an air of detached curiosity. "How do you know them?"

"Sholto used to be a maenad."

"He's retired?"

"Retired early. He's only a couple years older than me."

"Really?" Nemesia blurted.

"We go all the way back to the reformatory."

"But you don't want him to see you."

"He hates me with a passion."

"Why?"

No answer.

"Did you steal his wife? His daughter?"

Eden peevishly brushed invisible dust off her epaulets. "What do you think of me? No—I had an affair with his sister. Er, sisters."

"Multiple sisters? Not at the same time?"

Eden slumped. "I may have doubled up for a bit. Purely by accident. The Warden manages my work calender, but he never helps me juggle dates."

"Did you apologize?"

"I've tried, in my way. Sholto remains unappeased. His sisters are a lot more agreeable, honestly."

At one point in her life, Eden had seemingly formed intimate relationships with half the city without even trying. Nemesia, for her part, couldn't open up to a single soul without fretting about their ability to endure a confrontation with the Snake.

She felt the sting of injustice in her four stigmata—and a renewed sympathy for Daiya Sholto. He might seem petty and humorless, but perhaps he had a point.

Eden rallied, turning away from the poetry stone in a swirl of orange-gold robes. "Never mind all that. The King won't be free to see you till later. Let's have a look at the main event."

25

And Then They All Die

NEMESIA HAD NEVER seen a snake silkmoth, although she'd touched fabric made from their caterpillars' secretions. The moths were large and unwieldy, had no mouths to eat with, and only lived a few days after emerging.

In preparation for the Snake Moth Gala, royal lepidopterists cultivated hundreds and hundreds of fist-length cocoons. All in hopes of hatching as many as possible at just the right time.

Now moths filled their namesake garden, resting on trees, rocks, and the hands of thrilled ladies and gentlemen. Their bodies were plump and bee-like, with reddish stripes. Their wings were grotesquely out of proportion, with bulbous tips patterned like the head of a snake.

"We come and look at them," Nemesia said, "and then they all die?"

"They breed first," said Eden. "Allegedly."

"Allegedly?"

"They might not be very good at it. They get exhausted from flying short distances."

"Seems a little morbid, making them hatch just for the equinox."

"It's all about the ephemerality of beauty. Nobles love that stuff. Want to hold one?"

"Let them conserve their energy."

"What, for mating? You're a gentle soul, Nemesia."

They sat (cautiously—the moths lurked everywhere) and watched snake head wingtips peep out from behind branches and leaves.

"You might like these better," Eden said once they moved on, lining up for a series of exhibits inside soaring glass conservatories.

They met a variety of snake-mimicking caterpillars, some of which swayed as if threatening to strike.

Jewel beetles of every imaginable hue crawled in a heated room that had been magically drained of color. Everything—from leaf matter to Eden's robes—turned shades of sepia. Everything except the brilliant beetles.

After they stepped outside, the moss and grass seemed to scintillate. Nemesia lost her balance. She clung to Eden, who murmured approvingly that they would appear to be very much in love.

They were on their way to get tea when—for the first time—they saw a non-retired maenad.

It was the boy who'd made a sinkhole full of spicy tofu stew. He loitered alone in a leafy nook, holding a stemmed glass. He looked just as young in formal robes. Maybe eighteen or nineteen. Spots peppered his chin.

Eden's steps slowed.

"Go on," Nemesia said.

"I'll just be a moment."

The boy startled as Eden came up to him. She plucked his drink away, sniffed it, then poured it out at the base of a plum tree. "They shouldn't have served you that," she told him calmly.

Nemesia pretended to be fascinated by long-branching arms of bright yellow forsythia.

The boy said something inaudible.

"All maenads make mistakes. Just the other day, I almost turned a bluebird human."

More murmuring.

"Giving advice is the easy part," Eden said. "Doesn't cost me anything to tell you to stop beating yourself up. Thing is, if you're all beaten up, your magic will find it easier and easier to slip out through the cracks. That's a problem for everyone."

Nemesia made a furtive hand signal—she couldn't be sure if Eden saw it—and snuck away to give them privacy.

At the nearest tea pavilion, a loud-voiced woman regaled a rapt audience with tales of Oddscale's adventures.

Recently, Oddscale had broken into the home of a corrupt businessman and read him terrible poetry until he fell to his knees and begged for mercy.

Last fall, the King's favorite courtesan had been the victim of a terrible theft. Her face had been magically stolen by a conniving rival. Oddscale worked tirelessly to steal her face back. (A heckler piped up to say that facelessness would've made her the ideal candidate to become a new hero herself.)

Nemesia had missed out on ten years of Oddscale news. When she alluded to how little she knew, the orator launched into a rousing recap.

One popular running theory was that Oddscale had switched out about four or five years ago. The Oddscale behind the decade-old reformatory kidnappings had been a traditional sort. Very stealthy.

Older folk sipped their translucent green tea and nodded piously. A proper Oddscale would go unseen. One ought to never glimpse much more than a scarf swishing away into a foggy night.

The new Oddscale—the one who had theoretically taken over in recent years—appeared more frequently. So much so that at least some of their appearances had to be fake. Was an impostor running around, or were these deliberate decoys? No one could say.

The loud woman declared that Oddscale was a handsome man with blood-red hair. Others seemed just as certain that Oddscale was a spry old lady with a humongous nose.

Nemesia, contrarily, wondered if Oddscale might have always been the same person—one just pretending to change from generation to generation. Putting on a show for centuries.

The Snake had dominion over time. Kings were replaceable, and so were Brides. But maybe Oddscale had won, by dint of sheer heroism, the boon of neverending life.

The world was full of improbabilities. Women from outside could sprout horns and living chains. The existence of the Shell—and the Snake itself—was already a miracle. People lived here like magical flames inside a snow globe, a fire kindled among the ashes of a collapsed empire.

Why couldn't Oddscale be eternal?

"You're Eden's wife," said a voice of amazement.

Nemesia looked up. A middle-aged woman in svelte green robes beckoned her to a less populated end of the pavilion. Fancy fish circled in the pond behind them, hoping for crumbs.

The woman introduced herself as Daiya Anis. "I was hoping Eden would bring you by. Did Sholto scare her off?"

"Sholto?" Nemesia said, playing it safe.

"My little brother. He has a bone to pick with your wife. And it doesn't"—this she added with sudden vehemence—"have anything to do with us Daiya sisters."

"Um," Nemesia said weakly.

Daiya Anis had a head of perfectly average size, coarse gray-streaked hair, and a light rumpling of good-humored wrinkles. She wore them well.

"He and Eden used to be great friends, you know."

"But you..."

She fixed Nemesia with a hawk-like gaze. "Some claim that Eden ruined me and my sisters. Do I look ruined?"

"No," Nemesia said hastily.

"She was a real rake back then. We knew what we were in for, thank you very much. At any rate—after we won the nobility lottery, none of us wanted to participate in the usual activities. Sholto was very upset."

"The usual activities?"

"Getting paired off, forming marital alliances, all that good stuff."

"He should've gotten married, then."

Anis's mouth curved. "He already had a wife and child before we ascended. He lamented the fact that none of us had eyes for any man."

Nemesia's newfound sympathy for Daiya Sholto began rapidly dropping.

"If no man can live up to a dissolute womanizer like K. Eden, then it's men who need to start meeting a higher standard. Or maybe you need to find us a suitable woman. That's what we told him."

"What'd he say?"

Anis lowered her voice in a parody of manliness. "Where else can anyone find a woman like *that*?"

She broke out coughing. Nemesia offered her tea. She declined with a wave of her hand. "K. Eden broke many young ladies' hearts. Can't defend that. But for us, it was all in good fun. We fought duels in her name, yes, but everyone does that."

"They do?"

"Nobles, and aspiring nobles. We duel over matters as trivial as the beauty of the sunset. It's just entertainment."

"I see," Nemesia fibbed.

Anis looked out past the pavilion, past golden banks of forsythia. "Ah ... I've kept you too long." She used her sleeve to point the way. "Better head back now. Be quick."

Nemesia hastened along the forsythia-lined path just in time to see Daiya Sholto bearing down on Eden and the younger maenad.

"What," Sholto said tautly, "are you doing with my son?"

26

The King of Now

DAIYA SHOLTO's maenad son had a hangdog look. The end of his robes floated a finger's width above the ground. Anis's robes had been the same, come to think of it. Sholto's floated, too.

"He's not even twenty," Sholto said in that same dangerous tone.

Only a madman could have perceived any impropriety in Eden's posture. But she drew back with the deliberate motion of someone lowering a fatal weapon. She didn't laugh it off.

"D. Sholto," she said. "What are you implying?"

The son spoke up. "Dad ... it's not—"

Sholto moved his hand.

It was a gesture almost too small to mean anything at all. There certainly was no special power in it. Sholto might once have served as a maenad, but he must have been cauterized when he chose to retire. He had no magic left now.

Still, his son shut up instantly. The only sound to emerge was the gurgle of an attempted swallow.

Eden looked at Sholto as if she couldn't see that he was considerably taller and wider than her.

Neither of them glanced at Nemesia

"You're a married woman," he said. "Do I have to warn you off my own son?"

Frost stiffened the grass underfoot. Someone on the other side of the garden cried out in delight.

Sholto's son gave Nemesia a beseeching look, then seemed to realize that he had no idea who she was. There was a note in the air like a plucked string, a string close to breaking.

"I'm offended," Eden said. "I'm offended, and you're a noble." She spoke as though she'd made a fascinating new discovery. "I think this calls for a du—"

Nemesia's hands formed fists. The frosted grass went limp with melting dew. A blizzard of white fluff continued descending on the four of them, so slowly as to seem mocking, but the flakes had turned into milkweed seeds rather than snow.

Eden, cut off from her magic, touched her stomach as if expecting to find that someone had stabbed her. She and Sholto looked at Nemesia at the same time. Sholto's son braced himself, confused.

Nemesia ignored the Daiyas. She went up to Eden. "No time for dueling," she said. "You're supposed to escort me."

Sholto's eyes tracked them, but his head remained preternaturally still, as if screwed into place.

Eden started when Nemesia's arm came around her back. Nemesia nodded at the young maenad and then at his father. She pushed Eden away from them, across the damp grass that now gave off the heady smell of rain.

She didn't dare glance over her shoulder. Sholto's gaze seemed to follow her until they were far out of sight.

Pipe music rose and fell. Worm dancers and worm tamers performed in front of a lake that faithfully reflected every detail of the blue castle and the featureless gray-white sky.

From the corner of her eye, Nemesia found it hard to tell whether the dancers were imitating the gyrating worms, or the other way around. The largest worms were as thick as her wrist.

The reflected palace looked like an optical illusion. So did the original, for that matter. It could have been a bare-scraped swathe of naked sky, the only place not covered by clouds.

The music receded as they left the worm tamers behind. A broad glass bridge led across the lake. Nemesia told herself it wasn't actually glass, just some other substance rendered clear. Like the view from inside the front wall of the Facade Theater.

The water had appeared as still as ice from afar, but it puckered and rippled beneath the transparent floor of the bridge. She stopped and released her hold on Eden's robes.

"You extinguished me so thoroughly," Eden said. "Felt like I'd never had magic at all."

"Did I overstep?"

"You did it without touching me. Did you know you could—? Ah, of course you did."

"It's not a common ability," Nemesia said carefully. "But not unheard of, either."

They weren't the only people who had come to admire the lake. The bridge was so expansive, though, that no one else seemed close enough to eavesdrop.

Eden began picking fluffy white seeds off her epaulets and sleeves, where they clung like a dusting of snow. "Sholto let you off easy."

"He hardly even saw me."

"If he wanted to provoke me further, he could have insulted you. Not sure why he didn't."

"You wouldn't lose control over—"

"Wouldn't I?" Eden said, with a sharpness that bordered on suspicion. "Wouldn't it be in my interest to defend my vulnerable new wife?"

Nemesia kept her eyes on the castle mirrored in the water. "He must have heard that I came up from Below."

"So?"

"His family has good relations with the Brood."

"That's why he left you out of it? In the spirit of diplomacy?"

Eden let that hang in the air for a bit. She drummed her fingers on the glassy handrail. Then she pivoted. She rapidly plucked milkweed off Nemesia's robes, too, making her turn around for a thorough examination.

"I'll spare you the speculation," she said decisively. "First off, that boy isn't my child."

"That—you mean the younger Daiya?"

"He's just the son of an old friend. I last saw him when he was around eight or nine. He doesn't even remember me—he thinks we first met at the hotpot incident."

She gestured for Nemesia to do another rotation. Liberated milkweed seeds drifted out across the water, sinking gradually lower.

"You look skeptical," she accused.

"I didn't say anything."

"Sholto and I never saw each other that way, not for a moment. Not when we were schoolmates, and not after we graduated. He may have a stick up his ass, but he was practically born to be a faithful family man. Any questions?"

"No questions," Nemesia said meekly.

Eden smoothed the colorful inner layers beneath Nemesia's collar.

"I'm sorry," she said, newly dispassionate. "I'm sorry you had to bail me out, and I'm sorry my magic leaked. How embarrassing! Like wetting the bed.

"If nothing else, I'm glad to have been a living example of what I was telling Sholto's son. We're all fallible. I'd better cool my head while you talk to the King."

They waited on the palace side of the lake. Several nobles fished peaceably off the edge of a boardwalk. A distant thunking turned out to be the sound of an archery contest.

Palace officials came to collect Nemesia when the King was ready.

"Don't be scared," Eden began, followed by: "Why'd I say that? You haven't even broken a sweat."

Nemesia touched her brow to ensure this was true.

"Most people are intimidated by the King," Eden said.

"Are you?"

"I consider him a friend."

"How do you get friendly with royalty?"

"Did him a personal favor." She clapped Nemesia on the shoulder. "Well—I'm glad you're not rattled. Have fun."

Nemesia left with her guide.

From what little she glimpsed of it, the palace seemed desolate. The floors were very cold, especially compared to Below.

The King lived here—where else would a king live?—but Eden had told her that most nobles preferred their own domiciles to staying at court.

The halls leading up to the throne room were heavily decorated, with coffered ceilings painted bluish-green and yellow and red. She'd seen a robe like that in Eden's drawing room.

Equally colorful tiled channels ran down both sides of each hallway and antechamber. They were filled with water, like miniature canals. Once in a while, a toy boat or a rubber duck sailed past.

The throne room must have been grander still, and probably contained fewer toy boats. Nemesia was too preoccupied to take notice. Her guide pointed her through a door, then closed it behind her. The noise of running water vanished.

Her stomach dropped as soon as she stepped inside.

The King was not alone.

Vesper and Char lounged on either side of the unoccupied throne. Magic fell about them like a full-body veil.

Today Vesper's horns were thick and curled, akin to the horns of a ram. Char's chains wound around her limbs like docile serpents. She raised a finger to her lips.

Nemesia despaired of speaking freely. The Snake tolerated their presence, but this didn't mean they weren't spies from outside. After all, Eden tolerated *her* presence.

There were things she wanted to say to the King—things she could only have said to the King, and not anyone else Above—but now she restrained herself.

On the floor below the throne rested an inflatable pool. The same type of pool that she'd played in on hot summer afternoons at the crèche. It was bright blue, much bluer than the turquoise patterns on the many-layered ceiling.

This King of Now had been ruling since before Nemesia first went Below.

Which would explain why he felt more comfortable wallowing in water. Like all great kings, he was slowly turning amphibious.

"Welcome, Maiden of the Snake," he said. He sounded less like a frog than the Abbess. Granted, he appeared to be in the process of becoming something more along the lines of an enormous axolotl.

He still had human lips, although they were very long. And human eyes, although they were very far apart. As were his nostrils.

"Nice to meet you," said Nemesia. The Brood hadn't taught her courtly manners. Ordinary manners would have to do.

Lying in that temporary pool of his, he couldn't see the strangers lurking by the vacant throne. Perhaps he'd let them in himself; perhaps he hadn't. If she drew attention to them, her royal audience might come to an end right there. She kept quiet.

The King asked, with his elongated lips, about her health and happiness. There were other perfunctory questions, too, mostly pertaining to how well she got along with Eden, and the state of Eden's house. It felt like talking to a doctor right before his lunch break.

He had a robe draped over him. It was a dark sodden mess. His glistening limbs and thick tail fit the general framework of an axolotl body, but his toes were too long and too jointed.

Nemesia mentioned, tentatively, that he could have met her in a more comfortable location. She didn't feel great about making the King of Now squat in a blow-up pool for children.

He blinked wet lids at her. Another vestigial human feature.

"During the Snake Moth Gala, the King receives honored visitors in the throne room. It's tradition."

"Still—"

"It was easier, granted, when we were bipedal."

Casting about for a different topic, she asked whether the problems caused by Eden's liaisons had really been so severe.

"Has anyone challenged you for her hand, or demanded that you divorce?"

"No, Your Highness."

"Then your marriage is being accorded the respect it deserves. All is as we anticipated."

"Was there ever any serious trouble in the first place?" Nemesia pressed. "Maybe you simply thought having an extinguisher spouse would better position her to—"

The King shifted. The pool squeaked. Water spattered the floor.

"We can't entertain you much longer. It won't do to let the public think they can interrogate a king at their leisure."

Vesper, bored of listening, had drifted high above the throne behind him. She executed a controlled turn near the ceiling, like a swimmer doing laps.

"Your Highness," Nemesia said, composing her thoughts, "did Oddscale ever save your life?"

His black eyes narrowed as if in contemplation of something bright. "Twenty years ago," he said.

"There was an assassin."

"And a dramatic rescue."

"Staged by the Snake?"

"If it was scripted, no one informed us. It may very well be a rite of passage. But at the time, it was our one particular life that young Oddscale fought to protect. We will never forget our gratitude. Is that all you wished to know, Maiden of the Snake?"

"Yes," Nemesia said through the catch in her throat.

As she left, the two intruders—who still levitated near the throne like hungry flies—waved a silent goodbye. Char looked as if she meant it. Horned Vesper seemed sardonic.

The King wished her a happy marriage. As before, his voice was neither booming nor portentous nor especially moist. It was the sort of voice that might easily get lost in a crowd.

27

One Night at Home

SOMEONE BUMPED Nemesia after she left the palace.

She spotted Eden immediately, even surrounded by other celebrants. Those dark yellow robes with birds drawn in red, the golden hair interspersed with slashes of black—she stood out like the dazzling goldfish that swam below the clear bridge.

Because Nemesia was looking at Eden, she didn't see the boy come up beside her. He shoved her, then squeaked an apology when she staggered.

She sighted a fleeing figure as she righted herself. His hem skimmed the path without ever quite touching it.

He'd crammed a brief note in her sleeve. The paper was so thin that it had already started dissolving. She dropped it in the lake before going to meet Eden on the bridge.

The Snake Moth Gala would keep going well into the night. Around sundown, Eden—along with the few other maenads in attendance—was called away to work supportive enchantments.

Eden excused herself, grumbling, and Nemesia made her way back to the Moth Garden. The last hint of reddish gloam on the horizon reminded her of the rage at the bottom of maenad eyes, the magic that fought to be cut free of its moorings.

Snake moths were not ordinarily luminous. But on this one day, in this one place, they had been magicked to leave glowing trails of light.

The garden was as packed with humanity as the market by the stairs to Below. The crowd spoke in a hushed, sleepy rumble. It was in the midst of this that Nemesia looked to her left and saw Daiya Sholto.

"You've done well," he said.

She had yet to tell him anything important, but she refrained from saying this.

A moth perched on the railing of a nearby pagoda. With its wings open, it was wider across than both her hands put together.

The snake head formations at its wingtips seemed to droop downward, exhausted. Each stared out with a single black eye. Those eyes reminded her of the half-amphibious King of Now.

"Your guard assured me she would take a liking to you," Sholto said. "He was right."

"My guard?"

"The one with the sign of the bird."

"Roc."

"Always a helpful source of intel."

"You know who he—you know him from Above?"

"No," Sholto said curtly.

The snake moth twitched, as if debating the merits of flying.

"You don't need me to do anything special?"

"What are you imagining?"

"Like … planting evidence of a crime. Publicly denouncing her."

"Don't get creative," he said, scornful. "Carry on: continue what you're already doing. Whatever it is, it's working."

Warm air pooled around their calves. An enchanted heat, generated for the comfort of the King's guests.

"You'll know when I have further instructions," he said with finality.

What would he tell her to do, in the end, and when might that message reach her? Weeks from now? Months from now? In the final days of her sabbatical?

"Your son," she said.

Sholto looked at the nearest moth with disdain, as if disappointed in its lack of mobility. "What about him?"

"What's his name?"

"Does it matter?"

"I already met your sister Anis."

"D. Iori," he said tersely. "Keep your wife away from him."

Daiya Iori. She attempted to recall his face. On the day of the hotpot accident, he'd been blotchy and tear-streaked. Here at the gala, he'd mostly looked down at his toes.

Shortly after parting ways with D. Sholto, she almost walked straight into Eden.

Eden had tied her hair back in a swishy tail. A couple loose hanks fell to frame her face. Her eyes skated past Nemesia, as if to watch someone leave. As if she might have seen Sholto.

"You seem tired," Nemesia said.

Eden held up one of her little paper parasols as though to smell it like a flower. She twirled it between her forefinger and thumb. Magic glimmered like an eruption of startled fireflies.

A snake moth flapped heavily past them, as erratic as a fruit bat.

"Heat and light," Eden said. "Easy stuff. The painful part is trying to coordinate with other maenads. Ugh. Everyone expects the most powerful person to be good at taking charge. If I could govern, the Snake would have appointed me King, not—"

She crammed the rest of her complaints into a single incoherent mumble. Then she straightened up, stashed her cocktail umbrella in her sleeve, and smiled so brilliantly that a number of nearby nobles forgot they were supposed to be pondering the beauty of snake moths.

"Enough of that," she said. "Let's find something to eat."

They left the Moth Garden and all its trailing lights, but it didn't get any darker. Outside, gourd-shaped lanterns bobbed overhead like a fleet of miniature hot-air balloons.

It was altogether too well-lit to see much in the sky. The cloud cover would have spoiled most attempts at stargazing, anyway.

Eden was visibly wilting by the time they arrived home. Nemesia couldn't tell what had taken more out of her: using magic, or putting on a constant show of friendly charm. She'd entertained neverending questions about the lanterns and moths. She rarely repeated herself—half her answers sounded made up—but everyone walked away satisfied.

The Warden had already turned in for the night. They took the elevator to the top floor; Eden leaned on the wall with her eyes closed. Nemesia had to prod her to leave.

At the door to her bedroom, Eden balked. She yawned extravagantly, eyes tearing up. "You sleep on the second floor," she said. "I can put myself to bed, dear wife. I'm not drunk."

She stretched her hand out toward the shadows of the hallway as if expecting to catch something.

Pimiko plummeted from a corner of the ceiling. Fuzzy pink-toed legs walked up Eden's arm, then settled neatly on her right epaulet.

Eden (together with Pimiko) peered at Nemesia as if wondering why she hadn't left yet.

"Every night since I moved here, I've slept in the bedroom you gave me," said Nemesia.

"On the second floor."

"What about you? Have you spent a single night at home?"

Eden's eyes went to her shoulder, as if hoping that Pimiko might answer for her.

Pimiko retreated into the depths of her glossy shell.

Eden stifled another yawn. "Where I sleep has no bearing on—"

Nemesia backed her up against the closed door.

"It's not any of my concern if you keep a dozen mistresses in the city. But sleeping everywhere except your own bed hasn't done you much good, has it? Are you at peace? Are you well-rested?

"Go through that door"—she pushed it open, and Eden staggered at the loss of support—"and go to your loft, and put your head on your pillow, and pass out."

"Can I undress first?" Eden asked dryly.

"Make it quick."

The yellow robe and her crimson sash and various other accoutrements got tossed across the seat of a chair. Pimiko went on the hammock below the loft.

Reduced to a see-through underrobe, Eden crawled sleepily up to her bed. She loosened her hair. She shot Nemesia a vengeful look.

Even on the verge of collapsing, she must have known what sort of picture she made up there, wearing a single layer that served as more of a misty suggestion than actual fabric.

"Anything else?" she said.

"Good night," Nemesia replied rigidly. "Don't flee."

Eden laughed, not unkindly, and burrowed under the covers.

Nemesia stole away to the second floor. She changed to an underrobe of her own, which was far more suitable for company, and sat in the middle of her sunken bed. She wondered if Eden's demonic-looking guests were still prowling around the royal palace.

Her heart was going too fast to have any hope of falling asleep.

She listened to the sounds of the house while she waited. The drip-drip-drip of phantom water. The buzzing of phantom wasps.

She didn't have to wait long.

28
Leakage

First, the house shook.

It was a protracted swaying, like a boat on stormy water. Nothing fell down.

After the shaking stopped, magic sniffed around the perimeter of the room, a carnivorous animal circling a tent.

As Nemesia moved toward the door, that magical presence rushed to meet her. It was wolfishly muscular, blinded by hunger.

She extinguished it.

Eden had asked her—more than once—how, exactly, she extinguished magic. What did she have to do? How did it feel? Wasn't it difficult?

The truth was uninspiring. Nemesia couldn't speak for others, but for her, extinguishing demanded no exertion. It wasn't like physically scaling a wall. There was no sense of a battle, of wrangling magic until it surrendered.

The way she saw it, her mind could slice paper cuts in the thin skin on top of reality. Nothing so drastic as a wormhole. What she created were cracks so slim that only magic could filter through. The magic she targeted would have no choice but to drain away, just as water could not choose to remain in a sieve. In that sense, extinguishing was as simple as removing a plug from a bathtub.

Where did extinguished magic go? Maybe it vanished, snuffed out like a flame. Or maybe dregs of power slipped down into the waiting gullet of the Snake.

She knew other tricks, too. She could mute magic without destroying it, as if gagging a shrieking mouth. She could alter its flow as if putting her thumb on a hose to change how the water sprayed.

So: she'd banished the wolf at her door. But the space beyond was still rife with magic.

She stepped out. The corridor had grown even longer than usual.

A solitary marble rolled past her toes. It soon veered off course, pinging from wall to wall like a pinball.

Nemesia turned left. Every so often, another stray marble rattled down out of the darkness.

Her bedroom door had disappeared. There were many other doors now, but they had the uncanny appearance of stage props.

Off to one side of each door was a small white dish. In each dish nestled a molded mountain of protective salt. The sort that people might put outside shops, or at the top of a staircase to nowhere.

Some of the salt mountains were sharp-edged pyramids, and some were smooth cones that came to a flawless point. One or two had cocktail umbrellas sticking out at a jaunty angle—which was not, Nemesia thought, strictly traditional.

The hallway continued at a steady incline: enough to make her legs burn.

The parade of fake doors came to an end. In their place appeared an equally improbable series of portholes. She saw no garden, no angle trees. Lit by an unseen moon, the midnight land bulked up into shapes like the remnants of an earthwork fort.

When she stopped to look out, a clacking rhythm echoed off the floor. It was precisely the sound she would expect to hear from someone in a pair of wood-soled sandals.

The phantom footsteps paused right next to her. Then they multiplied, as if whole families of spirits were clopping along, lining up to pay for groceries. They went in the same direction as the marbles: down and away from her.

Nemesia hadn't been strolling aimlessly, either. She'd tracked all this flooding wild magic like a plumber pursuing the source of a leak.

Almost there.

She extinguished the footsteps, and the solid wall, and the yellow light pouring in through suddenly enormous windows. The air tasted sharply of salt.

She plummeted—as if jerking on the verge of sleep—and landed, knees jarred, in Eden's bedroom.

The lone hammock had grown into a spiderweb, new ropes springing taut from every corner. She had to climb across those shifting nets to get to the loft. At least it wasn't sticky.

That didn't mean it wasn't dangerous. If she weren't an extinguisher, she might have been turned into a tumbling marble, or a trudging pair of empty wooden sandals, or a pristine mound of salt. She might have been trapped in the endless steep corridor, huffing and puffing.

But she could take care of herself, and so could the Warden.

Pimiko, who had swollen to the size of a six-year-old child, crouched on a swathe of netting by Eden's vanity. She didn't seem to be in distress: she was just very large.

Eden's parasols were tangled willy-nilly in the hammocky web. Some had been cocooned like trapped insects. Fireless pillar candles had been caught up in it, too, jars and all. They still glowed weakly from within.

Nemesia managed to reach the loft without touching Pimiko's prey. She sat lightly at the edge of the bed, her feet on the steps.

Eden was upright, eyes unseeing, blankets coiled around her hips. She grimaced. She began tugging something out of her chest.

It was anchored in her flesh like one of Char's living chains. As she pulled, it kept unspooling—a pale squirming thing, a stretchy cord. Finally she yanked the last of it free, and it went still, piled dead all over her lap. Not a white snake, but a limp wormlike parasite.

There was a moment of magical silence.

Before anything else could start—the second act, another movement, another verse—Nemesia extinguished the entire invasive dream.

Eden sat empty-handed. No wound in her chest, and no tapeworm on her bed. The parasols were back on their hooks, and the room was no longer swaddled in rope.

Pimiko (back to her usual size) rested stonily on the vanity. Her coiled shell glistened like a smoky bottle of perfume.

The house sighed and sank a fraction lower on its foundations.

"Your dream leaked all the way down to my room," Nemesia said.

Eden raked her hands through mussed hair and breathed as if emerging from a long dark swim without air. She pulled a blanket around her shoulders.

Nemesia continued her confession. "I didn't erase it right away. I watched you to see what would happen."

"You didn't watch for long." Eden was hoarse.

"How can you tell?"

"Doesn't feel as awful as usual," she said practically.

She rested her chin on her knees and whistled softly.

Pimiko's shell clinked against the vanity table. Not much later, Pimiko scurried over the loft railing. She took up a position near Eden's ankle, facing Nemesia like a pint-sized guard dog.

"Where were you every other night?" Nemesia asked.

"Remember the house near the bus stop?"

"The abandoned one?"

"The one covered in vines, like a bird nest. It's nicer on the inside. I have a mattress on the floor."

"So you weren't camping in the hills."

"In summer, I'd consider it."

"You slept at home till I moved in," Nemesia said. "Were you just too proud to be seen as…"

Pimiko bristled. Eden laid a soothing hand on her shell.

"As a failing maenad?" she said gently. "Some nights, I did have genuine business elsewhere. That's no crime."

"Your dream leakage seems sort of severe." Nemesia didn't add: *for your age.*

"If you're powerful, even the earliest symptoms pack a punch. Sorry— wait here."

Eden shivered. She got up and brushed past Nemesia, hugging her thin underrobe around her, dragging her blanket like a train. She left the room.

During her absence, Pimiko mounted the empty pillow and began to rise up on long, long legs like a telescoping umbrella. She loomed high enough to scrape the ceiling.

When Eden returned, Pimiko's legs instantly collapsed to their usual length. She drew back inside her shell with her fluffy pink toes pressed together like the paws of a cat. Nemesia let out an uneasy breath.

Eden was in a fuzzy robe now, bare-faced. Her hair fell in a damp coil over one shoulder. Wetness had made it darker, a deep gold shading into brown. "Makes me a bit sick to let my magic out without a parasol," she said.

"Even by accident?"

She smiled—more to herself than at Nemesia. "At the reformatory, they compared it to getting toilet trained. Any maenad can unleash magic without their chosen props. Just like how anyone can go pee in the middle of the sidewalk. Most of us would really rather not."

"Why parasols?" Nemesia asked.

The majority of maenads would pick something less flashy. Like popping a particular type of breath mint, or tossing a coin, or turning a ring.

"I was eight when I learned I had magic."

"That's—"

"Quite old, yes."

Eden spread out her hands and examined her nails. They were painted some indefinable shade on the border of red and brown and black.

"Mastering berserk magic involves burning up your old self until almost nothing is left. But I remember having a mother. A real lady. She always carried a parasol. Then she saw my magic, and she gave me up like a midwife handing over a baby.

"That's how it goes. No regrets. No attachments. A lot of people carry parasols, or umbrellas. I stopped noticing them years before I picked my name."

She wouldn't have been born as Kuchinashi Eden. Students at the reformatory were referred to without surnames. Most would be conferred with a new surname upon graduating—and most would have nothing to do with their birth families. The disinterest became mutual.

"You still chose parasols," Nemesia said. "When you could have chosen anything."

"They're mine now," Eden said. "My symbol. Not hers."

Nemesia gazed at the ceiling beams as she listened. She couldn't imagine them having much structural purpose.

Those earthworm ridges ... like a horizontal combination lock. Stacked rings. She'd already touched them to wipe off dust. None of the segments had turned, or even wiggled suggestively in place.

But there hadn't been much dust to wipe, either.

"What did Sholto promise you?" Eden asked.

Nemesia looked down, caught off guard. Eden held Pimiko in cupped hands. Pimiko flashed a hint of claw like a hooligan with a knife.

"I was wondering who might come see you at the gala," Eden said. "He didn't try very hard to be stealthy. Bet he hoped I'd make a scene."

A lucky guess?

Perhaps. But Nemesia wouldn't waste time on denial.

"I could tell you I've decided to throw him over," she said cautiously, testing the waters. "Would you believe me?"

Eden set Pimiko on the railing. "Will he try to bribe the Snake for you? Sounds like a losing strategy."

Pimiko abandoned ship, scrambling down a bedpost and then dropping dramatically into the hammock below.

Eden watched her go, oddly blank-faced.

Time to leave.

Nemesia intended to steal away from the loft, to follow Pimiko's lead.

Her body flouted orders. She moved the wrong direction—towards Eden. She was halfway on the bed.

Eden took one of her hands, turning her wrist to expose the bite marks, sliding her sleeve up her forearm.

At times her stigmata looked like black tattoos drawn on with never-drying ink. At times they looked like fierce red puncture marks. At times they gleamed like nacre.

Tendrils of white smoke rose from the bared snakebite, as if her arm was the bough of an incense tree. Nemesia wanted to hide it, to smother it, but her upturned wrist and the inner crook of her elbow felt incurably weak.

"There are things I've always wanted to say to the Snake," Eden murmured.

"You—"

"You want someone to petition for you? Take me to the Snake, and I'll ask for your hand. For real. It would be the perfect chance for me, too. I'll say my piece to—"

"Don't." Nemesia found her voice again. "The Snake won't take kindly to pranksters."

Eden dropped her hand, looking sulky. "Wouldn't D. Sholto be the very definition of a prankster, too? He doesn't seriously want to plead for your release. Certainly not any more seriously than I do. It's all part of his give and take."

"Yes," Nemesia allowed, "but he started this."

"And you like me enough to try and spare me the lash," Eden said sourly. "How flattering."

Nemesia was close enough to glimpse her single crooked tooth. It felt like an inside joke—such a frivolous thing to want to see more of. She wanted to cut her thumb on it, to taste it. She wanted a lot of things she couldn't name.

Gradually, Eden's face cleared. "If I slept at home, I knew my dreams would leak. If my dreams leaked, you would notice."

"The Warden and I have an understanding. He won't go rushing in. But you would, even if I forbade it. I knew you'd come."

They weren't touching anymore. Eden just looked at her.

The pillar candles (with their pristine wicks) emitted only a whisper of light. Strange shadows fell through the greenery-covered skylight, moving over Eden as if the plants on the roof were dancing.

Nemesia's fingers were icy; her face was hot. Her voice came out shrill. "You think anyone who comes up here will—fall into bed with you? Lap from your palm?"

Eden held out her hand with an implied air of command.

Nemesia choked on the emptiness of her own mouth. She coughed painfully.

Eden cracked a smile, fingers curling into her palm. "Plenty of fine people have no interest in maenads, or women, or dyed blonds, or me. But"—this came out with an air of apology—"you aren't one of them."

Nemesia's embarrassment sloughed away. In its place came an arresting sensation of full-body fragility: her blood melted like snow becoming clear water. Eden was holding her wrist again. Eden's lips touched the snakebite. Eden's lips touched her veins.

"There I go again." Eden sounded faintly appalled. "Shall I send you away?"

Only stony pride kept Nemesia from diving over the side of the loft.

"Brides aren't celibate," she said.

"I'll assume you're referring to Brides of the Snake," Eden said slowly, "and not brides in general. All right. Brides aren't celibate. Are you?"

"...It's been a long time."

"Then—"

"I'm staying."

Her hand twisted to grip Eden's forearm, but there was no strength in her, just a cold febrile trembling. Eden's scent had gotten beneath her skin and nails without her knowing it. Eden had gotten inside her like a slow-acting poison.

"You can extinguish magic with or without direct contact," Eden said. "But touch is best at extinguishing thoughts."

"Prove it."

"Now, now." How infuriatingly self-assured she was. "I don't care much for challenges. This is a cooperative endeavor."

"Such sensual language," Nemesia said.

Eden leaned in and kissed away her sarcasm.

29

That Old Mistake

SHE GRASPED AT the back of Eden's neck. She pulled Eden's cold damp bundle of hair like a rope.

Eden stopped first. "You're sure?"

"We're married."

"Well, in that case..."

Nemesia's hands ran down Eden's soft-robed sides as if they had a mind of their own. She thought, despairingly, that she was less perceptive and less intelligent than a common crabantula.

"Wait," she said, half to herself. It came out all breathy. Eden, obedient, went as still as a mannequin. "Daiya Sholto—"

"Not really the name I want to hear now."

"He didn't give me new orders. *Carry on*, he said. That's all he said."

Eden stretched out on the bed. She cast her eyes up at the obscured skylight and the beams carved like massive fossilized worms.

"Ah," she said, lower than before. "Very telling."

She contemplated Nemesia again, no longer smiling. "What a poor spy you make."

Something—maybe the affection in her voice, maybe her trailing fingertips, maybe the robe coming off her shoulder, maybe sheer lurching gravity—pulled Nemesia down to her.

All along, Nemesia had told herself that if she admired Eden's figure, her magic, the sun on her skin—well, so did everyone else. She had that spark about her that made people stand up straighter.

But no Snake-ordained law of nature had obligated Nemesia to memorize the lines of her profile, or the set of her shoulders, or her nonchalant gait, or the sound of her voice, or the way she tied her sleeves back to show bare arms.

On the day they met, Eden had inferred that she was a plant—a mole, albeit an ambivalent one—and Eden had chosen her anyway.

Of course Eden would see through her in nearly every other way, too. She burned at the thought of it.

"Your eyes came back," Eden commented.

"My what?"

"Your snake eyes."

Nemesia's hands jerked with the impulse to cover her face. She made them stay down.

"Want me to check you for scales?"

She tried to match that silky tone. "You'd better make a thorough inspection."

It was a cold spring night, but they kicked the blankets off the end of the bed. "Nemesia," Eden murmured against her cheek, and that dealt the death blow to any lingering shyness. She wanted to hear it again. She might have demanded it, pressing her ear to Eden's mouth, limbs entwined.

"Snakes get tangled when they mate," she muttered, inanely, as they held each other. She didn't even know if it was true. The Brood was not a collective of herpetologists, and their Snake was not a literal reptile.

"I can do better than a snake," said Eden. "I have opposable thumbs."

"So do I."

"I also have a much more substantial tongue."

Nemesia heard herself make an unholy noise and then quickly stopped hearing much at all, or thinking, except to reflect on how glad she was that the Warden slept several floors down.

At some unknown hour, she lay like a puddle with her head on Eden's pillow. A finger ran thoughtfully along her lower lip.

She peeked at Eden. The finger stilled.

"Why am I dozing off?" she asked. "You're the one who hasn't been getting quality sleep."

"I've been thoroughly revived." Eden traced her mouth again. "Are you due for a piercing?"

"Under my lip? That's just for the Abbess."

"I wonder how it feels. I'd be afraid of causing an injury."

"What, while tonguing it?" Nemesia said, now fully awake. "Kiss the Abbess if you're curious."

"I'm a married woman, you know. I don't think she'd let me."

"She does have high standards."

They spoke of other things, most equally flippant, until Eden curled up against her and drifted off.

The most surprising part of it all had been how often Eden made her laugh—with comically widened eyes, or a deliberately silly voice, or an accidental bumping of heads.

The mood of desire didn't need to treated like a precious fragile thing, guarded jealously lest it break forever. You could shatter it with glee, and endlessly restore it.

While laughing, she'd lost her grip on all the old self-conscious fears. She knew already that she valued this comfort over grating attempts at perfection. But it came as a shock to feel it with someone who was in many ways still a stranger.

Eden was pragmatic, too, willing to revel in both the beauty and the strangeness of the human body. It had felt as if there was nothing to be ashamed of, no reason to hide.

All intelligent thought had flown out the window, leaving Nemesia's mind as bare as a fresh-washed bowl. Of course, now those abandoned anxieties came creeping skittishly back to their nest.

The meditations taught to Brides were never about releasing one's thoughts. Brood practices had equipped her with the ability to reinforce her mental borders. She'd learned to hold onto herself, to dig in deeper like Pimiko sheltering inside the cool, safe whorl of her shell.

Below, a Bride couldn't afford to lose track of any of the following: her time, her thoughts, her self.

Eden didn't seem to be faking sleep. Her breathing shifted from silent to labored and back again. She clung loosely to the arm that Nemesia had draped over her side. Sometimes she flinched, as if at the threat of an unseen blow.

With Tanyu, Nemesia had made the mistake of believing that little everyday offerings would be enough to compensate for her four bite marks. And for things she hadn't mentioned about what she meant to the Snake, and what she meant to the Brood.

She'd thought her own fundamental truth lay in the soft accumulation of loving moments. Fingers tapping the back of a hand, looking at hawthorn blossoms together, sharing a honey-soaked slice of baklava, trying not to smile all the time like a fool.

She'd thought Tanyu truly knew her—all the parts of her that mattered, beneath the trappings of the Brood. The repeated greetings and giggles and spilled drinks and stubbed toes that came together to form a person.

She would never make that same mistake with anyone else. She couldn't possibly make it with Eden, who had knowingly welcomed her into a marriage built on a foundation of practicality and mutual deception.

She'd meant to keep vigil all night, but instead she'd slept deeply. It was morning now. She inhaled the scent of Eden's sheets.

Eden, stirring, turned trustingly towards her with half-open eyes. Between the exposed beams and the skylight screened with a thin mess of roots, it felt as though they were nestled in a forest bower.

"Sleep well?" Nemesia asked.

"I didn't dream." Lines appeared on Eden's forehead. "No—maybe I dreamt. But I didn't leak. You smothered my magic. You put out my fires."

She sat up, folding her arms around her knees. The fluffy robe fell to her waist. It had gotten tangled under Nemesia.

"Did you know you kept extinguishing me?"

"Must've done it in my sleep."

Eden bit her lip, just for an instant. She dug around at the foot of the bed, then tossed something backwards. Nemesia dodged before recognizing it as her own wadded-up underrobe.

She'd originally had on a pair of drawers, too, and a loose front cloth that tied halter-style with string. Those appeared to have leapt down from the loft like fleeing thieves.

"I'm going to have to ask you to do it again," Eden said as they dressed. "See why I stayed away? One thing leads to another."

"If I can stop your magic from bleeding out just by lying next to you, why wouldn't I?"

"I don't like asking favors," Eden said crossly.

"Are you always this negative on the morning after?"

"I used to drink a worrange tincture every night before bed. You should've seen me then." She grinned, her bad mood flitting up and away through the dappled skylight. "That post-worrange sleep is very restful."

Nemesia found her drawers hiding in Pimiko's hammock. "Should you be telling me this?"

"It's not as if I've handed you a signed affidavit. I won't shut my mouth for fear of Sholto, and I'll make love to whoever I like. Well—whoever I'm married to."

Eden sat in front of the vanity to brush her hair. She scooted over so Nemesia could squeeze into half of the one-person chair.

Nemesia blinked at the mirror. Her eyes were normal again: no snake pupils. She wondered, fleetingly, if Eden had lied about seeing them revert in the throes of passion.

"Did you get taller?" she asked once they stood.

"You're just newly impressed by my physique." Eden hiked up her deep sleeves and flexed one arm at a time. "Did I wear you out so much that you shrank? Let me get you some water. You need to rehydrate."

"Like a strip of dried radish?" Nemesia said tartly. "I can reconstitute myself without help."

"Let me get you water anyway," Eden said. There was something so tender in her voice that Nemesia clammed up and sat right back down to be waited on like a coddled princess.

30

No Physical Evidence

THAT SAME DAY—the day after the Snake Moth Gala—the Warden called them to the scriptorium. His goal: discuss Eden's application for an extension of her right to use magic.

Pimiko rested in front of him like an implacable secretary. Eden lounged with her hip against the writing desk and looped her hair into a knotted bun that seemed highly unlikely to hold together.

Nemesia interrupted before the Warden could say anything further. "I want to clarify something."

She didn't make eye contact with him or Eden. Or Pimiko.

"I have no physical evidence," she hedged.

Eden's hair came loose. Her hands hovered by the crown of her head, forgotten. "That's quite a way to start a conversation."

"It's about…"

Eden lowered her arms.

The Warden pursed his lips.

"It's both of you," Nemesia said.

They didn't react.

"I thought it might be one or the other. But it's both."

They exchanged a glance.

"You're both Oddscale," Nemesia finished.

She clasped her hands. She was absurdly nervous. Dizzy, short of breath. As if she were accusing herself instead.

The Warden started to say something.

Eden spoke over him. "How do you figure?" It was the same tone she'd take when asking for a restaurant's daily special.

What was I doing? Reciting poetry by moonlight.

So she'd said, late at night, when Nemesia summoned her with the Warden's emergency egg.

At the gala, someone had told the farcical tale of how Oddscale tortured a mafioso with bad poems.

Daiya Sholto had complained about Eden frolicking at brothels, teaching board games to resident courtesans.

When the King's favorite courtesan lost her face to a rival, Oddscale had schemed to steal it back.

Eden claimed that the King supported her because she'd done him a personal favor.

It was our one particular life that young Oddscale fought to protect.

At the time—twenty years ago—Eden would have been only eighteen.

These were slender connections. But every strong thread had to be spun from a mass of fine fibers. "The public thinks Oddscale changed about five years ago. The previous player—the one who protected the King, and kidnapped young maenads—that Oddscale retired. A new vigilante emerged. Right around the time you"—she faced Eden—"went missing. That's when your Warden took over."

The Warden wore an expression of studied neutrality. "I'm a humble old man."

"Not as old as you like to pretend."

"I can't use magic."

"Oddscale doesn't have to be a maenad. You've made a lifelong study of practical effects. Wigs, prosthetic noses, an altered voice, an altered gait—the stage already trained you to be a master of disguise."

She met Eden's eyes. "You, too," she said.

Oddscale was the role of a lifetime.

So—had the public character of Kuchinashi Eden been crafted in careful opposition to Oddscale the hero? A vivacious woman, a shallow woman, a maenad with more power than sense.

How many of her tales of heartbreaking charm had been real, and how many were stories seeded by Eden herself? Brawling suitors, unforgettable duels—had some been staged? She and the Warden knew plenty of aspiring actors.

Oddscale existed outside the law, in the same semi-real space where people tucked their thoughts about demons.

If Eden were exposed, she wouldn't be punished. She would likely be lauded. But everyone would start to view Oddscale's actions not as the work of a Snake-blessed trickster spirit, but as the work of a single specific human being. One with a name and a reputation and an address.

A certain sheen of impartiality would be lost. Some feats might come across very differently if you were forced to consider their human author.

A player who took the role seriously would understand that much of Oddscale's power lay in mystery.

"The Warden worked hard to fill the gap. Three years later, you reappeared," Nemesia said to Eden. "But you had to be careful. Couldn't make it obvious that any change in Oddscale might correspond perfectly with your years of absence."

Eden was looking at the reflections on the glass-fronted bookshelves. She absentmindedly tapped her index finger on a corner of the desk. Pimiko marched over and touched one pink-tipped toe to her fingernail, making her stop.

The Warden looked winded.

"It's all right," Eden told him. "She doesn't have proof."

She stood before Nemesia, head tilted wryly. "I'm Oddscale." She made it sound like a joke. "Our Warden is my gracious understudy. You're the most beloved Bride of the Snake. Now it's all out in the open."

If only.

"What makes you say I'm most beloved?"

"You have four bites—that's a lot, isn't it?" She gave an exaggerated shrug, playing to an absent audience.

"Who else knows?" Nemesia asked.

"Just us three. Plus the King."

"Not Char and Vesper?"

"If they've figured it out, it's not because anyone told them."

The Warden put his hands together and said, dourly, that they would clearly have to talk about Eden's application at some other time.

He steeped clear green-gold tea and poured it into lumpy ceramic tumblers that he'd taken a class to make himself. He'd painted them with line art of inquisitive animals: a frog, a mudling, a puppy.

Nemesia helped produce more chairs. The three of them clustered around the scriptorium desk. Pimiko surveilled them from a corner of the ceiling.

Rain struck the windows. Just an irregular spattering, carried this way and that by the wind.

Eden poked at a small dish of salted nuts.

"So," she said. "Will you try to tell Sholto?"

Nemesia looked at the wide-eyed frog on her cup. She had to bite back the perverse desire to lie.

"Unveiling you would shape how several generations see Oddscale."

"Eventually they'll forget."

"Still. It'd be unfair to whoever succeeds you. Besides, Sholto has a problem with Eden the maenad, not Oddscale the hero."

A peculiar look crossed Eden's face. "He isn't fond of either."

The Warden took out his scrollworm tattoo kit. He inventoried its contents, then began pulling open drawers and muttering under his breath about the need for supplies.

"How long have you known?" Nemesia asked him.

He glanced at Eden. "Only since her absence. Pimiko showed me her will."

"Wrote it ages ago," Eden cut in. "Back when I thought serving as Oddscale might bring me in conflict with the government or the Bitten Brood. If something happened, I wanted a way to pass the torch myself. By the time I went missing, I'd forgotten all about it."

"You never suspected?" Nemesia said to the Warden.

"I wouldn't have thought of Oddscale in connection with a girl I've known since she was a sullen teenager."

"I was *not* a sullen teenager."

Nemesia spoke before they could start bickering. "You stepped in for her without guidance from the Snake. Without magic of your own—just Oddscale's scarf. And you succeeded."

Eden raised her cup in a mock toast. "People think magic solves everything. The best way to catch them by surprise is by not using magic at all. If I want to know what's being said behind my back, I don't eavesdrop with enchantments. I attend parties in disguise."

"That's just how you have fun," the Warden retorted. He turned to Nemesia. "She's always used minimal magic as Oddscale. Less risk of being recognized. Truthfully, until I read her last testament—until I saw the scarf—I didn't suspect her at all."

"In your defense," Eden said, "you never had time to play detective." She added, for Nemesia's benefit: "Because I bequeathed him the role of Oddscale, he stopped taking roles on stage. Not enough hours in the day."

"What do you do now? Take turns?"

The Warden laughed dryly. "I try to avoid going out in the field. It's easier to manage her schedule when I know why she misses appointments."

Nemesia thought of the three lonely years when he'd filled in for Oddscale. He—and everyone—must have assumed Eden was dead. He'd had no one to tutor him on the art of being a legend. Had he been prepared to keep up the charade until his body failed him?

But the same could be said of Eden. She'd only confided in him by accident: she hadn't removed herself from the stage on purpose. Her secret testament had been a fail-safe. She hadn't imagined anyone actually reading it.

Maenads left the reformatory after a transition period of greater freedom. At the same time that she started working with the Warden's troupe, had she also been wrapping her mind around the notion of embodying Oddscale?

She'd saved the King at eighteen—perhaps not long after graduation.

Nemesia stared down into the greenish sediment at the bottom of her cup. All that time, Eden had been acting on her own. All through her late teens and her twenties and her early thirties, before she allegedly slipped outside the Shell.

Eden had fished a cocktail umbrella out of her sleeve, though she didn't open it. She pressed its point to the desk and turned it in her fingers like a drill.

"Any other questions?" she asked sardonically.

Nemesia kept her voice steady. "Will you erase my memory?"

The finger-length umbrella fell over. The Warden closed a squeaky drawer.

"Could I?" Eden said with a sudden smile. "Would you let me?"

"I ... don't think I could."

"Don't think I could, either," Eden said thoughtfully. She righted her little umbrella and spun it against the desk again.

"I'd try, if you weren't an extinguisher. I'd try—although I might turn your brain into a bluebird. I don't have any experience with mucking around in someone's memory. Unless I did it to myself—there's a thought, huh?

"You already said you won't tell Sholto. That'll just have to be enough."

"You could keep me prisoner," Nemesia offered.

"Sounds tiring. I would know—I'm an experienced kidnapper."

"I saw you."

Eden almost lost control of her umbrella-drill. "Really," she said, not looking up. "Where?"

"Downcastle Street. I didn't know it was you," Nemesia hastened to add. "I saw Oddscale by the reformatory. Just for a moment. It must have been right before the kidnappings."

"Ah." Eden rose from her chair. She downed the rest of the her tea in a single swig. "This is nice, actually. Won't need to make up excuses when I flit off to do heroics."

Nemesia caught at her sleeve. "Tonight—"

"Yes?"

"Sleep at home again," Nemesia said. "If you can."

Eden's demeanor softened. "I'll consider it."

She sauntered out of the scriptorium, her footsteps swiftly fading. Nemesia strained to listen for doors closing. She heard nothing further.

31

A Lost Cause

NEMESIA WASHED their cups while the Warden cleared the dish rack, humming melancholy show tunes.

She apologized for hijacking the conversation in the scriptorium.

He sighed theatrically. "Something always comes up."

She considered his youthful glasses, his precisely gelled hair, the deep lines around his eyes and mouth that could project emotions distinct enough to reach the very back row of seats.

Right now he wasn't trying to project anything. He just looked resigned, and vaguely sad.

"I don't understand," Nemesia said eventually. "She wants to keep using magic. She wants that extension more than anything. Unless she's been lying."

"No," said the Warden. "I don't suppose she's ever lied about that."

"Why won't she sit down and work through the details?"

"Have you ever wanted something so badly that you can't quite bring yourself to actually face it?"

He grabbed a clean towel and vigorously wiped the teacups, although there was no reason they couldn't have been left to air-dry.

"I've seen brilliant young actors stay out all night carousing right before a big audition. Making themselves sick for no reason. A lot of people wreck their own chances."

He put the cups in a cabinet. "There's no system for appealing a rejected extension. She'd have to stop using magic, or go rogue. Which would mean making an enemy of the King and the Brood, and every other maenad, and the ordinary citizens she swore to defend as Oddscale.

"Her fate will be in the hands of a single committee. She doesn't like to think about it. So she doesn't. She puts it off. Daiya Sholto won't have to lift a finger, will he? She'll achieve better results with self-sabotage."

"Daiya…" Nemesia said dumbly. "You knew?"

The Warden scoffed. "You think we wouldn't monitor outbound mail? Your inscription technique needs correction, but I guess it's good enough for covert messages."

She almost flushed. "Not that covert, after all."

Just a few minutes ago, a patch of sunlight had opened over the house. Warmth had bled through the kitchen windows. Now a confused rain lashed about again, rising and falling.

Have you ever wanted something so badly that you can't quite bring yourself to actually face it?

Now that she was back Above, she wanted to stay. She'd known she would want that, and so she'd halfheartedly sought a way to avoid going Above at all.

Well, here she was. She'd done the next best thing. She'd taken a position in which she would have the perfect excuse not to forge any lasting connections.

Eden did return home that night, and the following night, and every other night to come. Sometimes they slept on Nemesia's sunken bed, and sometimes in Eden's loft. When dreams seeped out from under Eden's skin, Nemesia would smother them as if hitting a snooze button.

Most days, Eden could spring out of bed the moment she achieved consciousness. Nemesia took longer to get situated. Eden would wake her by opening the shutters to flood her with light.

One such morning, Nemesia asked: "How did you first become Oddscale?"

"The heavens parted, and the scarf fluttered down to me," Eden said playfully.

"Did you hear the voice of the Snake?"

Eden laughed as if she'd said something hilarious.

As an older child at the crèche, Nemesia had taken younger classes out to the park. Everyone wore matching hats. The littlest ones got rolled along in wheeled crates: open boxes like shopping carts that could fit eight kids apiece. Others walked in a line, clinging to guide ropes.

She'd fought to be allowed to do the same at the reformatory. She borrowed one of those nostalgic trolleys. She spent her stipend on colorful fabric hats.

Once, on the way back to the reformatory, she'd ground to a halt. Her trolley of three-year-olds kept babbling. Someone's bright orange hat slipped off. She retrieved it, and then she saw—

There was something sitting on the lamppost across the street.

Two long black tails danced, weightless, in a nonexistent breeze.

No, not tails. A sinuous scarf.

She rushed her charges through the reformatory gates. When she glanced over her shoulder, the lurking figure was gone.

It took some time for her to recall that Oddscale the hero was famous for wearing a mysterious scarf.

Even once the kidnappings started, she didn't tell her coworkers. What would they do, post a guard around every street lamp? Her memory took on the feel of a hallucination. No one else ever saw anything similar.

Perhaps Eden hadn't anticipated anyone other than a groundskeeper near the front gate. Deliveries went through a different entrance. When she was a student, no teachers would have dreamed of carting untamed maenads around in a giant stroller.

After the first abduction, all children had been barred from leaving the grounds. The risks were deemed too great.

Nemesia returned her borrowed cart to the crèche. From then on, her class could go no further than the gated garden. Tanyu helped keep an eye out to make sure they didn't munch bugs or plants.

Ten years later, on nights when Eden fell asleep before her, Nemesia lay awake and thought about the Warden's words.

A lot of people wreck their own chances.

She didn't have any real chance of being granted the boon of a life Above. Tanyu hadn't been capable of facing the Snake. Daiya Sholto couldn't do any better. He, too, would lose his nerve at the last moment. She knew it.

Never again would she crush anyone with the weight of unfair—and secret, and impossible—expectations.

So she could write her own desires off as a lost cause.

Eden was different. Eden had never previously failed to get her permit extended. She'd never been old enough to need it.

Every so often, the Warden nudged Eden to buckle down and get to business. He grimaced when Nemesia asked why he didn't push harder.

"I'm not her father, and I'm not her keeper, and I'm not her boss," he said. "I promised to treat her as an equal adult. Not as a madwoman on a leash. Not as a child in need of discipline. She got plenty of that at the reformatory."

There was another way to look at it: he and Eden were closer than many blood-related families. She felt utterly safe with him—safe to ignore his advice, safe to destroy her prospects, safe to be a failure, safe to fall apart.

He retired extra early one April evening, complaining of back pain. Nemesia and Eden found each other in bed. Eden bit each of her four stigmata, on both wrists and both ankles, as if trying to overwrite the mark of the Snake.

That, for some reason, was what pushed Nemesia over the edge. She sat up, nearly kicking a startled Eden in the face.

Eden asked, rather plaintively, if she had done something wrong. Nemesia feigned having a cramp in her calf.

She couldn't take it anymore. She wanted to march Eden to the scriptorium and make her fill out that stupid application right then and there. But they needed the Warden's help.

If she brought it up now, she thought darkly, Eden would slink away before dawn. She'd stay out until nightfall, untraceable, and another day would be lost.

"Stay with me," Nemesia said, putting her arms out.

Eden frowned, probably because it had come out with decidedly menacing undertones. Still, she obediently wriggled into her usual position.

If pressed, Nemesia would have to confess that she had no idea what they were doing. Play-acting at being loving wives?

Sleeping in the same room eased Eden's symptoms. Nothing beyond that would contribute to strengthening her control as a maenad, or any other conceivable goal.

Yet here they were again.

She toyed with Eden's hair, she massaged Eden's legs, she chased Pimiko out of the room to get some privacy—and she couldn't even claim she was acting on orders from Sholto, who remained as hands-off as ever.

It was all so pointless. It was all so senseless. She did it anyway, and Eden leaned into her like a cat in sunlight.

32

Great Deeds

SHE AMBUSHED Eden the following morning.

The Warden dished out bowls of reddish-purple rice. He'd made a spicy rolled omelette for Eden, and sweeter ones for himself and Nemesia.

The meadows nearby were shaded purple, too, with countless stems of wild hyacinth. A few stood proud in a vase on the counter. Nemesia had gone out to collect them the day before.

She waited until everything was plated, pickled bracken and miniature meat buns and all. She laid her chopsticks to rest on a small ceramic hedgehog.

"Tell us exactly what this application involves," she said to the Warden.

Eden had raised her soup bowl to her lips, and so could not afford to splutter. She meekly took a sip.

"The papers are in the scriptorium," said the Warden.

"Explain from memory. Don't give her a chance to sneak away."

"I can vanish whether or not you give me a chance," Eden said, indignant.

Nemesia looked up. "Pimiko, make her listen."

A shadow plunged down from a dangling plant. The plant went swinging wildly. The Warden jumped on his chair and reached to steady it. Meanwhile, Pimiko crash-landed on Eden's left epaulet. She flashed a claw large enough to close around Eden's wrist like a pair of pruning shears.

Best not to ponder where she normally stored her weapons. Nemesia knew one thing for sure: "Pimiko wants what's best for you."

"How touching," Eden said faintly. "Also a bit infantilizing, wouldn't you say? Ah—no, Pimiko, I'm not complaining."

The Warden climbed down off his chair. He'd made a big show of groaning over a pulled muscle. Probably so Eden wouldn't catch him snickering.

He turned back to the table. His expression was irreproachably bland. "The basic application packet is fairly straightforward. You'll need to write your name and address in triplicate. Most fields can be copied from existing documents. I'll collate the required attachments."

"If that's all it took, we would've already turned it in," Eden said gloomily. "What's the rest?"

"There's an oral exam—an interview with the panel. It'll get scheduled after you submit your documentation."

"Who sits on this panel?"

"That's kept secret. Which doesn't mean we can't try to find out..."

"But I'll get disqualified if the committee catches me doing reconnaissance." She lifted a single grain of rice with her chopsticks and held it up to her eye like a jeweler. "So it could be a whole team of folks who already loathe me."

"Or it could be the King and the Abbess," said Nemesia.

"I don't consider your Abbess an ally."

"She would try to judge fairly."

The Warden stroked his bearded chin. "The most important component of the application is a written summary of key accomplishments. A kind of resume. It has to cover the last five years."

A series of birds flickered past the windows; they were barely more than shadows.

"Well, that's bad," Eden said flatly. She faced Nemesia. "For three of those years, I was missing. Absent without leave. I remember nothing, and so I have no way to defend myself."

"You've been back for two years now."

"...I spent a lot of that time catching up as Oddscale."

"Excuses aside," said the Warden, "you have no significant magical achievements from the past five years."

Eden grumpily added a pickled plum to her rice. She grumpily drank from her soup bowl. She grumpily chewed a steamed bun.

"I lost three years from the prime of my life with nothing to show for it, and by no choice of my own," she said. "By the time I found myself back home, there was another maenad living here. It was a huge mess to sort out who would stay and who would go."

"That must have made it difficult to play Oddscale," Nemesia said to the Warden.

He demurred. "The house stayed empty for nearly two years. It was only toward the end that they replaced her."

"He kept my things in storage," said Eden. "He stepped into Oddscale's shoes, and he took care of Pimiko."

The Warden coughed. Gratitude seemed to embarrass him. "I inquired about whether you could submit earlier accomplishments. Considering the circumstances."

"They said no, of course."

"They said no."

Eden placed her arm on the back of Nemesia's chair, as if it was just the two of them arrayed against a hostile world. "This fall will be the last equinox before I turn thirty-nine. For some Snake-forsaken reason, the application has to be turned in over a year before the results become relevant."

"It's to give you time to plan your retirement," the Warden said. "In case your request is rejected."

Eden shuddered.

"In short," Nemesia said, by way of confirmation, "you have until the fall equinox to achieve five years' worth of great deeds. That's five months from now."

Eden's eyes strayed to the cabinet with her stash of worrange derivatives. "No," the Warden said. "There's a drug test."

"Oh, come on."

"It'll be around the time of your interview. Stay clean until then, to be safe. No more bagels."

Eden clutched her heart. "That's too cruel!"

"I've never seen you eat a bagel," Nemesia said, puzzled.

"There's a place in the city—I'm a regular. I always get poppyseed bagels with smoked trout."

"Eat the trout," said the Warden. "Skip the seeds."

Nemesia eyed the red-tinged broth of Eden's soup. "You fixed Daiya Iori's sinkhole. Would that count as a worthy accomplishment?"

Eden looked doubtful.

The birds outside the kitchen windows sounded as though they were making pointed remarks about the conversation within.

Suddenly Eden sat up straighter. "Let's be clear. I *am* a peerless maenad. I made my name back in my twenties. I dispatched three dragons, you know." She thumped Nemesia's chair for emphasis. "Three! All by myself."

"Dragons? From where?"

Eden shrugged. "From underground."

That was the usual way of things. Mythical monsters didn't often emerge. When they did, they clawed their way up out of old caverns or new crevasses. They came from below, but not Below. The Brood had never been disturbed by angry land krakens or armored tigers.

Even as such monsters appeared to climb out of an abyss, where they truly came from was a different time. They were ancient, or unfathomably futuristic, or both. They materialized among modern humans of the Shell only because the Snake (in a fit of ennui, perhaps) granted them passage.

A furious magical creature was like a bad winter storm. When one came through, it was all anyone would talk about. But soon afterward, they would move on with their lives.

Which would account for why Nemesia hadn't heard a peep about these three dragons. She must have been Below.

"How did you vanquish them?" she asked.

"I sent one back where it came from. I killed one—didn't like that. The last one really wanted to stay, and it was fond of ruins. I turned it into a palace cat."

"And you've rested on your laurels ever since," Nemesia concluded.

"I had other things to do!"

"Like courting the Daiya sisters?"

Eden held her head high and cleared the table with the air of a martyr.

They moved to the scriptorium, where the Warden made her fill out forms. Her penmanship was sharp and professional.

"You've trained as a scribe," Nemesia said. Oddscale had left scrollworm notes after each abduction.

"Courtesy of our Warden, yes. It's a valuable skill."

Eden finished writing, and the Warden began checking her work. She cast a sly look at Nemesia. "It would be helpful if another dragon could pop up for me to defeat."

"You want me to ask for intercession?"

"Please."

"The Snake doesn't take much interest in individuals or their prayers."

"Except its chosen. Like the King of Now, and Brides."

"And Oddscale."

"I've already prayed enough for a lifetime," Eden said grimly. "I'm only useful to the Snake as long as I continue playing my assigned part. I'm one in a long line of actors. You're different. The Snake loves you just for existing."

Nemesia tugged her sleeve down to hide the marks on her wrist. "The Snake won't intercede for Brides, either."

"I'm not talking about Brides in general," Eden said. "I'm talking about you."

Nemesia looked at the plants bathed in light by the window. One amaryllis stood so tall that the Warden had added a splint to support its stem.

"The Snake is our audience," she said haltingly, "and we're the ones on stage. The audience has preconceived notions about fairness, and rightness. And how stories should go. And who makes a deserving heroine."

She trailed off, losing confidence. How many plays had she seen in her life? Maybe two or three total, including *The Archetype*.

But Eden and the Warden were nodding along.

"The Snake is our audience," Eden repeated. "We're players, and the Shell is our stage. Yes, I can see it. But what does that make..."

Her voice softened.

Nemesia's head snapped up in reaction to some indefinable sense of alarm.

"Never mind," Eden said lightly.

A muted scratching emanated from the walls. Just the ambient magical noise of the house.

Nemesia recovered her composure. "We can't conjure a dragon. But your guests might as well be mythical beasts."

"They'd fight me if I asked them to." Eden sounded dubious. "On the other hand, I'm pretty sure I'd lose."

She heaved a sigh. "If opportunities to do great deeds came by so frequently, they wouldn't be great deeds. Should I hire a marksman to aim at the King? I'll relive my glory days, this time without hiding my face. Good plan."

"Grab all the hardest unassigned tasks," Nemesia said. "Ones that other maenads would struggle with."

Pimiko clacked her claws in agreement.

"I can arrange for that," said the Warden.

"You'll have to help fill in as Oddscale," Eden told him.

"If I must."

"I'll need time off, too," she warned. "That's one of the things they really drill into us. Neglecting yourself creates an opening for magical mutiny."

"Fine," said Nemesia, "but we can still get started today."

33

Mother of Thousands

THE WARDEN prepared a cheat sheet of difficult jobs waiting to be claimed by some dutiful maenad. His first recommendation sent them to the suburban outskirts of the city.

Nemesia had gotten better at convincing local mudlings not to stalk her. They still popped their heads up like prairie dogs when she passed.

Eden brought along her favorite oil-paper parasol; she claimed it would boost morale. Tassels and gauzy streamers dangled from the tip of each wooden rib. Somehow, they never blew into her face.

She had a flower behind her ear but was otherwise dressed plainly, all dark robes beneath that scarlet umbrella.

Together they mounted the crest of a faded hill. Gangs of children were sledding down the smooth-worn slope. They rode flat sheets of cardboard, sometimes falling off halfway through.

"Ever go grass sledding?" Eden asked.

"A couple times."

"Teach me how."

"It doesn't take much skill," Nemesia said.

"Then—"

"Get through your task list first."

Eden pouted, then moved on.

They came up to a series of lots at the end of a run-down street. The fencing was haphazard: two horizontal strands of wire bound to tilting wooden stakes.

A printed board announced that the property beyond had been claimed by the government, and listed various penalties for trespassing. There were a couple wooden houses, complete with rotting stairs to nowhere. Between them languished an empty plot like a punched-out tooth.

Further back lay a white-painted apartment, long and low-slung. The steps and railings were mottled with patches of rust like black mold.

Everything—the apartment, the houses, the vacant lot—was madly overgrown with a single type of plant. Acidic magic bristled through the wire fencing: a kind of ethereal herbicide.

"Mother of thousands," Eden said.

It had meaty tongue-shaped leaves, each lined all the way around with innumerable bud-like plantlets. Fallen plantlets clustered to fill every conceivable crack, even hairline seams in barren pavement.

"It's gone feral. A wild growth like this—it'll take root in flesh, too."

Something lumpy had died inside the fence, coated in green buds. A small wild boar, maybe.

"There's no smell," Nemesia said.

"The mother plants drank it all up." Eden handed over her parasol. "Hold this—it'll offer some protection. Just in case. The fence should shield us."

"What will you do?"

"Burn it down." Eden wrinkled her nose. "Which is trickier than it sounds. I'm supposed to leave the housing intact."

She put her hands together inside her sleeves and stepped up to the crooked wire fence. "Enjoy the show," she said pertly.

Silent fire tore through the massed mothers and their myriad plantlets.

Harsh gusts of magical wind almost ripped the streamers off Eden's parasol. Nemesia's ears felt defective, her senses anesthetized. She gasped for breath, but the air was cool and smokeless.

The woody stems of the oldest mothers writhed. Their tongue-leaves curled in agony. Rooted plantlets crisped and blackened like charred cabbage.

Flames throbbed inside windows—some half-boarded, some barred with metal. But the buildings themselves hadn't caught fire. Eden was merely scourging the growth inside them.

As more and more stalks succumbed, tiny plantlets leapt free. They pinged off the air above the fence in rat-a-tat bursts like popcorn.

Eden's flames sank, dwindling together with their fodder. The popcorn noise slowed. It felt like waiting for the final beat of a dying heart.

Between one belated *pop* and the next, the magic on the fence fizzled out.

The fire instantly soared higher.

But one last plantlet arced past the fire and the fence. It was just a cluster of leaves and questing air roots, smaller than a fingernail.

It zipped around Eden. It dodged the flailing ribbons and tassels attached to the oil-paper umbrella. It buried itself in Nemesia's hair.

Roots found skin. It didn't hurt, exactly, but she felt them burrowing. She could picture a capillary-fine tracery spreading rapidly around the side of her head.

She had to scratch it out, uproot it. Yet her fingers stayed glued to the umbrella's bamboo shaft. She couldn't drop it, she thought inanely. It was Eden's favorite.

Eden shouted something she couldn't hear.

Then Eden tore the umbrella from her and threw it aside. No hesitation. She raked her fingers through Nemesia's hair. It tumbled loose; hairpins dropped to the sidewalk.

She pinched something budding in Nemesia's scalp. Now it hurt—now it felt like getting a tooth pulled from the side of her skull.

The plantlet had already grown several times larger, and was sprouting new plantlets—children, or grandchildren—of its own. It burst into flames as Eden chucked it over the useless fence.

Nemesia's hearing returned in fits and starts. Eden kept finger-combing her hair, extracting lingering roots. Some stringy bits were white like dental floss, but the bulk had turned red.

"You should have extinguished it," Eden said. Her voice was unnaturally steady. "Did the roots make you freeze?"

Nemesia's lips felt clumsy. "How much of it was magic, and how much was..."

"Extreme tenacity?" Eden suggested. "Hard to say."

Her mouth formed a moue of disgust. She lobbed one final spaghetti-limp glob of roots through the fence. It spat fire like a sparkler.

She stooped to collect the pins scattered about their feet. She wrapped them in a handkerchief before handing them back.

"Was it only one?"

"What?"

"Just one plantlet struck you? No orphans fell in your clothes?" She searched Nemesia's face. "It all happened too fast. We have to be sure."

Nemesia's brain was slow to catch up. "How...?"

"Take off your clothes."

"Can't you check with magic?"

Eden hadn't lost the flower behind her ear, but it was severely wilted. "After all that"—she flung an arm at the smoldering plots—"my magical fine motor skills aren't at their best."

Nemesia looked helplessly at the occupied houses down the street.

"No one will see you." The air blurred around them, an effect like frosted glass.

Nemesia disrobed numbly. Eden shook out all the folds of her outer and inner robes, checking for passengers. She plucked at Nemesia's undergarments, too.

It wasn't a magical examination. Even so, a brief touch behind her neck seemed to ripple invisibly to the ends of her toes. She shivered, and tried not to show it.

"All clear," Eden said at last. "No more stowaways." She held out each layer for Nemesia to slip her arms through.

The fabric—which should have cooled by now—felt as warm as a shared bed. Nemesia fumbled to secure her garments.

Meanwhile, Eden retrieved her parasol. One sheer ribbon reached out and made a pass across Nemesia's head like a hand delivering a blessing. The stinging left her scalp. Her skin itched as if freshly grown. Half the streamer turned pink, although it hadn't quite touched her.

"It's stained," Nemesia said, horrified. "Eden—"

"Doesn't matter."

The conflagration hadn't left substantial piles of ash. A clinging grayish residue turned every fenced-off structure the same color, from wood-sided houses to the once-white apartment.

No plant life remained: no weeds, no children, no mothers. They'd finished early, but as it turned out, they weren't in the mood for sledding.

34

On Downcastle Street

AFTER SIX SOLID days of magical problem-solving, the Warden told Eden to take a day of rest.

Nemesia assumed she would stay in and laze around. Instead she was up like a rocket, tugging Nemesia back through the wormhole to Yolk City. She wore wrap-style pants and a look of glittering determination.

"Free time is a precious commodity," she said. "Can't waste it."

They went to the rumored bagel shop, which had rickety outdoor seats.

Eden got a forbidden poppyseed bagel and watched enviously, chin in her hands, while Nemesia ate it.

The shop signboard was too old to be legible. A bicycle leaned near the window where an assistant took orders. The entire thing, from seat to chain to spokes, was coated in a dense layer of neon yellow paint. Ivy spilled from a pot in the basket up front.

Nemesia was bemused to find that Eden didn't even know the shop's name.

"It's the Bike Shop," Eden said.

"But is that its actual—"

"Of course not. They sell bagels."

A couple came over with a trio of long dogs: one red, one black, one dappled. Eden gleefully entertained them while the owners studied the menu. This new commotion bought Nemesia just enough time to finish her bagel.

Next, Eden hustled her off to buy first-harvest tea for the Warden. One errand led to another, and by early afternoon, they were both carrying multiple bags.

They passed a park where small children played with cooking pots in a sandbox. Others scampered around collecting twigs.

All wore soft lavender hats. Several child carts, currently empty, were parked near a bush.

"Got any pictures of yourself as a kid?" Eden asked.

"The Snake has no use for photographs."

"Forget the Snake. What about you?"

"What would I do with old pictures?"

"Give them to me," said Eden, with apparent sincerity. "I'll preserve them."

A few blocks later, their path intersected with Downcastle Street. On the corner, a magnificent pine tree menaced a four-story building.

The patio beneath the pine had been claimed as public land. They sat on a bench with a placard thanking a once-noble family for funding.

Flowers filled long boxes. A sign stuck in the dirt listed the current varieties, and credited a local class of elementary schoolers with their planting and care.

Most children had families. Most children never set foot in either a mage reformatory or a crèche. If their teachers knew anything of Below, it was only because they'd been there as tourists.

"The picture in your room," Nemesia said. "It's by this tree."

Eden stretched her arms out along the back of the bench.

"The first time I got permission to leave the reformatory grounds on my own, I didn't know what to do. I walked up and down the street. Eventually I just stood here. It was before they put this new bench out. The old one was rotted through."

She tipped her head back, looking at the red brick wall of the anonymous building. Its stairs to nowhere were made of industrial steel.

"Sholto saw me wasting my free period. He threw up his hands. He told me how to find the Warden's troupe."

"Sholto took your picture?"

"We were best friends," Eden said simply.

They could have gone anywhere in the city today. Eden hadn't wandered over to Downcastle Street by accident. She was in an expansive mood—she was ready to talk.

About what?

"You played Oddscale for years before you targeted your reformatory," Nemesia said. "Maybe over a decade."

"Yes."

"You never wanted to see that place again," Nemesia guessed. "But you couldn't forget it."

Eden crossed her ankles. "Crushing the rebellion out of a berserker's magic could never be a painless process. But the teachers made it worse. They absolutely made it worse."

"You don't regret anything."

"I regret waiting," said Eden. "The kids kept asking why I hadn't come sooner."

"Where'd you hide them?"

"A magical pocket of space in the countryside. Like a camping trip." She smiled humorlessly. "That's how I know I'm unbeatable, as far as maenads go. No one else was skilled enough to find it."

"Do I…"

"What? Spit it out."

"Do I remind you of your teachers?"

Eden had her umbrella of the day propped up against the armrest. It was translucent, drenched in watercolor hues, designed to meld with the sky.

She turned toward Nemesia. "Being extinguished by the Warden feels like a bracing smack on the back." She gave the air a mock slap. "And you—"

"Is it bad?" Nemesia asked.

"You scare me," said Eden. "It's too total. Too peaceful. Makes me feel like I could live without magic, and not hate it."

Pedestrians meandered past. A harried young person with a rolling suitcase. Stylish middle-aged women in open coats.

"Here's a secret," Eden said. "I let you see me."

"When?"

"As Oddscale. Did you really think I slipped up?"

"You didn't?"

She laughed ruefully. "I was doing surveillance. I'd learned about a teacher who took the littlest kids out in carts. That was a shock, let me tell you. My class once spent a year locked indoors."

"They didn't let you use the grounds?"

An elderly man creaked along on a rattly bicycle.

"It was punishment," Eden said. "A girl tried to kill herself by eating slugs. Almost worked. A child infected with a horrible parasite doesn't act much different from a child drowning in their own magic.

"They saved her life, and they barred us from going outside. They tried to make us blame her. Bad strategy. If they'd succeeded, we might've killed her.

"The administration was always like that. Magic can only be mastered by the individual, they'd say. You can't help anyone, and no one can help you, either. Which is true. But they didn't have to make us miserable just for trying."

She flexed her fingers. "So I had to see this weird new teacher for myself. I spied on you. I recognized you."

"…What?"

"That's why I showed myself. Wanted to see if you would know me, too."

A sickening centrifugal force tugged at the whirl of Nemesia's thoughts. "We've never—"

"We did meet before," Eden said. "Just once. Never exchanged names. I'm not surprised you forgot."

"How long ago?"

"I was sixteen. Still in school. I'd just seen Withers performing at a park."

"So I was—"

"Around twelve, I guess."

Nemesia couldn't stop shaking her head. "I became a teacher at twenty-three. You couldn't have known me on sight."

"There are parts of the face that change with age, and parts that don't."

Her stomach tightened. "This year—when we met Below…"

"I knew you," Eden said. "I remembered you."

There was a hollowness in Nemesia that might have been filled with shock, anger, confusion, betrayal. Except that she had no right to any of those, and so she stayed empty.

She had come to Eden as a traitor in the guise of a wife. Eden, conversely, had always been open about not telling her everything.

She couldn't even act surprised.

"I won't hold out on you," Eden said, her mouth quirking. "Not here. Want to know how we met?"

All Nemesia could do was nod.

"It was somewhere between your crèche and my reformatory." She gestured at the street. "You called out to me on the sidewalk. You ... gave me a bit of life advice. I must have been looking really down, to get a pep talk from a passing twelve-year-old."

Nemesia's childhood memories had always been fuzzy, patchy, lacking in continuity. But it wasn't extreme enough to qualify as a type of amnesia. She was just more forgetful than most.

She could recall plenty of broken moments. Colorful corners of the crèche library. Picture books full of animals. Mudling-shaped crackers.

She'd seen huge fluffy snowflakes falling past a casement window—but had that really happened, or was it part of a story? How often did it snow in Yolk City, anyway?

Three loud kids took turns kicking a pebble down the street. They sang with gusto—snippets of a tune the Warden had taught her. An oddly upbeat song with violent lyrics. She couldn't remember which show it came from.

"What did I say?" she asked Eden.

"You didn't seem like yourself."

"How would you know? We were strangers."

"You didn't sound like a kid."

Every now and then, a hint of fragrance reached them from the planters.

"Keep going," Nemesia said.

"You asked me what was wrong. I mentioned the reformatory. Didn't go into detail. You told me to go to a place near the Shell after graduation. You rattled off exact coordinates. You said a crabantula would be there, lost and abandoned. You said if I took care of her, then Oddscale's scarf would come find me. A gift from the Snake.

"You told me to become Oddscale. *Don't seek vengeance in your own name*, you said. *Seek it for me.*

"I couldn't forget those coordinates." She recited a string of numbers. "I scoffed. Then I resented it. Then I turned around and embraced it. I graduated. I went to find Pimiko. I was grateful."

She put a steadying hand on Nemesia's back. "You told me my fate. I thought I should look for you. I thought I should thank you.

"I also thought—if the Snake had seized you, possessed you, maybe you wouldn't appreciate being found."

Nemesia squeezed her eyes shut. When she opened them, the world was still there.

"The Snake can speak through Brides." She felt distantly hysterical. "But it shouldn't happen like—that. They didn't realize how susceptible I was. I didn't get the right kind of training till I went Below."

Her stigmata burned with a feverish heat.

As the Abbess was fond of saying, Brides had no natural predators. Thanks to the Brood, Nemesia had never wanted for anything. The only thing she'd learned to fear was total sublimation by the Snake. Which had already come to pass—at least once in her life—and she'd never even known it.

She was lucky to have come back from that.

Had she come back as herself?

If something else had quietly replaced her, like an actor being recast, who would notice the difference?

No. The Abbess had told her not to think like that.

Insects came to investigate the flower boxes, drab coin-sized butterflies and bees and flies. Down a side street, construction workers holed up in the skeletal shade of a half-built house.

"I owe you my entire career," Eden told her.

"One of your careers. I didn't make you a maenad."

"Still wish I had a way to thank you for it."

"Thank the Snake," Nemesia said shakily.

"I have, in my heart. I'll keep trying. I'm sorry you weren't a willing participant."

What had Eden felt, gazing down at her from that lamppost? Disappointment, surely. At twenty-three, Nemesia had turned her back on Oddscale and fled. She'd been clueless.

Ten years later, Eden had lifted her veil in the Abbess's chamber of contemplation. What had she thought upon seeing Nemesia again at thirty-four? How could she reconcile prosaic human reality with the prophet who had ordered her to become an avenging hero?

That wasn't me, Nemesia wanted to protest. She wouldn't let herself say it out loud. Eden had already understood and accepted it—accepted her, who had done nothing to earn anyone's gratitude.

35

Yesterday, Today, and Tomorrow

THE JOBS KEPT coming. Eden didn't always request extinguishing after unleashing complex magic. She noted (a bit testily) that she'd gotten by without immediate staunching for years. But she did admit that she could never have maintained such a hard-driving pace on her own.

In the wilderness near the Shell, she fought and banished a spiny monster—albeit not one of particularly epic proportions.

She answered a summons from the King. The palace cats were yowling: their ruins had been infested by ghosts.

The cats were very angry, and very jumpy, and kept swiping ineffectually at thin air. Eden exorcised the infestation. Even after bathing, it took a while for her and Nemesia to stop catching phantom whiffs of feline musk.

Then she solved the mystery of several drowning deaths on dry land. The bodies had been strewn along a scenic path paved in artificial snakeflint, which had a certain softness to it. Good for joggers.

A-frame wooden signs exhorted cyclists to get off and push their bikes. (There were also boards that cautioned against feeding birds and touching fruit.) The path was lined with decorative trees and flowering shrubs and family gardens.

Many decades ago, before the city government filled it in, this route had been a waterway. In the realm of the Snake That Ate the Roots of Time, the old water could still be alive, Eden said. It could still take revenge. It could drag pedestrians down into solid ground, and it could spit them up looking as though they'd drowned in a well.

Eden laid the spirit of the waterway to rest.

A day later, she built a bridge between two rural towns, far out of sight of the city.

Both towns had a single-digit population. There was no conceivable economic reason to connect them. But offspring from one family had settled on the opposite side of the river, and it was an arduous journey back to see their grandparents.

So they'd put in a request. Eden came, and a bridge constructed itself out of growing branches, like a self-weaving basket. The walking surface was as smooth as a mat of fine-woven rushes, the kind you could fill a house with in lieu of flooring.

"Won't win me any plaudits," Eden said over dinner.

The Warden ceremoniously served them filets of eel over rice. He'd toned down the sweet sauce to suit Eden's palate.

"All the same," he said, "you're in a good mood."

Nemesia had been thinking the same thing.

"Yes, well." Eden sounded philosophical. "I can't act less optimistic about my prospects than the enemy embedded in my own house." A nod to Nemesia. "I ought to be able to outdo anyone for false cheer."

"That's the spirit!" crowed the Warden.

In free moments, Nemesia began reading her way through the scriptorium shelves. She was looking for ideas of what might constitute a great deed.

"Here's an easy one," said Eden. "Fighting dragons."

Nemesia cleared her throat. "I'm hoping to find scenarios where nothing gets killed."

"There's a complete catalog of titles over here," said the Warden. She turned to him gratefully.

More days passed, and Eden kept working. She contributed substantially to magical upkeep at the Facade.

The Warden grew masses of daylilies around the front stoop. Next came tall stalks of agapanthus, each topped with a bristling blue-violet sphere of clustered flowers.

"I call them morning stars," Eden said. "Like the weapon."

Leafy green shrubs massed in irregular shapes along one side of the house. Nemesia had never noticed them before, but in late May, a sweet scent filtered through open windows.

She sniffed her way outside. The bushes were rife with flat-petaled flowers—some rich purple and some snowy white, all mixed together, even on the same branch.

They turned out to be a plant known as Yesterday, Today, and Tomorrow. "Or Kiss-Me-Quick," Eden said drolly. Each individual blossom lost its color over time.

The Warden kept cooking eel dishes—smoked, jellied, marinated, stewed.

By early June, Nemesia figured out that eels were an auspicious food. The Brood had never indulged much in superstition, since those Below already lived side-by-side with the Snake. No need to invoke further blessings.

As the weather grew warmer, the sunlight around the cottage began to change. In winter, it had stretched deep into every room, heating window glass like the front of a fireplace. Vivid yellow blankets of light had laid on the floor—although Nemesia never saw signs of fading.

April became May, and May became June, and no more direct sun touched any windows, no matter which way they faced. Even on hotter days, it stayed impeccably cool indoors.

After another meal of eel strips on rice, Nemesia found Eden sound asleep in the middle of her sunken bed.

Eden's solemn face made laughter fizz up in her. She tucked herself in, struggling not to giggle, clenching her belly to keep quiet. The windows were open, the shutters cracked to let in starlight.

She inhaled a wandering note of Yesterday, Today, and Tomorrow. Or it might have been the warm aroma of Eden's neck.

She was wordlessly, foolishly, indefensibly happy.

This realization came like a missed note at the heart of a melody. She stopped laughing. The silence ached, a neverending echo in a neverending cavern. It would have been far better, she thought, to stay oblivious.

36

The Broken Maenad

NEMESIA WOKE, blearily, and knew only that it wasn't yet morning. A growl of faraway magic disturbed the air.

Eden was already up on her knees, fully alert. "There's a siren."

"I can't hear—"

"It's tuned for maenads." She left the bed. "Come down once you're ready."

Nemesia hurriedly got dressed and rinsed her mouth.

Downstairs, the Warden bent low and marked up a worm. He wore a headlamp like a miner.

Eden shifted Pimiko to an unused corner of the scriptorium desk. "It's my neighbor," she said to Nemesia, who had just come in. "He's losing it."

"You have neighbors?"

"Anyone can be a neighbor if you hike far enough."

"I've walked all over," said Nemesia. "I never saw another house like this."

"You wouldn't have," Eden agreed. "He likes his privacy."

The Warden slotted his finished worm through the lotus pod. Eden told him to deal with any incoming messages. She rapped her knuckles on the desk, saying goodbye to Pimiko.

And that was that. No more time for preparation.

The front door closed behind them. Nemesia rubbed her arms. She couldn't tell if her goosebumps came from a physical chill or the low-level rumbling of unfamiliar magic. It was like being snarled at by an unseen wolf.

"Now what?" she said.

Eden rested a closed umbrella on her shoulder, like a sheathed sword. She guided Nemesia away from the stoop, then tilted her head back and yelled.

"Vesper! Char!"

A sleek shadow popped into view, hanging upside down from the eaves like a bat.

Somewhere above came the sound of chains clinking. A languid greeting. But only Vesper had shown herself.

"We aren't dogs who come when called," she griped.

Eden gracefully neglected to point out that she had just done exactly that.

Vesper's eyes gleamed golden in the dark. She had vertical pupils. Yet—and it would have been hard to explain why—she made Nemesia think more of a palace cat than a snake.

Eden pointed her umbrella out into the nighttime landscape. "We're going to patch that up."

"Took you long enough."

"It's a bit of a trip. Know any shortcuts?"

Vesper licked her fingertip and held it out as if testing the wind. "No need," she said brusquely. "Walk in the right direction, and your neighbor's territory will be drawn to your power."

"Wonderful," Eden muttered.

Vesper was already gone.

Eden opened her umbrella. A glowing trail snaked away from her feet, an inversion of her shadow. It kept going on and on, tracing a wavy route between tree-stippled knolls.

"Shouldn't be far," she said.

The path was like a stream of stars enmeshed in topsoil. They followed it for a few minutes, Eden keeping a half step ahead.

And then it was as though someone peeled night away from the scenery. The horizon took on the burnt colors of late sunset. The persistent magical growling went silent, but only because they stood in the middle of it, in the eye of a storm.

Nemesia recognized the terrain—a certain tree with feathery leaves, a certain hillock.

The house, however, was new to her. The entire structure had been elevated on stout wooden stilts and stacked rocks, leaving an empty black space beneath. The bottom floor would start above her knees.

There was a wood-shingled roof. There were shapes that resembled doors, but they appeared to have been painted over; the paint still glistened. There was the black scorched hulk of a ruined staircase to nowhere.

"Should I extinguish anything?" Nemesia asked. Truth be told, she didn't know where to start.

"Might hurt him. He's gone completely berserk." Eden huffed out a breath. "Let's find him first."

She uncurled her fingers, releasing her umbrella. It wafted up into the sunset sky and circled the rooftop as if searching for prey.

"Don't be shy," Eden said to the shadows, hands on her hips.

A fleshy hoop came bouncing around the side of the house, as sprightly as a mudling.

It was taller than both of them. Moreover, it was composed entirely of human hands clasped together so tightly that they had no visible end. The fingers of one swallowed the wrist of the next, and so on.

"Stop with the dramatics," Eden scolded. "Let us in."

The wheel rolled sulkily away. It fitted itself to the painted-over outline of a door frame at the front of the house. Suddenly there was an opening—a round emptiness akin to a moon gate.

Eden's umbrella watched from above, coasting like a kite.

Eden went through first. She reached back to pull Nemesia up onto the elevated floor. The wreath of hard-gripped hands made a sound like knuckles cracking.

Nemesia wore wood-soled sandals. She hesitated at the threshold. It would be quieter (and more courteous) to remove them.

Eden guessed her thoughts. "Don't. Look."

The only light came from Eden's epaulets. She brushed them with her fingertips, as if flicking off dust, and they turned a color like hot metal in a forge.

The floorboards were wide and dark. Old wood. The seams between them gaped large enough to see right down to the crawlspace.

Parts of the corridor glistened wetly. Gelatinous amphibian eggs—translucent spheres with black staring dots—were massed in corners like melting snow.

They gingerly went forward. Eden swore when she trod on a stray cluster of eggs. She guiltily met Nemesia's gaze. "Hope this doesn't count as a form of regicide."

Nemesia had to press a fist to her mouth to keep from laughing.

The hall dead-ended at a linen closet. Eden haggled hotly with the walls, which were loath to reveal other rooms.

They ascended a staircase made of tight-packed stacks of books.

Upstairs, they discovered a huge funereal gallery, as large as a ballroom. It was crowded with old-fashioned refrigerator cabinets. They stood on proud clawed feet—some of which were human, and shoeless, and looked exceedingly awkward next to elegant carved talons and hooves and paws.

The refrigerators were positioned in angled clusters, with occasional solo cabinets caught between one group or another. It was a perfect imitation of how humans would behave at a party.

Eden looked increasingly unhappy. She grabbed Nemesia's hand.

None of the refrigerators had moved. Had they?

Wetness leaked from around the edges of closed cabinet doors.

Eden put her mouth to Nemesia's ear, keeping her eyes on the room, and said without sound: *He's here*.

Doors banged open. Eden thrust her away. Nemesia stumbled noisily—she really should have picked softer shoes.

Eden's epaulets had lit up like a stun grenade. Nemesia's eyes smarted; she couldn't see a thing.

She heard scuffling. Her vision started to return in painful blotches.

Magic—Eden's magic—quivered palpably throughout the room, coating every inch of space like the slime on the hallway eggs. It had a sort of cushioning effect, blunting danger.

A man had lunged out of one of the refrigerator cabinets. Now he was on the floor. White fangs grew from his naked palms.

"Extinguish those before he stabs an eye out," Eden told her—unhurt, but breathing raggedly.

Relieved to have something to do, Nemesia neutralized the maenad's hand-teeth.

He had hair as long as Eden and half-shaven gray stubble. He shrieked and babbled, spitting as he spoke. He called someone a viper. It wasn't clear who he meant.

Red lines scored his throat. These, at least, seemed to have been made with regular fingernails.

"I looked through time sideways," he said. "I saw it. I *saw* it. A billion stacked sheets of mica. Seeds of it grew in my—"

"Seeds in your throat, yes," Eden said. "Don't scratch them."

In a far corner of the room, the floor abruptly gave way.

Several refrigerators crashed out of sight, as if vanishing into a pit trap. Nemesia choked down a yelp. The house shuddered.

The man started scratching his throat again. His nails drew blood.

"Nemesia," Eden said. "I'm going to take all this uncontrolled magic and roll it up like a carpet. I'll roll it back up inside him. Stop me if it looks like I'm about to get us killed."

"Um—"

The features of the gallery shifted like a kaleidoscope. For an instant, all the refrigerators were made of stained glass. The man moaned and tore at his throat. Frog eggs surged from the floorboards, first foaming like bubble bath, then subsiding into featureless puddles.

The entire chamber dropped, jarringly. It felt as though multiple floors—or multiple layers of reality—had merged into one.

Eden's epaulets radiated a molten light. The refrigerators had shrunk to the size of toys. A buzzing sound drifted in through screen-covered windows. Late-night insects, not wanton magic.

The maenad was no longer scratching himself. He'd developed a cold sore; it looked like an egg tooth.

The lingering puddles on the floor let out a series of coarse, mocking ribbits.

"This is the best I can do," Eden said, strained.

Her magic stretched all around like a network of intangible tendons, bolstering the ceiling and walls and floor.

She'd kept the house from developing more new rooms like tumors. She'd closed his power up—as much of it as she could—as if locking a dog in a crate.

"Your turn," she told Nemesia.

Most of the magic was now contained to a single room in a single house. Even so, dousing it felt like switching off the lights of an entire city.

The lights did go out, in fact, because she forgot to spare Eden's shoulders.

The maenad made an appalling noise. Nemesia backed off in a hurry. Eden's magic revived, shedding a ghostly glow on his face.

He'd crumpled up with his arms around his stomach. He was unconscious. Still breathing. Nemesia felt sweat all down her back. Her ankles came close to giving way.

"Not bad." Eden caught her elbow. "We saved his life."

The wooden floor was unpleasantly sticky. Eden tied her hair up and began sliding open every door, lighting lanterns as she went.

When she found a small, ancient writing desk (complete with the requisite lotus pods), she dashed off a message. She worked almost as fast as the Warden.

Over the next few hours, a handful of officials and emergency responders came by to see them. Some were maenads, some were Brood sisters, and some were neither. They collected the long-haired man, who had yet to come to, and gently took him away.

Eden gave an oral report to their highest-ranking visitor. For the most part, though, she and Nemesia were left to sit waiting on the narrow veranda out back.

Eden's umbrella descended from the sky to meet her. Said sky was now properly starry.

Nemesia learned that the maenad they'd rescued was only thirty-seven. After this incident, he'd be compelled to retire early.

His warden had come down with a sudden illness and was currently hospitalized in the city, leaving him to stew alone. He had an acute phobia of Below. He'd muttered often about his terror of being forced to live there post-retirement.

"There are sanatoriums Above, too," Eden said, exasperated. "Not as many, granted, but it wouldn't be impossible to lock in a slot. He didn't tell his warden just how badly he wanted to stay. Maybe he didn't have the words for it, or he didn't think his pleas would matter."

She hopped off the veranda. Nemesia followed her to the front of the house.

The stairs to nowhere would need to be replaced—they were still a burnt heap of charcoal—but the main door had rematerialized. It was encircled by clutching carved hands, which looked considerably worse for wear. Many had broken nails, or missing fingertips.

"Not my idea of soothing decor," Eden said.

"They're not animate anymore," Nemesia said. "That's something."

They were released from duty around dawn. Eden proclaimed herself too worn out to tunnel a wormhole, so they walked the long way home.

"Was this a great deed?" Nemesia asked.

"To that maenad, sure. To everyone else..." Eden swung her closed umbrella back and forth, ambivalent. "I don't know. It's the closest we've come so far."

37

Eden's Key

EDEN HAD HANDLED the broken-down maenad with professional aplomb.

Accompanied by a gifted extinguisher, she could have taken the easy way out. She could have asked Nemesia to level all the magic eating away at the wood-shingled house, like heavy machinery leveling a hill.

But such a thorough and sudden extinguishing might have shredded their neighbor's psyche—like wet toilet paper, Eden said crudely.

Instead of calling immediately on Nemesia's abilities, she had used advanced magical maneuvers. She'd limited the mental damage to him as much as humanly possible.

And she received plenty of praise. In the days that followed, though, she seemed more irritated than proud.

She broke into occasional rants about it, unprompted. One afternoon, for instance, the Warden sent her to deal with a giant lake carp with delusions of grandeur. It thought it was a great king of the sea.

She stood on the shore with a deep blue parasol shading her face. It was covered in intricate embroidery of pale foaming waves.

"In the reformatory, they teach us to endure alone," she said to Nemesia.

The lake roared and parted. The carp twisted unwillingly into the air, held aloft by an invisible fist. It was black with striking orange blotches like fallen leaves, and it was at least the size of an omnibus. Water fell from its scales in glittering strands.

Eden didn't even look at it. "Then, as soon as we're cleared to graduate, everything changes. We're supposed to report all our smallest problems. We're supposed to ask for help."

The surface of the lake churned as if it, too, were in pain.

"Er," Nemesia began.

"Oh, right."

Eden's magic lowered the carp back into the water. It thrashed in fury. She angled her parasol to deflect the spray.

"No more scaring children," she called. "And definitely no more attempts to swallow them! I'll come give you another shakedown if you misbehave again. Got it?"

The lake moaned out a sound reminiscent of wind in a cave. The water's surface puckered like goosebumps.

"Good," she said.

At home, the Warden kept them informed about their neighbor's fate. His permit had been revoked, of course. He'd put in a request to have his magic cauterized.

With time, Nemesia came to understand that neither Eden nor the Warden (nor most of their colleagues) had ever seen a full-grown maenad in such a state.

Everyone knew it was possible, but the rules usually prevented it. Reformatory training; careful monitoring by Brood-educated wardens;

no recreational drugs; government housing in peaceful surroundings; mandatory retirement at forty.

The scruffy man in that hidden house was a year younger than Eden, and he had utterly lost his grip on his magic.

One evening towards the end of June, Nemesia stepped into Eden's room with a towel around her shoulders, flushed from a prolonged bath.

Eden sat in the hammock below her loft, scrutinizing Pimiko's spiral shell. When she got up, the hammock swung wanly with the loss of her weight.

"There's something I want to show you."

She tossed Pimiko up like a ball.

Pimiko landed on one of the ridged ceiling beams. She scampered along the length of it, starting and stopping.

She hooked delicate claws into the invisible seams between each ringed segment. The rings turned as she passed.

An opening appeared in the opposite wall.

Nemesia had poked at those grooves before. They hadn't budged, not one bit. Human hands—and even human hairpins—were too crude a tool to replicate Pimiko's work.

"Crabantulas can do that?" she said, amazed.

Eden answered with a winsome smile. She raised her arm, standing on tiptoe, so Pimiko would have an easier route back to her shoulder.

A split curtain hung from the other side of the secret doorway, hiding the space beyond. Eden lifted it to let Nemesia through.

The walls were a confusion of lit-up mirrors. The mirrors reflected, among other things: an antique sink that resembled a birdbath, a hat stand, clothing rods, bins, shoe racks, wigs of all colors on faceless stands, an enormous beanbag, jars of cold cream, a filing cabinet. And a lotus pod, which protruded from a metal tube attached to a trough.

The doorway clicked shut, closing them in. The privacy curtains hung like a tapestry.

"It operates on a timer," Eden said. "We're not trapped."

Nemesia looked in the mail trough. At the moment, there didn't appear to be any new letters.

"Seems a little inconvenient," she said.

"That wasn't always there. We moved it up from the scriptorium right before you became my lawfully wedded wife."

"Oh."

"Pimiko pokes the Warden when fresh messages come through."

The closed door made Nemesia uneasy. She kept shifting her weight from foot to foot. "Why show me now?"

"No one knows what will happen to any of us in the future." Eden paused and reconsidered. "Maybe the Snake knows, but we can't count on being informed. You, me, our Warden, your Abbess, the King, Sholto—we all have our plans, and all our plans could shatter tomorrow."

"What does that have to do with—"

Eden held out a hand. Something leapt to her like an animal pouncing. It happened so fast that Nemesia couldn't tell where it came from. A half-open drawer? The pocket of a hanging jacket?

It was a scarf of indeterminate length, and it wound up her arm like a living snake. Its dark gray scales shimmered, prismatic.

Eden spread part of the scarf between her fingers and cocked an eyebrow in invitation. Nemesia put her palm on the taut scaled fabric. Or skin. It was as warm as a fevered forehead.

"There's your physical evidence," Eden said with relish. "Can't let you keep it."

"I wouldn't ask to."

She spun on her heel. "And here's a wig I used to wear. You'd look good as a redhead."

She went on in this vein for a while, pointing out various components of nonmagical disguise. Some belonged to the Warden. It began to feel as though they might spend hours in here, like kids playing dress-up.

"I like seeing this," Nemesia said helplessly. "I do."

"As you should. It's the most exclusive backstage tour in all the Shell."

"But I don't understand why you let me in."

Eden shrugged off Oddscale's scarf. She twisted her hands, and it vanished. Mirrors reflected her at too many angles to count: big wall mirrors and small makeup mirrors mounted on metal goosenecks like eyes on stalks.

"I don't really care about Sholto's machinations," she said. "I don't think you do, either. You might leave when your year is up—nothing to do with him. You might decide to dissolve our marriage. As is your right."

The air felt too humid. Maybe it was the lack of windows. Maybe it was the wet hair getting in Nemesia's face. Eden reached out and adjusted the towel around the back of her neck, slow and patient.

Nemesia involuntarily stepped forward. As though Eden had taken both ends of that towel and tugged her. But there was nothing involuntary about it, not really, and Eden never pushed or pulled her against her will.

The tug-of-war was wholly internal. She wanted to shut her ears and flee. She wanted to hear every syllable Eden would ever have to say to her.

"This room is my last secret," Eden said. "If there's anything else I haven't told you, that's only because it's not my story to share. Wherever you came from, wherever you plan on going, I consider you my wife. I hope you'll think of me as yours. But I don't expect any kind of answer."

She lowered her hands. "I'm saying this today because I truly don't know if I'll be in my right mind tomorrow, a year from now, ten years from now. I don't know if I'll even be here. That's equally true for all of us, Above and Below, human and ... whatever Char and Vesper are."

"I'm not a good Bride," Nemesia blurted. "I'm only a Bride because no other role would fit."

This wasn't much of a secret. But it was all she could bear to give.

Eden kissed her forehead. "Then I'll call you my bride, not a Bride of the Snake."

They tried on assorted wigs and costumes. Eden showed her the mechanism to open the room from within. Pimiko scurried out past the curtains.

They flopped down on the beanbag, which was spacious enough to accommodate both of them. Like a human-sized cat bed.

Eden kicked off her slippers and stretched her toes. She had beautiful feet. Nemesia drew idle circles around her ankle bone until Eden laughed and told her it tickled.

Eden spoke wistfully of how human sorcery operated in other lands (with the caveat that her knowledge came largely from Vesper).

"Maybe the rest of the world is how things should be," she said. "Is that sacrilegious? Don't let the Snake get me."

"What do you mean?"

"They use rules-based magic."

"Could you learn it?"

"No," Eden said at once.

"Why not? You're good at magic. Better than anyone else."

"Berserkers, maenads, raging mages—whatever you call us, we're stuck like this." She bent her arm. "Imagine a broken limb getting deliberately twisted to heal wrong. We can't untwist ourselves. We can never undo what the reformatory did to us. I'll be a maenad until I die, or lose my wits, or get cauterized."

"But you might have gone outside the Shell," Nemesia argued. "For all you know, maybe you did use foreign magic."

Eden gave her a knowing look. "Ever hear Vesper's thoughts on that?"

"Briefly."

"She tells me I'm delusional. In fact, she says most adult maenads would shatter like dropped teapots if we ever left the Shell, or if the Shell ever left us. It's like—the Shell is something that exists inside us, too. A membrane installed by the Snake. Our wild magic should destroy everything, but it doesn't, and not just because of individual willpower."

She held Nemesia closer, heedless of damp hair. "I probably never left. So for three years, did I simply drift sideways out of existence? What's stopping me from slipping away again at any given moment? It's too frightening to think about."

Nemesia sympathized with that more than she could say.

"Let's talk about something else," Eden said. "Do you miss Below?"

"Not really."

"That was fast."

Nemesia sat up to adjust her robe. The top of her head skimmed the array of repeating mirrors.

"I love sunlight," she said. The easiest answer. "I love everything that grows Above. And rain, and mudlings, and mammoths in the distance."

She stopped herself from going into a litany of all the things that didn't exist Below. Soon her list would touch on the cottage, and the Warden, and Eden herself.

Only one loose thread nagged at her: the fact that none of her letters had produced a reply from Roc.

Then again, Brides on sabbaticals weren't supposed to waste time corresponding with acquaintances Below—guards or otherwise. Brides were supposed to focus on experiences unique to Above.

A breeze on her cheek. Dappled shadows from hedges. Families blowing bubbles. Open-air terraces full of noisy fountains and children and curious dogs. The fragrance of Yesterday, Today, and Tomorrow. Eden's hand against her heartbeat.

Every sensation was fodder destined to be milled through the vast imagination of the timeless Snake.

38

Summer in the Shell

In July, linden trees bloomed all over the city. Back home, the Warden maintained a constant stock of cold-brewed tea. Nemesia shyly asked if she could start walking around the house without slippers. The floors were soothingly cool in this season, rather than freezing.

The countryside insects should have been deafening, but they seemed oddly muffled. Inside—even with windows open—they were reduced to a soft hypnotic hum. Only on longer strolls away from the house could she hear how they really sounded.

"It's to protect my delicate sensibilities," Eden said, rolling her eyes. "Can't have sheltered city maenads losing their minds over rural cicadas."

In spare moments, Nemesia practiced climbing up to the turret. Eventually she got the hang of stomping to call the ladder.

Around mid-July, she stood facing the ladder alone. Eden had left for an Oddscale mission that had something to do with police corruption. It was one of her rare days off from maenad work.

Nemesia summited the turret, then made her way to the balcony. A hot wind buffeted her; sweat trickled down her back. It wouldn't be unbearable if she remained perfectly still in a patch of shade, but there wasn't any shade here.

She called out quietly until chains rattled in greeting. She craned her neck.

Char sat on the turret roof, silhouetted against a backdrop of mountainous summer clouds. Vesper bobbed judgmentally in the air beside her. Neither of them appeared to notice the heat.

Nemesia wished, too late, that she'd brought a pitcher of olive tea. Did they drink tea? Or a plate of snacks. Something to offer them. Instead, all she came bearing were words. They owed her nothing, but she had come to ask an enormous favor.

Later that same week, she and Eden sat out back to admire the shadows cast by angle trees.

"I should have asked this much earlier," Eden said.

"Mm?"

"Is there anyone from the gala you'd like to see again?"

"Huh?" Nemesia hadn't been listening.

A butterfly swooped past drunkenly. "The Snake Moth Gala. If there's anyone you thought was pleasant company..."

"Are you trying to set me up with someone?" Nemesia asked blankly.

"Just to be clear—you can go to town whenever you want. You can meet whoever you like. Signing on to marry me doesn't mean you have to devote your entire sabbatical to chasing my dreams. Whether you do it seriously, or for the sake of your cover story."

"I know."

"All right, then."

Nemesia studied the picture frame wormhole that stood half-concealed by trees. "I'd like to talk with Daiya Anis."

"Sholto's sister?" Eden was visibly curious. "I can't join you—Sholto might have a stroke if we're seen together."

Even when suppressed, the sinuous thrum of summer insects made it hard to think.

"He didn't always hate you," Nemesia said.

Eden had been drinking bitter lemonade—made by blending an entire lemon, skin and all. There was nothing left now but ice. When she tilted her sweaty glass, it made a sound like Char's chains.

"Maenads are notoriously bad friends," she said meditatively. "Except for Sholto. He graduated first, but he kept looking out for me. We stuck together when everyone else scattered. I went to his wedding, and I made him promise to come to mine."

A sharp smile crossed her face. "He did deliver me a bride in the end, didn't he?"

"But you never told him about being Oddscale."

"Once you start telling people, where do you stop?"

"The King—"

"Guessed it on his own, like you." She swirled her glass of melting ice. "Our dear Warden learned about it through ... if not an act of god, then an act of Pimiko."

Shortly after this, the Warden scheduled Nemesia for lunch at The Over-Under with Daiya Anis. Eden, who had other business in Yolk City, offered to escort her into town.

"You won't need that," she said as Nemesia checked her wallet. "Anis will treat you."

"Even if it's my invitation?"

"Noblesse oblige," Eden said gleefully.

"I thought the Daiyas' term was almost over."

"Not quite yet. They won't step down till the end of the year."

Nemesia still made sure to have plenty of cash ready, just in case.

They made their way to the restaurant through a series of back streets. Nemesia counted no less than fifteen long-bodied dogs out on walks.

They were supposed to be auspicious. Like all the eel filets the Warden kept feeding her and Eden. To her eye, however, those dogs looked more like furry, leg-wearing mudlings than a glorious serpent.

Just outside the building, she faltered. "This isn't inappropriate, is it?"

Eden snorted. "Wives are allowed to have friends."

"People might think—"

"That you're stepping out on me? Not unless you make out with her in full view of the restaurant. Anyway, let them think what they like. Who knows? Sholto might embrace it. He'll root for his sister to steal you away."

"Could get complicated."

"Anis knows it isn't a date," Eden said. "I might sabotage my career, but not my chances with my wife." She grinned irrepressibly. "That's your job, isn't it?"

"Eden!" Nemesia hissed, although no one was close enough to listen in.

"I mean, look—life is plenty ridiculous even if you disregard spying wives and self-important heroes and the fact that our god is a colossal snake. You've got to laugh at life before it laughs at you."

With those words ringing in her ears, Nemesia went up to find Daiya Anis.

39

The Daiya Family

"I'M DYING OF curiosity," Daiya Anis declared.

She wore cool-toned layers. A clip pulled back much of her hair: the rest fanned out by her neck, stiff as a paintbrush. She gave Nemesia a pitying look, then ordered for both of them.

"Whatever it was you wanted to chat about," she said decisively, "you'd better catch your breath first."

In the meantime, she launched into idle talk about the recent heat wave. She ran through the names and ages of her younger sisters. She critiqued a popular city tabloid.

Nemesia, for her part, didn't talk about Eden, and she didn't mention being a Bride. Which left her without much to say.

She waited for Anis to bring the conversation back around to the Daiya family, and everything involved with their impending descent from the nobility.

She seized her chance. "How's your nephew?"

"Iori?" Anis's face sharpened. "Oh, so that's what this is about. How well do you know him?"

"To be honest ... not at all."

She waved a manicured hand. "No matter. You know maenads—aside from K. Eden, they're basically all prickly hedgehogs. Iori, he's more like a hedgehog without spines."

"He's quite young, isn't he?"

"Only eighteen." Anis sighed. "It's hard for civilians to relate to a maenad. Sholto was standoffish around the rest of us siblings for years. Can't blame him—he did try to come back after graduation. Our parents wouldn't even look at him. Each time they closed the door in his face, they almost forgot they had a son."

"You remember him."

"Maybe it affects siblings differently." Anis tapped her temple. "Maybe it's because we all decided to start fresh as adults.

"Or maybe"—she gestured delicately with her wineglass—"our parents took some kind of curse with them when they died."

"You haven't rejected Iori, either," Nemesia ventured.

The glass in Anis's hand was textured with a pattern of scales, although their shape seemed more fishy than reptilian. She studied the way light played across the etching. Her expression clouded.

"Few maenads contact their old families. Your wife, for instance—she wouldn't even dream of it, would she?" She looked keenly at Nemesia. "Is it any easier for those called to the Brood?"

Nemesia admitted that she'd never felt any desire to find the people who birthed her.

Anis nodded. "Sholto is unusually stubborn. Or freakishly family-oriented. For better or worse, he never lets anything go. He found his way back to us. He's one in a million."

On the plate before her gleamed an assemblage of hyperrealistic cakes crafted to resemble fresh produce: grapes, kumquats, baby corn, cabbage sprouts, blackberries. She seemed reluctant to cut into them.

"The truth is, we did abandon Iori," she said. "All of us except Sholto. He's not a bad father, I promise. I know he and Iori seemed uncomfortable at the gala. But Sholto would never hurt his own child."

She offered to share her dessert. Nemesia declined. Her thoughts teemed like a cloud of gnats.

Daiya Anis took ladylike bites. Nemesia felt as she had in the moments before accusing Eden and the Warden of being Oddscale.

No—this time she felt sicker. But how could she untangle anything in the present without understanding the knots that lay in the past?

Eden, speaking of Daiya Iori: *I last saw him when he was around eight or nine.*

Now he was eighteen.

Only Oddscale's very first abductee had been the right age at the time. An eight-year-old girl.

"Did Iori attend the same reformatory as Sholto and Eden?"

Anis said nothing.

Nemesia forced herself to sit still. "I worked there," she continued.

"How long?"

"A year. I don't condone anything they ... I'm sorry I didn't see it, or stop it." She raised her eyes. "I was there when Oddscale told us to change. The first child to vanish—her name started with S. Can't remember the rest."

"Daiya Shiori," Anis said, very softly.

Nemesia stumbled through an apology. Then she shut up before she said anything worse. Anis filled the silence. "Sholto had to enroll his daughter at four. I mean—at the time, we thought he had a daughter. So I heard all of this much later.

"That reformatory was built on the principle of not listening to children. Their misery, their wildness—all things to be pulverized and overcome. The staff would only call Iori by the given name they had on file.

"Among other things, Oddscale refused to give Iori back until they respected his wishes. If Oddscale hadn't stepped in, he'd have been stuck as Shiori till graduation."

"So Oddscale—"

"May very well have saved Iori's life," said Anis. "Sholto understands this. He embraces having a son.

"But think back to when the kidnappings started. Sholto's child disappeared, and he didn't find out for weeks. The administration didn't keep parents informed—most of them wouldn't care to know even if their little maenad died in an accident.

"Sholto's own wife couldn't understand why he was so hung up on it. It wasn't her fault—she didn't stop caring on purpose—but he almost divorced her.

"We sisters weren't much comfort, either. No one knew how to talk him off the ledge. The second he stopped bringing it up, it totally slipped my mind. Like an unimportant subplot from some play I saw years ago. It just wouldn't stick.

"He couldn't rally other families to his side. He was the only father in living memory to raise a fuss about his maenad child. The reformatory even threatened to report *him* to maenad authorities."

"He didn't..." Nemesia struggled for words. "He didn't trust Oddscale?"

"In retrospect, it's easy to say that Oddscale didn't cause any lasting harm. Oddscale got results. In real time, though, those children were held hostage for months. Oddscale made it fun for them, I'm sure—a grand old adventure. Iori looks back on it fondly.

"But Sholto had no way of knowing that the kidnapper was the real Oddscale—or that this Oddscale meant well. Anyone can call themselves a hero, can't they? Fear ate at him until there was hardly anything left."

Anis pushed her plate away. "My brother isn't an easy man to like," she said. "But he's always tried to do right by his son. That's the beginning and end of it."

After that, they spoke only of inconsequential topics. With wicked delight, Anis described the peculiar rituals and pretensions her family had been expected to partake in as nobles.

"They give you a giant handbook when you're selected," she said. "A how-to manual. And one of the rules is to never let a commoner pay."

She winked. Nemesia tucked her wallet away, conceding the battle.

After saying farewell to Anis, who departed in a shiny vivitaxi, she waited for Eden beneath a lamppost. She kept waiting until half an hour past their agreed-upon meeting time.

Tired of standing around, she wandered off into the market by the stairs to Below. If needed, Eden could find her anywhere.

Her coin purse and billfold were still bursting at the seams. She continued to receive a modest stipend from the Brood, but she'd spent hardly a single scale of her own money since coming Above.

Her mind glazed over as she ambled along at the same pace as the rest of the crowd. She eyed antique scrolls, handwoven baskets, used clothing, animal carvings, small potted succulents, ceramic bowls, celadon vases, chopstick rests....

She kept stopping by racks of vintage robes. She could afford something really nice. But Eden already had a wardrobe so extensive that she kept a constant rotation on display in the drawing room.

A boisterous vendor made her try bouncing a series of coiled, springy toys. One had the head of a mudling; one had the head of an eel. Their swaying reminded her of her first day at Eden's house—snakeskin streamers fluttering from the front door. She moved on. At a booth selling jewelry, she fingered silvery necklaces meant to look like a worm draped gently around the wearer's neck.

Hours passed before Eden showed up. Long enough for anxiety to seep right up to the back of her throat.

She was on the verge of heading home alone when someone caught at her from behind.

Eden was panting and unusually disheveled. She tugged haplessly at her clothing—a summer robe with unobtrusive geometrical patterns. It looked as though she'd thrown it on in the dark.

"What a day," she said at last. "I'm so sorry."

40

Old Friends

THEY THREADED their way out of the marketplace crowds. Eden produced a cocktail parasol, flicked it open, put an arm around Nemesia, and magically shifted across the city. It felt like being tugged behind a curtain.

They emerged outside Eden's secondary property. The outlines of the house had been smothered by a fresh layer of leaves. Pale pink roses bloomed all over the barbed wire out back.

"I was supposed to stop an arranged marriage," Eden said.

"As a maenad, or as Oddscale?"

"As Oddscale. That sort of matchmaking is purely a noble thing. It's usually not so serious. But the families were being pushy, and the kids—they're both twenty—seemed very unhappy."

"What happened?"

"Oh, they called it off. But then there was a runaway omnibus, and a bank robbery." She took a breath. "And *then* some hooligans hijacked a vivitaxi and went joyriding all up and down Jigsaw Boulevard! Didn't run anyone over, thank the Snake, but that's a cut-and-dried case of animal abuse. So I had to chase them down, too, and rescue the taxi, and make sure no one got wounded. I hope your afternoon went better?"

"Um," Nemesia said. "Well."

Her traitorous hand held out a little brown paper bag sealed with floral tape.

Eden looked questioningly from the gift bag to Nemesia's face.

After a moment, she carefully opened it.

"Nemesia," she said, with equal parts delight and disbelief.

She drew out a slender chain. At the end was a teardrop pendant that held a bit of molted snakeskin under glass.

"You don't have to wear it," Nemesia said. "If you do, it'll be easy to hide in your clothes. I can't cook eel like the Warden—maybe it'll bring you another kind of good fortune. It can't hurt, at least. The Brood wouldn't approve of using real snake sheds. But the Abbess isn't here to judge us."

She felt like a geyser of useless words; she wished someone would stop her.

"Put it on for me. Please."

"What?"

"Your gift. Put it around my neck." Eden lowered her head, waiting.

Nemesia hesitantly guided the necklace down into place. She was afraid, all of a sudden, that the chain might break in her fingers. It looked so slight.

Eden lifted her hair free. The necklace remained intact. "If this can't bring me success, then nothing will."

She looked around. "Let's enjoy the roses," she said. "We've earned ourselves some lingering."

She parted the vines and slipped inside the house before Nemesia could react. A minute later, she reappeared lugging a sizable sun parasol.

The parasol could have shaded at least two restaurant tables. They held it to the ground as if planting a flag. It opened with a shudder, smelling of old dust and magic.

The pole winked out of existence, but the canopy stayed aloft.

The weeds throttling the garden parted like green velvet curtains. The hoary lump beneath the hovering sunshade turned out to be a couch hewn from rough natural stone. It was lined with inexplicably clean, fitted cushions.

"See, this place is actually quite well equipped," Eden said.

From the couch, they gazed out at the thicket of roses. Eden kept touching her necklace.

"Are you naturally more social than other maenads?" Nemesia asked.

"As opposed to what?"

"You could have made yourself that way. For your work as Oddscale. For gathering intel."

Eden tilted her head. "I was frantic, in those early years," she said slowly. "I don't know if I remember."

She turned the pendant. Lacy scales glistened beneath their shield of glass.

"Before I knew I could be Oddscale, I had a very different plan."

There was a low, hypnotic note to her voice.

The sun parasol rotated like a lazy ceiling fan. The warmth, the shade, the glinting of Eden's necklace, the bees among the roses, the summer sky like a painting—Nemesia had been getting sleepier and sleepier from the moment she gave her weight over to the outdoor couch.

Now she came fully awake again.

"What would you have done?" she asked.

"If we never met? I didn't tell anyone, but I was already thinking about what comes after graduation. I thought about it all the time. I knew what I had to do."

Eden sounded as if she were reading calmly from a book. "I would graduate, and then I would go back to the reformatory, and then I would kill my old teachers one by one. Without magic. Extinguishers require different tactics."

The roses stirred beneath the weight of crawling insects.

"You can't have been the first to think that," Nemesia said.

"Must be a reason no one ever goes through with it. Maybe the rage fades too fast after graduation. What's the point of reforming ourselves as containers for power if we can't even use it to slaughter our enemies?"

A half-smile tugged at her lips. "I wasn't a very nice kid. No one asked me to be nice. Maybe the Snake picked me for Oddscale because I would otherwise have become a mass murderer. Maybe that's how the Snake keeps this realm peaceful—switching one destiny out for another. But I'm happy with the life I got." She gestured vaguely. "Now my only concern is keeping it."

Passing clouds dimmed the midsummer sun.

"We'll make the committee grant your extension," Nemesia said.

"I wasn't just talking about the extension." Eden leaned back into her corner of the couch. She contemplated Nemesia from behind lowered eyelids. "You got what you wanted?"

"What I wanted?"

"From lunch with Daiya Anis."

It would have come up eventually. Nemesia related what she knew. She didn't hold back.

"I thought I was doing Sholto a favor," Eden said distantly. "I got his boy out of there first."

"You couldn't give him any clues about—"

"That's the fundamental principle of being Oddscale. Never name yourself, and never explain yourself. Don't show up to take blame, and don't show up to take credit."

Birds rustled amid weed-choked bushes.

Eden's hand closed in a fist around her necklace, as if she thought someone might steal it.

"You had a falling out," Nemesia stated.

"We sure did."

"Was it about Iori?"

"It's a dull story."

"Tell me."

"Sholto seemed to age years after I kidnapped Iori," Eden said. "I wished I could drag him outside and punch him in the head and somehow just make him believe his kid was safe. If human magic worked for stuff like that, no one would ever eat worranges."

She uncurled her fingers, releasing the pendant. "One day, I told him to trust Oddscale for the thousandth time. Then I kept going. I made light of his most unspeakable fears. Dark humor used to be a big thing for us, back at the reformatory. But I should have just shut my Snake-forsaken mouth. It wasn't funny anymore.

"Anyway. He blew up. I got defensive. It got ugly. By the end, he would've sworn I said I hoped his spawn was dead. There's no coming back from that."

"Sholto went through the same things you did." Nemesia felt herself growing more animated. "And he enrolled his own kid there? It's not the only reformatory in town."

Eden stared into her hands. "The other reformatories could've been worse. Adult maenads are all prone to the same fallacy—we think what we experienced was livable, because we lived through it.

"He still doesn't even know why he lacked the ability to give up on his child. Maybe because he was born a maenad himself. Maybe there's just an exception to everything. Like how some people don't respond to anesthesia." She kicked her sandals off in the grass and tucked her legs up under her. An ant had found her instep; she flicked it away.

"He's nursed his grudge for a decade," Nemesia said.

"Time flies when you're plotting vengeance."

"Did he ever do anything to you?"

"Nothing of note." Eden pulled at the thin chain around her neck. "To be fair, he's had a lot on his plate. Worrying about his kid. Keeping an eye on the reformatory. Applying for early retirement. Didn't have to fight very hard for it—they saw his attachment to Iori as a kind of disability."

"Then he got selected for the nobility," said Nemesia.

"Almost immediately after resigning as a maenad. Unbelievable luck. He welcomed Iori home last year. But it's been difficult."

"You've kept tabs on them," Nemesia said, in what she considered to be a remarkable understatement.

"I keep tabs on a lot of people. Goes part and parcel with playing Oddscale."

That evening, Eden climbed to her loft in the cottage. Nemesia sat reading, with Pimiko crouched on the railing like a guardian hawk.

"You're wondering why Sholto never made any big moves before," Eden said, picking up the conversation from hours earlier.

Nemesia had been working her way through an old journal from the scriptorium—tales from a cartographer who'd devoted his life to surveying the border of the Shell. She reinserted the crumpled tissue she'd been using as a bookmark.

"He had other stuff going on, and for three years of the past decade, I was totally out of reach. If I had to guess, he's acting now because he's coming to the end of his term as a noble. He'll lose a lot of influence once he's no longer titled."

Or maybe Eden herself now had more to lose than ever before. She loved magic, despite everything. She was almost thirty-nine.

"Could he suspect you of being Oddscale?"

"It doesn't matter," Eden said.

"How could it not matter?"

"I mocked him at the lowest point of his life, when he didn't even know for sure if his child was alive."

"That's—"

"What's unforgivable is that I had endless chances to make it right. Both before and after our fight. I could have told him Iori was safe. I could have arranged a stealthy visit. But Oddscale's secrecy was the one thing I chose to hold sacred above all else."

She put her hand on Nemesia's book, keeping it closed. "So. Don't get any bright ideas about arranging a reconciliation. We're long past that."

"Noted." It was not in Nemesia's nature to meddle.

Eden seemed satisfied. She played the railing like a piano to say goodnight to Pimiko.

Once the lights went out, she tugged Nemesia's silky robe off one shoulder. Nemesia fixed it, just to see if she would paw absentmindedly at the same place again. (She did.)

"I didn't tell you all this because I expect you to do anything about it," Eden said.

"What could I have done?" Nemesia said honestly.

"I won't underestimate you. And you can't trick me into giving out hints."

The ends of her hair brushed Nemesia's skin. It felt like a taunt. Nemesia shivered, toes curling, then clutched at her to make it stop. She sensed a bottomless relief in the soft punctured-sounding gust of Eden's breath.

Beyond the ceiling beams and the skylight, insects hummed even under the cover of night. It was a noise like the echo of blood in covered ears.

41

Off-Roading

It was much too hot to sleep tangled together. They would start off on opposite sides of the bed, sheets kicked down to their knees.

By morning, their bodies would inevitably migrate into the same tight spot. Someone (usually Eden) would wake first, sweaty and laughing at the stickiness of it all.

Whether in the city or the country, everyone moved slower in August. Nemesia was intensely grateful for the shady shelter of the cottage. Ceiling fans appeared where none had existed before. The Warden dragged floor units out of storage, too.

He and Eden repeatedly holed up in the scriptorium to argue about which feats to include in her application, and what references she might need to provide for them.

"It's all the same," Eden would say fatalistically. "Doesn't matter whether we put in the new bridge I built or the case of the screaming cats. Won't be good enough. You know it. I know it. She knows it."

This last bit came complete with a theatrical gesture at Nemesia, who was pretending to scan the scriptorium shelves.

"There are still two months left," said the Warden.

"Not even. Six weeks at best."

"Regardless, you've got to make a final list. Or you won't have anything to turn in at all. Perhaps you don't mind wasting your time, or my time, but what about hers?"

Now came his turn to fling a dramatic arm in Nemesia's direction. Her primary role in these debates was to stand about looking stoic.

There were two lotus pods posted next to the desk now. They'd moved the receiver and its trough down from the hidden dressing room upstairs.

Eden scowled. "The bridge," she said finally. "I'm prouder of that."

The Warden pushed up his glasses. "The panel might be more familiar with the ruckus caused by those palace cats."

"Depends who's on the panel."

"Precisely. Now, one solid strategy would be to...."

On what was supposed to have been Eden's next day off, someone started screaming in the scriptorium.

Nemesia and the Warden had been outside watering plants. They dashed indoors, straw hats flying.

Eden had slept late for the first time in memory. Even so, she got there first. She stood by the receiving pod with her hair hiding her expression and her robe half off.

Nemesia halted. "Is that scrollworm trying to bite you?"

Eden had already unwound its tattooed skin. Worms would not normally react to handling—no more so than the wooden stave at the end of a handscroll made from silk. This one, however, kept screeching shrilly despite its lack of a larynx.

The Warden strode over, confiscated the worm, and pacified it with a goopy brown solution from his toolkit.

"Trouble at the border," Eden said.

He flashed the worm's contents onto paper. "What kind of trouble?"

"There's a hole in the Shell. Perhaps the largest ever seen."

"You've already worked the maximum number of days you're allowed to go without a break."

"They must be desperate," Eden said. "If they want me there, I guess it's legal to report for duty." She scraped hair out of her face. "How am I supposed to get to the scene?"

In typical fashion, the Warden had already read the message more closely than her. "They've sent an off-roader."

"A what?" said Nemesia.

"An off-road vivitaxi." Eden gave her a worried look. "Want to stay home?"

"It's not an omnibus," Nemesia said stoutly.

She regretted her bravado as soon as they got in. It was excessively large for a vivitaxi, with a blinding golden sheen that made her wonder if the King had donated one of his personal vehicles.

The interior was cool and dry and scentless, in the way of a well-kept vault. The curves of the passenger compartment seemed to apply a warbling effect to sounds from outside. When the Warden waved and shouted to see them off, she could barely understand him.

Then the vivitaxi jumped. Nemesia grabbed at Eden as if grasping the edge of a cliff. Her innards wobbled like big trapped bubbles of air.

Eden, unruffled, murmured about how cushioning magic would protect them every step of the way. And how ordinary little crickets could jump fifty or sixty times their body length ... but an athletic off-roader could make jumps well over two hundred times its own (much greater) length.

Somewhere in the middle of this series of awful heaving leaps, Nemesia opened one eye. They were surrounded by translucent chitin panels like gray-tinted windows.

She retched. She focused frantically on the steady patter of Eden's voice. Eden narrated the look of the sky, the prodigious clouds, the valleys and forests and farms and hillocks and veins of water that fell away rapidly and then surged up to meet them.

"It's as if we're hovering in place—doing nothing—while the land moves beneath us," Eden said. "Just a matter of perspective. Ah, here we are. Look, it's already over."

Nemesia couldn't unfasten herself; Eden had to do it for her. She doddered out of the vivitaxi with Eden gripping her forearms to keep her from falling.

42

The Hole in the Middle of August

THE OFF-ROADER had deposited them at some sort of encampment. Eden handed Nemesia a water bottle, and she drank greedily: it helped settle her stomach.

Meanwhile, a man came to see to their vivitaxi. It trailed away, glittering like a golden idol.

At first glance, the pavilion-style tents reminded Nemesia of an outdoor festival.

Last month, Eden had taken her to see the Warden's old troupe perform a comedic whodunit. The audience held up colorful light sticks to influence plot points and, ultimately, vote on the culprit.

There had been food on skewers, which Eden fanned out like a set of impractical throwing knives. There had been fireworks after dark, and a smog of magic-tinged incense meant to repel biting flies.

The scene before them now was more like a field hospital. Many tents bore the ammonite sign of the Brood. But not all the workers milling around were clerics. Some wore gear marked with a tailless salamander—the universal symbol for second chances, used by all manner of emergency services.

People without visible wounds had been laid out on blankets and tarpaulins. Attendants gave them cold tea and salty crackers and rice balls.

A maenad paced the sunny ground around the perimeter of the open tents. Dandelions sprang up in her wake. Each flower reached full bloom in a matter of seconds, then withered shut, then reopened as a white puff of seeds. The puffs exploded one by one. A fine mist of water burst forth, evaporating to create a cooling breeze.

Other maenads sat dazed among long rows of civilian patients.

Eden walked between tents with a few quick greetings to nurses along the way. Her parasol was already propped on her shoulder. It had a colorful bulls-eye pattern that sucked in gazes like a whirlpool.

She caught Nemesia's eye and gave the parasol an ironic twirl. "Flashy, isn't it?"

Eden understood the opportunity at hand. She would make sure to be seen and remembered.

"You," croaked a voice like an accusatory frog.

"Venerable Abbess!" cried Eden, smiling widely.

Nemesia had never seen the Abbess in summer clothing. Veiny forearms protruded from loose half-length sleeves. Her lower jaw jutted, emphasizing the piercings under her lip. She had a stranglehold on her staff of twined worms.

It hadn't even been seven months since their last meeting. Maybe she seemed shrunken because this was Nemesia's first time facing her beneath open skies, away from cavernous snakelight.

Before briefing them on the situation, she eyed Nemesia up and down. Her only comment: "Hmph."

They were a few minutes' walk from a border settlement; she pointed with her staff until they saw it. The breach was located just past town. It must have happened yesterday, or at most a day earlier.

Minor cracks in the Shell usually went away on their own, healing with time. They were known, however, to have a soporific effect. In this case, the hole was so large that the entire town had been put to sleep.

"Like a gas leak," Eden muttered.

"No big injuries," said the Abbess. "Just scrapes. Some of them remember slowly lying down in the street. Felt like they were being tucked into bed."

Early this morning, a Brood rep had come to take a look at new artifacts from outside. Instead, finding everyone sleeping, he'd put out a call for urgent backup.

Only extinguishers could enter the danger zone without immediately dozing off. Which was why the Abbess herself had come to oversee the evacuation effort.

Eden surveyed the town rooftops. "Any other maenads try to fix it?"

"Several. All failed."

Eden let out a quiet whistle of sympathy.

The Abbess bared her teeth. "The breach looks highly unnatural."

"Do holes in the Shell ever look natural?"

"Most of the time, they're too small to see. A subtle splintering. Like cracks in dry skin."

"An attack from outside?" Eden suggested. "But no soldiers came pouring through."

"Nothing of the sort," the Abbess said grouchily. She warned them that Nemesia would have to constantly stave off the ambient sleeping spell—without suppressing Eden's magic. A finicky task.

"Go with the blessing of the Snake," she ordered. She tended to make blessings sound like a curse.

Orange flags marked the area where anyone without a Brood escort would grow too sleepy to follow instructions. Eden took Nemesia's hand as they walked past.

Even animals weren't wholly immune. Dark churning circles writhed on a paved road, like geometrically perfect swirls of ink. The circles were all made up of ants in constant motion.

Nemesia concentrated on the stones of the street. Yellow, white, off-white, yellow-brown. As if they were treading on teeth the size of bricks.

They reached the other side of town in twenty minutes. Yards and fields gave way to wild brush, which should have been rife with insects (and toads, and digging creatures, and mudlings). But not one single cicada chirped in a bid for attention.

Eden made a face. A broad swathe of low-growing foliage flattened to form a path for them, as if someone had taken a huge box and laboriously shoved it inch by inch along the ground.

They proceeded down the damp, fragrant road of pulverized grass.

The repulsive field around the Shell had become visible, almost tangible, a silver undulating mist.

Eden coughed. She waved her parasol about in annoyance. The obscuring fog dissipated as if blown away by a fan.

The air was still denser than water, hard to wade through. Nemesia's thighs burned. Eden wasn't breathing lightly, either. Something told them to turn back, to avert their eyes, to sleep it off.

It was much cooler here than on the sun-heated streets. But the chill felt more sickly than soothing. They trudged through a stand of stunted trees that had dropped all their leaves in a fresh green carpet, brighter than newly grown moss, almost glistening.

The Shell reared up before them like a broken mirror.

As usual, its visibility decreased as it arced toward the sky. The highest parts were presumably still intact.

"Looks like a piece peeled off a hardboiled egg," Eden said.

The gap—a jagged hole—started right where the Shell met solid ground.

The Abbess had told them to look for a place where the reflections stopped. She hadn't told them what they would see on the other side.

Wilderness. A desert. But not a wasteland.

The ground was a light sandy color. Spiky shrubs grew in patches that made the landscape appear to be balding, interspersed with austere trees crowned in porcupine-quill leaves. They cast almost no shade.

A mote in the sky might have been a faraway bird. A mountain range jutted from the earth like a naked lower jaw: teethy thrusting columns of rock with near-vertical sides.

Eden pointed out more strange formations in the foreground.

"Imperial cannons," Nemesia said automatically. "And railguns." And other esoteric artillery, all half-buried.

"How do you know?"

"I'm in the Brood."

So much weaponry. It might have been abandoned as the last remnants of the Blessed Empire retreated inside the realm of the Snake. It might have been stationed there later, in futile hopes of assaulting the newborn Shell.

Time has no place.

Disembodied thoughts trickled through her.

Time has no border.

The roots of time went much deeper and further than the land inside the Shell. The roots of time bound the entire world, parts known and unknown. One day the Snake, having consumed all there was to consume, would encircle the world and replace the roots it continually ate.

A shell is a mere beginning.

Eden leaned back, scrutinizing the upper edge of the rift.

"A hardboiled egg," she said again. "But snake eggs are nothing like poultry eggs, are they? They're usually leathery. And long, like cocoons. Some snakes don't lay eggs at all.

"This is only a metaphorical Shell. Still—makes me wonder how much of it we could peel away in one go…"

Eden chuckled dryly at her own joke.

What was there to laugh about? Eggshells were meant to be broken. It was just a matter of when. And in the eyes of the looping god that ruled this place, *when* was a very flexible notion indeed.

Why not here? Why not now?

Nemesia's old guard Chameleon would give up years of his future in service of the Brood. Below, it had already happened. Above, it hadn't yet come to pass. Two sides of the same coin. A question of angles.

From one perspective, the Shell was more or less intact. From another perspective, it hadn't finished forming yet. From still another perspective, it had hatched long ago. All those perspectives belonged equally to the Snake That Ate the Roots of Time.

Tilt her head back like Eden, and she could see more than a single angular opening. She could see every crack that had ever formed or ever would form in the Shell. Most would come and go without anyone noticing.

One day the Shell would finish incubating. One day it would crumble away into fragments and vanish, no longer needed.

Why wait?

There came a muffled noise. Eden's parasol tumbled down. It landed with the handle pointing skyward, then tilted like a spinning top.

Nemesia stumbled. Eden's arms were around her, crushing her. She couldn't see the broken aperture in the Shell anymore. Eden had turned her away.

"Your eyes," Eden said, squeezing her harder.

"My ... eyes?"

"I've seen you with snake eyes. But not like this. Not since the first time we met."

"Below?"

"Above. When you ordered me to be Oddscale."

Pressed in so close, she felt smaller than usual. Nemesia's arms tentatively circled her back.

She touched the thin line of the lucky necklace under Eden's collar.

"You have to leave," Eden told her.

"You said I can go anywhere I want." *No forbidden rooms in this house.*

"Something else is taking over you. Seeping in, or seeping out." She held Nemesia as if she could physically stop it.

"You can't do anything alone," Nemesia said reasonably. "You'll fall asleep."

"Make the Abbess send someone to carry me out."

"This is your last chance to—"

"There's a whole month left." Eden shrugged a little. She still hadn't let go. "I don't care if I miss a chance to pad my resume. I can live without magic. I don't want to—but I can. I can live without a lot of things."

She pulled back just enough for Nemesia to see her. Her voice was immaculately controlled. But the stain of magic in her eyes looked feral.

"You're about to lose yourself," she said.

"You're one to talk!"

Nemesia lost her breath as she spoke. A cold, shocking clarity enveloped her. Eden wouldn't hesitate to send her away. Eden would instantly give up on the hole in the Shell.

She would turn her back on it without even trying.

"Wait." Her voice cracked horribly. "Eden, wait."

Eden waited.

Now Nemesia was the one drawing her close.

Her cheek against Eden's cheek. Short nails digging at her back. The smell of Eden's hair. The trampled path they had walked to get here.

She reeled herself back into her body, into reality, into the present, all the way down to the palms of her hands and the soles of her feet. Eden breathed in her arms, trying not to move.

She turned her face up.

"How are my eyes?"

Eden studied her. "Like Vesper in a decent mood."

"Is that an improvement?"

"It's closer to when I met you Below."

"Don't make me leave," Nemesia said. "Please. The worst already passed."

"What if you start teetering again?"

She clung to Eden's sleeves. "I won't look at it. I won't even turn around."

"If you do, I'm getting you out of here."

"Just hurry up and deal with the hole."

They glared at each other. Eden laughed in a huff of breath without sound. She picked up her parasol.

Nemesia kept her gaze averted from the Shell. As Eden worked, she sensed a great coalescing of magic behind her. Her neck tingled sporadically; so did the beds of her nails.

"Don't patch the gap with power alone," she advised. "The Shell can eat more magic than you'll ever dredge up in your life."

Eden paused. They stood side by side, facing opposite directions. She had an arm around the front of Nemesia's shoulders.

"What should I do, then?"

"The Shell always heals over time. The edges want to come together ... it's just going very slowly. Accelerate it. Be the wind, not the sails."

Nemesia stopped, trying to figure out if this statement made sense. "I get it."

"You do?"

"Think like the Snake, yes? You're right. The broken part wants its time to pass faster." Eden tensed with effort. "I'll just give it a good—hard—push."

Layers of time ground together with the sound of a thousand forks scraping a thousand plates. There rose a smoky, choking scent like malfunctioning machinery and burning grass.

Eden began to say her name—a cry, a plea. Nemesia extinguished her as if shoving her out of a moving vehicle.

The acrid smell dispersed. The broken squeaking ceased.

Eden sagged. She closed her parasol and planted its tip in the ground like a cane.

"Look," she said.

The Shell was whole: a seamless unbroken mirror reflecting lush thickets and leggy wildflowers and prematurely denuded trees. A green panorama devoid—as always—of animate life. No invaders had broken in, and nothing had hatched.

43

Those Who Never Sleep

AFTER EDEN REPAIRED the Shell, a Brood team went to confirm that the oozing soporific magic had cleared out.

Then the long-suffering evacuation workers had to do everything in reverse, escorting all the locals back home. Nemesia took detailed notes for an entry in the town logbook.

"Didn't think you could resolve it today," the Abbess begrudgingly told Eden. "Well done."

Nemesia—who had been drinking from Eden's refilled water bottle—nearly choked. The Abbess never praised anyone lightly.

"My wife gave good advice." Eden smugly patted her bicep. "All I did was provide some magical muscle."

The Abbess whacked Eden on the shin with her staff.

"Ow! What the—"

"Humility doesn't suit you."

They helped take down the tents and pack up supplies. A group of reenergized locals began planning to throw a feast for weary first responders. Given the belated start, it looked as though the cooking and drinking and revelry would keep going till morning.

Eden lingered just long enough to leave everyone with an impression of her dazzling smile and her vivid bulls-eye umbrella, which she let the crowd pass around like a holy relic.

The golden vivitaxi was waiting again. Garbled hoots of applause fell away below them as it bounded off. Nemesia shut her eyes. Eden, sapped, limply massaged her clenched hands.

The Warden had stayed up late to welcome them back. He seemed tickled to hear that they'd seen the Abbess.

"This will clinch your application," he said to Eden.

"Sure hope so. Let's not get overconfident."

Nemesia stumbled off to take a long, mindless bath.

She returned to her room clad only in fresh drawers and a towel.

Eden lay sprawled diagonally on her bed, accompanied by a smattering of books and scrolls. A gooseneck lamp peered over her shoulder, trying to follow along as she read. She flipped pages without much apparent interest. "These are my books, from my shelves, and yet you hid them like contraband," she said.

The half-open windows let in a restless nighttime breeze.

Eden rolled onto her back, holding up a thick tome with both hands. The lamp craned its neck to keep a spotlight on the cover.

"Tales from the Membrane, Volume 6: Memoirs of a Traveling Veterinarian," she read. "Made his living going from one border village to another. How adventurous!

"Some interesting stories here. There's one about a mystery illness striking camelids—a sleeping sickness. Or maybe the culprit was gas from an abandoned mine...."

She sat up. She set *Tales from the Membrane* down with a thump. The lamplight swiveled around wildly, unsure what to focus on next. Finally it settled on an empty swathe of wall.

"So much covert research," she said admiringly.

"Bedtime reading," Nemesia corrected. "I'm not a scholar."

"You were trying to learn more about cracks in the Shell."

Nemesia wrung the ends of her hair in her towel. Her pulse floundered. Guilt welled up in her so readily, even when nothing went wrong.

Eden spoke again, unbothered by her lack of response. "You quite literally made an opening for me to seize greatness. You would've been hopping mad if I threw it all away, huh?"

"I did nothing."

"You called in a favor."

Nemesia turned her back and tied on a sleeping top. She felt Eden's gaze as a hot light between her shoulder blades. Like the lidless yellow stare of the lamp.

"It was well thought out," Eden told her. "Very dramatic. Frightening. But no one got badly hurt, and there were plenty of people to witness our triumphant return."

Having run out of reasons to delay, Nemesia folded herself down onto the sunken bed. The top of the mattress lay flush with the wooden floor.

Eden pushed her trove of books and scrolls into a corner. She reached around Nemesia to bop the lamp. It curled its long neck in like a sleeping heron, then shut off.

Splotchy darkness slowly yielded to familiar shapes. As Nemesia's eyes adjusted, she located Eden's nose, the edge of her ear, the dim gloss of eyes and teeth.

"Did you give them anything in exchange?"

There was no smile in Eden's voice.

"Nothing," Nemesia said.

"You didn't make any promises?"

"No." She wasn't lying.

"They wouldn't just volunteer to help. They aren't running a charity."

"You've been a good host," Nemesia insisted. "They're being good guests. They don't want repayment."

Eden smothered a laugh with her fist. "Somehow, I don't think Vesper would have felt very cooperative if I went swaggering up to her and asked her to throw me a bone."

That was hard to argue with. "Maybe not."

"You pleaded on my behalf. Without my knowledge. Guess they found that more compelling. Or—"

Nemesia stiffened. Eden pretended not to notice. She kept speaking in the same smooth, proficient voice. She could've made a living as a master of ceremonies.

"Or," she said, "they agreed for diplomatic reasons. Because you were the one who came and asked."

Even though they were in shadow, Nemesia wanted to pull the sheets up over her face. "They might have some misconceptions about what it means to be a Bride of the Snake."

"Don't suppose you ever tried to correct them. How naughty."

"It's not—!" She lowered her voice. "They think I'm more important than I really am. More—"

"Unique? Singular?"

Eden's breath touched her temple. A hand glided along the skin of her back. Her voice dried up somewhere near the entrance to her throat, which jerked futilely, even though there was nothing to swallow.

"But you are," Eden whispered, as if confessing a secret. "You're the only wife I'll ever have."

Some time later, they lay listening to wind prowl along the sides of the house. "You made our foreign friends swear to keep the townspeople safe," Eden said.

There were things Nemesia would never have uttered if it wasn't already over. If she weren't already relaxed to the point of melting.

"I was worried," she admitted. "They didn't seem like they'd lose much sleep over tragic accidents."

"They don't sleep at all. They don't need to. But they wouldn't break their word to you, either."

After Eden drifted off, Nemesia kept watch for errant dreams. Once it seemed safe, she crawled out of bed, padded silently down the hall, and crept back up to the turret.

She didn't expect acknowledgment. She didn't expect an answer. Still, she wanted to say something. After all, they could have refused her.

Last month, she'd gone up the turret alone. She'd peppered Vesper and Char with all kinds of questions about how they infiltrated the Shell. They'd described making a slit in it, as if slashing a tent with a knife. It was such a fine cut that it started healing over before they both slipped fully through.

She'd asked if they could punch a much bigger hole. A hole that would take decades to heal on its own. She'd asked them to do it by early September, but not to tell her when or where. It would seem more authentic if she found out at the same time as everyone else.

The August breeze plucked at strands of hair around her face. She held the railing of the turret balcony and murmured her thanks.

No one said anything in reply. The bushy roof rustled and creaked like a huge fidgety beast.

As she turned to duck back inside, chains clanked delicately in the dark of night. A low stirring like laughter, so brief that she might have imagined it.

44

The Otterdog Masquerade

EDEN WANTED TO submit her application immediately. "I fixed a giant hole in the Shell," she said. "I saved an entire town. Let's tack that on as my crowning achievement. Won't do anything more impressive within the next couple weeks."

To Nemesia's surprise, the Warden convinced her to wait.

A week later, they received word that the King wished to award her a prestigious royal medal. An event called the Otterdog Masquerade would be held at the palace grounds in mid-September. Eden was to present herself there to be honored.

"Otterdogs, hm?" said the Warden. "Maybe he'll give you Best in Show."

"Hah."

The worst of the summer heat had passed. For a time, they had all gone around in sheer overrobes. Solid fabric now became more appealing.

For the Otterdog Masquerade, Eden donned an eye-catching robe in one of the looser styles she tended to favor. Nearly every inch was covered in brilliant stencil-dyed mountains and clouds—red, purple, blue, yellow, gray, green. Water flowed beneath, rendered in vibrant snaking lines.

She and Nemesia both wore black surgical masks. Everyone in attendance came similarly protected.

This show was not the sort of masquerade where anyone would attempt to hide their identity. Nose coverage was advised because some featured animals were known to be unbelievably stinky.

The titular otterdogs turned out to be a type of low-slung lapdog frequently seen in Yolk City. They smelled like your average domestic canine.

But the Otterdog Masquerade was meant to celebrate all manner of long-bodied mammals.

River otters and miniature seals gamboled in artificial streams and pools. Part of the gardens had transformed into a water park built expressly for their use.

Elsewhere, zoologists introduced curious guests to weasels, stoats, ferrets, minks, and rarer creatures. Some were plated with keratinous scales; some had fur in banded or blotchy patterns like a snake.

The sickly sweet scent of early autumn flowers clashed with intense animal musk and trails of cloying incense. The incense was meant to help mitigate the overall funk, but Nemesia privately thought it had the opposite effect.

After an ill-advised attempt to sip from a thimble-sized cup of rice wine, she kept her mask on at all times. Magic in the lining made the air she breathed smell no mustier than a rainy day.

"My beautiful wife," Eden said without irony, introducing her to various people that she had almost certainly met before.

Eyes twinkled at Nemesia over masks of every color. Inexplicably, she felt more at ease when all these semi-strangers were reduced to half a face.

Someone who might have been Daiya Anis toasted her from afar. Near the temporary water park, Daiya Iori and another young maenad intently observed sinuous otters.

There weren't any other working maenads around. Just those two and Eden. Magic guttered in them like a trapped flame, although few passers-by took notice. It wouldn't be polite to stare at people's innards.

Iori's hair had grown longer and looser than before, down to the nape of his neck. He seemed just as quiet as he'd been at the Snake Moth Gala, but subtly more comfortable—his shoulders less tense, his head less bowed.

Nemesia and Eden let him be. They brushed their way through whispering aisles of ornamental grass. The stalks had reached full bloom, forming ethereal floating halos of pink and orange and lavender, forever dyed in the light of an aging day. Each feathery clump splayed out like bursting fireworks.

Eden touched Nemesia's hand and looked at her as if there was no one else in the entire garden. Her mask should have rendered her inscrutable, but instead it only made her more obvious. Her eyes were deep brown, unwavering, without any spark of scarlet magic.

The grass bowed and hissed, and expensively clad people glided by. Cloth masks muffled a banal comment, a tittering laugh. Dogs yapped madly in the distance. Eden canted her head as if conceding a point.

They watched spunky little otterdogs scamper through an agility course. They clapped politely as other otterdogs received prizes determined by exceedingly obscure matters of physical conformation.

Then it came time to give out the Royal Medal of Benediction. (This one was reserved for humans, not canines.)

There were three honorees this evening. An outgoing nobleman being recognized for his charitable efforts. A surveyor who had made an illustrious career out of mapping every single public wormhole in the city. And one maenad: Kuchinashi Eden.

About half an hour before sunset, officials came to whisk Eden away. Nemesia ensconced herself at the back of the dahlia-filled garden where the ceremony was scheduled to take place.

The King wouldn't appear in person; a representative would present the medals instead. No one would expect the royal body to reveal itself in front of so many people.

"She looks happy."

A man's voice. Nemesia needed a moment to place it.

She looks happy.

A non sequitur: Eden was nowhere in sight.

They stood side by side, facing forward, like strangers in an elevator. Sholto wore silk brocade in very deep shades of gray. He remained as still as a decorative rock.

"I've decided how to use you," he said through the mask over his mouth. For all the emotion he showed, they might as well have been discussing the coloration of well-bred otterdogs.

No one was interested in them; no one was listening. People fawned over the dahlias as they trickled in and searched for seats. Their murmuring merged into a meaningless susurration—a waterfall in the background, washing away whatever Sholto might say to her. Or whatever she might say back.

"K. Eden hasn't applied for her extension yet," he remarked. His mask made it seem as though his lips weren't moving at all. "Let me guess. She'll send it in tomorrow, having joined the illustrious ranks of medal recipients. Very strategic."

"How do you…"

"Has that Warden of hers managed to ferret out any committee members?"

"No," Nemesia said, and with that, she knew what was coming next. It clicked into place like the secret rotating segments of Eden's ceiling beams.

"The panel has slots for current and retired maenads," Sholto said. "There are also slots set aside for nobles, so I had multiple options. I pulled strings to get the seat reserved for a former maenad. Seemed fitting."

"And your son—"

"Didn't take much maneuvering. He had virtually no competition. There are few things your typical maenad hates more than going to meetings."

He looked at her briefly, as if noticing a common bird. Nothing worthy of prolonged study.

"Did you know," he said conversationally, "that the committee has to come to a unanimous decision?"

Nemesia blinked at the dahlias. They were as showy as Eden's robe—a robe she'd chosen to compensate for wearing a mask. She would stand up there, brighter than anyone, and she would be unforgettable.

"What do you want me to do?" She said it plainly. No dithering.

"You'll come with me," he said.

"When?"

"Tonight."

"Is this a kidnapping?"

"Told you everything, did she?" His voice was too empty for bitterness. "You'll follow me of your own accord. You might find it quite comfortable. Like a five-month vacation."

Five months. He meant to hold her until mid-February: the end of the year. The end of her sabbatical.

"No," she said.

Sholto betrayed no surprise. "If you wish. Her application will be denied."

"Four months," she told him. "Not five."

"It isn't negotiable."

"She still has to get through the interview," Nemesia said. "If I disappear first, she'll be distracted."

She regretted this the moment it came out of her mouth. He could create reasons for her to leave—even if the very act of leaving might ruin Eden's chances. He could cut funding to the Brood. He could target the Warden.

Did he see himself as a gentleman? What standards would he hold himself to? What lines wouldn't he cross?

"Leave a note for her," Sholto said, implacable. "Say you're in good hands. Say you never want to see her again. Word it however you like."

"That won't appease her." Nemesia twisted at her fingers as if turning invisible rings. The other figures in the garden were blurs of draped fabric at the periphery of her vision.

"I'll go wherever you want," she said, "on the day of the interview. Not a moment sooner."

Her thoughts kept doubling back. She wasn't supposed to be in a position to care. Should she have tried to deny it? Whatever he saw in her, she could've said it was all an act. She could've said it didn't matter one whit to her if Eden forever lost the right to use magic.

"The day of the interview," he agreed, though he had the power to drive a harder bargain.

Lights winked on at the front of the garden. The seated audience cheered. The standing audience swiveled forward. In the moments before the ceremony started, Sholto quietly told her what to do and where to go.

45

The Autumn House

THE FACELESS COMMITTEE booked Eden's interview for early October, two weeks after receiving her written application.

Nemesia didn't tell Eden or the Warden about Sholto's new plot. What could they do? Defying him would invite obvious repercussions. If either of them took action as Oddscale, they might as well whip the scarf off and confess their identity.

Was that Sholto's objective—to draw Oddscale out of hiding?

The panel was set to convene in an old government building near the noble district. Nemesia said she would accompany Eden to the city (for moral support).

She woke very early, up in Eden's loft, and found herself hugging all the blankets. She must have stolen them in the night.

Eden was, unusually, still sleeping.

Nemesia slipped away to get washed and dressed. Pimiko, who had followed her, squatted balefully on a windowsill.

"Don't say anything," Nemesia told her.

She'd weighed the pros and cons of leaving a message with Vesper and Char. It would be better not to owe them too many favors.

She took out her tattoo kit, which had gone unused for several months now. No need to search for scrap paper when she still had dormant scrollworms handy.

A sepia curl of sliced-off worm skin....

There would be unfortunate parallels to Oddscale's kidnapping letters. Well—as long as they found Nemesia's note within a day or so, the Warden could flash-transfer it to more a readable medium.

Anyway, she didn't have a whole lot to say.

She didn't want to leave any hints about her planned destination.

They'd see right through her if she made some overwrought attempt at false cruelty.

How much might her departure even matter? It would be embarrassing if people started saying that Eden's wife had run out on her. It would be inconvenient if Eden no longer had a top-flight extinguisher at her fingertips.

But Eden had weathered far worse.

She didn't think about how Eden had reacted to the snakeskin pendant—just a trinket, something anyone could have bought at the market. She didn't engage in pointless speculation. All she could truly claim to know was herself.

She couldn't inscribe gushing goodbyes. She couldn't inscribe even modest words of affection. Her hand locked up and refused to cooperate.

She wrote only this:

Wait for me. Wait as long as you need to. One day we'll meet again.

She placed it like a dead leaf on her neatly made bed. She hadn't slept here in days; she'd practically moved into Eden's loft.

Around the corner from City Hall, Eden stopped and bent to kiss her. Harsh-voiced urban birds squawked from a nearby roof.

"Wish me luck," Eden said.

She was dressed rather soberly, and she clutched a black folding umbrella like a nightstick.

Nemesia touched the chain around her neck. A discreet thread of silver. "You're already wearing all the luck I could give you."

"I'll stun them, won't I?"

"Of course you will."

"With amazement, I hope, rather than horror. Nemesia..."

"Yes?"

"Thank you for coming."

Another quick peck of a kiss.

She watched with folded hands as Eden climbed to the entrance. Her shadow lay staggered across the steps.

Once Eden and her shadow had gone out of sight, Nemesia shuttered her thoughts. Her feet ached, though she had long since grown accustomed to walking everywhere in shoes.

She carried herself to an address deep in the noble district, where every house looked different from the one beside it. Monumental concrete cubes hunched next to peaked roofs of green-glazed tile.

A woman in a high-collared suit shepherded her past a moon gate, then through a dizzying string of private wormholes. In a suburb she had never seen before, she rode a vivitaxi in circles. At least it wasn't the jumping kind.

Then came more garden gates and sliding doors and stairs to nowhere topped with secret portals. By the end, she understood why no one had bothered to blindfold her. She couldn't begin to guess where she'd landed.

Her escort delivered her to a one-story complex somewhere on the distant outskirts of Yolk City. She thought she saw a far-off shape resembling the palace, but it might have been a mirage.

It was a compound of extraordinary harmony. A timeless specimen of regional architecture, more like a temple than a regular house. It might have been constructed during the twilight of the Blessed Empire—or perhaps during the past decade.

Covered walkways ran through austere gardens. The ground beneath was carpeted in moss and crystalline gravel. Elsewhere, it gave way to still clear ponds and hushed streams.

Trees leaned steeply, casting reflections in the water. Others grew in bent zigzag shapes. They were spaced out like art pieces in an outdoor museum.

Servants nodded when she first stepped in, but after that, they ignored her. They said that Sholto would come by later.

As summer stretched into fall, Nemesia had more or less stopped feeding him information. What was there to say? If he had a problem with her lack of output, he could find a way to let her know.

He'd had them watched, she thought. In border towns and in the city. When they visited flea markets, and when they went to see plays. He would know about everything Nemesia had spoken of with his sister Anis, too.

She thrust Daiya Sholto out of her mind. She resumed her study of her immediate surroundings.

She'd left her shoes at the entrance. She paced the verandas around each building perimeter, and the wooden paths that connected one structure to the next.

The interlocking layered eaves and rafters and high coffered ceilings reminded her of the throne room. Here most were bare wood, unpainted.

Inside, light filtered through paper-screen walls and doors. Beyond the hardwood corridors, most floors were tiled with pliant woven mats.

Hanging scrolls displayed ink brush paintings—predominantly in shades of black and gray, but with occasional hints of color. A red-brown bird. A muted purple iris. She quizzed herself on the names of artfully drawn plants. Paulownia, flowering kudzu....

At last she settled down on one of the verandas facing a courtyard.

She used a trick that the Abbess had discouraged her from deploying Below. Too perilous.

She hadn't used it at all in Eden's house, either. She hadn't wanted to make anything go by quicker, not even the nights when she woke with a gasp and struggled to fall back asleep.

She would lie there listening to Eden breathe. With other senses, she would hear the house breathe as well, centuries of magic coursing through its walls like fluid through arteries.

Sometimes Pimiko would creep over to take a peek. She'd felt an odd camaraderie with this voiceless crabantula that scuttled around like a monster in the dead of night. Neither of them wanted to disturb Eden's sleep.

Now Nemesia mentally placed herself Below, wandering through familiar halls. In her mind, she walked barefoot. The snakeflint floor was warm and spongy. She conceived of herself as a solitary blood cell in an empty vein.

One step. In that single step, she imagined five minutes passing. Another step. Ten minutes passed. Her own blood quickened. She envisioned water lapping at the shore of a lake, faster and faster. She envisioned clouds whipping across a sky without anything to stop them—no fences, no Shell.

Step, step, step.

She opened her eyes.

Those were someone else's footsteps.

If the angle of the sun was anything to go by, three or four hours had passed. Her stomach growled softly in surprise. Her thighs were excruciatingly stiff.

She looked up.

Daiya Sholto looked down at her. He didn't sit.

"How was it?" she asked.

"The interview? K. Eden certainly ingratiated herself."

"You didn't—"

"It went as well as she could have hoped. I merely sat back and listened."

He stood with the brightest part of the sky behind his head. She could hardly see his face at all.

"Of course," he said, "I could be lying."

He gestured for her to rise. "This is our autumn house."

"Your what?"

"Nobles have a residence for each major season—and sometimes minor seasons, too. Never used this one as much as the others. Autumn always passes too quickly."

He cast a critical look at the contours of the landscaping. A few servants swept halfheartedly at fallen leaves.

"Offered this place to my son, but he didn't take it. Chose maenad housing. Perhaps that was wiser. He'd have needed to move out by the end of the year."

"You'll lose access?"

"To all noble properties, yes."

He made a disinterested motion at the sweepers. "Walk out whenever you like. No one will intervene. If you take a single step beyond the outer walls of the garden—"

"I understand," Nemesia said flatly. "But I came empty-handed."

"We'll provide all needed amenities."

Did Daiya Iori know about this? Probably not, she decided. Through sheer force of personality, Sholto might push Iori to join him in denying Eden's application. He would justify it one way or another. He wouldn't complicate things by telling his son the full story.

Sholto showed her how to take shortcuts around the estate. Certain sliding doors served as wormholes leading to the opposite side of the compound.

On most doors, the latticework was composed of sharp ninety-degree corners. Around the portals, it took on a curvy worm-like appearance.

"Eden might come for me," Nemesia said.

"Despite your best efforts?"

"She's very perceptive."

"If she shows up, you'll turn her away."

"She might not—"

"Has she fallen so far that she would drag you off even if you try to refuse her? Then she deserves to be stripped of her magic.

"Or will she turn on me instead? If she lifts a hand against me—or any of my employees—that, too, would disqualify her. In anyone's eyes.

"Or"—his voice became dangerously pleasant—"will she show up with a magical scarf? Has Oddscale ever been in the business of stealing back runaway wives?"

He didn't seem to genuinely believe Eden was Oddscale. But even if he meant it as a crass joke, he'd stumbled too close to the truth.

"This wasn't your original plan," Nemesia said.

He gave her what might have been a curious look, coming from anyone else. His eyes were like black chips of stone set in his too-small face.

"You changed your mind midway through," she said. "When? At the gala? You told me to just keep living my life with her. No other requests."

He sniffed. "K. Eden became enamored of you much faster than I could ever have guessed."

It felt as if the floorboards buckled underfoot. Nemesia didn't trust herself to say a word in reply.

Sholto brought her back to the central building, where his shoes awaited in the stone-paved entrance. Somewhere out of sight, servants were still sweeping away at already-clean corners.

"You must see that I've done you a substantial favor," he said.

She recovered her voice. "I married Eden as a favor to *you*."

"That was a business deal. The Bitten Brood has reaped the rewards. Your Abbess, your guards—they'll continue living in style. Just in time, too. Next year, I won't have so much wealth to spread around."

"I won't thank you," Nemesia said.

"It's been a burden for you, hasn't it?" He sounded almost sympathetic.

"I knew what I was getting into."

"You knew you were getting married. You saw it as a two-sided sham. You didn't think she would let herself care. You can't answer in kind, and it troubles you—you hold yourself back. You're a better weapon against her than any scheme I might have hatched on my own."

Brooms scraped stone. The noise of it grated deep in her ears. All her thoughts kept plucking the same insistent note.

What does he know? What does he know?

What does he know?

She must have said something, because Daiya Sholto spoke in answer.

"I've seen the way she looks at you." There was a curious lumbering grace in how he slipped on his shoes. "She wants more than you've given her. You've kept her waiting, wagging her tail."

Inchoate rage hit Nemesia like a hammer to the head, then immediately died away. Nothing he had uttered was false.

He slid open the last screen door. "She taunted me when Iori was missing. Later, she vanished for years without a word to anyone. Now she'll experience the other side of that. Poetic, isn't it?"

46

People of Leisure

DAIYA SHOLTO'S autumn house was empty except for Nemesia and the domestic staff. It felt like living at a ghost inn with no other guests.

The servants helped orient her if she got lost, but they refused to give her their names or answer questions. Her guards Below had been more personable, anonymous costumes and all.

Nemesia had the run of the place. It gave her the illusion that she was sneaking around in a historical estate maintained for tours. The Daiyas hadn't left behind any personal articles.

She didn't entertain thoughts of walking out. Sholto had—allegedly—refrained from disrupting Eden's interview. But the committee might take months to deliver a verdict. He could raise objections at any point.

Somewhere out there, Eden was turning thirty-nine.

Each night, a maid laid out a lavish floor bed. Each night, Nemesia wondered if Eden's dreams were leaking, spreading, searching for something out of reach. Had she retreated to the nest house to sleep alone?

Only someone with an inhuman sensitivity to magic could mentally grope their way across the entire city, like a bird of prey seeking Eden's signature. Nemesia knew better than to try.

Some cold part of her thought Sholto was right. He had done her a favor. Her provisional marriage was going to have to end eventually. At least his master plan didn't involve physical violence.

If anything, she fretted that Sholto would open his eyes and realize he hadn't done nearly enough.

How could his years of resentment be satisfied by hiding away a fake wife who was never supposed to have been anything more than a stage prop? How could he, of all people, compare that to the terror of losing your only child?

Even worse—at the time, everyone else who once cared for Iori had been neutered of their fears. The Snake spared them, and left Sholto to steep in panic alone.

Perhaps taking Nemesia felt more honorable than, say, threatening the Warden. After all, Nemesia had been personally implicated from the moment she and the Abbess began bargaining with Sholto. The Warden had never done anything wrong.

She asked for writing utensils. She received paper and pens rather than needles and scrollworms. She attempted to compose a letter to Eden. She could send it out next year, after returning Below. But she kept crumpling and discarding her drafts.

Extraneous memories bobbed up every time she knelt at a borrowed writing table and tried to wring out all the things she had never been able to put into words. Her own feelings hid like eels in silt, but Eden's voice came through loud and clear.

Once, while they peeked at a street of fancy residences, Eden had said: "Nobles are people of leisure. They've got lots of time to stew over old grievances."

"Is that a common hobby?"

"Oh yes. Definitely one of the top ten hobbies in the city. Maybe top five."

Nemesia gave up on letter-writing. She roamed in widening circles through the gardens and the various wings of the house.

The deciduous trees planted here and there were still mostly green. Burning bush shrubs and clumped grasses led the way in turning red. They formed collective streaks of color that, from above, might look like esoteric brushstrokes. What words would they spell?

The only part of the garden she'd been barred from entering was a corner with a tall quince tree. Misshapen head-sized globes hung like lanterns among its boughs. Sholto's crew had surrounded it with wooden barricades and handwritten warning signs.

This felt rather excessive; the yellow-green fruit didn't look ripe enough to drop.

Indoors, the complex had virtually no visible furniture. Everything was meant to be put away as soon as it lost its purpose, from the bedding that vanished each morning to the trays with legs used to serve her meals.

It was ingenious, really, how much storage space lurked below trapdoors in the floor, and in closets concealed by wall panels. The building seemed ideal for hosting giant banquets. The staff could open partitions to merge rooms. They could haul out an endless number of dining trays and bedrolls.

But there was no one to entertain except Nemesia. Having all this space to herself felt curiously like being Below.

The rooms were mostly interchangeable, anyway. They could be reconfigured on a whim, too, by adding or removing long rows of sliding doors. Guests were supposed to enjoy the interplay of light and shadow from the garden, the serenity of bare square spaces, the sound of water trickling over rocks.

Each night, serpentine lights uncoiled from the ceiling. They resembled the string you might pull to turn on a lamp, except there was no lamp attached—just the string itself, like a burning filament.

Sometimes they came down rather late. On cloudy evenings, she had to squint to make out her dinner. The servants seemed convinced that the snakes could not be persuaded to descend any earlier. They adhered to an internal clock that would brook no argument from mere humans.

If Nemesia were a head taller, she would have bumped those hanging strings. As things stood, she didn't have to worry about getting tangled. But they brushed at her mind regardless, fishing up thoughts of bygone days.

Up in the shelter of her loft, Eden had asked about Tanyu. An unfamiliar urgency permeated her voice. When was this—a month ago? Two? Summer felt as distant as childhood.

"I don't get why she was so reluctant to confront the Snake," Eden said. "What would it actually do if it denied her petition? Eat her? Laugh at her?"

"Most people don't feel ready to look divinity in the face."

"Sometimes we all have to do things we're uncomfortable with," Eden said acidly. "No one asked my opinion on getting shunted off to the reformatory."

"I think ... Tanyu may have been more afraid of success," said Nemesia.

"That doesn't make any sense."

It was easier to speak about these things in the dark. "What if the Snake gave her to me—and then, a couple years later, we fell out of love? What if we broke up?"

"What if you did? Would the Snake have cursed her? Would you have been forced to become a Bride again?"

"No," Nemesia conceded. "It doesn't work like that."

"Right? So what's the problem?"

"It's hard to take things lightly when there's a god looking over your shoulder. The whole notion of proving your love—that would make anyone think hard about their future. She would've felt responsible for me and my happiness for the rest of my life. Like a guarantor sworn to the Snake."

"But you're fine with Daiya Sholto petitioning for you?" Eden said, outraged. "In lieu of giving you a proper salary?"

"I don't necessarily expect him to succeed."

"*I* would succeed."

Nemesia had choked on her next words.

Eden rolled over, snuggling her back up against Nemesia, as if that was that. She didn't demand any sort of response.

47

The Scarf Wielder

She hadn't been at the autumn house all that long. A week—maybe two weeks? She kept using her secret trick to make the flow of time feel faster. As a result, she soon lost track.

The first change she noticed was an unusual stir among the servants.

It was close to dinnertime, and someone was cooking. She smelled vegetables searing, followed by a bloom of sweet sauce that gave her a powerful hankering for the Warden's eel bowls.

Voices echoed in the corridors. Several figures in the usual high-collared uniform came to shepherd her through a series of identical rooms. She thought she recognized the one where they stopped: here she had tried and failed to write letters.

There was no low desk anymore. No pens or blank sheets. Just a flat embroidered floor cushion, as impeccably square as the walls around it. Nemesia knelt there, a prisoner awaiting her sentence.

The servants told her to stay. Then they vanished behind one sliding door or another, putting themselves away like unwanted furniture.

Another door rolled open in an adjacent room.

It was as if she'd been plunged back through time and space to the Abbess's chamber of contemplation.

Here entire walls closed her off, rather than a single folding screen. But she could hear just as clearly. Sholto's footsteps, carrying his bulk with balletic surety. Eden's footsteps, and the radiant crackle of her magic, like a torch entering a midnight cave.

"That quince tree could've killed someone," Eden said casually. "What if it went feral?"

"In a single season? Unlikely."

"For the past six years running, you booked a maenad to deal with the harvest. Every fall. I suppose it slipped your mind this year? Must be very busy, what with your preparations to leave the nobility."

Eden talked as if she had never avoided him, or vice versa. As if they habitually exchanged barbs at parties.

Nemesia stared down at her fists in her lap. They felt weak—cold, bloodless, declawed. But her ears were burning hot.

She wanted to crawl across the woven floor. She wanted to nudge the nearest door open and put her eye to the crack. She wanted to see who was speaking. Even if it was only Eden's back. Half a heel concealed by robes. A sliver of bleached-blond hair.

Would she flick her hair contemptuously, eying Sholto, or would she turn and see Nemesia crouching like a monster looking out of a closet?

"No need to thank me for taking care of your quince," Eden said. "You're welcome. I've been quite the self-starter lately. At this stage in my career, I've got to set a good example."

"You look terrible," Sholto told her. There was no pleasure in his voice.

A pause.

"Overwork," Eden said briefly.

Nemesia was clad from head to foot in borrowed clothing. The draping layers should have been enough to warm her, but her hands and feet remained icy.

Dinner had been put on hold. Meaty smells faded. The faraway sizzling went dormant. The air grew dimmer, the shadows thicker.

"You went Below recently," said Sholto.

"Had a nice little vacation."

"Alone."

"No need to sound so judgmental."

"Were you planning to challenge our god right then and there?" he asked. "It's a shame that your wife only has eyes for the Snake."

Eden's voice dropped. "Of all the things you could say ... You've lost your touch, Sholto."

Nemesia wanted to bury her face in her hands. Why provoke him?

"Why are you still here?" he said.

"Why haven't you banished me? The least you could do is serve me some tea for my trouble."

"I wanted you to understand," he said.

In the silence that followed, pendulous lights unfurled from the rafters above Nemesia—and presumably in the other room, too. They swayed as if tasting an intangible breeze.

"Here's some unsolicited advice for you," Eden said tiredly. "Focus on your son, Sholto. He graduated in one piece. All this energy you've wasted on me—wouldn't it be better spent on him?"

"What a perfect maenad," he said. "Nothing stirs you. I could have sworn you were fond of her."

"You wouldn't sympathize if I wept and begged to see her. You wouldn't even enjoy it."

"I'll take more from you." His tone sharpened. "I'll get the committee to deny your extension. I'll raise complaints against your Warden."

"Right now," she pronounced, with the projection of an actress, "you could be having dinner with your family. You could be learning how to speak to Iori.

"You terrify him, you know. Your certainty, your focus, your strength of will—he can't imagine ever living up to you. He can't imagine ever making you proud.

"He has no idea how you broke down when you enrolled him at the reformatory. He has no idea how it destroyed you when Oddscale took him. He has no idea how fast you accepted him as your son. Your child was alive. What else could matter?

"Iori doesn't know any of this, and he shrinks at the sound of your voice, and he's given up on pleasing you. If you come off as forbidding and distant and disappointed with life, he's going to assume it's because of him."

Eden stopped for breath. "You can't pin that on me. Or on the actions of a vigilante. Every wall between you now—you built it all yourself. And—"

A crack.

Nemesia flinched, her heart in her throat. The lights went utterly still, so rigid that they looked like needles sticking down from the ceiling.

Through the walls, she felt Eden's magic turn about like the stirring of a wakening bear.

"You know, Sholto, you ought to realize that it's a really bad idea to slap a maenad."

Such an effortless voice. It put a tremor in Nemesia's shoulders.

"We're supposed to be serene and well-rested," Eden continued. "I haven't slept more than three hours per night in weeks.

"But I understand something new. Are you happy? I understand how incredible it was that you never lost control of your magic. Not even when Iori went missing. How did you do it?"

Nothing in Nemesia's room had moved. She should have been alone, just her and the stringy lights.

The shadows seemed denser in one particular corner.

"I guess you were always special," Eden said to Sholto. "You looked out for other students when most of us couldn't look past our own noses."

The shadow in the corner was Char, devoid of chains.

She wore something similar to the plain high-collared suits of Sholto's servants. Her hair was black and tousled, her eyes unreadable. She put a finger to her lips.

She had Oddscale's scarf tossed nonchalantly about her neck.

"The thing with me," Eden said in educational tones, "is that I never aimed to be kind or good. I could have been the worst maenad to ever awaken within the Shell. You want me to feel your pain? You want my unfiltered reaction? All right."

Eden's magic had begun to uncoil like a string light descending.

Char, off in her corner, looked distorted—inhumanly large.

Nemesia shook her head at Char. No time to reflect. She extinguished everything in the building, from floor to ceiling, as if slamming a lid on a coffin.

The lights went dark. Startled servants cried out. Eden made a noise as if she'd been punched in the stomach.

Nemesia couldn't see her own feet. She eased up on Char alone—only as much as she dared, which wasn't much.

Oddscale's scarf gave off a grayish phosphorescence. It made inquisitive movements, sniffing for prey. Char pulled it up around her face. She no longer appeared tall enough to shatter the ceiling.

All this had happened in too few seconds to count. Nemesia pointed at the wall between them and Eden. Char must have done something; the panels flung themselves away. She still stood half-hidden, her back to the others.

With Nemesia's permission, a single drooping string began to glow again.

In the other room, Sholto was sweating.

Eden pinched a broken cocktail umbrella. She appeared to have snapped it one-handed. When she looked at the missing wall, her eyes were as red as an open vein.

She'd given up on holding in her magic. But it had nowhere to go: all it could do was run crazed circles inside her. With Nemesia actively working against her, releasing her power would be like trying to light a wet candle.

The red-hot coals in her eyes went out all at once, leaving her gaze as dark as Sholto's. Her magic folded itself up, sullen and neat.

One by one, Nemesia let the other lights come back to life.

Sholto took a ragged breath. Abruptly he sat on the floor, grabbing at a corner of the low table before him. All the seat cushions had flung themselves up against random walls.

Eden took a halting step toward Nemesia.

That was when Char strode into view, trailing Oddscale's scarf like toxic black smoke. The air around her face looked distorted, glass too warped to see through. She bowed to Sholto. The scarf waved fretfully, refusing to bow with her, swatting at a nearby dangling light.

Upon straightening, she stood right next to Nemesia. No transition. She reached out and—without a moment's hesitation—lifted Nemesia off the ground, holding her bridal style.

Eden's eyebrows shot up. Sholto made a strangled noise. The black scarf lashed about tauntingly, like a pair of impudent tails.

Char dematerialized from the building, and Nemesia went with her.

48

A Better Person

THEY REMATERIALIZED near the top of an angle tree. Char set her on a bough as straight and sturdy as a city bench.

Nemesia tried to thank her, and promptly had a coughing fit. Her throat had forgotten how to process air.

Char unwound Oddscale's scarf from around her neck. She dropped it in Nemesia's lap, where it curled up, all but purring.

"Was it—safe to leave them?" Nemesia managed at last. "Eden—"

"Trust her."

Char's voice was husky, a little self-conscious, and perfectly comprehensible.

Nemesia didn't say: *You can talk?* Still, it must have been written all over her face.

"Ves is better with languages."

"You sound fine to me."

"Your spoken tongue hasn't changed in centuries. Ves calls it unnatural."

"She didn't come with you," Nemesia said.

"Didn't feel like getting involved."

"And you did? Now you're Oddscale, too."

"Just for today."

The scarf had a warmth all its own, even on a chilly autumn night. Clouds blotted out the stars.

Nemesia craned her head until she glimpsed Eden's cottage—the incongruous turret, the plant-furred roof. Heights didn't alarm her as long as she wasn't locked in the belly of an off-roader, leaping like a flea.

"You showed yourself so Sholto would see the scarf on you," she said. "Not on Eden."

"That's the idea."

They spoke for a few more minutes before Nemesia had to explain that she couldn't climb down on her own. At least not without breaking her neck in the dark.

Char picked her up once more. She gave the impression that she could have simultaneously carried Vesper, Eden, Sholto, and the Warden, all without breaking a sweat.

She deposited Nemesia on the front step, then faded out of sight.

The Warden opened the circular door to let Nemesia in. He nodded—as though she'd just come back from an evening walk—and asked if she'd had dinner. As soon as she answered, he put out a steaming bowl of stew.

She sat there, eyes stinging. At first she couldn't swallow. Her stigmata itched with shame and relief and yearning and guilt, all divorced from any coherent chain of cause and effect.

How unreal it seemed to breathe the air of this house. To listen with one ear to creaky sighs of ancient magic, and with her other ear to the Warden's humming.

Oddscale's scarf slipped inside her robes as if it wanted to feel her skin. All the clothes she wore were technically stolen. But she had also abandoned at least one full outfit back at the autumn house. Sholto would just have to consider it an equal trade.

Pimiko clambered over the edge of the table and watched her eat with an accusatory stare.

After she finished, something in the walls twitched like shuddering skin. Despite the leaden weight of her meal, she rocketed out of her seat. Pimiko dove into the opening of her dangling sleeve.

She held her forearm as if it were broken, cupping her sleeve so Pimiko wouldn't fly around like a flail. She rushed to the basement, and then down the stairs rife with sunless clover.

Those stairs brought her to highest floor. Eden was descending the steps from her bed. She'd taken her preferred passageway home, worming up through the sheets rather than walking in the front door.

Pimiko wriggled free, scurried across the floor, scampered up the railing, and took a flying leap. Luckily, she had excellent aim. She came to rest on her usual landing pad on Eden's shoulder.

"There, there," Eden said. "Still have all my limbs."

After barreling here fast enough to get a stomachache, Nemesia found herself at a loss for words.

She trailed downstairs with Eden, who said a quiet goodnight to the Warden. He sagged with relief and packed himself off to bed.

Nemesia numbly washed a few dishes that, all things considered, could probably have waited till morning. She started wiping countertops.

Solitude had peeled back her hard-won ease, the comfortable accumulation of time together that built up like rings around a tree. Now she was bare, uncertain, and Eden looked every bit as worn down as Sholto had joylessly implied.

"I'm glad you're back," Eden said, as if it were really that simple.

Eden poured herself a glass of water. She drank like it was the first liquid she'd tasted all day. Pimiko stared up at her with all twelve eyes, glossy and beady and so worried that they began to protrude on swiveling stalks.

When Eden put the glass down, Nemesia gulped a breath and pulled her in. Pimiko's tiny toes prodded her shoulder in warning.

Nemesia's body refused to interpret the message.

Oddscale's scarf snaked out and wound a figure eight around their necks, tying them together. Then it slithered away from Nemesia and clung solely to Eden. The scarf must have missed its true wielder.

Eden exhaled shakily. She felt thinner.

"He'll trash your application," Nemesia said hopelessly, her face buried in Eden's hair.

"Maybe." Eden spoke as if it didn't matter either way.

She led Nemesia across the hall to the drawing room. They fell onto an antique sofa with a frame of sinuous wood.

A fireplace had appeared in the middle of the floor. Flames licked at logs that, judging by their magical scent, would never fully burn to ash. Hollow robes on stands clustered in closer, seeking warmth.

Eden displayed her knuckles. No marks; no blood. "We didn't throw punches after you disappeared. Didn't even yell at each other."

"What happened?"

"Can you guess?"

Nemesia gave her a half-hearted shove. Eden slumped sideways on the couch, acting like she would never recover.

"Sholto started talking me through all the old mental exercises from the reformatory. Real basic stuff. Like musicians doing scales."

Nemesia attempted to picture this. It felt more surreal than Char dressed up as Oddscale.

"He didn't say a word about anything else until I'd solidified my grip on my magic." Eden placed Pimiko on the curved arm of the couch. Pimiko delicately picked her way to the floor. Then—avoiding the fireplace—she skittered off. She faded into the shadows beneath hanging robes like a spy in a crowd.

"He's a better person than I am, in that sense. If I saw my nemesis bleeding in the street, I wouldn't lift a finger to save them."

"How did you know I was there?" Nemesia asked.

"If Sholto wanted you to be difficult to find, he wouldn't have stashed you in a Daiya estate. That was part of his game."

The fire shone all the colors of a royal goldfish. Small fishy shapes did, in fact, leap among its waves. The closer Nemesia looked, the more it came to resemble a flaming aquarium.

"I waited long enough," Eden said.

Nemesia dragged her next words out. "You didn't have to come."

"I waited," Eden repeated, unmoved. "No one can accuse me of being impatient. At first I waited to see if you would wander back on your own. Then I felt compelled to wait by my own blasted sense of fairness."

"Fairness to who? Daiya Sholto?"

"Fairness to you."

"...I don't understand."

Eden made a flicking motion at the fire. It puckered and rippled, like she'd thrown a stone in a pond.

"You've lived in close quarters with me since February."

"I have a room of my own."

"Don't be pedantic. We've battled worranges and fixed the Shell and shared a bed."

If she still wore the snake pendant, it lay hidden beneath her odd-scaled scarf.

"Here's an experiment: make two people spend every single day together. For weeks. For months. If they're reasonable, they'll probably learn to be friends. It's a basic survival skill—becoming partial to whoever's nearest.

"That's what happened at the reformatory. No matter how our monitors set us against one another. Bonds can be forged in hell. Companionship kept us alive."

She twisted to look at Nemesia, the firelight soft on her face. "But you don't hear me saying much about pals from school, do you? No reformatory reunions. No one wants to remember. Only Sholto made any real effort to stay in touch."

"Being your wife has nothing in common with child incarceration."

"Doesn't it?" Eden said drolly. "A month felt long enough for a mental reset. My nerves were getting pretty frayed by the end, to be honest. Sholto wouldn't harm you—I trust him more than he ever trusted Oddscale—but it still ate at me."

"Wait," Nemesia said. "A month?"

"It's November now. I think I showed incredible restraint."

"Eden—"

"So. Do you want to stay?"

Nemesia was too taken aback to do anything more than stare.

"It'd be a shame to while away the rest of your sabbatical in Sholto's empty party house. But you don't have to stay here, either. Unless you want to."

"I want to. I want to, but—"

"You'll lose nothing by following your heart, instead of his."

"It's your extension on the line," Nemesia snapped.

Goldfish swirled around in their bath of flames, agitated. Showers of sparks rose and fell, and the fish swarmed to them as if they were edible crumbs.

"Sholto got what he wanted. Or a pale echo of it." Eden's voice was growing hoarse. "If he still plans to retaliate, there's nothing anyone can do to stop him. At this point, though, I bet he's had enough. He'll start skipping committee meetings. What can they do, fire him? He's already on his way out of the nobility."

After a moment, Nemesia put her head on Eden's shoulder. Oddscale's scarf cushioned her; it felt simultaneously cool and warm.

Eden's fingers found their way to the sensitive skin behind her ear and beneath her chin.

"I was clean for the drug test," she said. "But I gorged myself on worrange juice after you left."

"Did the Warden threaten to pour it all out?"

"Not just threats. He actually went through with it."

Nemesia captured Eden's hand and felt her unbitten wrist.

It was already November. Late in the month, too, judging by the fire in the room.

She'd leapfrogged too eagerly across time in the autumn house. She'd flung her senses forward like a skipping stone to avoid feeling it.

The remaining months would go by like nothing at all. Could she haul on the reins of time and make it slow to a crawl inside her? She'd never tried.

It might work. But she could only alter her own perception. Eden had tried to be fair to her, and now she had to be fair in turn. Which meant experiencing life at the same pace. No matter how rapidly it flowed away from them.

49
Parting Ways

"YOU'RE LEAVING," said Eden—a statement, not a question. In concession to the crisp air, she wore a lustrous black jacket with a gaudy embroidered phoenix on its back.

Vesper and Char had taken over the still-empty residence that used to house Eden's neighbor. Nemesia wasn't quite sure what they did there—float in the hallways as if swimming through underwater tunnels? But they seemed to like it.

The garden was beginning to go to seed. A host of imperial dahlias towered higher than the house itself, blooming on stiff canes like bamboo. The sky behind the flowers was covered with a veil of scale-shaped clouds.

Char descended from the roof without fanfare, as if stepping out a back door. Vesper followed, although she didn't touch ground. One of Char's chains wrapped around her to keep her from flying away.

"We've paid you back for your hospitality," Vesper said bluntly. "Any last questions?"

Was it Nemesia's imagination, or did her bone-colored horns look longer than usual?

Eden made a thoughtful sound. She crossed her arms. She peered up at the imperial dahlias whose weight made them bow toward the roof like the curve of a bow.

These guests of hers had shown up well before Nemesia. She must have already slaked her curiosity.

"*When* are you from?" Nemesia asked.

Vesper's face turned remote. "There were times when we soldiers vowed to never let your language pass our lips."

"Did you ever see the Antemaenad in person?"

"The what now?"

"The first maenad. Our forerunner."

"Oh. That." Vesper spoke to Eden, although she hadn't been asking. "You're nothing like the Anti-maenad, or whatever stupid name you people call her. You're nothing like either of them."

"Either of them?" Eden said suddenly.

"Forget it. Too early for you lot to worry about anything outside the Shell."

"That's where you're going, though."

"We'll go wherever we please."

"You stayed here longer than planned," Eden said. "Why?"

Vesper nudged Char.

"We were curious about the Shell," Char said, with her careful pronunciation. She cut a look at Nemesia. "And we were curious about you."

Nemesia didn't react until Eden clapped her on the back. "You, my dear wife. It's you they stuck around for. Not me."

"But—" Nemesia stuttered. "I can count on one hand the number of times we've even talked!"

"We came to watch," Vesper said, "not to chat."

"Families don't visit the city zoo to converse with monkeys," Eden muttered. "It's like that."

Char regarded Nemesia with, again, a distant hint of pity. "You're human."

"Unlike some of us," Vesper said under her breath.

Nemesia waited for more. But Char simply met her gaze with solemn eyes.

Apparently that was all she would get. She'd expected some kind of follow-up—perhaps a few words of otherworldly advice.

You're human.

"Want us to rip another mortal wound in your Shell when we leave?" Vesper flexed her hand. Her nails caught the light as if they were made of metal.

"Don't put yourself out," Eden said.

"We could go much larger than last time."

"No, really—please don't. Two unprecedented patch jobs in a row? People will definitely start to suspect me of rigging it."

After a few more threats to smash the Shell, Vesper lost interest. She said a cursory farewell. Char and her chains waved goodbye, too.

They would make one last circuit of the realm and then remove themselves by morning. They would choose a remote area to cut through the Shell—up by the peak of the sky, rather than on the ground near human settlements.

They would make a precise incision, and the damage would be limited enough to heal in days.

With that said, Vesper darted out of sight among the dahlia canes like a fish weaving a path among reeds. Gravity never seemed to know what to do with her. Char's chain trailed after her, stretching longer without ever running out of links.

Char nodded gravely at Nemesia and Eden. She stepped back—and she too was gone, as if she'd tripped into a hidden wormhole.

"Not too sentimental, are they?" Eden said wryly. "I'm surprised we all got along as well as we did. They've got long memories, and they don't look fondly on the Blessed Empire. Should count myself lucky that Vesper never got fed up enough to disembowel me."

"It would be very rude to disembowel a monkey at the zoo."

Eden cackled.

"Also, the Snake wouldn't stand for it," Nemesia said.

"Suppose not. Although our guests were certainly enthusiastic about punching holes in the Shell. If they've got enough power to break it, then..."

Nemesia's wrists flashed with a sensation like touching a hot pan.

"...Let's not waste time on heretical—and hypothetical—thoughts," Eden said quickly. "Our friends don't have any interest in fighting the Snake."

Nemesia managed a nod.

Eden changed the subject. "Why do you think Char said that?"

"Said what?"

"*You're human.* Seems a little obvious, no?"

"Maybe she was just expressing her opinion."

"About?"

"About how humans shouldn't be brides for divine snakes."

"Hm," said Eden. "She never struck me as being a particularly opinionated sort."

"Did you ever hear her talk before?"

"Now that you mention it, no."

50

Not Forbidden

HOUSE FIRES STARTED cropping up all over Yolk City. There were always more in winter, due to dry air, but this was shaping up to be the worst year in living memory.

As a maenad, Eden helped staunch the largest blazes. As Oddscale, she went back to track down the elusive arsonist.

In late December, Oddscale caught the culprit (and was much applauded). Still, that wasn't quite the end of it.

Natural wildfires swept across the terrain between the city and the Shell. Government policy recommended letting them burn out on their own. But Eden—along with a number of other maenads—got sent to construct protective magical barriers around villages and farms.

The air by the horizon turned hazy. One sunset after another presented a feverish, tortured churn of color. People covered their noses and mouths as if they were back at the Otterdog Masquerade.

All told, the fireplaces that had popped up in the cottage were beginning to make Nemesia uncharacteristically edgy. She strove not to quash each new blaze as if swatting a fly.

The floors emitted enough heat that she could walk around comfortably in bare feet. This was unnerving in its own way—when she brought her ear close to any given surface, she heard the avaricious crackling of trapped flames.

At least there wasn't much smoke.

It had been just as cold when she first arrived in February, and there hadn't been any friendly heat rising through the floors back then. Perhaps, regardless of weather, the house found it improper to keep winter fires going past the end of the year.

In all this, there still came no word about Eden's extension.

"It'll probably take a couple more months," Eden said glumly.

Nemesia couldn't understand why the committee had to drag it out. "How many maenads want to work past forty? There can't possibly be a backlog."

"That's the problem. They've got to revive rusty old bureaucratic mechanisms that have been all but forgotten. I should be grateful that at least they're going through the motions."

One frosty day, Nemesia helped the Warden bring in his weekly deliveries.

He made her carry the lightest box (filled with packets of tea leaves, dried fish, and other dessicated products—river vegetables, mushrooms, marbled beans, and so on).

When she came out to get another load, he pointed at the front step.

"Package for you," he sang. A popular anthem from a musical that had a whole lot to say about courier logistics.

"For me?" Nemesia said obligingly, because that was one of the next lines in the libretto.

The Warden went off-script. "No, really. For you."

Puzzled, she brought this next box into the kitchen, too.

Eden was already there, stacking arm-length lotus roots on the counter. They were made up of bulging links, like a chain of pale sausage.

The Warden carted over the last of his produce and promptly put everything in its place. He feigned a lack of curiosity about the mystery package. Eden didn't bother: she leaned over Nemesia's shoulder until Nemesia relented and started opening it.

"Wait."

Eden tapped an obscure code on the underside of the box.

"This is from the Daiya family," she explained.

"So—"

"From Sholto."

Nemesia continued prying at the flaps—now more gingerly than before.

Inside lay the clothing she'd worn when she first went to the autumn house. Professionally cleaned. Impeccably folded. Eden lifted the garments out piece by piece and sniffed them warily.

Underneath was a stack of paper—Nemesia's discarded letter drafts. They had been obsequiously ironed out to smooth perfection. She snatched them up, furious, and resolved to feed them to the fire fish.

Fortunately, there was something else to keep Eden distracted. A greeting card graffitied with spidery handwriting had fallen away from the top layer of clothing.

Eden made her take it. "Well?"

"You can read it with me."

"Give me a summary."

Nemesia tried. "He's releasing me from any obligations to him, real or imagined. He won't deliberately steer the committee against you. He won't petition the Snake for me, either."

Eden rubbed her temples. "Could be worse."

The Warden began decanting grains and seeds into tall glass jars. Eden made as if to assist him, but he waved her away.

Thus liberated, Eden scooped up the bundle of clothes again. "I'll take these up," she said to Nemesia. She elbowed her way past a swinging door.

Nemesia marched over to the drawing room and dropped her half-written letters in the central fireplace. Flaming yellow-red goldfish swarmed them like a pack of scavengers.

Then she went upstairs and, as expected, found Eden on her bed. Nemesia's robe was spread out beside her, a flat and silent companion.

"Didn't know where you want to put it," Eden said. She folded her legs under her, kneeling as demurely as any Brood sister.

"M. Nemesia"—her voice turned more formal—"Sholto won't speak for you before the Snake. But I will."

"It's not like being a barrister."

Nemesia cleared the clothes off the bed. Each piece of her outfit had its place in a heavy wooden chest. Sholto's card went in there, too, for posterity.

"Are you thinking about Tanyu again?" Eden asked. "This time will be different. I already know you're a Bride."

Nemesia hadn't been thinking about Tanyu at all.

Not once in her life had she ever owned enough physical possessions to fill all the polished chests in this room.

One of the empty ones radiated dry heat, although its metal fittings remained defiantly cool to the touch. Something pulsed behind its seams like lightning flashing through clouds.

A few nights ago, she'd pulled open the middle drawer and found it overflowing with merry fire. She'd immediately slammed it shut.

"You can't," she said.

"You mean you don't want me to," Eden corrected.

"I don't want you to," she squeezed out.

"Your choice."

Nemesia had been prepared for a fight—not this attitude of easy agreement.

"After you move back Below, I'll visit you," Eden said brightly. "It's not forbidden, is it? I'll befriend your guards. I'll take long vacations in the tourist district. If I get in the mood to retire, I'll find a spot at one of your maenad sanatoriums. Seems cushy."

"That's not how it—"

"Why can't it work that way? Has no Bride ever entertained a friend from Above? How different can it be from getting in a long-distance relationship with someone on the opposite side of the Shell?"

Nemesia, incapable of speech, heaved open the drawer of blazing fire.

Eden scarcely even glanced at it. "I'll release you if you want to end our marriage. I'll stay away if you hate me. If you don't, there's no need to avoid each other for ten whole years just because you're a Bride. You might be forbidden from venturing Above, but who says I can't go Below?"

Much to her own consternation, Nemesia had genuinely never thought of this.

"I wouldn't want to live out the rest of my life without seeing the sky," Eden continued blithely. "But Below has plenty to recommend it. For one thing, you'll be there. We can take all the time we need to make big plans for your sabbaticals."

All the flaming drawer had done was make Nemesia jumpy. She shut it.

"It could look bad for you if I return Below before the committee makes a decision," she said, thinking rapidly.

"That's irrelevant."

"How can it be irrelevant? I'm here because—"

Eden, hands on her knees, said: "Because I wanted to talk to the Snake again."

The pitter-pattering magic of the house shushed like a crowd shocked into silence.

It took Nemesia another second to realize that she had borne down on the magic around her as if pressing a boot to a neck. Eden, tight-lipped, still knelt there on the bed with immaculate posture.

Nemesia made herself stop. Magic whooshed back through the structure of the building as if freed from a tourniquet.

"You wanted to talk to the Snake?" she said querulously.

"You made it seem easy," Eden told her. "All those years ago. How old were you, twelve? You opened your mouth and let the Snake out like it was nothing.

"My disappearance gave me a new perspective on a lot of things in life. I've got questions for the Snake. Who doesn't, right? But I've actually spoken to the Snake before. I'm a chosen hero. Having a divine mandate is great and all, but I want answers. Or so I thought."

"I can't..."

"I know," Eden said gently. "I'm not asking you to lend out your voice. I'll gladly give up those lost memories if it means the Snake will authorize you to live however you please.

"I don't care if I never find out what I did to get spirited away at thirty-three. That's a tiny, tiny price to pay for the rest of your life. And I don't mean a life tied to mine. Be whatever you wish."

Nemesia walked a jerky circuit around the sunken bed. The sheets blurred like water in her vision. There was too much to take in.

"You and the King were in cahoots," she said.

"That's not news to you, is it?"

"The problems with your lovers—there were maybe one or two real incidents, decades ago, and then a whole lot of made-up stories."

"Convincing ones," Eden put in.

"What you really wanted was to partner with someone as close to the Snake as possible. Preferably one of its Brides. By royal decree, the King gave you a silly pretext to seek a bride of your own from the Brood."

"Wasn't expecting to find *you*," Eden said. "I almost laughed in your face. Would've been a great first impression, huh?

"You hadn't recognized me, obviously. I thought the Snake was taunting me. I thought this was the Snake's way of showing that it would never say another word to me."

Nemesia's head pounded as if it were trying to send her a message in code. The chest opposite her kept flickering with muffled fire.

"You still want to talk to the Snake," she said slowly.

"Not for the same reasons as before. Not for myself."

Nemesia brushed this away. "It's a bad idea. I can't ever endorse it." She spoke with as little emotion as she could manage. "But I won't stop you."

"I can deal with rejection," Eden said. "Even if the Neverending Snake shuts me down, and you officially remain a Bride all your life, I can still do exactly as I've said. Has the Snake ever barred a specific individual from going Below?"

"The Snake wouldn't. The Abbess might."

"Then I'd better stay on her good side. I'll come see you no matter what happens. For as long as you'll have me."

Nemesia stopped herself from asking why. Eden, who looked at her with suppressed amusement, knew precisely what she wasn't saying. It rang out louder than any of the words that passed their lips.

51

The Final Month

JANUARY: THE LAST month of the year. The recent spate of wildfires had mostly subsided.

They still hadn't received any updates about the status of Eden's application.

Now thirty-nine, Eden was officially one of the oldest magic-users on active duty anywhere inside the Shell. She thus became saddled with an important annual assignment—going around to check up on the youngest working maenads.

She trotted all over the countryside. Some of her junior colleagues were housed in ramshackle old mansions. One had been placed in a modern building that looked like a blade of steel and glass planted to its hilt among rocky moors.

On a rare snowy day, huge flakes floated around like tumbleweeds. They piled up on Eden's umbrella, just as they did on the meticulously bent branches of angle trees. Nemesia came along, too. She wondered if eventually they would visit Daiya Iori.

"Wormed my way out of that one," Eden said.

"How?"

"Conflict of interest—I know he's on the committee. Saw him at the interview."

Nemesia didn't listen in while Eden conferred with her juniors. A few houses already had a warden, in which case she would take tea with them, or do small chores.

Most wardens were happy to gossip about obscure personnel changes and other goings-on spanning Above and Below. They didn't often receive visitors who shared their intimate familiarity with the Bitten Brood.

But many younger maenads had no live-in guardian. Fresh out of the reformatory, they weren't yet of an age to require near-constant monitoring. They preferred solitude—and this was the first taste of true privacy they'd ever had in their lives.

In the absence of a warden to speak with, Nemesia would get permission to wander around looking for weak spots in the magic that supported each residence.

A couple times, she came across a different type of problem. Kitchens towering with precarious stacks of takeout containers and dirty dishes. Laundry trailing like molted skin in random hallways. Dust swirling so thickly that the air by sunlit windows looked like soup. Masses of brown-stained cups abandoned on every imaginable surface.

As for what she glimpsed behind bathroom doors—that was better not spoken of. Ambient magic had a way of making it all too easy to live in filth. The house would dutifully soak up offensive odors. It would zap swarming flies like a hungry frog, sucking their corpses into the ether behind its walls.

In the worst cases, Nemesia would wait until after Eden and the junior maenad finished speaking. She would give Eden a look.

Eden, in turn, would sunnily yet relentlessly insist that the three of them band together to do some heavy-duty cleaning.

"Take care of your house," she'd say with ruthless good cheer, "and it'll take care of you."

Nemesia avoided pointing out that the Warden took care of Eden's cottage. Furthermore, Eden was both disinterested in and frankly inept at all manner of housekeeping enchantments. Getting the whole mess dusted and laundered and sanitized invariably required a combination of oddball magical shortcuts and practical elbow grease.

"Doing dishes is good for the soul," Eden would declare (usually while her mentee—or Nemesia—tackled the actual dish-washing). "That's what my Warden always tells me."

Nemesia had never heard him say that. Possibly because she'd never tried to reason her way out of menial chores. Or perhaps it was just a quote from a play.

"Well, that was disgusting," Eden said after an afternoon spent battling a veritable jungle of mold. She drank in a loud breath of outdoor air. "Ugh. Was I ever that slovenly?"

"I'll ask the Warden."

"Anything but that. I'd hate to shatter your illusions."

"I don't think I have many illusions left."

It was cozy beneath their umbrella. If Nemesia stretched her arm out past its protection, it felt like running her fingers through freezing water.

They walked slowly towards the wormhole that would bring them nearer to home. No reason to rush.

After dinner (rich curry, this time without eels) Nemesia said: "You went Below while I was away."

"Did I?"

"Sholto said it to your face."

"Ah. Then I suppose I did."

"Were you trying to find out more about the petitioning process?"

"A little bit of this, a little bit of that," Eden said evasively. "Mostly just wanted to have a chat with the Abbess."

"Did you see Roc?"

"Who?"

"My guard."

"Oh—no, the guards all gave me a pretty wide berth. I think the Abbess warned them off."

She steered Nemesia into the scriptorium.

The Warden had put up a calendar featuring vintage poster art from classic theatrical productions. He'd bought it at a steep discount in early fall, over halfway through the year.

The January design was fairly abstract—large flat shapes in garish hues, like paper cut-outs. Two faceless figures appeared to be dueling with swords.

"I don't want to wait till the last possible day to throw myself on the mercy of the Snake," said Eden.

Nemesia stared at the calendar. Pimiko, sitting pretty on Eden's shoulder, appeared to glare at it, too.

"I thought we could go at the end of the year," Nemesia said.

"I'd rather not."

"Why?"

"Because you'll have to pack all your things and bring them Below, just in case. Not a good omen."

Eden lifted the page for January. The new year would come partway through February, and so the final page contained only a truncated block of dates.

"Besides," she said, "if the Snake tells us no, there's no rule against trying again."

"I've never heard of anyone asking for a Bride's hand more than once."

"Doesn't mean it can't be done. If we go early, there's a chance to regroup. I can go bother the Snake multiple times."

"How early do you mean by early?" Nemesia asked with trepidation.

Eden lowered the calendar page and pointed at a date late in January.

For an infinitesimal moment, Nemesia felt time roaring around her like wind in a blizzard. She couldn't grab it, as if grabbing someone by the hair. She couldn't snuff it out like magic.

"It's your decision to face the Snake," she said, eyes fixed on the duelists battling across their old poster. "You decide when."

52

The Bride in Question

SO THEY SET OFF around the end of January, when there were still a few weeks left in the year.

Nemesia wrote to the Abbess to let her know they were coming. She wore head-to-toe red: on this one day, it would be best to dress like a Bride.

She wouldn't normally have been allowed Below before the end of her sabbatical, but if someone wanted to ask the Snake for a Bride, they were welcome anytime. It was only fitting for the Bride in question to come along as a guide.

Rain started pouring when they reached the city. Her embroidered shoes were soon soaked through.

Eden had brought the same stained-glass style umbrella that she'd been carrying when they came up the stairs almost a year ago. They squeezed in shoulder-to-shoulder beneath it.

The stalls and carts around the stairwell were unusually deserted. Just a few shoppers splashed to and fro (armed with ponchos, umbrellas, or both).

"You peg your birthday to the start of the year?" Eden said in her ear.

Nemesia's mind had been wallowing somewhere Below. With effort, she made herself pay attention. Thin waterfalls streaked down off the edges of their shared umbrella, and the roofs of shuttered booths.

"It's the same for everyone in the Brood," she said. "You round your birthday to the nearest New Year."

"Why?"

"In deference to the Snake's conception of time." This answer could be repurposed to explain the majority of Brood rituals. "We don't make much of birthdays."

"After all, they all come at the same time."

Nemesia took a wide step to avoid planting her foot in a puddle. "Should I have done something for yours?"

"My what?"

"Your birthday." Of course this would only occur to her now that they were on their way Below.

"Oh, don't worry about that. You were busy being Sholto's hostage."

"But—"

"Maenads don't have much attachment to birthdays, either. They certainly didn't let us run around setting off firecrackers at the reformatory. I'd forget my own age if not for the whole thing about having to retire at forty."

She tilted the umbrella against a gust of wind. "If you'd like to make it up to me, let's celebrate yours instead."

"What? Why?"

"I missed my own thirty-fifth birthday. Let me share yours. Hm— when should we do it? Before or after the turn of the year?"

Nemesia tripped on nothing. Eden caught her.

Whatever happened today, there were still several weeks before the end of Nemesia's sabbatical.

Celebrate early, and she could promise to be there. Celebrate later, and she'd have already gone back down for another decade. Like a cicada waiting years to grow wings.

"After," Nemesia said.

"I'll hold you to that."

The entrance to Below yawned open before them. The entire Facade Theater could fit in that hole. Perhaps even the entire palace.

Rain appeared to fall over the stairs, just as it fell over the market. But it never touched the steps. It vanished as if showering into a horizontal wormhole.

By the time they reached the bottom, Eden's umbrella was completely dry. Nemesia's feet were getting there, too, although they still felt uncomfortably steamy.

She led Eden to a foot bath and paid a couple scales so they both could have a quick soak. Their shoes and socks went in sanitizing lockers that looked (and, for some reason, smelled) like a bakery oven.

Afterward, Eden borrowed a pair of ammonite-logo slippers. Nemesia went barefoot.

No one questioned Eden's presence, not even when they stepped into Brood-restricted areas. Anonymized guards watched without comment. The Abbess must have spread the word.

A few passing sisters waggled their fingertips in greeting. That was about the biggest reaction Nemesia got: Snake-bitten clerics were not naturally effusive. Especially not when in residence Below.

She sensed fellow Brides in far-off corners of the warren of stone. None emerged to say hello. She reflexively counted them as if counting rabbits in a hutch, making sure none were lost or hurt. Four, five, six...

Had the Abbess kept Brood guards at a distance because Eden might recognize one or more of them?

This seemed increasingly plausible. Eden knew a lot of people, and she had extremely sharp instincts.

They proceeded single-file down narrow paths around gravel gardens. Next to never-opened doors of inhuman proportions, doors so high that you couldn't even make out their top edge, they ducked to crawl through rough holes bored in rock.

Sometimes it seemed as though the Eternal Brood dwelt like a colony of mice in a human house.

She kept asking how Eden felt. Some from Above found that their vision and balance became impaired Below. This could strike anyone, even those who had never suffered on previous trips.

Vertigo, headaches, eyestrain, difficulty distinguishing distances ... there were a few different names for it. Many tourists called it Staircase Syndrome.

At last they came down to one of the lowest levels. Here were all the Brood vaults, as well as the decorative stone door that walled off the undersky.

"Is that where we're going?" Eden asked.

"The undersky is only for Brides."

Nemesia took her in the opposite direction.

There were few obvious signs of how much deeper they'd come. The passageways only sloped subtly, if at all. They hadn't taken any other grand staircases, or gotten on an elevator, or climbed a ladder down a shaft.

Those not of the Brood would have to ride silent, intimidating magical escalators to get down to this level. If they were even allowed here in the first place. The escalators were poorly lit and so mind-numbingly tall that, at first glance, most newcomers thought they looked like death traps. Nemesia had spent enough time Below to know shortcuts.

Eden kept tilting her head as if she had water in her ears. Some force adjacent to gravity seemed to come down from above and flatten all attempts at thought. It pressed your mind and feelings through a sieve. This was quite soothing, if you knew what to expect.

"What's that growling?" Eden said.

"Growler snakes."

"Right. Of course." She plucked at Nemesia's sleeve. "To face the Snake, do I have to dive in a literal pit of living snakes? If so, I'd like to know sooner rather than later."

"Probably not," Nemesia said.

"*Probably* not?"

The low growling came through the walls around them. The walls were much, much farther apart than any two walls in the palace, or the Facade Theater, or any other grandly proportioned structure Above.

And yet the growling still reached them. It was more of a tingling, hair-raising vibration than an outright sound.

"That seems," Eden said, with the air of a doctor making a diagnosis, "like a lot of snakes."

"They stay in designated chambers."

"Even if they're hungry?"

"They're scavengers."

"But what do they—oh. So this is what it means to have your dead interred by the Brood."

"The Snake provides," Nemesia said automatically.

They entered a crenelated natural cathedral of pink and white and yellowish stone, ridged and glossy in a way that suggested moisture.

Eden gazed at the ceiling. "It can't be coincidence that this looks so much like the mouth of a—"

"It's just rock," Nemesia said.

They were alone. The Abbess would ensure that no one could come to interrupt.

There was a certain candlelit quality to the cathedral's edgeless illumination and deep inky shadows. The snakelight around them didn't have any identifiable origin. It was simply there, woven into the heavy air of the depths.

Like a tour guide, Nemesia named objects on the altar. One was an automatic toothbrush from outside the Shell.

The realm of the Snake had never been truly self-sustaining. People only exited in fables or freak accidents. But magical resources regularly surfaced along the border. Pallets of spices, dunes of pure salt, barrels of chemicals.

Overtly foreign artifacts would be requisitioned by the Brood. Books in illegible writing, archaeological remnants like shards of pottery—and occasional curiosities like this toothbrush, or a single sock, or creepy jewelry made of human teeth.

Every now and then, animate creatures got stranded, too. In the Abbess's youth, a pair of lonely land-walking dolphins had been added to the royal menagerie. They'd failed to produce offspring (which was probably for the best, given the lack of a native population).

"Outside the Shell, human magic doesn't last beyond the death of the mage," Eden said. "Isn't that sad?"

She reached for the enshrined toothbrush. Nemesia stopped her, and then kept hold of her hand, for good measure.

"So," Eden said.

"So," Nemesia echoed meaninglessly.

"Is there anything else I need to do to speak with the Snake?"

Nemesia narrowed her focus to the shape of Eden's knuckles, the familiar warmth of the floor under the soles of her feet.

She didn't know what she would have done if not for the sedative effect of the caves. Their enormity rooted her in place. Without that, would she have been breathing? Would she have been standing?

"You came to tell the Snake to let me go." Her voice sounded profoundly unreal. She squeezed fitfully at Eden's hand, but she couldn't raise her head. She swallowed convulsively and, horribly, almost broke out laughing. "You came to persuade the Snake that your love is true."

"Nemesia—"

"I'm the one you need to convince," she said miserably. "I'm the one who needs to believe you."

"You're a Bride of the Snake." Eden stretched out each word as if testing its logic.

This was why Nemesia had always tried to downplay (or outright conceal) her status as a Bride.

It was the only role she could possibly claim. She strove to live within the stated parameters. She followed the rhythm of ten years Below, one year Above. She stuck to all the rules even when the Abbess reminded her that she didn't have to. Exceptions could be made—for Meifu Nemesia, if no one else.

Strictly speaking, she had lied every time she called herself a Bride. But she had done her absolute best to make it true.

Eden touched the side of her neck, her face.

Eden made her look up.

"Eyes like a snake," Eden said. "But you aren't the only one whose eyes change Below. You aren't the only one with multiple bite marks."

And then, almost accusingly: "Char called you human."

"I *am* human. My ... my body is human."

"I've noticed."

"I'm also the—"

"Not just a mouthpiece? Not just a conduit?"

"I'm the Snake in human form," Nemesia said, loud enough to echo.

53

The Snake That Ate the Roots of Time

To HER UTMOST astonishment, Eden grabbed the toothbrush off the altar and hoisted it overhead like a trophy.

"Eden!"

"What are you going to do, smite me?"

"I'm serious! Put it down!"

"I'm serious, too." Eden returned the toothbrush. "You can't just claim to be the Snake incarnate and leave it at that. Walk me through the implications."

Nemesia had stayed up half the night agonizing over where to start. How to confess to being the Snake. Part of the Snake. An offshoot of the Snake. There were many ways she might describe herself, and none of them seemed right.

Tanyu had never come this far. She'd backed out, and so Nemesia had never told her. Or anyone.

Within the Brood, the Abbess decided who to inform.

Wrinkled rock formations grew around the fringes of the cathedral. They cupped shadows like dark liquid, rivulets and goblets and cauldrons of unspilled ink.

Everything she'd never dared to say seemed to have dissolved in those waiting crevasses.

She'd swayed without knowing it. Eden steadied her. "We should sit down."

Nemesia took her around behind the altar.

A matrix of fungi and mineral deposits curved into cups like molded seats. The seats held a lingering heat from countless other bodies that had occupied (or would come to occupy) the same spot. Like an empty bed where someone had been lying moments before.

"You aren't very surprised," Nemesia finally said.

"I came braced for anything. And it makes sense."

"It does?"

"This explains a lot about Vesper and Char. They hung around my land, sure, but you represented their host—their true host. Besides ... I could tell something was weighing on you."

"I wasn't going around sighing and moping," Nemesia objected.

Eden raised her hands in surrender. "We've been together all year. I knew from the way you held yourself. The sound of your voice. I just knew."

The snakelight on this side of the altar had a lavender tint. Nemesia tangled her fingers together as if weaving a net.

"You're more like a child of the Snake," Eden said, "than a Bride."

"No." This she could state with vehemence. "I'm not the Snake's human daughter."

"Then what are you?"

"You can take a bucket of water out of a river. What's inside is still the river. It's just isolated from the rest." She mimed overturning a bucket. "If you pour it back, you can't ever retrieve it. The river flows on. Fill your bucket again, and it'll be a different haul of water."

Eden felt the sides of her warm cradle of a chair. It looked as if she were rubbing the back of a pet.

"You're the water *and* the bucket," she said. "Your human body is a container for a cupful of the Snake. It's similar to being Oddscale."

"It's nothing like—"

"I've been Oddscale to some people, in some situations, at some times. I'm a transient vessel for something that can't be contained in a single body. One of many incarnations."

But she didn't fear losing her mind to the Oddscale of history and legend.

More than anything, Nemesia dreaded being subsumed by the Snake.

Not because she wasn't already part of it. Because if she dribbled out of her bucket and trickled back into that wide, immeasurable river, the being once known as Meifu Nemesia would melt away forever. Nothing left but water mingling with more water, inextricable.

She wasn't the first human incarnation of the Snake. They tended to manifest once every few generations. They usually disappeared— rejoined the Snake—at a young age. They left no particular mark on society. The Brood had never found it difficult to protect their secret.

According to Brood records, Nemesia was the oldest ever. She attributed this to the Abbess.

"If you want a long human life," the Abbess had said, "you'd better work hard at living within human boundaries."

Breaking rules that no one else could break felt like a surefire way to dive back in that river. It would mean embracing everything about herself that never really fit in human form.

When Nemesia related this, haltingly, Eden sat forward.

"That's why you're so strict about following the rules that govern Brides. Even if it makes you unhappy."

Nemesia winced. "In the Brood, you're either a Bride or you're not. I can go to the deepest places. I meet all the criteria."

"And if you call yourself a Bride, you've got to live by their laws. Can I register a complaint?"

"Uh—"

"The Snake sure seems like a stickler for arbitrary regulations. Why do we need a King? The noble class—what are they for? Aren't there other ways we could rule ourselves, for good or for ill?

"I suppose we don't rule ourselves at all. The Snake rules us. You don't, so long as you choose to stay in your bucket."

"If I leave my bucket," said Nemesia, who was growing tired of the word *bucket*, "I won't be myself anymore. Or ever again."

Disconnected sounds welled up in the space when neither of them spoke. Breathing and rustling: a crowd assembled for a religious service. Hushed singing, and the twang of plucked instruments.

In the deep reaches of Below, noise from other times and places might sweep through like wind in a valley. But not everyone was attuned to it.

Eden had paused with her head tilted back.

"Those things like stars ... are those eyes?" Before Nemesia could answer, she shuddered and glanced away. "Never mind. Let them look."

Stalagmites and stalactites surrounded the nook behind the altar. Some had elongated far enough from the ceiling and floor to meet in the middle, forming twisted tornadoes of stone.

There were caves Above, too—spaces below the earth that weren't part of Below. Stone icicles there looked different. They didn't contort like wrung-out rags.

Eden stared most intently at the protrusions that hadn't grown long enough to touch. These were forked—yes, like the tongue of a snake.

The completed columns looked as though upper and lower tongues had twined torturously together, wrangling like the worms on the Abbess's staff.

"I have a confession, too," Eden said. "Sometimes your tongue becomes forked."

Nemesia's fingers leapt to her lips. What did she plan to do with them—pull her tongue out? She pressed it against the backs of her teeth. It wasn't split.

Eden preempted her before she could argue her innocence. "You never notice. Personally, I love it."

"When does my tongue—"

"When do you think? When you're using it. I could show you"—she started to lean in—"although it might be hard to get in the mood with all those eyes hanging over us."

"You still..."

"What?"

"You still want to touch me?"

"I mean, you're not physically a reptile."

Creatures like clear barnacles grew in clusters around the base of the altar. Nemesia used to spend hours on scraping duty, listening to lost sounds from other shards of time.

Her fingers itched to scour off all that crud, but she didn't have any tools.

Eden frowned. "There's something else you're afraid of."

Blood ebbed in her veins. Whatever filled her seemed contemptibly shallow.

She hadn't wanted to spell it out.

"If you're born with a snakebite, or you turn out to have magic, the Snake can make your family reject you."

"The Snake does that," said Eden. "Not you."

Nemesia kept going. "I've never used the Snake's power on purpose. But how can I prove I've never done it by accident? What if I made you want to be here? How can we ever know I didn't?"

"Does the Snake force love?" Eden countered. "That's the opposite of severing parents from children."

"You can't swear I never—"

"You already said it yourself. If you abused your power, you wouldn't stay human much longer. You'd merge back into the body of the god.

"For now, you're still you. Sure, maybe you're also a bucket of water drawn from the well of the Snake. So what? I can be in love with a bucket. And the water inside it, too."

"Um," said Nemesia.

"That isn't usually what I say to seduce people."

"No?"

"I adapt to the situation."

Eden was making light of it to take the pressure off. But something pierced straight through to parts of Nemesia that she had never learned how to defend.

She felt newly hatched, or flayed. Exposed to air for the very first time. She covered her eyes, unable to look any longer at the lavender light.

Eden's voice came closer.

"Guess I'd better lay it all out. Prove myself worthy."

"You don't have to prove anything," Nemesia mumbled into her hands.

"But I will," Eden said right by her cheek, deadly serious. "Whatever you are or wish to be, I love you. Will you marry me?"

"I already did!"

"Can't hurt to double-check."

Nemesia uncovered her face. She glared; she'd been disarmed and cornered all at once.

Eden's lips twitched. "Anyway, that was provisional. Do you want to stay married? Think before you answer. Don't throw a *but* in there."

"...Yes."

"Really?"

"Yes!"

Eden studied her with such intensity that it was hard not to avert her eyes again.

Then she let out what sounded like a long-held breath. She planted her hands on either side of Nemesia's makeshift chair. She kissed the corner of Nemesia's mouth—just a touch. She was beginning to withdraw when Nemesia, indignant, hooked the back of her neck and dragged her down for more.

Eden made a noise halfway between a guttural guffaw and a squawk. Nemesia felt the sound of it in her own mouth. A hot pang of laughter curled in her belly.

"See," Eden said, once Nemesia finally let her break free. "Your tongue—can you feel it? Hate to say I told you so, but—"

"I don't want to hear it."

Eden pulled her out of her stony seat. Her legs felt giddy, as if she'd run miles all day.

She didn't question where they were going until Eden stopped in the middle of the chamber, back in front of the altar.

The muffled voices—and other scraps of the future and past—gradually died down.

"I still have a choice to make," Eden said gravely.

Nemesia's ankles and wrists felt abnormally heavy. Bound in iron cuffs, as if someone had tricked her. Imprisoned her.

Her lips parted to speak. She detected the way the skin stuck before separating. The slick presence of her teeth. The exact weight and thickness of her tongue—no longer forked. The sensation of air pushing words.

The cathedral flickered in shades of black and white. The voice that came out of her chest said:

All your choices are as real as anything inside the Shell.

She lost a few seconds after she said it.

When she came to her senses, Eden was holding her up.

"Well," Eden said. "That's either reassuring, or absolutely terrifying. I'll try to look on the bright side. Why wouldn't my choices matter? The Snake can reverse cause and effect, past and present. Whichever way lies forward, I know what I want."

"Eden," Nemesia said raggedly. She didn't have enough breath left for more.

Eden spoke in her most formal and beautiful voice. She could have been an actress for the ages.

Here she played to an audience of one.

"To you, the Snake incarnate, I give what could have been the best three years of my life as a maenad. From the age of thirty-three to thirty-six."

"Eden—"

She rolled on, unrelenting. "I'll offer up my years in service. A fitting marriage gift for a time-eating Snake. That's how I'll prove myself. Nothing less weighty would do—no flowers, no jewels."

"You can't!"

"I can, and I will, and I did."

Nemesia cast about wildly for a way out. The pain in her stigmata drowned her thoughts like an army of drums.

"Wait for me," Eden quoted. "Wait as long as you need to. One day we'll meet again." There was a slight edge to her smile.

She pointed at the entrance, where the otherwise natural cathedral was fitted with unnatural doors of solid bronze. To the left, behind curtain-folds of stone, was a humble saloon flap for human visitors.

"You have to spend the final weeks of your sabbatical Above," Eden said. "I have a promise to keep to the Snake. You'd best get out of here before your river gets to work."

Nemesia started to babble. "I'll stay. I'll stay until…"

"You like sunlight," Eden said with implacable patience, "and the sky. And me, if I'm lucky."

She kissed Nemesia's hands. "Time to go."

Nemesia's stigmata stopped hurting, or feeling anything at all.

Time to flee, said the heart knotted inside her breakable human body.

She saw herself as if she'd become a disembodied eye glistening at the peak of the cavern. A figure in crimson, small and meaningless, numbly retreating.

54

As Above, So Below

NEMESIA DIDN'T look back.

As she left, her mind swelled with unseen images. Eden waited by the altar. Except the altar had become a hungry door. Or a wormhole stretching like a spiderweb between two vast broken pillars.

She rushed blindly toward the upper reaches of Below.

"Don't cry," Eden said in her imagination, sounding pleased.

Eden had spoken so matter-of-factly of love. Why hadn't she been able to say anything back? Why had it been so much easier to wrench her lips apart and release the prophetic voice of the greater Snake?

At the lockers near the foot bath, she went to take Eden's shoes. Partly out of consideration, and partly out of spite. Who knew how long Eden might be trapped Below?

But they'd kept their locker keys separate. Nemesia could only open her own.

Inside were her embroidered dress shoes, and her loose ribbon-tied socks. And Eden's stained glass umbrella, folded down into a tidy cylinder.

She took the umbrella out. Rage vibrated in her, brittle and tremulous.

Eden had known she might need it. Eden must have distracted her with some flippant comment and then slipped the umbrella in her locker. Just another sleight of hand trick.

On the way out, she drifted like a red-clad ghost past guards and tourists and Maidens of the Snake. She ascended the stairs to Above without any conception of how long it took to get there.

It was raining more softly now, but the market remained quiet. She opened Eden's umbrella. Her fingers were painfully cold around the handle. Should've brought gloves.

She ought to be capable of understanding what Eden had offered the Snake. And how the Snake would take its due.

She blocked out all such thoughts. She filled herself with the sound of raindrops on Eden's umbrella, and the dicey work of skirting puddles.

She mindlessly retraced the route they'd taken when Eden first brought her Above. The little city park was still there, just as worn down as before. The broken bench was swaddled in caution tape.

It had more or less stopped raining by the time she reached the bus stop across from the nest house. Icy water still dripped irregularly from the roof of the shelter.

She started to sit. Then she stood again, clutching Eden's half-folded umbrella.

Eden hadn't brought her here with serious plans to ride the omnibus. Its route wouldn't take them anywhere near her cottage. She'd shown Nemesia the bus to rattle her—perhaps having already pegged her for a Bride. Always one step ahead.

At the far end of the street, an omnibus clacked its numerous legs.

Nemesia had heard somewhere that they were capable of moving in absolute silence. They made noise because they liked to. Or to warn off oblivious pedestrians.

She stepped out of the shelter.

If the greater bulk of the Snake saw fit to reabsorb her, it could do so at any time. No need to wait for public transportation. She'd feared buses, obediently, because Brides were taught caution. How much had that gained her? What was the point of fearing anything?

Lasting connections were supposed to serve as protection. Would her year with Eden and the Warden shield her?

All of a sudden, she wanted to test it. If she vanished at the back of the omnibus, maybe she would end up wherever Eden had gone. A purgatory without time, or full of too much time. A place where one might look upon the true body of the Snake.

For people outside the Brood, the Snake was an implicit presence, a twisted coil of invisible gravity. They took it for granted, but they never saw it in person.

Even for the Bitten Brood, the Snake existed primarily in the repetition of daily rituals. They circled through endless sacraments, and their circling became the Snake's slithering. The human mind could not otherwise conceive of it. No human mind could truly go to meet it.

The omnibus lurched to a halt right in front of her.

An aperture slicked open, chitinous panels sliding smoothly aside. Nemesia kept still. New passengers had to wait to board.

A man in a bowler hat stepped down. He gave her a puzzled glance. The omnibus shifted minutely, its black iridescent parts sighing with friction. Goosebumps prickled her forearms.

The next passenger to descend was a woman in a deep blue robe. With black streaks in her hair. With an epaulet on each shoulder.

Whether out of fury or terror or incredulity, Nemesia's first reaction was to hurl the compact umbrella in her hand like a rock.

Eden caught it just before it smacked into the innocent omnibus. She eyed Nemesia reproachfully. She moved to let the living door snick shut behind her. The omnibus—which had evidently had enough of all this—trundled off, gradually picking up speed.

Eden turned the umbrella about, checking for injuries. It was still damp with leftover raindrops.

The man in the bowler hat had long since hustled away down the sidewalk.

Nemesia accused Eden of heartlessly fooling her, playing cruel pranks, exacting revenge for her time in the autumn house. She said all kinds of things.

Either Eden didn't hear her, or didn't take it to heart. She tugged Nemesia into the bus shelter. Open walls framed their view of the vine-wrapped house across the street.

Nemesia found that she'd wormed a hand inside Eden's low-hanging sleeve. Her fingers must have been chilly, but Eden didn't complain. She had her other arm curled tight around Nemesia's waist.

"You snuck out right after me," Nemesia said.

"Had to ride the bus to catch up."

"But nothing happened. Nothing could have happened." She felt her face heating. "You gave up your years from when you were thirty-three to thirty-six. You didn't go anywhere *today*. You weren't in danger. You weren't swallowed by the Snake."

"I never meant to be in danger," Eden protested. "It's not that nothing happened, either. I made my choice. After you left, time clicked into place like the tumblers of a lock. The past became real.

"You—and all the rest of the Snake—you accepted me and my offering. You're not a Bride anymore. The Brood records have already changed. I asked your Abbess. It worked, Nemesia."

There was an insurmountable gap between wanting to believe something and actually believing it.

"Your three years have always been missing," Nemesia said. "Was it ever a choice at all?"

"Those years aren't lost anymore." Eden glowed with triumph. "I remember everything. I only remember now because nothing really came true until I chose it."

Her arm squeezed Nemesia's side. "I used to be very angry about my vanished years. My own decision! Can't believe I wasted so much time on regret."

"So where were you?" Nemesia demanded. "What were you doing? No one saw you, not even the Warden. Were you outside the Shell?"

Eden smirked.

She started laughing.

Nemesia tried not to seethe. She gritted her teeth. She held her tongue. The peals of laughter kept coming. Eventually she extricated herself and thumped Eden on the back.

"Hey!" Eden said, still hiccuping. "No hitting. I deserve better than that. I've made a mind-bending demonstration of undying love and affection."

She fought to master herself. She wiped the corners of her eyes. "You can't guess where I was? I gave the Snake three years of service."

Half-formed thoughts bloomed inside Nemesia, wordless shapes like ink in water.

She watched in disbelief as Eden tugged at her blue robe, indicating a spot by her collarbone.

The spot where a Brood guard would wear their badge.

Without once breaking eye contact, Eden raised both hands with her thumbs linked together and her fingers outspread. She flapped them in a farcical imitation of wings.

55

Deep Cover

"Roc," Nemesia said.

Then: "You're kidding."

And then: "Please tell me you're kidding."

Eden just sat back, smiling.

Nemesia was a living splinter of a god that held time itself in thrall. As a result, she couldn't raise any of the standard objections. It wasn't impossible for Eden to be Roc. In fact, it was entirely feasible.

Chameleon—the other guard she'd been fond of—had donated part of his future Above to serve in the past Below. The flow of time could change from person to person.

Eden had vanished at the age of thirty-three and reappeared at thirty-six. She hadn't spent those years in hiding. During her absence, she hadn't existed anywhere: not Below, not Above.

Her term of service had been shifted forward. Closer to the present.

Roc had begun working for the Brood three years ago, in what would have been winter Above. In fact, Roc's term must have ended very recently. Yesterday, perhaps. Or even today.

When thirty-nine-year-old Eden ventured Below with Nemesia, her thirty-six-year-old self might have been watching from the shadows, disguised as a guard.

She would complete one final day of service. Then she would evaporate, whisked back into the past to resume living a seemingly consecutive life Above ... without any memory of where she'd been, or why.

Until now.

Nemesia smoothed the sides of her pinned-up hair. She couldn't will herself into being less frazzled. "Why didn't you leave?" she said.

"And go where?"

"You just opened your eyes and found yourself dressed like a guard? You had no reason to stay with the Brood."

"I was confused," Eden admitted. "But I had vague memories of my future. Of committing myself to this course, and to you."

"Why'd your period of service get moved? Did I ... did the Snake demand it?"

"Oh, that was my choice," said Eden. "First of all, as a supremely powerful and glamorous maenad, I was—and continue to be—a figure of no small importance."

"...................."

"I'm not joking. My disappearance was a pretty big deal. People searched all over the Shell for me. They even went Below. I needed to be totally gone—unfindable.

"So I chose to serve in a time when no one would ever go looking. Because I was already there. Living out my future life Above. Turning thirty-seven and thirty-eight and thirty-nine. No one would hunt for me when I was no longer missing.

"Also," she said slyly, "I wanted to meddle."

"...With what?"

A wet wind gusted down the street.

"I gave Sholto a few tips."

"You pushed me to take his offer, too." How very absurd. "You pulled every string you could get your hands on."

"I hoped I'd have all three years with you. But maybe that would've been a less convincing sacrifice. After you went Above for your second sabbatical, I kept toiling away in the caves. I was an excellent guard."

"You spent a lot of time slacking off."

"Watching over you," Eden said piously. "And I was always a perfect gentleman, wasn't I? I pined after you—muddled memories and all—and you had no idea. I was just one of the guys!"

Indeed. Her uniform had concealed her magic just as thoroughly as her voice and face.

"Could the Abbess have figured it out?" Nemesia asked.

"Mm. Maybe. She did work me like a dog."

Many guards were debtors, or had other reasons to seek shelter from hardship. The Brood took stringent measures to honor their privacy.

Since Eden had been covertly inducted by the Snake, maybe she had no identity papers at all. Or maybe they'd materialized out of nowhere and stayed in a file collecting dust.

She shot Nemesia a sheepish look. "Before any of this came to light, I was jealous, you know. Of myself."

"You never—"

"I just didn't show it."

"But I hardly ever talked about Roc."

"You hardly ever talked about anyone. I kept reassuring myself that you must've seen him—hah!—as a brother."

"That *is* embarrassing." Nemesia's exasperation bubbled over into laughter. "All along, you were just competing with—"

"Yes, yes, laugh away. I won in the end, didn't I?"

They both chuckled fitfully, jostling each other. One would erupt in stifled giggles as soon as the other settled.

"This is unbelievably stupid," Nemesia said.

"I think it's quite touching."

Someone had stapled a new Oddscale caricature to the wall. This figure was masculine, with a scowling face on the back of its head.

"That's our Warden for you," said Eden. "Sometimes he gets overly creative."

"Does the government ever actually hunt you?"

"Not in earnest. This is a fan-made poster, anyway. Not a legal notice. See the disclaimer?"

"Oh."

"That being said..." Eden tipped her head sideways, as if perceiving a secret in the portrait. "I didn't spend my entire time as Roc mooning after you behind my magical mask. I learned all kinds of things I could never have discovered Above. The Brood's archives are something else."

She tapped the jagged brushstrokes of Oddscale's scarf. "Our hero was originally meant to be a villain. In the oldest tales, Oddscale is a frightening reaper, a boogeyman. A shadow that breaks the laws of the Snake."

"Wanted posters are a modern remnant of that?"

"Could be. Over time, Oddscale evolved into a champion of the oppressed. The public loves an antihero, and so Oddscale grew more heroic."

Jewels of water beaded along the overhanging roof. Across the street, the nest house appeared pleasantly desolate.

The Snake controlled everything down to civilians' ability to digest imperial history, and how parents reacted to magical children. Yet the populace had subconsciously willed Oddscale to become more of a mysterious hero than a mysterious monster. People weren't powerless in the world of the Snake.

When she voiced this, Eden agreed. "Over time, maybe we collectively shape the Snake's thoughts more than it shapes ours."

Nemesia absentmindedly picked at a corner of the poster. It felt as if she'd left part of herself behind to stumble around the city in confusion. She was only just beginning to catch up with the events of the day.

"You aren't going anywhere," she said.

"Already did my time."

"I can stay Above."

"As long as you like." Eden poked a finger at her breastbone, grinning. "You thought I was just going to soliloquize about my devotion, didn't you?"

"I was trying not to think about anything."

"No, you were sure I'd face the Snake with talk alone. Like giving an audition for the biggest role of my life."

"Well—it was hard to picture anything else."

Eden nodded sagely. "Even if you were desperate to believe every word, something in you would have felt it wasn't enough. You'd have been compelled to judge as fairly—as harshly—as possible. You wouldn't ever bend the rules for yourself.

"I'm just glad my three years were a sufficient contribution. They were prime years, perfectly ripe. Plucked straight from the golden age of my life."

She ran her thumb along the thread-thin chain of her pendant. Ever since Nemesia gave it to her, she hadn't gone a day without it.

"Hope you don't feel cheated," she said, "if the years to come are even better."

"They will be," Nemesia said impulsively.

"They're all yours, regardless."

The sky resembled a torn sticker, white and gray shredding away into startling blue. The fullness of the moment quivered around them like those droplets clinging to the edge of the roof.

If Nemesia let herself be more than human, she could twist that brilliant moment off the vine and keep it forever. There was such a simple wonder in the way Eden looked at her, the cleanness of the damp cold air, the warmth that came from sitting close.

But she was human, and because of that, irretrievable seconds flicked by with every breath.

Drops fell, splatting. The pavement was plastered with flat wet leaves spaced out like footprints.

They got up and left for home, arm in arm, sometimes snorting quietly with remembered laughter. How ridiculous it was to have walked such corkscrew paths—only for their chronology to dovetail right back in the same place. Still married. Still together.

56

The Entire Time

THE NEW YEAR came in the middle of February. Nemesia persuaded Eden that she didn't want anything elaborate for her birthday.

"You spent three irreplaceable years for me," Nemesia told her. "That's worth more than any valuable."

"Oh, I bet economists could convert my time to scales."

"Doesn't mean they're right."

They hung shed snakeskins around the front door again. At the top of the staircase to nowhere, they placed birdseed and suet cakes. On lower twigs of the nearest angle tree, they speared sliced-open halves of winter citrus.

A few days later, the fruit had been scraped down to skeletal white pith. The stairs to nowhere were littered with droppings.

After cleaning up the leftovers (Eden did slink out and help), Nemesia brought a saucer of rice wine to the wooded yard behind the house.

Mudlings hopped over to lap at it. "Didn't realize they were such drunkards," said Eden.

"Landscapers put out alcohol to make them easier to trap alive."

"Does it work?"

"Seems to make their wits sharper, if anything."

"I don't know if the world is ready to deal with smarter mudlings."

"That's why it has to be an occasional treat." Nemesia tipped her bottle over to refill the saucer.

The mudlings ricocheted about like acrobats doing circus tricks.

"How festive," Eden said. "This is better than fireworks."

Finalizing their provisional marriage took only another simple act of paperwork, with the Warden as their scribe. (A second warden bore witness; they'd met him while visiting a junior maenad.)

"Happy anniversary," Eden said afterward, hugging her close.

How wonderful it was to taste everyday minutiae without a looming countdown.

Even criminals and scoundrels seemed to get lazy around the turn of the year. After digging up evidence to free an official wrongly accused of embezzlement, Eden didn't have much left to tackle as Oddscale. Most maenads were supposed to be resting, too.

Which left plenty of time to sit the Warden down and tell him everything.

He said nothing during their first attempt to explain it: who Nemesia was, the whereabouts of Eden's missing years, et cetera. He just looked intently at Pimiko, who waved her front legs as if to inform him that he was on his own.

He got up, hauled out a big roll of butcher paper, and made them go through it again. Now, at his insistence, they added supplementary illustrations and annotated timelines.

"All right," he said at the end.

"You followed all that?" Eden said eagerly.

"I get the general idea."

After this grand confession, Eden could participate much more actively when Nemesia and Warden spoke of Below.

Now that she remembered living there, she knew firsthand what it all meant—their talk of sages, and rude tourists, and the Abbess's refusal to give up her bark pipes. She knew what Brood maidens called various chambers closed to the public, and the names of the biggest players in vertical commerce.

She, too, could grouse about how much the Brood relied on sales of snake water: a placebo that contained little other than ordinary drinking water. Plus a drop or two drawn from private mineral springs Below.

The ingredients were written right on the bottle, as was the fact that it guaranteed no effects whatsoever. But it was an unassailable tradition, centuries in the making. Tourists always brought back cases of snake water. There would be riots if the Brood stopped selling it.

Later in February, Eden talked Nemesia into going back to the clothier. She didn't mind letting Eden dress her like a personal stylist. It was just as much a present for Eden herself; she collected robes the way some people collected music boxes or decorative teacups.

As part of this project, they often went together to the secret dressing room.

On a day when the floors were frigid enough to merit two pairs of socks, Nemesia glanced at the translucent clothing bins stacked in a corner. Eden had left one with the lid askew. Empty limbs of fabric hung over the side, struggling bonelessly to escape.

"You've got to be joking," Nemesia said.

Eden was behind a clothing rack. She stopped pushing hangers around. "You've been saying that a lot lately."

Nemesia stalked over to the bin, plunged her arm in, and yanked out every last piece of a Brood guard uniform. The real thing, not a costume.

"This was here the entire time?" she cried.

Eden came over to inspect it. "Guess so." She sounded impressed. "I must've stolen—er, inadvertently borrowed it. Retiring guards are allowed to walk off the job in uniform, though. For privacy's sake. So I really didn't do anything wrong."

"You're supposed to mail it back."

"I caught a case of chronic amnesia, dearest. The Snake strangled my sense of time like a python."

"You never even questioned this being here?"

"Never noticed it," Eden said ruefully. She swept her arm about like a ringmaster. "In my defense—just look around."

The room was packed with esoteric garments and disguises and uniforms for every conceivable occupation within the Shell. As well as others from realms of fancy.

"I'll have to hang onto it a little longer," Eden said. "Might raise questions … unless I pay someone to send it anonymously. We can figure that out later."

She no longer voiced anxiety about her still-pending extension. But it was evident in the ferocity of her dreams. Sometimes she took refuge in the turret, which she had strewn with cushions and diversions.

She knelt to fiddle with glue and colored paper and needle-thin bits of wood, laboriously constructing mini umbrellas. Or she noodled away at a book of number-based puzzles. Or she doodled in the margins while deciding Oddscale's next move, which often involved scaring the living daylights out of city bigwigs.

"Every year," she said, "someone from the new crop of nobles gets too into their role."

"If your application gets rejected…"

Eden rolled over to stare at her.

"I'll appeal for you," said Nemesia.

"They don't take appeals."

"I could pull rank. I'll make them listen."

"And what rank," Eden asked, "do you have to pull on them?"

She sat up before Nemesia could answer. "Don't," she said. "I might lose my right to practice as a maenad. But even if I don't stop at forty, I'll have to stop someday. And even once I lose magic, I'll still have Oddscale. I'll still have you."

"People so rarely want to continue. They should value you more. They should—"

"Nemesia," Eden said, "you wouldn't twist the rules of Bridehood. You'd better not twist the rules of magic licensing, either. Might as well pour yourself back into the river you came from. I want you here with me, not gnawing at the roots of time."

Nemesia could recognize a losing argument. She didn't push it. "The roots of time must be tasty."

"I'm tastier," Eden grumbled.

They were just leaving the Bike Shop in Yolk City, arms full of bagged bagels, when Eden tripped on the sidewalk.

Nemesia tried to catch her. She faltered: Eden's left leg had plunged down to the knee, buried as though the pavement were made of sucking quicksand.

"Bite me," Eden snarled. "Now? Really?"

She glared at the ground. She had already begun sinking deeper. Magic yanked at her like a leash.

Nemesia would have extinguished it—but Eden shook her head. She stuffed both bagel bags in the crook of her elbow and beckoned Nemesia closer. Only their fingertips touched, which was apparently more than enough. A well of magic snapped them up like a trapdoor spider on the hunt.

57

The Next, and the Next

THE NEXT THING Nemesia knew, she was embedded to her waist in the scriptorium.

Eden hauled herself out of solid hardwood and carpet as if as ascending a flight of stairs on her hands and knees. Then she turned and freed Nemesia, too.

The floor looked unchanged, aside from having been anointed with several dropped bagels. Eden sprang to rescue them, shook them off, shrugged, and dropped them back in one of her bags.

"You egged me," she accused the Warden at his desk.

He handed her a message that had already been flash-transferred to archival paper.

Eden went rigid, pinching the edges of the paper as if afraid to mar it.

"This is real," she said.

"Yes."

"This is final."

"Yes."

"Look, Nemesia." Eden's face was unreadable. "I got a year."

"Your permit … got extended?" The words came into clearer focus. "With the option to apply for future extensions."

"One year!" Eden squawked.

"Uh—"

"I applied for two, and they gave me one! I'm not geriatric!"

"By maenad standards—" the Warden started to say, but he closed his mouth when Eden whirled on him.

"Now I have to apply all over again *this* year!"

Her howl died away.

The walls burbled with indigestion.

On the desk, Pimiko angled herself to avoid eye contact.

The Warden looked expressionlessly at his houseplants.

Nemesia made sure the sacks of bagels had been put down where no one would kick them.

By the time she turned back, Eden was shaking with silent laughter. The Warden bowed his head in prayer. His facial hair was too neatly trimmed to hide how his mouth twitched. Pimiko had gone all the way in her shell, leaving the humans in the room to their foolishness.

"What fun," Eden said. "Wow! I love bureaucracy."

"You have until fall," said the Warden.

"Again? How generous. So I'm currently covered till I turn forty-one—"

"Your next application will be for the years after that."

"Right."

"Perhaps they'll expedite the process."

"But I was enjoying it so much." Eden placed the message on the desk.

"At least Sholto won't be on the committee again."

"You can start racking up accomplishments now," Nemesia said, "instead of procrastinating till summer. That might help."

Eden gave her a look of abject betrayal. The Warden bobbed his head in approval.

Other notes trickled in not long after. One came from Daiya Anis, congratulating them both for their anniversary (belatedly) and for Eden's extension (right on time).

"Someone tipped her off," Eden muttered.

Another came from the Abbess. The Warden brought her letter to the kitchen, where Nemesia and Eden were bottom-watering a jungle's worth of potted plants.

He turned sideways and shuffled daintily between colorful rubbery tubs. "Old Balsa is extremely suspicious."

"What'd we do this time?" Eden asked.

He spoke to Nemesia. "The artifacts we inquired about last year—they weren't missing then. They *are* missing now."

Eden cut in. "Does the Abbess think I pilfered them when I went Below to plead for my wife?"

"Didn't you?" the Warden said baldly.

Nemesia must have made a sound, because they both pivoted. She raised her hands in self-defense. "Wasn't me."

"It wasn't—fine, it must have been me," Eden conceded.

"You don't remember swiping them?"

"It's all rather blurry."

The Warden wordlessly walked out of the kitchen. They followed him to the scriptorium. He took a roll of butcher paper from a cabinet: the one where they'd previously scrawled all sorts of time travel diagrams.

"Feels like three years ago," Eden said. "In terms of my own chrono-logical experience."

Nemesia pointed at her notes. "But your thirty-six-year-old self was Below until very recently. You finished serving as Roc, and you vanished—"

"And went back in time to resume living in order."

"Before you left, you snatched two artifacts out of the Brood's vault," said the Warden.

"You stole them in January or February," Nemesia continued. "They came back in time with you afterward. Like your guard uniform."

"They've only been missing from Below for the past month or so. But they've simultaneously been lurking in this house for years." Eden pulled a face. "My head hurts."

"You'll get used to it," the Warden said pitilessly. "Imagine how I felt when I first heard all this nonsense." He smacked the end of the paper roll.

"You should thank us. Mental exercise is good for aging brains."

"On the contrary—my cognitive health is in shambles."

While they bickered, Nemesia went over and pulled the unreadable book off its shelf. She slipped away upstairs and retrieved the necklace of metallic teeth from her bedroom, too.

She called Pimiko to the basement by knocking at the walls with a particular rhythm. They went down the stairs to Eden's room, where Pimiko manipulated the lock hidden in a ceiling beam.

Nemesia came back to the scriptorium with Roc's guard uniform draped over one arm. By then, Eden and the Warden had mostly stopped sniping.

"Let's return everything," she said. "It belongs Below."

"How will we explain ourselves?" Eden asked.

"Only one way."

So they told the Abbess the full truth, too.

She brought them into her chamber of contemplation. They drank from small steaming cups of green tea.

They were at the same low table where Nemesia had first parleyed with Daiya Sholto. Behind the Abbess stood the folding screen where she'd crouched like a child playing hide and seek.

The Abbess puffed incessantly on her bark pipe. Eden, grimacing, alternated between fending smoke off with her hands and burying her face in the steam of her teacup.

"I knew Roc was up to no good," the Abbess said with grim triumph.

"How perceptive," said Eden. "Wouldn't expect anything less from our venerable Abbess. Of course, it'd be more impressive if you'd spoken up earlier."

The Abbess snorted. "You never change. Insolent in every guise. And an unrepentant thief, to boot."

"We're repentant now," Nemesia said hurriedly. "Very repentant."

Eden gave the Abbess her most soulful look. "Sholto aside, I'm not used to being disliked. But I get it. No one could ever be good enough for your favorite pupil. Shall I bow down and vow to make her happy?"

"Uh," said Nemesia.

"Urgh," said the Abbess, muffled by the pipe in her lips.

Eden remained undeterred. "I respect you more than you think. I've always respected the elderly."

The light of glee in her eyes was downright evil: no two ways around it.

"Venerable Abbess," she said grandiosely, "it would be my honor to call you Venerable Mother."

The Abbess sucked so hard on her pipe that the bark curled up like a snail shell.

Nemesia laughed weakly, since no one else seemed willing to. Better get back to business before Eden invented other ways to torment her elders.

She presented the Abbess with Eden's guard uniform (flawlessly folded), and the book written in a language no one could read, and the eerie necklace of human teeth.

"Fine," the Abbess told them, following a cursory examination. "You're absolved." She had never been a very ceremonious sort.

"And—"

She exhaled; her bark pipe crackled like arthritic knuckles. She squinted at Nemesia.

"Yes," she said, unsmiling. "I remember every word. Scribes will record your story for posterity."

Nemesia started to thank her, but she was already shooing them up and away from the table.

They had set down far greater burdens than the weight of a single outfit, and a book, and a necklace. Relief made Nemesia buoyant, as though she could drift up through the stairwell and into the skies of Above like a lost balloon.

There had been other human incarnations of the Snake before her. More would surely come after her, too. Still, it might not happen until they were all long dead—Eden and the Warden and the Abbess, and certainly Nemesia herself, if she stayed human to the end.

The next incarnation would have no living guides.

There had been no one living who knew how to guide Nemesia, either. But the Brood kept excellent records.

The Abbess had recognized her for what she was. She'd taught Nemesia techniques to protect the contents of her bucket: her one and only self. A self that existed solely in the intersection between divinity and human flesh. She was a candle that the greater Snake might snuff by sighing in its sleep.

Yet she'd lasted longer than any of her predecessors. She felt more secure in her self than ever before. When another incarnation came around, her story would be waiting in the Brood library.

They would be their own person—someone different from her. But she might be able to help them without ever knowing it. She could pass down an inheritance totally separate from what the divine Snake would bestow on them.

She could serve as an example for one way to live, and keep living. She could become a spark of hope to be shared with the next incarnation, and the next, and the next.

"Why did you take them?" she asked Eden as an afterthought.

"The book and the teeth? Goodness knows. I'm usually the one catching thieves in the name of justice."

"Sometimes you pull off heists in the name of justice."

"That, too. This was more of a whim. I remembered stashing them at home in the future—must've felt like a prophecy I had to complete."

Her epaulets glittered as they climbed the spiral stairs to Above. She gave Nemesia a sidelong look. "Maybe I did it because keeping them would give you another reason to visit Below. Just in case you ever needed it."

58

A Worthwhile Life

A WEEK BEFORE the next Snake Moth Gala, a vast crevasse cracked open just outside the city.

No one could see to the bottom. All they knew was that it didn't connect to Below. Echoes moaned out of the depths even when no one standing on the edge had said a word.

Soon enough, titanic limbs jutted out and started scrabbling to escape. They looked uncannily like crab legs, but there were far too many for a single crab: the new canyon was two miles in length, and legs filled it from end to end. They seemed to be heaving up a creaking, dripping body of unfathomable size.

Eden put a stop to that.

She slammed the walls of the abyss together like a pair of cymbals, sealing the earth without a hint of a scar. After that, her magic bravely attempted to merge several harmless hills and bluffs, for good measure.

381

Nemesia extinguished her just in time.

The air rang with something you couldn't call an actual sound. It buzzed in their bones. The aftertaste of magic flooded their mouths; today it seemed unpleasantly reminiscent of soap.

"You could just turn in your next request for an extension tomorrow," Nemesia said, "and be done with it."

"I'll consider it," Eden panted. She looked as if she'd run a marathon.

When the gap in the ground roared shut, it had severed a number of protruding leg segments. They toppled like logged trees, one by one, making the earth shake again.

After falling, they took on an angry orange tint.

This was around the time when fascinated onlookers grew bold enough to move closer. They came bearing all manner of deadly tools: pruning shears, chainsaws, pole saws, pitchforks, shovels.

"They want to know if it tastes like regular crab meat," Eden said.

"Could it poison them?"

Backup maenads were already running to meet the crowd of civilians.

"My coworkers will take care of it," Eden rasped. "Let's get away while we can."

From the way the smiling mob brandished their weapons, it did feel as though they might also develop a taste for human flesh.

But Eden didn't want to step in a wormhole, or hail a vivitaxi, or board an omnibus. She wanted to walk, she said, and feel the unmoving ground underfoot. Her mind expected it to jiggle like pudding.

With frequent breaks, they made their way to an intersection near Downcastle Street.

"Back again," Eden said under her breath. It was the same way she spoke when she talked in her sleep. Nemesia eased her onto a bench.

A street stall across the way sold rice cakes drenched in red sauce. Nemesia bought a paper cup to share. They took turns eating their stick-shaped cakes, blanketed in a silence born of contented exhaustion.

They weren't within sight of Nemesia's crèche, or Eden's reformatory. But Eden looked down the street as if she could see past all those other trees and buildings.

"I was wondering," Nemesia said. Her lips burned with lingering spice.

"Mm?"

"Why don't adult maenads teach at reformatories?"

Ordinarily, Eden would have teased her for asking something so obvious. She must have been too tired to bother.

"Same reason we don't have textbooks, or professional conferences. Our magic is completely intuitive. We can't explain it. What kids need are extinguishers to keep them from killing each other by accident."

She grew more animated. "Taming berserk magic is different from using it. Like the difference between forging a sword, and fighting with it. They haven't even tempered their swords yet—what good would it do to hear the bragging of a duelist? Besides, no one who graduates from a reformatory ever wants to go back."

"You've already been back."

Eden blinked at her.

Nemesia pretended to wind a scarf around her neck.

"That was very much not in an official capacity."

"You did the rounds of junior maenads. What's the difference between them and the ones who haven't graduated yet? A year? A couple months?"

"Magically, they have to—"

"—get through it all on their own," Nemesia finished. "The forging part of the process. I know. No one can make it less painful. But do they have to feel alone in every other sense, too?"

Eden peered into the cup of rice cakes. All that remained were dregs of sauce. "If anyone does this," she said morosely, "it's going to have to be me. I'm the only one with decent social skills."

"Retired maenads could get involved, too."

"Most of them aren't any better than..." Eden trailed off. "You're thinking of Sholto."

"It's probably better if you don't go at the same time."

"No kidding." She spoke as if resigned to her doom. "Oh, he'll definitely want to participate. So long as the idea doesn't come from me."

"We can make it seem to come from the Abbess."

Sunset inched its way across the sky behind city rooftops. This neighborhood had peculiar stairs to nowhere: tall spirals that rose from the ground like a drill.

"Sholto's been spending more time with his son." Eden gently crumpled the wide paper cup in her fist. "The one thing no maenad has is a good parental role model. So it's hardly surprising that he fumbled. He'll do better."

She opened her parasol with a button press. She blew at the cup like a stray eyelash.

The crushed cup wafted down the street, bobbing, distracted by smells on the breeze. It made its floaty way over to the black garbage bin next to the rice cake stall. It pitched itself in with all the flair of a high diver.

"I never thought it was possible for the parent of a maenad to care that much," Eden said quietly. "I didn't want to believe it was possible."

She cracked a lopsided smile, sensing Nemesia's eyes on her. "Hey. We're still alive and healthy, all these years later. I'll be happy for him from a distance. Not everyone has to be friends."

Nemesia had been rather lacking in friends herself.

It became easier to remember names and faces when she knew she could stay Above for more than a year.

She ducked backstage with Eden and the Warden to meet the cast of community plays. She went on her habitual long walks through the wild meadows and dells around the cottage. Sometimes alone, and sometimes with company.

Every now and then, she walked to another maenad residence. Most were impossible to locate unless you knew where to look. She'd stop by and catch up with friendly wardens. She might exchange words with a shy maenad, too.

What would happen when the holy Snake finished growing and hatched? What would become of everyone when the Shell broke open for good?

That was like wondering when the end of the world would arrive, and what might come after. Personally, she hoped to never find out.

At the Snake Moth Gala, they received an invitation to see the King. This time, an official took them much deeper in the palace.

They stopped at the sweeping glass wall of an aquarium that wouldn't have looked out of place Below.

The water continued so far back that Nemesia couldn't guess where it ended. A nearer wall held dark shapes that might have been the mouths of submerged tunnels.

A man-sized axolotl drifted towards the glass. Its four-toed front feet seemed to gesture at them. But maybe it was just swimming.

The King of Now no longer looked remotely human.

They watched the axolotl paddle about. Once or twice, before performing a particularly dynamic maneuver, it came right up to the glass and flailed its tail. *Look what I can do!*

"He seems happy," said Nemesia.

"It's hard to tell with amphibians."

"He swims like a professional."

"Would be pretty disheartening if he couldn't." But Eden's mood had softened. She smiled at the slippery King. She pantomimed clapping so vigorously that there was no way he could have missed it.

On their way out, they stopped on the shores in front of the palace. Couples lingered on the glass bridge that spanned the lake. It was already dark, and gourd-shaped lanterns flew in radiant flocks over the royal gardens.

"Eden," said Nemesia.

"Yes?"

"Why did I decide to become me?"

"Instead of—what, an axolotl like the King?"

Eden reached for her hand. She didn't have to reach far. Without looking, Nemesia had detected the faintest movement of Eden's shoulder. Without thinking, she'd sought Eden's hand in turn. It all seemed to happen at once.

Eden rephrased her question. "Why would the Snake decant its essence into human form? Maybe it's the godly version of a hobby."

Something splashed in the lake.

"Maybe," Eden said, sounding inspired, "the Snake lives as all kinds of creatures. Caecilians and mudlings and camelids and mammoths."

"And actual snakes?"

"Sure, why not? Another smidgeon of you might have been decanted into a moth over yonder. Or some noble's pampered otterdog. I've always thought that Pimiko is suspiciously smart."

"Isn't Pimiko a refugee from outside?"

"That's what I was led to believe. You wouldn't necessarily recognize yourself in other forms, would you? Looking yourself in the face—really looking—might bring you closer to becoming one seamless whole again."

"I won't go looking," Nemesia said.

"Taking mortal form could be how the Snake learns what makes us tick. Maybe it's a necessary rite of passage for the Snake to swell to its full potential."

"I haven't done anything special, though. I'm not a king or a hero."

"You appointed me Oddscale, which I'm still very thankful for."

"That didn't have to be me."

Eden rubbed a thumb over her knuckles. Snatches of music and revelry rang out across the lake.

"Yours is the life a god chose," Eden told her, "and it would be worthwhile even if a god hadn't chosen it. No one has to prove themselves worthy of living. It's not like working off a debt.

"You're already thinking further into the future than most. I've only ever worried about myself—about growing older, and what it might take from me. You're looking out for the incarnations to come. The next generation of maenads."

"The Shell has been kind to us." Nemesia's voice caught. "I hope it'll be kind to them."

The lake lapped at the pebbled shore just beyond their toes. In a different garden, unwieldy snake moths were careening from tree to tree. Each hour of the evening represented a substantial portion of their lives.

Eden had on an irrepressible smile. "We came back here for a second year," she said. "To more years to come."

She toasted Nemesia with a nonexistent glass. She squeezed their twined fingers, and Nemesia squeezed back. A lone lantern flitted closer to light them.

As far as they knew, it was a night devoid of fistfights, or corrupt backdoor deals, or assassins gunning for the amphibious King, or eldritch monsters crawling out of cracks in the earth.

Eden slept without dreams. Nemesia slept just as soundly, pressed against her back. She saw a future brimming with joy and astonishment and an abundance of quiet, loving repetition. She woke with tears crusted in the corners of her eyes.

She would have made a poor archaeologist. She couldn't even begin to reconstruct the skeleton of her dream.

Maybe it was just her bleary morning brain, but she had a hard time coming up with anything more fulfilling than Eden snoozing obliviously in her arms, slow and deep and peaceful. Plus the knowledge that Pimiko watched over them like the world's smallest bodyguard.

Love wove itself like a web from one day to the next. It wove itself into the most boring routines, and into jokes that no one else would laugh at. She understood the shape of it as if through a fogged-up window, but she couldn't make out the details. She just had an awed sense of that intricate weave spanning moments and hours and weeks and years, and years, and years.

She couldn't risk peeking forward through time as if putting a telescope to her eye. She couldn't.

But it had felt like such a marvelous future. And she was already losing her grasp on its giddy edges. She was already drifting back into the dimness of sleep.

Well, there was nothing else to be done.

If she couldn't imagine it, then she would just have to live it.

A Note from the Author

THANK YOU for traveling to the realm of the Snake! (If you feel moved to leave a rating or review, thank you again! It makes a massive difference to the success of my books, and I couldn't be more grateful.)

I've always been a voracious reader. But this year, I've read more novels in rapid succession than at any other point in my life. It felt like having some sort of nutritional deficiency. All those stories fed me in a way I must have really needed at the time.

My greatest hope for *Masks Worn by Magical Wives* is that it manages to fill a similar need in at least a few readers. This book turned out to be a lot gentler than much of my other work, but it's no less sincere.

In case you were curious: the story takes place several years after *The First and Last Demon* (although time gets a bit wobbly inside the Shell!). Speaking of which, that's the novel to read if you're interested in seeing more of Char and Vesper.

One last note: I like to think of all my novels as having been rather generously translated from their original (fantasy) language into English. So the characters don't really measure distances in miles or use Gregorian calendar months—imagine that these terms have been substituted in as part of a heavy-handed localization process.

As for my next story, it'll be another entry in the Clem & Wist series. I can't wait to get started!

Follow my Author Page for future updates if you'd like to see more: **https://amazon.com/author/hiyodori**

Hope to see you again next time!
– Hiyodori

Novels by Hiyodori

The Clem & Wist Series

Prequel: No One Else Could Heal Her

Book 1: The Lowest Healer and the Highest Mage

Book 2: The Reverse Healer Case Files

Book 3: Clematis and the Queen of the Void

Book 4: Three Murdered Mages, Two Broken Bonds

Set in the World of Clem & Wist

The First and Last Demon (Standalone)

The Forest at the Heart of Her Mage (Standalone)

Carrion Saints (Standalone)

Masks Worn by Magical Wives (Standalone)